THE MISSHAPES

THE COMING STORM

THE MISSHAPES

THE COMING STORM

ALEX FLYNN

Copyright © 2014 by Stuart Sherman and Elisabeth Donnelly
Cover illustration by Sebastian Ciaffliogne
Logo design by Eamon O'Donoghue
Interior designed and formatted by E.M. Tippetts Book Designs

ISBN 978-1-940610-31-3
eISBN 978-1-940610-12-2

First hardcover edition October 2014 by Polis Books, LLC
60 West 23rd Street
New York, NY 10010
www.PolisBooks.com

POLIS BOOKS

To Abby

"Mis-shapes,
mistakes,
misfits,
Raised on a diet of broken biscuits.
We don't look the same as you and we don't do the things you do
but we live around here too,
oh really."
—Pulp

PROLOGUE

I DON'T REMEMBER how old I was the first time I saw a man fly. I was very small; I remember that much. My arms were tightly locked around my dad's neck. He was giving me a piggyback ride through our perfectly ordinary town center.

It was a crisp and cold fall day. Our heads craned upward as we tried to name the various clouds in the sky, giving them shapes, personalities, and identities. Mom still lived with us. I didn't know about her abilities yet.

I can remember pointing to one cloud and told Dad it looked like my teddy bear Winston. Dad tried to say something in return but the sound of an airplane drowned him out. Or so I thought. A gust of wind plastered my shirt to my small body. I felt my head rip forward as something moved past it. A man. He was in the air, just clearing the tops of people's heads. His feet pointed behind him like an Olympic diver and his arms pointed forward, ending at balled fists.

He was headed straight toward Old Mrs. Galloway. She shuffled slowly down the sidewalk, juggling her grocery bags, a cane, and an enormous purse. The old woman wobbled like a top that was ready to fall over.

A loud baritone bellow of "Never fear!" came from the flying man. I screamed.

Dad stopped short. We watched as Freedom Man scooped her up

in just one arm. "Freedom Man can handle that!" he announced in a deep, leading-man voice that seemed to echo off the buildings.

"To my house, please," Mrs. Galloway wheezed.

And just like that, the man in the shiny green cape whisked the old lady right over the town center and above the trees. My world had turned upside down. If a man could fly through the air, something as basic as gravity meant nothing. I didn't know it at the time, but everything was going to change.

I watched them fly off into the clouds that we had named.

"Honey," my dad said, setting me gently on the ground, "I have something to tell you."

SUMMER

ONE

I T WAS the best birthday gift of my life. No matter what season, it had a place of honor on my nightstand. A tiny altar, my tabletop humidifier, glowing with an eerie blue light. The perfect tool. Dad got it for me when I started to train for the Academy admissions test.

Most kids like me were in Academy admissions prep. Some even managed to get practice time at the Academy, in crazy simulator rooms the size of football fields dedicated to recreating weather conditions. These days I'd be laughed out of those rooms, considered a bad omen.

I saw those simulators once, when Mom was still around. She took me to the Academy, for Bring Your Daughter to Work Day. Those rooms didn't mean anything to me back then. I didn't know that Heroes like the Black Zephyr learned their tricks in rooms like empty warehouses before getting out into the world. Back then, I was too young to appreciate Mom's position at the Academy, too young to even think about my powers and when they'd appear. I didn't understand that I could've gotten in easily if she were still around. The test would've been a formality. But I couldn't think like that.

It was time to practice. I perched on the side of my bed, my back straight, knees pointed out, feet planted on the carpet. I put my hands on my thighs and took three deep breaths. My mind needed to be clear to use my power. I flipped the switch on the humidifier. The plastic mechanism inside it whirred. A warm skein of moist air poured out of the nozzle. I waved my hand through it a couple of times and tried to focus my emotions on the jet. With a small dark thought and a little tension in my muscles, I was able to shepherd the rising moisture and form a small cloud. It looked like a floating pile of marshmallows.

Another few twitches and the cloud was drizzling. I looked down. A dampness crept up my socks. In fact, my entire carpet was soaked. I grabbed a bucket from underneath my bed and put my feet in it.

For the past year, I'd been trying to see if I could make it snow. If I could pull it off, it was the type of talent that would definitely get me into the Academy. I had no luck so far. Snow required a perfectly calm mind. I needed to relax my muscles, let all thoughts—good and bad— leave me, and be at peace. A state of total Zen. Basically, the opposite of me. The best I could do with my racing thoughts was slow them to a jog.

I took some deep breaths. I watched a yoga video that said soft eyes help relaxation. YouTube videos on acting, yoga, and anger management were crucial for learning to control my powers. I liked the anger management ones best. This yoga one had a stoned-sounding guru squinting at the camera, spending ten minutes describing the action. How to be completely chilled out. I squinted my eyes and took a deep breath, letting the air fill my lungs and expelling it in a sliver of noise. I put my hand up to the cloud. The air was cooling. I looked at my hand again, trying not to feel anything. One of my problems with my whole emotion-controlled power was that I couldn't respond when it was working. Even a positive thought like, "Awesome job, Sarah" screwed the whole thing up.

A minute passed and one single snowflake dropped in the bucket. I watched it begin to dissolve in the water. The crystal's arms disappeared first, followed by the granule in the center. A smile crept across my face. Another snowflake. Then another. They were fat and fluffy and floated slowly into the bucket. I pumped my fist with excitement and accidentally thrust it into the cloud. Ice quickly formed on it and I yelped in pain. I pulled it away quickly. My hand felt like it was on fire. A small white patch with yellow spots appeared on my skin. It felt numb. I was terrified it was frostbite, which meant a trip to the hospital and a grounding.

I winced at the sight. The cloud grew enormous. It puffed outward until it almost filled my entire room. My hand throbbed. I wanted to run downstairs to get the first-aid kit, but knew if I left the cloud alone it would cause unaccountable damage. The moisture made my Black Zephyr poster curl up on the sides.

The doorbell rang. "Sarah!" my brother yelled. Shoot. I looked at the clock. Probably Betty. We had a date. I had completely blanked out on when she was picking me up for the Harpastball game. I shook my fist at the cloud, trying to will it to disperse. It didn't.

I yelled, "I'll be right there" but my words were stopped dead by the dense moisture. I couldn't see anything. It was just white all around. Fighting my way through the fog, I ran to my window and opened it. The cloud billowed outside, but my room was still cloaked in white. Maybe a fan would work. Betty kept ringing the bell. Everything was drenched. This was going to ruin my room. Of course Johnny couldn't bother to open the door. I grew anxious and the cloud grew more. It was starting to rotate. Like a tornado. It was getting harder and harder to stand upright.

I opened my closet and felt around for my fan. It had to be somewhere. My hands moved over a box, old clothes, a pile of books, my numb finger following along clumsily. I inspected my fingers closely. It was only a spot of frostnip and not frostbite. I could have lost the finger. Most Academy students have at least ten fingers.

No luck, and no fan. I furrowed my brow, looking over at my desk, where the fan sat mocking me. I took one leap to get there and snagged my foot on a power cord. It sent me toppling face first onto my squishy carpet. When I looked up, the cloud had disappeared. My humidifier lay on the floor, unplugged.

I surveyed the damage. One ruined poster, one very wet carpet, and a few sodden books. My computer looked okay, luckily. I was about to check on it when the bell rang again.

"Door," I heard Johnny yell.

I ran downstairs to let Betty in. "I'm so sorry!" I said. "I was in the middle of something and you know Johnny, he hasn't been trained."

"He's the worst cousin, Sarah."

"But you're the best, Betty," I replied, batting my eyes. I felt bad that she had been sitting out there. She gave me an appraising glance.

"Have you been wrangling tigers in your room? You look pretty intense. You might want to change," Betty said.

In all the drama, I didn't realize my clothes had gotten damp and dirty. She had me pegged. "Yes. Of course. But come in!"

"Sure!" Betty said. "Thanks so much for letting me in, *Sarah*," she said, flashing a dirty look at Johnny. He grunted a greeting and slumped down farther on the couch. He was bookended by two friends, Kurt and Hamilton. Kurt was pale and wiry, a wraith in plaid. Hamilton had on his shutter shades, flecked with paint. A trail of hot-pink paint drips polka-dotted his brown arm. They were all drinking out of large cups and watching the Maximum Fighting match blaring on the TV.

"The bell's ringing, dude," Johnny said. His friends laughed. Ever since he got kicked out of the Academy he's tried to be a rebel. New friends and new clothes. He traded his Academy uniform of navy pants and a white button-down shirt for jeans and a series of rotating T-shirts, homemade and stenciled, ratty and worn-in. Today he had on a red shirt that said, THIS IS NOT A RED SHIRT.

"Thanks for the help, Johnny," I chirped.

"Ladies," Hamilton said, "you're kind of messing up the Maximum Fighting match."

I dragged Betty upstairs. I probably looked like a soggy wreck next to my cousin, perfectly put-together in her usual prim cardigan and matching tank top, her straight brown hair catching the light. She was so together that she even made her AlcoMeter belt look like a stylish accessory. On Johnny the belt just looked silly.

Betty was my closest friend, and I wouldn't have said that a year ago. As my cousin, she had to be my friend. It's weird how that got more important once my mom left. But when everything was crazy and scary, Betty was there for support and reliability, which was ultimately pretty okay even if she kind of drove me crazy sometimes. The last few years had been rough. Family drama. All of my friends from school going off to the Academy. My ex-best friend, Lindsay, promised that she'd write every day, but I hadn't heard from her in a year. That's what the Academy did to people, apparently.

Betty took over my room, rifling through my drawers looking for something that would make me look semi-presentable. The Harpastball game was a big deal. It was the town religion. I couldn't show up looking like a mess, especially in front of Heroes and Academy students. I had to make a good impression. Soon enough we'd be on the same team, saving the world.

TWO

I CHECKED THE mailbox as we left. Nothing. It shut with a groan. "Yeah, I haven't got mine yet, either," Betty said, blue eyes twinkling. She got the Robertson genes. Dark hair, blue eyes, fine features. She looked more like Dad than I did. It was totally unfair. I got my mother's wild, kinky, and uncontrollable hair. I heard clouds rumble overhead. Thinking about the application process made me nervous.

Betty had also applied to the Academy. She has the same power as Johnny. They can both convert water into alcohol. It's good for making fireballs but it can take a toll on the body. Especially if you want to be a rebel. Betty handled it well. Johnny didn't. And since Johnny was kicked out, she was probably a shoo-in.

My street was already packed tight with cars. Some people had put cones out on and lawn chairs on the few slivers of sidewalk. Betty looked at the street. It was clogged with fans, food trucks, souvenir booths, sidewalk vendors, children running circles around their parents, and bumper-to-bumper cars. She shrugged. "Let's walk."

The Summer Spectacular was a gigantic deal. People came from far and wide to check it out. It had gotten even bigger since they started showing the game on ESPN-H. Maybe because it was the two oldest

Hero Academies in the country locked in a centuries-long duel. The Hero Academy of Doolittle Falls—my future Hero Academy, visible from my house, perched on the top of Marston Heights—versus the Charleston Heroes Academy, the second oldest Hero Academy in the country.

Charleston didn't have a chance. Everyone knew the Hero Academy team was unstoppable, especially this year, with Freedom Boy as a starter. He was from a long line of Freedom Men, the signature Heroes of Doolittle Falls. I had to admit, I had a huge crush on him. But then again, America had a huge crush on him.

We passed a little kid walking to the game with his mother. He looked up at a rain cloud and frowned. I stopped and turned toward him.

"Want to see something cool?" I asked.

"What?" he said, glumly.

"Keep looking up at that cloud and smile."

He tilted his head up and smiled. His mom glared at me. Even though there are a lot of Heroes in this town, parents are still pretty mistrusting of strangers. A town with Heroes can draw villains out of the woodwork.

I took a deep breath and stood still, focusing on my excitement about the game. The cloud moved toward the sun, spreading its fingers. If I could get it just right I could…Yes! A small rainbow appeared. It was faint, a thin line of colors, but clear. The kid's smile grew and his eyes lit up.

"That was for you," I said, and continued on with Betty.

"Show-off," she said.

I just smirked.We took a right on Main Street, heading north toward the field. Our sleepy little town was buzzing with people. There was a line out the door at Seymour's Scoops, filled with people looking for ice cream. Hero paraphernalia stores advertised huge sales, trying to capitalize on the big game. We went by Hiro's Heroics and I stopped short.

She was glaring at me from the window, nearly popping off the poster. It was like I could touch her. She had on a white skintight uniform with a matching white cape. She looked strong. And angry. The poster had her facing off against Freedom Man. They were in the air, locking arms as bright red bolts flew off them. Freedom Man's green cape shimmered. A worried town looked on from below. The caption read, FREEDOM MAN BATTLES THE NEFARIOUS LADY OBLIVION.

Lady Oblivion, archenemy of Freedom Man and the Order of Justice. Lady Oblivion, the scourge of Doolittle Falls. Lady Oblivion, enemy of all that is good and pure.

Everyone knows her as the woman who nuked Innsmouth.

I just know her as mom.

Betty yanked my sleeve. "Don't let it get to you. It's not something you did," she said.

I wished it could be that easy. The image tore me apart. I could feel the sky fill with clouds. I couldn't see her, I couldn't talk to her, and yet, with her image everywhere, I couldn't avoid her.

Betty led me toward the game. "See? We're almost there."

I managed to change focus. The clouds drifted away. "Oh, we're close. Cool. Let's go to the game."

We were near the entrance gates, behind a pushy scrum of people. The gates were enormous, fifteen feet of towering iron, topped with busts of famous heroes who'd attended the school throughout history. We could see the field beyond the gates. People, as far as the eye could see. It was packed.

The crowd was thick. It felt like shopping on Black Friday. There was no semblance of order. Betty clasped my hand tighter.

"Hey! Stop it!" someone to my left yelled. It was Tom Doodlebug. He was surrounded by some Normal jocks, who towered above him, wearing their Harris High letter jackets. One kid held a bottle of water over his head. "We got special powers," they said. "Doodlebug powers!"

Doodlebug was a target. He couldn't help it. The whole town knew about his crappy power. His ancestors were the original settlers of the town and known dowsers. Dowsers can find water—and sometimes other elements—by using their special intuition. All of the Doodlebugs are dowsers. And, lately, they were considered Misshapes. But that was a whole other thing.

Without thinking, I yelled, "Cut it out."

It wasn't the smartest move. I wanted to take it back. I wasn't Doodlebug's friend and I had no particular interest in incurring some bully's wrath by defending him. But the way Misshapes were treated bugged me. The jocks jostled their way over to me. One of them dragged Doodlebug by his collar and pushed him next to Betty and me. We both said "Hey" but they just laughed.

"Look, you and your new friends found water!" said one jock, who then poured the water over Doodlebug. Some splashed on us.

They formed a circle around us.

"Jerk!" I cried. At the sound of my voice, a smile curled across their faces.

"Well, if it isn't the spawn of Satan herself," a jock sneered.

"Has your mom destroyed any other towns? Maybe she made a flock of dead birds fall from the sky. Just for fun," said another. The jocks hocked loogies at Doodlebug and me. One hit. It was disgusting, wet, and squishy.

Suddenly a large blob, which looked like a basketball made out of blue glass, flew through the air, passing in front of my face and hitting one of the bullies in the head. He was knocked to the ground and covered in water. More giant balls flew at the kids and smashed into them. The impact sent the jocks flying left and right, falling to the ground. A girl shouted at them, "So, you want to have a water fight?"

They got up and ran in the other direction, shouting, "Whatever, Hero!"

The girl approached me. She was fit and confident, her long blonde hair spilling out of a knit cap. She had a scowl on her face. A gold Academy pin, a simple A that caught the light, sparkled on her shirt.

"How have you been?" Lindsay asked.

THREE

LINDSAY PUT her hand on my arm. "Sarah, I'm sorry we didn't see each other much this past year. Things were pretty crazy. I really miss, like, just getting ice cream with you. Now all I do is worry about the fate of the world."

"I love ice cream," I said, thinking wistfully of a giant cookie-dough sundae that we shared. I missed Lindsay too. We were inseparable last summer.

She was wearing her Academy uniform. A crisp white blouse and a black-, blue-, and gold-checked skirt with pleats. She pinned the skirt up midthigh. We fell into chatting as we stood in the scrum, waiting to enter the stadium. The old patter made it feel like Lindsay never went off to the Academy last year. Betty coughed next to me. Doodlebug followed us, swearing allegiance to Lindsay for saving his life. "Don't mention it," she said and gave him a look that said, *Seriously, please stop mentioning it*. He got the point and fell behind.

"Remember in seventh grade," Lindsay reminisced, "when you sat with Tyler Friedman during lunch for a week and you thought you guys were dating but then he asked Lily to that stupid dance instead of you?"

I nodded. "Not my finest moment."

"Then you freaked out and there was a hailstorm in town? That was kind of amazing. What was the name of that dance?"

I thought for a second and then remembered it—"Snowcoming!" I yelled, right along with Lindsay.

We both broke out into hysterics. Betty kept quiet and played with her phone.

"I think Tyler lost his dog in one of those mini-tornadoes," I said.

"Served him right for messing with my girl," said Lindsay.

"How's the Academy going?" I said, trying to keep the jealousy out of my voice. I always pictured it like a non-stop training montage set to the *Karate Kid* theme song.

"It's amazing," she said. "Although it would be better if you were there. Sorry I've been crappy at keeping in touch. Sometimes we're just locked away up in that school, you know? Eating, drinking, breathing all sorts of Hero stuff. My mind's blown every day."

"I can't wait to go," I said.

Betty shot me a look. She had been subject to enough rants about how terrible Lindsay was as a friend to just let it slide. She was about to say something when a large man in a Red Cyclops shirt slammed into her. He apologized. The gate was jammed with people. We squeezed through it like tiny fish and showed the man at the booth our tickets.

Lindsay looked at our tickets. They were general admission. "You can't sit there. You won't see anything."

They were the best we could find, and so expensive. Fifty dollars apiece. And that was after camping out in line overnight so we didn't have to pay scalpers.

"They're not that bad," I said.

"No, seriously, they are. You two are coming with me. I'll get you into the stands."

"Seriously? You can do that?" I asked.

The stands were off limits to regular folks. Only Academy students, alumni, and the ultra-rich could get into them. I was able to sit in them once when my mom was dean, and it was one of the best experiences of my life. I was eight and it was a practice or scrimmage. They weren't even moving and I loved it. But even she couldn't pull strings for the Summer Spectacular.

"My friend Christie will hook you up," Lindsay said. "She has the skills, and the guard already has a crush on her." She pulled out her phone and typed a text. Like lightning, her friend appeared in front of us, a skinny reed with long red hair, glasses, and a scarf wrapped jauntily around her neck. She seemed to make up for the Academy uniform with a lot of accessories. I saw a black choker of some kind peeking out from underneath the scarf.

There was a reason that Christie looked familiar. Her mother was Ann Glanton, the WXBS reporter who covered the destruction of Innsmouth with a blonde bob, a hazmat suit, and a smile. I sat in the den with my dad and my brother, glued to the TV and Ann Glanton's chirpy news reports from Innsmouth—the only reporter allowed in— talking about the horrors perpetrated by Admiral Doom and Lady Oblivion.

"How can you get us in? Your power must be amazing," Betty asked.

Christie Glanton slid the thick cherry-red frames of her glasses down the bridge of her nose with her index finger. She looked at us with her large brown eyes. "Telepathic hypnosis," she whispered. "Clap four times."

Betty and I clapped four times in unison, unaware of why Christie smiled. She said, "I also run a gossip blog and have dirt on everyone. It's actually way more useful in high school then the silly clapping trick."

"You don't even want to know how many hits she gets," Lindsay said.

"Wow, that's quite a power," I said, looking down at my hands for betraying me.

"Come on," she said. "The game's about to start and Luke's at the gate for only ten more minutes."

She pulled us over to an entrance manned by a gangly boy holding a scanner. He was wearing a black shirt that had a logo of a shoe with wings on it.

"Who is Luke?" I whispered to Christie.

She did not whisper back. I guess when you're a hypnotist you don't have to be subtle. "Luke Markowitz is, like, one of the fastest living creatures in the world. He was on this episode of *Hero vs. Machine* where he beat a Porsche in a hundred-yard dash. And he's got a huge thing for me. It's kind of dorky."

Christie and Lindsay showed their student IDs. Luke scanned them and waved them in.

"Our two friends left their IDs at home, Luke," Christie said.

He was shocked that she knew his name, stumbling over his words. "Well, I could get in trouble, and how do I know they're students? But you know if I could help out…Um, I could call and have them checked by security. It would only take a minute."

She lowered her glasses. "That shouldn't be necessary. Remember,

Luke, they're Academy kids. Betty and Sarah. You had class with them last semester, and you ate lunch with them. Of course they're students."

His eyes glazed over. Then he said, almost confused, "You're right. I remember them! We had lunch together a few times. Good to see you, Sarah and Betty. Go right ahead."

We walked down the hall.

Luke yelled after us as we made our way to the stands, "You should come to my place after the game. I mean, my parents' place. They're not home and …" He stopped and started again. "I'm having an after-party. You should come."

"Can my friends come or is this a party of two, Luke?" said Christie.

He turned bright red. "No. I mean yes. Of course they can."

She smiled at him and he melted to the floor. Not literally though. That power would be gross.

"So, you two want to go to a party after this?" she asked.

"Isn't that for Academy kids only?" Betty asked.

"No. And besides, you two are shoo-ins for next year. It's like you're already honorary Heroes."

I couldn't stop smiling in return. Being a Hero was going to rule. I could almost feel the acceptance letter in my hands.

FOUR

HE STANDS were enormous—three stories high and fifty yards long. The entire rafter hovered above a large metal track, which ran the length of the one-thousand-yard field. It worked on magnets or something, like one of those Disney monorails. It enabled the whole thing to zoom back and forth at a speed close to eighty miles per hour. If the action took to the sky, it could hover higher so the audience could see what was going on.

Lindsay and Christie led us to the far end where there were some empty seats in the front row. Normally, I'd be afraid we were taking someone's seat but I felt that Christie was convincing enough.

It was hard not to stare as we made our way through the rows. People flew across the country to get to this game. Some in planes, some in capes. Everyone I'd ever idealized or envied was in the stands. The Black Zephyr, the world's greatest weather controller. Freedom Man, surrounded by the Freedom family in prime seats. They were there to cheer on Freedom Boy, their son. Some people would say he was the golden boy in town. He was the best-looking boy in town, for sure, and I could only admit it when I was alone in my room. Ever since my mom and his dad battled in Innsmouth, the family Freedom was basically a forbidden word in my house. We lived five miles apart, but the last time we were anywhere near each other was when we went to Hero Camp together, back when we were ten.

People dressed fancy in the stands, like they do for horse racing. Academy students had to wear Academy uniforms, and most people had on their best business casual. Lots of sport jackets. Women who were old enough to drink were required to wear skirts. I heard that people used to wear their fanciest hats, but that tradition had to end because the hats would eventually blow off people's heads. There were even security officers there, which Lindsay said were secret service men for the Vice President Bergeron, who loved Harpastball.

We passed the president of PeriGenomics. He didn't have powers, but his company focused on harnessing them for practical and profitable uses. He didn't notice us, but his daughter, Megan, gave me some serious stink-eye. She was the head cheerleader and head B at Harris High. She's hated me because I wouldn't let her cheat off my test in geometry last year.

We got to our seats just as the game was about to start. I idly picked at the seat belt for the seat, wringing it back and forth. I could see the hordes of people on the other side of the field, packed together in normal-size static stands or sitting on lawn chairs on any available patch of green. There were people standing packed together all along the sidelines. The crowd on the sidelines was bigger than our whole entire town. They had on Hero fan shirts, Academy Harpastball jerseys, knock-off shirts sold by vendors, and some even were wearing the costumes of their favorite Heroes.

The mass of fans stopped at both ends of the field where there were two identical swimming pools. Above the pools were, I was told, some kind of force fields. At the ends of those pools were the goal posts. They were so far away that they were a little blurry.

To be honest, even though I'd been to countless games since I was a little kid, I still wasn't one hundred percent sure what the rules were. They involved getting a ball to the opposing side's end, facing down obstacles, fighting, and piling on top of each other. I once looked up the rules, and after scrolling down for two hours and still not half finishing I was so confused I gave up. Really, I just liked watching the men in their little Hero outfits flying around and beating the crap out of each other. Especially when Freedom Boy was playing.

When the announcer introduced the Academy Team, the roar from the crowd was deafening. The players paraded onto the field in their blue and gold Lycra uniforms, a menagerie of shapes and sizes.

Charleston Academy, in red and white, walked out next to jeers. We stood for the national anthem.

After the song, Lindsay and Christie clicked the safety belts around their waist. Betty and I copied them, nonchalantly, like it was an everyday thing. The stands began to rise, slowly, swaying back and forth. It was like being in a cradle. A twenty-ton metal cradle with one thousand other people. My anticipation was rising.

The game started with a *boom*! In the middle of the field, the Harpastball shot out of a cannon and flew straight up into the air. Freedom Boy and the Charleston Academy player flew up into the sky to grab it. A quick second later, we shot up like a rocket after them. The cradle was now a roller coaster.

Betty and I shrieked.

People in the stands turned and laughed at us. We must have been the only newbies.

In midair, Freedom Boy and the Charleston kid were fighting over the ball. Other kids leaped or flew up after it, but they seemed to be the only ones who could stay aloft that long. Maybe they were the strikers. The strikers flew and were kind of like quarterbacks or something.

People scored points by getting the ball into the end zone, like football, and they also could get points by passing certain marks throughout the cube. "The cube" was the field, back and forth, up and down, what they called the three-dimensional space considered "in bounds." The most confusing part was the difference between legal and illegal fouls. The game got rough. Whistles and flags were blown regularly, with possession changes and sideline throws in a fluid progression that didn't stop the action.

All I could see were flashing capes and Lycra. Then Freedom Boy popped out of the scrum, the victor. He flew toward the opposing team's goalpost and we sped along beside him. I looked downward. We were hovering above the huge crowd. They looked small. We must have been pretty high up. "Are you okay?" asked Betty, looking at me with concern. "I didn't know you could look green."

I nodded.

When Freedom Boy was within a hundred yards of the pool, a large body spun up through the air and hit him like a tank. The player who hit him grabbed him in a bear hug and dragged him back down to earth in his enormous arms. As we plummeted along with them, I let out another excited yell. A woman with a diamond-studded brooch turned around and glared at me. The stands would take some practice.

Another Academy team player, who looked like an enormous muscular baby, grabbed the other player and ripped him off Freedom Boy. The game moved on and the giant baby continued to beat up the opposing player until the ref threw a flag and he finally stopped.

"That's Humungulous," Lindsay whispered.

After a few more changes of possession, Freedom Boy was rushing down the field again. Opposing players were in hot pursuit, grabbing at his feet as he ran and flew, leaping and dodging. Suddenly he was right in front of us. So close I could reach out and touch him. He was amazing in person. His huge shoulders popped out of the shiny fabric. He breathed heavily, every muscle in his body pushing him forward. His perfect, wind-swept sandy blond hair flew back, revealing eyes as green as mountains.

I shouted, instinctively, "Go, Freedom Boy!" As I shouted, a powerful gust of wind blew from behind him. It gave him a huge boost and with the tailwind he was able to escape his pursuers, swoop through the pool, and fly into the end zone. My shoulders slumped. My body was exhausted. Without meaning to, I think I created the wind. And I think we were winning.

Freedom Boy slowly flew back toward the middle of the field for the next toss-up. He was all grins, waving at the adoring crowd. I felt flushed. He paused when he got to our seats. He turned and looked directly at me. My face turned bright red. Then the son of my mother's archenemy said with a smile, "Thanks for the help."

I turned to putty.

I just stared at him like an imbecile for a long ten seconds while thousands of fans, and everyone in my town, watched.

Finally Betty elbowed me and I shouted, "Don't mention it, Freedom Boy!" like a fangirl idiot. I blushed. I know I blushed. I looked down at my feet, and I felt the air start to get warmer and warmer, like we were in the tropics.

FIVE

THE REST of the game was amazing, even though I had trouble focusing on it because I kept thinking about Freedom Boy. My brain didn't want to think about him but I couldn't stop my heart. I'd never seen a boy as dreamy as Freedom Boy. Despite myself, I guess I was just one of thousands of women screaming and tearing at their clothes whenever he got in their airspace.

Every time the Academy team scored, the crowd would go wild and the people in the stands would applaud. It even felt like the stands applauded quietly and classily. I didn't know how to do it right. The Academy won in a narrow 46–49 victory in the last quintile over Charleston. Throughout the game Freedom Boy would occasionally give me looks when he passed us and I would turn the color of a tomato.

When the game ended, Lindsay offered us a ride to the party. We slivered our way through the departing crowd. "Are you seriously considering not going?" I asked Betty.

"I don't know. I don't really like parties. And I don't know anyone. It'll mostly be Heroes. Won't you feel awkward?" she asked.

"This is a huge opportunity to hang out with Heroes. Don't you want to meet them if you get in? And all the hot Academy boys will be there," I said. "Please, Betty, I can't go without you. Family has to stick together, right?"

"I'm beat, Sarah. Have fun. Maybe I'll see you later," she said, then walked off.

She was so weird sometimes. We couldn't really be related, could we?

Lindsay drove out of the underground parking lot and weaved through the crowd of people in Academy Harpastball shirts holding up foam fingers and signs. She thought it was funny, seeing all the Normals and Misshapes coming out in Academy gear. "What's that guy's power?" she said, pointing to an obese man in an Academy shirt. "Eating fast food at lightning speed?"

She took a right up a secluded street that wound its way through Marston Heights. The Academy is located on the hill's peak. Along the ridge, farther west, that's where the wealthy Heroes of the town live, side by side with the executives from PeriGenomics, in enormous estates hidden behind high walls.

I'd never really spent much time in the Marston neighborhood. When I was a kid my parents drove me through it to show me some of the historic sites, although it was nothing like those creepy Hero tour buses that sometimes crawl through. The neighborhood felt different from mine, even if it's the same town. There was so much space between each giant gate, and so many trees. It was like a forest with the occasional mailbox and driveway. They must have kept the trees up to hide the large mansions and properties from gawkers. There was always the occasional rogue fan or stalker. Or supervillain.

The gates bore the insignia of the Hero family who lived there. Giant letters embedded in circles, square, triangles, and other assorted shapes next to hammers and lightning bolts, swords, and axes. Occasionally one of the giant houses could be seen above the tree line or from the base of the driveway. I noticed a large iron gate with a tremendous golden F inscribed in a pentagon. It was Freedom Boy's house. It had to be. That was his family insignia. My cheeks bloomed red at the very thought of him. I couldn't believe he had talked to me at the game.

Soon enough, we were at Luke's. What he called home looked like a palace to me. A balcony topped the entryway, with rows of white Roman columns welcoming you inside. It was sunny and warm when we arrived. The perfect day and the perfect weather. Christie ran over immediately to say hi. She put me in a chokehold of a hug, like we were suddenly best friends. Leading the way out back, she had secured us three primo lounge chairs next to each other by the pool. This required her to convince a girl with green hair that she didn't really like the sun that much anyway. It took about two minutes. Green walked away, shaking her fist.

Seeing all the future Heroes in person at this party was so weird. I knew them from reading about them in the paper and on the Internet. Christie talked a blue streak, gossiping about Heroes and her famous friends while I tried to subtly people watch behind my sunglasses. She was so worldly. She knew everything about everyone.

My phone vibrated with a text. Betty. *Hey, Sarah, where's the party?*

She must've changed her mind. I didn't get it, but whatever. Hopefully she wouldn't be a drag. I texted her back with the address and moments later, her reply came. *I'll see you there.*

The day was getting more humid and sticky by the minute. The fact that I was so excited and nervous at the same time probably had something to do with it. My skin was starting to sizzle. I walked over to the edge of the pool and dangled my feet in the water. It was perfect.

"Out of my pool!" said the Aqua Kid, midstroke. "I'm not responsible if your leg gets ripped off!" He was swimming laps, undulating like a dolphin. The silvery sheen of water on his skin glistened. I almost dropped my phone. I barely had time to register his words or movements, or even realize that he was talking to me when he snapped—

"Don't swim in the shark tank unless you're a shark!!!!" Aqua yelled at me.

I was frozen in place.

"Are you deaf?" he huffed. I jumped up, feeling like a criminal as I retreated back to the lounge chair. I had offended an Academy kid. A famous one at that. Lindsay and Christie came to my defense.

"What a pool hog," Lindsay said.

"Yeah. Who does laps at a party?" Christie added.

Behind me, a deep voice joined their chorus. "He can be a jerk. He usually is."

I turned around to see who was talking to me. My heart skipped a beat.

It was Freedom Boy. "Besides," he said, "you did more to help us win that game than he did." He smiled at me and offered his hand. "I am Freedom Boy. Nice to meet you again."

I shook back and he almost turned my fingers into dust with the sheer power of his force. He apologized when he saw me wince in pain. As much as it hurt, I didn't want him ever to let go. "Sorry, I sometimes do not know my own strength."

He looked like a statue of a god up close, all blond and hunky. The girls giggled beside me. "Again?" I asked.

"Yes. We went to Hero Camp together," he said. "Though I do not recall your name at this moment."

"I can't believe you remember me from Hero Camp. I'm Sarah Robertson," I replied. "I don't go to the Academy. Yet." I prayed he didn't say anything about my mother.

Instead, he said the next worst thing. "Oh! Your brother is Johnny Robertson, right?"

"Uh, yeah, did you know him?" I asked.

"Yes. I will not hold it against you." He winked at me. "I have to go make the rounds, but you should give me your number. We could fly together."

"Yeah?" My eyebrows rose. Was this really happening, I thought. Was Freedom Boy asking me out? I typed my number in his phone and then, without thinking about it, scrolled through his messages. I mean, how could I not. I had Freedom Boy's phone. There were numbers from various police commissioners, some from Dr. Mann and other Academy people, and I felt like Christie, getting access to the many different female Heroes he was connected to in the blogs, like Dangerous Girl and Foxy.

"Maybe I will use it sometime," he said, snatching his phone back. I shielded my eyes from the sun and Freedom Boy and lay back down on the patio chair. Every cell in my body was buzzing. The temperature ticked up into the hundreds, but I hardly noticed. I fell into the most pleasant sleep of my life.

I was rudely awoken by the sound of Megan's whiskey-tinged drawl. "Well, well, well, if it isn't the Bane of Innsmouth's little daughter. Oh, and let's not forget, the sister of Stupor Man." She lowered her sunglasses and glared at me. "You know no one wants you here. Half their parents tried to kill your mom, and with your brother drunk all the time your family doesn't have the best rep."

It was a rude awakening, to say the least. "Well then, why are you here, Megan?" You've got no powers." *Other than being a total bitch,* I wanted to add. "I'm applying, at least."

"My boyfriend, Alex, over there," she said in a "duh" voice. "Nice job almost getting killed by the way. He just loves it when people swim with him."

"Alex?" I asked, and then realized. "Wait—the Aqua Kid?"

"Such a lame name," she said to me, like I had made another major faux pas. "His name is Alex Vodianoi. His dad is, like, one of the richest men in Russia. Only a fangirl would call him by his Hero name."

"If I'm a fangirl, you're a groupie," I said.

"Don't think I don't see what's going on between you and Freedom Boy. He does that with every girl. He probably just wants to see if he can get his hands on the daughter of the villainess who escaped his father's clutches. I bet that's it. It's, like, Oedipal," she said.

She made me so mad. I wanted to make lightning strike her down or something. But nothing happened. The more I looked at her, the more I realized that even though she was a Normal, she totally had superpowers—she was super hot, she was super rich, and she lived in this super neighborhood.

"You should check on Stupor Man. I just saw him and he wasn't looking so good." She walked off. I didn't believe her. Why would he be here? My head thrummed. It always did anytime Megan and I talked.

Lindsay and Christie came back to our patio chairs, with weird purple drinks in their hands. "You know," said Lindsay, "when you get there, you should totally stick with me. I'll show you around. Like, some teachers you gotta avoid. Professor Cyclopso is so creepy. He always stares at the girls with his one eye. Or Mrs. Leach, but that's kind of self-explanatory. And Dr. Mann."

"I love Dr. Mann. He's so hot," Christie added. "He's hot like a man, not a stupid boy playing action-figure games like Freedom Boy or my brother."

"Admit it, though, you love Freedom Boy," Lindsay added.

"Sort of, but Freedom Man is even better, don't you think?" Christie said.

"Who's your brother?" I asked.

"J5 over there," she said, motioning to John Joel Glanton V, aka J5. He was holding court on the other side of the pool, murdering people in various board games. His pasty skin sparkled in the sunlight, except around the thick black collar that wrapped around his neck. The same one Christie had. It must be a mind-control thing. J5 played simultaneous games of Risk, Battleship, Scrabble, and chess. "I sunk your battleship!" he yelled. A scrawny kid yelled, "J5, you suck!" and slammed his hands down on the table in response. The kid's hands went through the table and straight to his lap, like the table was a hologram.

Someone was tugging on my sleeve. "Hey," said the girl. "Are you Johnny Robertson's sister?"

I pulled her over to the side, excusing myself from Lindsay and Christie. "Who's asking?"

"I thought you were. You look like him. Um, you're going to want to come downstairs."

I followed the mystery girl to the back door. "What's your name?"

"Rosa. I was friends with your brother before he got kicked out." I should mention that my brother was the Academy's first expulsion in a decade. "He's in the basement," she said, leading me through the throng. It felt like scrum at a big stadium concert, except in this case I was pushed up against people who were levitating or made out of material that wasn't quite flesh.

The basement was totally different than the rest of the house. It was a wood-paneled seventies-style temple to male pursuits, like weight lifting and video games. There was a small crowd gathered around the sofa in the center of the room.

I had a queasy feeling that Johnny was the reason for the crowd. As I got a closer look, it was pretty clear that I was right.

My brother was at the center of the commotion, with a horde of jocks flying around him like little imps. He was lounging across the couch, a lion napping after a great feast. His black hair askew, his red T-shirt dirty and smudged. At some point, someone had drawn a mustache on his face in Magic Marker. My eyes were instantly drawn to his AlcoMeter belt, which was beeping and blinking bright red.

One of the downsides to his power—Betty's, too—is that their bodies are constantly making alcohol out of any H20, whether it's inside or outside them. If they don't take their medicine, their alcohol level might get too high. First they get drunk and then they get alcohol poisoning and then they may die. The AlcoMeter monitored this, and if you're Betty, you kept track of it. Not so much if you're Johnny.

I fought my way over to the couch and felt for a pulse. Not dead.

Good. He had a small stream of drool running out of the corner of his mouth. I felt his forehead, to see if he was feverish. He seemed okay. I searched his pockets for pills, shoved one in his mouth, and forced him to swallow it.

Dad was going to kill him. I hoped he didn't need to go to the emergency room again. Johnny's screwups were a touchy subject in our family. Particularly his expulsion from the Academy. I didn't know too many of the details. It's just—one day he was going, the next day he wasn't. He acquired a leather jacket in the interim and a white T-shirt with New Kid written in Magic Marker. Everyone at Harris High called him a Misshape and disliked him even more because he was once in the Academy.

"Can I give him something too?" asked some Hero in a stupid varsity jacket.

"No!" I said, firmly. "He's not in good shape. This isn't, like, a party trick."

Rosa glared at the Hero.

While we were occupied, some of the Harpastball team snuck up behind Johnny. Bearing a Big Gulp cup filled to the brim with ice-cold water, a kid slowly flew in my brother's direction so that Johnny's dangling hand fell inside. Johnny jerked back but it was too late. The clear liquid clouded up, swirling with dark colors, and transformed into a deep red wine. The senior held the Big Gulp cup up like a chalice. "To Johnny Robertson," he yelled with a flourish. "Keeping the parties alive!" He downed a swig of the liquid, gagging slightly on its acrid taste. His face curled in a frown, looking at my passed-out brother. "That boy must be hammered! This stuff tastes terrible, Robertson."

Johnny mumbled, "What the hell is going on, boys?"

The jock said, "Just looking for a top-off, Johnny. Was hoping not to bother you too much. You're a busy guy."

"Not a problem, my man," my brother mumbled, then slumped backward.

The AlcoMeter on Johnny's belt was still blinking red. "Hey," I said, nudging him in the ribs. "Sit up." He straightened up on the couch, head wobbling. I handed him another pill and he begrudgingly took it.

"I'm fine," said Johnny. "Hi, Rosa." He perked up. "I like your hair. Today," he added. "At this party."

"You're not fine. You're drunk," I said. "And you didn't tell me you were going to this."

"I had a message to deliver." Johnny pulled an envelope out of his back pocket with a flourish. "This came in the mail for you. I thought you might want to see it." It was slightly scuffed from the journey, but it was the envelope. My envelope. The culmination of my summer, of all my work and all those tests. The Academy emblem was embossed on the front, a fancy silver shield.

It was my letter from the Academy. The one that would change my life.

I grabbed it from him. His AlcoMeter turned to yellow. I should have waited until it was green but he was getting better and I had a letter to open.

"I'll be right back," I said and ran upstairs to open it. I was going to open it in private. Maybe a bedroom no one was using. But Lindsay spotted me.

"Oh my god, is that your letter?" she asked.

I nodded, shrugging my shoulders. Lindsay's face lit up. "Sarah's opening her letter, everyone. Check it out," she announced.

Before I could even tear open the envelope, a group of kids had formed behind me. Some looking over my shoulder, others flying above to get a better view. It should've felt like a hug, but the vibe was weirdly competitive. They were on my side, right?

I closed my eyes, held my breath, and tore it open. A single piece of paper was inside. I unfolded it and read it aloud.

> *Dear Miss Sarah Robinson,*
> *We have received your application and were very impressed with your abilities and your passion for the Academy. The Academy has received a record number of applications from very qualified students this year. We regret to inform you that we can not accept you for admissions at this time. Due to the large number of applicants, we can't discuss individual applications.*

By the time I got to the last sentence the letter was hard to read. My eyes were tearing up and my voice felt wobbly. They rejected me? And I got to find out in front of the whole Academy? This was the worst day ever. I was crushed. I felt like the world was pushing on my chest. I barely noticed the small handwritten note in the bottom corner that said CALL ME! —DR. MANN, followed by his number. The impromptu audience began to walk away. I heard someone say, "Of course, they're not going to let in the kid whose mom destroyed an entire town."

My life was over. Everything I planned, my dreams, it was all crushed. I made a beeline for the bathroom, looking for some privacy. Before I could escape, someone pawed at my sleeve. It was Betty.

"You'll never believe it," she said, "I came here to show you." She held up a letter, oblivious to the tears streaming down my face. "I got in! I got in!"

Of course you got in, I wanted to say. But I didn't say anything. This just felt like she sucker punched me in the face. She was flushed with excitement. I probably looked worse than Johnny.

"Are you okay?" she asked. "You look sick."

I fled into the bathroom. There was a clear view of the sky through a little porthole window: little fluffy clouds sped toward the sun, smashed together into massive dark forms and blocked out the light. The wind picked up and blew towels off the deck chairs and onto the lawn. I could hear people talking outside the bathroom.

"I miss Sam," said Christie, her distinctive purr ringing out over the din. My ears perked up. "He knew how to make the weather fun."

"Sorry! I thought this would work," Lindsay apologized.

My shoulders tensed. I continued to eavesdrop through the window.

Christie sounded bored. "The weather would've been nice without her. It's not like she's got real powers. Just a Misshape who isn't a criminal yet."

It came as a shock. They were talking about me. My heart sank. I had gone from friend and potential classmate to Misshape in an instant. Was that why they had invited me? To try and scam great weather, like I was just a tool—not a real person, or even a friend. Suddenly, my sadness snapped into a toxic cocktail of anger.

Thunder growled overhead. Huge lightning began to strike the backyard. Trees shook and the ground rumbled. Someone knocked on the door.

"Hey, sis, you okay?" asked Johnny.

"No. I'll never be okay again," I said.

"You have to come out of there sometime," he said. "Get yourself together and I'll take you home."

I was pretty sure I was going to escort his staggering ass home, but I had to take what I could right now.

SIX

I DON'T KNOW what came first: the town or the weirdness. Mom said that Doolittle Falls has always been a town rife with rumors, reports, legends, and fantastic events that can't be explained away.

Some historians claim that the founders of Doolittle Falls came over on the *Mayflower*, rogue Heroes who fled King George's wrath along with the Puritans. Others reported that they were kicked out of Plymouth Plantation and sought refuge along the hills of the Miskatonic River. The only thing that's consistent is that every story involves the persecution of people with powers by those weaker than them. That's how the town became a Hero haven and the location of the world's first Hero Academy in 1656.

Mom said that Heroes have been around since the dawn of time. Throughout the ages, people have held them in high esteem and great disdain, depending on whether they're fighting in a war or trying to rule a country. Kings are notorious for using them to conquer lands and then exiling or killing them. It's hard to run a proper monarchy when one person can fly over your knights and behead you with their eyes.

Once Doolittle Falls got a reputation as a hotbed of witches and warlocks, incredible people made the pilgrimage to live here. It was sort of like a self-inflicted penal colony: hordes of fantastic, super people committing themselves to live in the wilds of Massachusetts.

It is hard to tell if a townsperson had a power just by looking at them, although some are more discreet than others. Some of the national celebrities wear their capes around town, like Freedom Man, but almost everyone else Clark Kents it. Though not since olden times do people have genuine secret identities. Those that do use them mostly to make their docs more interesting.

Mom explained it like this: Everyone is born without powers, but as they grow older, they develop. And once puberty hits, *boom*, you're a full-on one-person crime-fighting machine. Or, in some cases, crime-causing. But until that point, you're in limbo, with some traces of powers to come. Some may find that they can control the elements, like turning rocks into liquid. Others may just be able to fly, although very few can without some assisted propulsion. For Mom, it came on suddenly, in a matter of a day. Then her life unfolded, perfectly: acceptance to the Hero Academy, a glorious Hero career, and going back to work at the Academy as dean once she had two small children.

I asked Mom once if I would have powers. She patted me on the head and said, "Maybe, maybe. But you'll always be amazing. No matter what."

She tried to explain how superpowers happened once. They're the result of a small rogue chromosome that broke off from the rest of the genes thousands of years ago. That was all well and good, but when some virus interacted with this chromosome, it transformed it into a source of potential superpowers. That's how Heroes came into existence, and that's how they marry other Heroes and they pass down powerful powers from kid to kid.

The process of finding out who was going to have awesome powers, the right kind of powers, was similar to finding a prima ballerina. Prima ballerinas are discovered when they're young, when experts check the make of their feet and their legs to determine whether they'll develop into sylphs that you can throw around. The Academy system keeps its eye on kids around the world in a similar way. All of the tests and physicals that these kids take are supposed to one day pay off with the ultimate golden ticket, admission to the Academy. In Doolittle Falls, however, all the Hero parents, Hero genetics, and Hero money stack the deck for the majority of students.

If you're in, you receive a big envelope in the mail. And then you're pretty much a Doolittle Falls ghost: You're not normal anymore. You're one of "them," one of the elite, and your teenage shenanigans include flying, super-strength, and amazing eyesight. Every day you're Superman. You appear publicly as a Hero, and are way more likely to depend on Lycra fabric or shiny lamé as fashion choices for everyday wear.

I always thought that lamé was lame with an accent mark.

The week Mom left was the worst week of my life. One day she was packing us lunch and sending us off to school, and the next she was all over the news and on the cover of every paper. The day the Mayflower Nuclear Reactor exploded started out normal, and then the news hit, and I knew that nothing would ever be the same again. It destroyed Innsmouth, a town twenty minutes north of Doolittle Falls. They had to evacuate the town. It was left in ruins. Thousands were left homeless. People aren't even allowed to enter it anymore. The pictures were devastating. There was so much destruction. Reports focused on the seven people who failed to get out in time. They disappeared. They're presumed dead. But there were no bodies.

When we heard about the explosion, we were sent home from school. I huddled in front of the TV with Johnny, Mom, and Dad, watching the news updates. Ann Glanton on WXBS put on her best frowny face and told us about expected death counts and contamination areas. When the phone rang, Mom grabbed it and immediately suited up. She had to run out to help with the Academy's response to the crisis. I figured it was the Hero "bat signal." Soon she'd be on TV, part of the Heroes, containing the problem and rescuing people.

That never happened.

The next morning, when I woke up, she wasn't home. Dad and Johnny were still asleep. I turned on the TV to get updates. The newscasters looked happier. They said a suspect was in custody, and a picture flashed on screen. My mother, in full costume. For a minute, I forgot what the word "suspect" meant. It was so incomprehensible. Then a stream of reports filled my ears about her role in the explosion, how she was a supervillian, how she had escaped and was being hunted by Heroes. "It looks like the dean of Hero Academy is more like the fiend of Hero Academy," someone quipped. It was that day she stopped being Outstanding Lady and became Lady Oblivion. It didn't make sense. It felt like the walls in the house were moving, like the ceiling was falling down and crushing me in the rubble. When the smack of the morning paper hit our door, I padded out to get it and saw my mother, once again: SUPERVILLIAN TERRORIZES MASSACHUSETTS. WORST NUCLEAR DISASTER IN US HISTORY.

School was canceled. The town shut down. Most of New England shut down as well. We had to hide out. Vandals threw trash on our front lawn. Somebody spray painted our garage door, writing "Fiend." The Doolittle Falls cops did nothing. We just watched TV, waiting and waiting for the phone to ring. A few unmarked black cars showed up across the street, and never moved. It wasn't long before reporters showed up. They camped outside our house. When we tried to step outside, they rushed at us with microphones and cameras with glaring lights.

So we stayed inside. The town flooded twice that week. A hailstorm nearly killed one of the reporters for WXBS news. I didn't know about my powers. I thought it was just coincidence.

The news was the only thing keeping us tethered to the world. Every night they updated us on Mom's escape. They showed her in battle with her former allies. When she fought Freedom Man, it was sold as the battle of the century. Good versus evil. It took the heat off our house for a couple of nights. When her former students mounted an assault, we unplugged the TV. Dad was like a zombie. Johnny, too. I cried every night.

She never came home. After a week, she disappeared. After a month, the news coverage finally let up. After three, the last reporters left our front yard. After four, we packed up her belongs into boxes and put them into the attic: the costumes, weapons, pictures of her receiving medals from the president, news covers, plaques, all of it. I took one of her boxes—the one with her main costume—and I kept it hidden in my closet. One day, someone from the Superhero bureau came to confiscate her classified equipment. We handed over a brown box with HERO SUPPLIES written on it in black marker. We didn't ask any questions.

They never found the box in my closet.

Johnny and I went back to school. Johnny was in his first year at the Academy. I can't imagine the grief he had to deal with, but he never said anything to Dad or me. I was in seventh grade. The Normals stopped talking to me. A lot of the Heroes (or future Heroes, since none of us had powers yet), like Lindsay, were still friendly.

Dad, who ran a division at PeriGenomics, was demoted. He has super-eyesight and is really smart. He rose up in the PeriGenomics ranks quickly. But then Mom became the Bane of Innsmouth and he fell down the ladder. People started calling him a Misshape. Given what happened to Mom, he didn't protest. He still needed the job. We thought of moving, but in spite of everything, we had too many ties to Doolittle Falls. Besides, how could Mom find us if she came back?

A week after the men came to get the boxes, our family, all three of us, went for a walk. Dad's suggestion. We strolled downtown on a hazy, humid summer day. Across the river, workers were changing a giant billboard that stood above the PeriGenomics factors. A billboard that Dad had to see every day when he went to work. They took giant sheets of paper and plastered them down with paintbrushes that telescoped to reach the height of the billboard. We stood up to get a better look.

The first thing we saw were the words, in red letters: WANTED: FOR MASS DESTRUCTION, TERRORISM AND ACTS AGAINST THE STATE. Our hearts stopped, collectively. And then, with a few swipes of the brush, a giant picture of Mom was pasted up next to those words. I stood next to my father and my brother feeling nothing, save Johnny's hand on my shoulder. I couldn't cry.

I ran down through a small wooded area to the banks of the Miskatonic. Shivering in my pink hoodie, I settled down on a rock and watched the rush of the river. I could hear Dad and Johnny in the distance yelling, "Sarah!"

I stared into the river. The temperature had dropped at least ten degrees. I felt the day switching from summer to fall, in an instant. Then I felt something. My cheeks were getting wet and I put my hand to my eyes. Was I crying? I looked up to the sky. Sleet was lapping at my face. Sleet in August. It was so heavy I couldn't see past my own nose.

That's when it hit me: My powers had developed. That weird weather when Mom was under attack? Me. My fault. I had waited for it to happen for my whole life. And when it did, the one person I wanted to share it with was gone.

FALL

SEVEN

A WOMAN IN a white blouse and red pencil skirt led me into Dr. Mann's office. He was on the phone. I could see only his neatly shaved head, looming above the enormous leather chair like a small globe. Out of politeness, I tried to ignore the call. I'm not very good at that.

I hadn't seen the office since Mom left. All her diplomas and family photos had been taken down, burned, probably, and replaced with Dr. Mann's paper pedigree. The room was large, with high windows and enough space between the door and the mahogany desk that I had to take a few paces to get to the small black chairs across from him.

I sat down and smoothed out my black skirt. I had no idea what to wear to this interview. I had been working through the stages of grief at the loss of my Academy acceptance. I sulked and nearly flooded downtown on three occasions. Dad said a black skirt and my purple sweater would be fine and serious enough for Dr. Mann. I felt overdressed. It may have been the first week of September, but the summer heat still lingered.

"He's not Academy material. I don't care that his grandfather is Gold Lightning!" Dr. Mann said, then paused while someone spoke on the other end. "Yes, I understand. Big donors, they're all big donors. Do we have to take their incompetent progeny?" He went silent. "Look, I know his parents think he can walk on water." He paused. "Okay, fine. So he *can* walk on water, but it has to be purified with a pH of exactly seven point five. Is that really a superpower worthy of the Academy?" Another pause. "A new training facility in the Antarctic? Fine. But no more of these, these...Misshape children of rich Heroes. It dilutes us!"

He slammed the phone down and rubbed his temple, then swiveled around slowly to face me. He had a square jaw, a broad face, and sharp cheekbones. He smiled at me. His teeth were as white as paper and perfectly lined up. He looked like an advertisement for something expensive.

"Sorry about that. I didn't realize you had come in. Sarah Robertson, is it? Great to meet you," he said and thrust out his hand. I felt at ease around him. For a millisecond it seemed like the skin on his hand turned scaly and green. Like some kind of lizard. It felt coarse, but it passed so quickly, I could hardly register it.

He glanced at his hand and apologized. "Oh dear, I'm sorry. It's a saurian tic I have. Goes with my powers and pops up on occasion."

"That's okay," I said, pretending I knew what "saurian" meant. "If you don't mind my asking, what are your powers?"

"Besides fundraising and listening to the complaints of the school executive board?" he said, chuckling. "De-evolution is my power. I can transform into many sorts of lesser creatures, from dinosaurs to a bacteria colony. It was useful when I was younger and into fighting and vigilante heroics, like so many people with new Hero Cards, but now I mostly prefer to keep myself as a human. Devolving has its drawbacks. Not the least of which," he said, while scratching at the lizard hand, "it's itchy."

His expression changed to something serious. He clasped his hands together on his desk. "Sarah, I asked you here to discuss your application to the Academy."

You mean my rejection, I thought.

He pulled out a folder and flipped through it. From what I could see, it was all the materials I sent in, as well as pictures and graphs I'd never seen before.

"You were a special case. While your powers put you on the borderline for admission, they were not strong enough to guarantee you a position. I shouldn't admit this, but since you required a scholarship, that worked against you. But based on our readings and testing, you have enormous potential. Unfortunately, I couldn't convince the board that your potential was enough to grant you admission. First, there's your family situation. We can get over that—we did with Johnny, before he made his own mess. But also, there's the fact of Sam Albedo having just graduated. He came in with your same power but with significantly more control to start. You're powerful but untamed, and they weren't sure, based on the results, that you could be tamed."

It was heartbreaking to hear. I almost preferred it when it was some vague reason and I could blame them for making a mistake. But knowing it was my powers was different. Something that was part of who I was wasn't good enough for them. And that someone named Sam was better than me. I clenched my jaw to keep from crying. I had to be strong. Heroes don't cry.

He put down the folder and looked me in the eyes. His stare was intense. "I'll be honest with you. Now, this is very confidential. If it were any other case, you would have been let in and watched for progress. We do it all the time." His voice took on a radio announcer's gravity. "But you have to understand, given your family's history, and the unfortunate situation with your mother, we just didn't have that kind of flexibility. But I believe in you. You are not your mother. And from the fact you have yet to spit on me, you are obviously not your brother. Just because you didn't make it in this year doesn't mean you won't. We accept new students—up to the age of eighteen, even."

I sat there, blinking. It was a lot to take in. I wasn't sure what to say. He continued: "But what happens next is up to you. Being a Hero is more than flying around and fighting supervillains. It takes a lot of hard work, not just in the body and mind, but in the heart. A Hero is not just someone with powers."

I nodded.

"Being a Hero means being a person who knows when to use those powers and to what ends. Most important, it's about making difficult decisions, and when the time comes, making the hard choices that others are too weak to make. At some point, Sarah, you will have to make a choice. Do you really want to be a Hero?"

"I do," I said. My voice came out so small, it surprised me.

Dr. Mann grinned back. "I know you will. And when you do, I'll be glad to have you as one of our students." His voice grew quiet. "I can't do anything about this semester. It's a wash. But we'll keep in touch. Great things will happen for you, Sarah Robertson."

I didn't know what to think. It was like Dr. Mann had given me a kernel of hope that I could get into the Academy. His secretary escorted me out of the building, leading me down a series of secret stairs and hallways that cut through the hill of Marston Heights. It spat me out a few hundred feet below onto the Harpastball field. I turned around so I could remember where the elevator was, but when I did, it had disappeared, covered entirely by very realistic-looking rocks that blended into the cliff face.

The Harpastball field was eerily empty. Every time I'd been there it had been overrun with players, fans, bands, and all sorts of revelers. Seeing the field without players made me feel like I was already a part of the school. I passed by the enormous stands and skipped over their magnetic track. Without people on the stands, it looked like a giant ship floating at sea. A wind blew by and the stands creaked slightly. My heart raced at the thought of them toppling and I quickened my pace. Even the slightest movement made an enormous sound.

The more I thought about meeting with Dr. Mann, the more excited I got. In my dream world he would have apologized and told me to show up to class on Monday, but short of that, the meeting was perfect. Dr. Mann was nice. But some of what he said was confusing. What choices? I didn't know what else I could do to get into the Academy.

When I got to the main entrance, the gates opened automatically. I wanted to explore but I didn't want to get in trouble. And trouble was definitely possible, especially now that I knew they were watching me. I walked home. I cut down Main Street and took the left toward my house. As I walked, it felt like someone was behind me, but also hovering above me. I turned around just as Freedom Boy landed gently on the ground.

"Hi, Sarah," he said. I looked up into the greatest smile I have ever seen. "How have you been?"

I fumbled for words, and after an awkward silence finally announced, "Good!"

"Glad to hear it. Were you just at the Academy?"

"Yes. I met with a Mann," I replied. "I mean, a doctor."

"Well, which one was it?" he joked.

"Dr. Mann. I met with Dr. Mann," I finally said.

"He is a great guy. Probably telling you about how they screwed up and are going to let you into the Academy."

"Kind of?" It came out as a question. I didn't want to tell him anything more. I didn't know what was happening, exactly.

"Sorry I did not call, by the way. I dropped my phone while flying home from the party and had not backed up the new information."

I didn't believe him for a minute. "I have more numbers. You can have some if you want. If you want to call me, sometime."

"Yes!" Freedom Boy enthused. He seemed so happy. Maybe he wasn't lying. Hmmm. "That would be great." A pause. "So where are you off to?"

"Home," I said. "I was walking home. It's not far."

"Oh. Great. Mind if I walk you home?" he offered.

Mind? Mind, I thought. "No, I think that would be okay," I said.

And like that, I was walking home, escorted by Freedom Boy. He talked endlessly about school, but I wasn't quite sure if I heard anything over the drumbeat of my heart. I was trying hard to act as normal as possible.

EIGHT

A WEEK LATER my alarm clock woke me up with Florence and the Machine. The sun streamed through my bedroom windows. I opened my eyes and turned my head toward my humidifier. It looked like it smiled back.

The first day of school was upon me. I had been dreading heading back to Harris High since the rejection letter, but now I had a new purpose in life. This year was going to be different. So I wasn't going to the Academy. I knew my path. Dr. Mann said I needed to make a choice, and I was ready to make it. I needed to choose to be a Hero. I needed to try harder, work harder, focus harder. If I wanted the Academy to accept me and make me a Hero, I had to show them that I wanted it. I looked at my humidifier again, willing snow to rise from it, like magic. It stared back at me. I was going to need something bigger. Much bigger.

I rose from my bed, rubbed my eyes, and attempted to hype myself up for the day. Every Hero needs a good origin story. Every day was a new opportunity for the great Sarah Robertson. Any day could be the day that I'd meet my nemesis or get bitten by that radioactive insect. Doolittle Falls is lousy with radioactive pests just ready to grant powers like little nuclear fairies.

My phone blinked from my desk. I had received one text message since falling asleep. It came in at three a.m., something from Freedom Boy. He'd been sending me flirty texts ever since he had walked me home, though they always seemed to straddle the line between wanting to be my new platonic male friend and my new sweep-me-off-my-feet boyfriend. I assumed it was platonic. I mean, why would Freedom Boy, America's biggest heartthrob, want to date me? I looked at the message.

Good luck at school! Want to celebrate Friday night?

Eep. I didn't know what to say. I tried to think of responses as I prepared for school. I went through my desk, pulling out school supplies and throwing them in my bag. I wrote back, feeling bold.

Like a date?

Before I could even put the phone down, it buzzed in my hand.

Yes! Buzz Man. 8:00. I will be one in the corner enjoying my Freedom Fries.

"Awesome!" I thought. Now I couldn't wait for the week to end. Five days and Freedom Boy might literally sweep me off my feet. This was already turning out to be the best year ever.

When I came downstairs, Dad was already up and about in the kitchen. He was making some coffee and glancing over at the morning paper on the table. He has the eyesight of an eagle or something. I was always really jealous of it. He's a skinny redhead. I get my freckles from him, but my curly hair and curvy figure is all Mom. At least that's what he told me. He's Irish and she was Iranian so it makes sense.

"So what's the plan?" Dad said.

I stuck an English muffin in the toaster. "Do well at Harris High and practice my Hero skills so I can reapply to the Academy."

"Yes," he said and nodded, excited. "But remember, the Academy isn't the be-all and end-all of life. Focus on what you can control in the world. You can do well in school. Albert Einstein didn't need an Academy to change the world."

The buzz of the toaster drowned me out as I added, "Yeah, but

I don't think Albert Einstein had a brother who got kicked out of physics."

I wanted to talk more to Dad about my plans for sophomore year—Study, Practice, Eat Well, Train, Check In monthly with Dr. Mann to remind him how great I was – —but we were interrupted by Johnny, who stomped down the stairs and fell like a sack of flour into a kitchen chair.

"God, do you have to make breakfast so loudly?" my brother said and groaned. His voice had slowed down to a drawl. He was fiddling with the saltshaker, and it slipped from his fingers and went skidding across the floor, spilling everywhere. Johnny wasn't particularly functional in the morning. Part of the disorder, Dad said.

"Hey, brother!" I chirped.

"No, Sarah," he complained, watching me chew my muffin. "I can hear you masticating from here."

"It's important to chew my food, bro. You couldn't save my life if I started choking right now," I said, pantomiming gagging and making my brother turn greener. "Right, Dad?" I asked, looking for backup. He nodded with a smile and went to clean up after the spilled salt on the floor.

Johnny continued with his groans. "The sun! God, why do you curse me?" He pulled out his aviators and placed them over his squinting eyes. "It didn't have to be sunny today, sister. You could've made it rain. I would've done that for you!"

I ignored him, asking Dad, "Hey, can I steal some of that coffee?"

"Sure," he said, with the dustpan and brush on the floor. "Johnny, you are especially klutzy this morning. Would you like some extra pills? I have some Tylenol. You should take it with your meds."

Johnny held his hand out like an orphan begging for food. Dad pulled out Johnny's meds and handed him two bright yellow pills. Johnny swallowed them down with his neon-green prescription pill as a chaser.

Dad glanced at his watch. "I'm late," he said, and ordered me to take Johnny to school. "Make sure he gets there. He seems a bit boozy this morning." Boozy was the term for when Johnny's condition made him act like he was drunk. His AlcoMeter was blinking yellow.

"Guys," Johnny whined, "still here, still in the room!"

Dad and I exchanged a grin. For a self-proclaimed rebel, Johnny can still act like a needy kid. The quirkiness and unpredictability of a disease like his kind of kills the whole "cool punk-rock loner" shtick. It'd be like if James Dean needed an inhaler.

Harris High stood before us. The gray school looked like a squashed cement pancake. On the field, members of the football team were finishing their morning drills. The welcome sign had a cartoon of an angry old woman wielding a club—the school mascot, the Harris High Harridan—and read WE RESPECT ALL BUT FEAR NONE.

We went into the front entrance and parted ways, pretending not to know each other as we walked toward our respective lockers. Mine was empty. Just another reminder that I thought I'd be spending this year at the Academy. I stuffed my things in and thought that it wasn't empty; it was…full of possibility.

The slam of a locker interrupted my daydreaming.

"Great, another year of this," muttered my neighbor. He kept talking to himself. "Three more years and I'm free." Noticing my stare, he wandered off, still grumbling.

After my first four classes, my backpack was so laden with textbooks, I felt like I was going to snap like a twig. AP European history shouldn't take a thousand pages and ten pounds to explain. Europe is one of the smaller continents. Whenever I got bored, I would start to imagine the magical date I was going on with Freedom Boy. Sure, it was only to a coffee shop, but it was with Freedom Boy. I looked down at my outfit. My favorite red skirt was looking kind of dingy. There was a small tear in the hem, and a stain on the thigh. I hadn't gotten any clothes for the year, and I had nothing that would let Freedom Boy know that I was a confident, sexy, and hot future Hero. Honestly, I was counting on the comfort of an Academy uniform to solve my sartorial uncertainty.

Fifth period was my favorite subject, English. I went into Mr. Schwartz's class expecting greatness, clutching a dog-eared copy of *Cat's Cradle*. Most of the same kids from my other classes filtered in.

I saw one girl shudder when Matt Butters strolled in with his backup singers, the three gray Spectors. Undeniably full-grown women, they were tough and pretty with loads of eyeliner, darling little dresses, and spectacular beehives. Everyone in school called Butters a Misshape. He mostly stuck to himself, and he was rarely alone. Getting three backup singer ghosts who project your thoughts was one of the weirder powers around Doolittle Falls. What could you do with it?

I felt bad for the kid, but Harris High had rules. If you wanted to survive, it was best to keep your head down and follow them.

Number one: Don't let people know that you have powers. Even if they are Freedom Man–level awesome (although, more than likely, they are super lame). Kids with powers went to the Academy. Kids with any powers that didn't make it to the Academy were targets. Normals lorded it over kids with powers.

Number two: If the Normal kids at school get wind of your powers, you are through. Labeled a Misshape and shipped off to social Siberia. Misshapes who can't hide their powers have their own little corner of the cafeteria.

Number three: If you are a known Misshape, keep your head down and don't cause any trouble. Misshapes aren't allowed on any sports teams because of rules against powers in Normal sports. Since athletes and cheerleaders are the top of the social heap, it already puts Misshapes at a disadvantage.

Number four: If you are an unknown Misshape, try to blend in. Distinguish yourself in something other than sports (claim to hate athletics) like academics or art.

A few kids were exceptions to the rules. Butters wasn't one of them.

I had no idea where I fit in on the social scale. I always thought that I was going to be a Hero. But now that I was rejected, I wondered if that made me a Misshape. I hoped not.

I had no one to talk to. It used to be Lindsay, and then it was Betty. Nobody ever bothered to talk to me. I don't think they ever thought about my powers. It was like I had my very own invisibility cloak. But this year, I would be alone. My friends had dumped me to become Heroes. Then there was my slacker brother making the Robertson name look bad. I didn't know what would happen.

Mr. Schwartz came into class and immediately grilled us on our summer reading. "Sarah Robertson, I see that copy of *Cat's Cradle*. Why don't you enlighten us on what Mr. Vonnegut thought about the nature of science?"

I fumbled in my bag for my notes. "In *Cat's Cradle* the author is critical of science's notion that all discoveries are good for mankind."

Mr. Schwartz nodded. "What discovery is discussed in the book?"

"A weapon called ice-nine, which would freeze all the water it touched, and it froze all the oceans in the world."

Butters' Spectors burst into song: "You're as cold as ice! You're willing to sacrifice!"

"Very good," Mr. Schwartz said. I didn't know whether he was speaking to me or the Spectors. He turned his attention to a girl sitting in the back. "Alice, what book did you read this summer?" I knew who she was, since we were in classes together every year—Alice Lofting. She had on a plaid shirt opened to show a ratty band tee underneath. Her short hair was dyed jet black.

"*Another Bullshit Night in Suck City,*" she said, savoring all the bad words. I think she chose the book just so she could say its name in class.

"Not on the list. But I know that book," said Mr. Schwartz, barely concealing his smile. "Since you took so much joy in the title, could you tell us where it comes from?"

Honestly, I could barely hear what they were saying. Butters' Spectors were continuing with the whole "ice" theme. They had gotten to that cheesy old song "Ice Ice Baby."

"Da-da-da-da-da-dum!" one sang, imitating the bass. The others chanted, "Ice, ice baby, too cold, too cold."

Alice and the Spectors were interrupted by the ringing of the bell. Before I could even make it to the door, the loudspeaker kicked in and the principal announced, "Will the following students please report to room twenty-four-A for next period."

He droned out names. I heard Matt Butters, some other familiar ones, and a weird array of kids I barely knew. Alice Lofting. Johnny Robertson. And me.

Alice gave me a nod as she passed. "Come on, Robertson. We all screwed up somehow."

"Yeah but—me *and* my brother?" I muttered. I didn't get it.

NINE

LICE AND I got to twenty-four-A at the same time and grabbed seats in the middle of the classroom. Butters followed behind. Some kids were there already, but the room itself was empty. No signs of any teaching going on at all. There were no READ! posters, no prints of the American Constitution or the periodic table of elements.

Some of the kids in the classroom were familiar, but I didn't recognize many of them. There was a freshman acting bizarre in the back of the room. His eyes were darting everywhere and his body kept flickering on and off at random intervals like he was a strobe light or something. Anytime he looked at a girl, he disappeared. He'd reappear soon after, staring at his shoes.

My brother's buddy Markus walked into the room and gave me a big smile. "Sarah!" he said, and took a seat in the front row. A girl came in with him and took the desk right behind him, giving him puppyish glances. I hadn't ever seen her before. But I knew Markus.

"Hey, Markus!" I said. "I haven't seen you all summer. You probably stayed out of trouble if you avoided Johnny."

"Not really. Finally, I realized my true talent. Romancing the MILF."

"Ew!" Alice blurted, raising her eyebrows at me. I shrugged. Markus was a known Misshape. He could read the minds of women—but only women who had been pregnant. He never mentioned his other power, but Johnny told me about it. I guess in second grade Markus was bitten by a radioactive chicken at a petting zoo, which was subsequently rated the worst petting zoo in New England. After the incident, if he flapped his arms spastically for a few minutes he could fly. Then he'd crash down hard looking terrified, just like a chicken. He had gotten to play for the Harpastball team at some point thanks to the flying, but that didn't last.

The girl behind Markus introduced herself to me. "I'm Wendy," she said, and she shook my hand. I wondered if she had a power.

"Alice," I said, "why do you think we're here?" It was pretty much the first thing I'd ever said to her.

"Between Butters and that strobe light of a freshman, it's a weird-kid roundup," she said.

Minutes after the second bell rang, the classroom was still relatively empty and the teacher's desk was unoccupied. Then the usual suspects slouched in and sat in the back. Harris High's most frequent detention-goers, whose mere existence contributed to the bad rep that Misshapes had throughout Doolittle Falls. They wore that rep like a crown. They were all Johnny's new best friends, of course. Super delinquents.

"Hey, Hamilton," I said. I had to say hi. He practically lived on our sofa this summer. His cheap plastic shutter shades looked like half-closed venetian blinds. They were always dripping thick paint. Today it was red. He walked by us and a paintball shot out of his eye, hit his glasses, and dripped down into a huge puddle on the ground.

"Argh," he said, taking a bandanna out of his back pocket and frantically cleaning up the mess.

"Hamilton, Hamilton, Hamilton," said Henry "Backslash" Pap, one of the delinquents. He was wearing his trademark T-shirt with a giant backslash on it. Backslash was one of the only Misshapes who took on a Hero name. "You know what I'm teaching you this year? How *not* to get busted for graffiti."

"Yeah, but whatever I do, at least I won't look like your punk ass," Hamilton replied, glancing up from his effort.

Backslash poked Hamilton in the side. "Come on, that's a total lie. I look way better than you when I'm running from the cops." His skill was somewhat useful: a really fast runner, but he could run fast only when he was escaping from something, whether it was a bully, a dog, or, in most cases, the law.

"Nice job, Hammy-Ham," said Kurt. I shivered when I looked

at him. He may have been my brother's friend, but I didn't trust the guy. There was something cold about his eyes. Unfeeling. He could freeze water. He should've been in the Academy, but they didn't let him in because of his family. He was the result of a secret affair between a famous Hero and his Normal mother. It would've been too controversial. He used to live in Innsmouth, but after the disaster he moved to a trailer park in East Doolittle. He never mentioned the disaster in front of Johnny and me, which is why my brother liked him. I felt differently.

My brother walked in and sat in the back with them, like he was looking to be crowned king of the rats. Johnny was too much of a punk-rock nihilist to care about the social trivialities of high school. He spent his days skipping class and ignoring teachers while he read or studied whatever he wanted. He even wrote MISSHAPE in White-Out on one of the sleeves of his black leather jacket.

"Misshapes. These are the Misshapes," Alice said to herself. "Just because I can talk to small woodland creatures—"

"That's your power?" I asked.

"Whatever. I thought your power was being, like, an Academy fangirl, or nerd," Alice replied. "You're a Misshape?"

I stayed quiet. Maybe she'd stop talking to me. I didn't want to say anything. I didn't know what the deal was.

I looked around the room, and I realized Alice was right. My secret was blown. Here I was: not in the Academy, and in a class with a bunch of superfreaks. Everyone at Harris High was going to think that I was a Misshape.

When Principal Holloway entered, with Tom Doodlebug slouching behind, the room snapped into attention. Doodlebug nodded at me.

The principal waved someone inside. Dr. Mann. I was so excited to see him I waved to him like an idiot. Everyone else just stared. Why was he here? For a brief moment I fantasized that he was going to pull me out of the class and take me to the Academy, where I should be, while patting my head and telling me the rejection had been a huge mistake.

Holloway shook his head. "This is my friend Dr. Mann. He's the new head of the Hero Academy and wanted to trail me today so he could meet all of you. Say hi, everybody!"

"Hi, Dr. Mann," I said, the class droning behind me. My brother was grumbling something in the back, flipping through his book loudly. I got the sense he wasn't on Team Mann.

"Hello, children," he said in the most charming fashion, following it up with a beatific smile. "It's a pleasure to meet you." I hung on his every word. Alice was blushing.

Principal Holloway took the reins, while Dr. Mann stood behind him like a guardian angel. "So to get to the point, there's been a change in your schedules that's occurred after the paperwork for the year was sent in the mail." He coughed. "According to new federal guidelines all people with...your abilities are required to take a civic responsibility class with a standardized curriculum." Holloway was looking down at his notes, avoiding eye contact. "Students at schools all across the country will be taking this course, as well as the children in the Academy." He glanced at Dr. Mann, who nodded in confirmation.

Alice raised her hand so high I thought her shoulder would come out of its socket. "Miss Lofting, I'm not really prepared to answer any questions," said the principal. Dr. Mann interrupted: "Oh Holloway, I don't think it should be a problem. Lofting, was it?" Alice said yes, sheepishly. "What was your question?"

"I thought all school regulations and policy were set at the state level of government, so how can the federal government set a requirement on education standards?"

Someone in the back coughed the word "nerd."

Principal Holloway looked confused. Dr. Mann was quick with a response. "The requirement is set by the Bureau of Superhero Affairs. It has jurisdiction over things related to people like us. People with gifts. And while it may be a violation of federalism, it does have the ability to require mandates on Heroes pursuant to authority granted by Congress."

I swear Dr. Mann looked at me when he said "powers like ours." I felt a thrill flutter in my stomach. Maybe this class would be my chance to prove myself to him.

"The Bureau has specific constitutional authority that enables it to go over the heads of a lot of other agencies and governments," he said. "For example, it administers the Hero Card program, even though it involves military and police involvement."

Butters stirred in his seat, about to raise his hand. His backup singers sang, "Question! Question!"

"Yes, Butters," Principal Holloway said.

"Who's going to teach this class? You?" he asked. "And also, what is civic responsibility?"

The Spectors started to spell out responsibility. "R-E-S-P-O-N-"

Butters blushed. "Quiet, ladies!" he hissed.

"First off," said the principal, "one of our new teachers will be covering the class. Ms. Frankl. She was recently informed about all this. You'll meet her tomorrow."

Alice muttered, "I wonder if she's a Misshape, too."

Principal Holloway continued: "And the class itself is going to go over some of the history of people with abilities in this city, and the country, and the world at large. It will also cover, umm, it will cover..." He looked around for help.

Dr. Mann took over. "The course is designed to help you explore the role of special people like yourself and those at the Academy in the world. The great responsibility and duty that comes with your powers, if they're spectacular or kind of silly." He looked around, staring at each of us in turn. "You may think such lessons are only for the elite up on the hill at my school, but they're not. You, too, are powerful. Consider yourself the Academy C-squad. You face the same restrictions in society. The class will review basics like Hero Cards and the associated draft and history that isn't covered in public school." He paused, chuckling. "Don't look so worried. The goal is to make you better members of society by harnessing your powers for good. To be honest, I don't know why this wasn't offered sooner."

I was on board with this class. It was exactly what I needed. It was exactly what Doolittle Falls needed. Something like this might make powerful kids at public school feel better about themselves. And that would mean that Misshapes could just be normal at some point, instead of hellions. That's what my gut said, at least. But there was a tiny little voice in the back of my head asking, why?

Alice smiled at me. I think she was into it, too. The other kids looked confused, and Johnny was just griping about "Misshape apartheid" or something. "This is how it begins," I heard him say. "C stands for condescension."

To be considered a part of the Academy was fine by me. If Johnny had my weather gift, it would probably be storming outside. But it was my power and the weather was stunning: sunny, with bright yellow beams hitting the parking lot like tunnels of light.

TEN

A COUPLE OF days later—my Freedom Boy date tantalizingly close—it was time for the mall. I couldn't quite believe that it was happening. Girls had Freedom Boy posters in their lockers at school. He grinned on their iPhone cases. He was on screens and billboards, in glossy, alien perfection, reminding me that our date seemed like a weird, half-remembered dream that I made up. Like that old song asked, "Is he really going out with her?"

When school got out I ran to Main Street. I had to meet Betty at three o'clock, and I was worried that I might end up late. My phone vibrated.

I'm sorry. Too much school stuff. Can't make it, Betty wrote.

Typical. Betty used to be reliable. Now she was always too busy with some Academy thing. Orientation, registration, parties. Betty was suddenly invited to parties.I wasn't happy. The sketchy bus left from downtown every half hour for the mall and took forever. The walk was an hour or so. I decided to walk. Maybe it'd give me time to figure out the perfect outfit. I was so distracted I didn't even notice the car slowing down next to me. It was a beat-up old gas-guzzler, which rattled as if it wanted to break into pieces. The window rolled down. It was hand cranked. Alice looked at me from behind the wheel.

"What's with the face, Robertson?" she asked.

"What? This is my face," I replied. "My cousin was supposed to give me a ride to the mall and she just bailed in a super-lame way," I said. "So now I am walking. Slowly."

"That sucks. My cousin did that to me the other week. Turns out he was busted for pot so it was okay, but I was stranded waiting for a tow truck while he was being arraigned." She leaned over and opened the passenger door. It made a loud creaking noise as it swung outward. "Hop in, I can give you a ride," she offered.

"Thanks," I said. "Is this thing street safe?"

"Safer than walking there, ingrate," she replied. "You know you'd have to cross a highway if you keep hoofing it."

Alice was so deadpan I had a hard time figuring out whether she was angry or making fun of me. By the time we got to the mall, I realized that was just her sense of humor. We pulled up in front of the sleek, futuristic entrance.

"What are you doing at the mall?" she asked.

"Oh, I have this, umm, date tomorrow. And I need to find something to wear."

"You look fine to me," she said, and then looked befuddled. "Really, wait, who dates these days? What are you even talking about?"

"Um, it's with a Hero and I thought I should put some extra effort in. He's surrounded by hot women in tight clothes flying around all day."

"Oh, this changes things. You need me," Alice said.

She took a hard left in the car, parking it while simultaneously cutting off an angry man in a Jeep. He honked and cursed at us as we walked toward the entrance.

"Should we meet up somewhere?" I asked her.

"Meet up?" Alice said, shaking her head. "I can't let you go off on your own in the dangerous world of chain stores. You may wind up looking like a total skank for your date."

Right. I did want to look honorable.

"Or even worse, you might *not* look like one," she added.

We walked into the mall together and she led me down the main hall. We dodged kiosks ready to spray us with perfume or offer us e-cigarettes. The Doolittle mall had some specialty Hero boutiques, native to the few American cities with Hero Academies. These stores were the Hero-themed versions of the usual mall fare: AeroHeroLe, which sold a wide array of capes and flying accessories; H&K, with its sexy assortment of skin-tight, bullet-resistant costumes and masks; and the best store of all, Captain Bearshark's Tools of War.

We passed by Bearshark. There was a gaggle of boys drooling and gaping at all the toys outside the windows. The store encouraged this window shopping with its spectacular displays: large hand cannons that fired grappling hooks, retro fluorescent ray guns, quark grenades, and a whole panoply of colorful yet dangerous devices. Any Hero necessity you could imagine. I had a wish list of goodies from the store that I'd get when I became a licensed Hero with a Hero Card: a cute red laser gun and waterproof ballistic clothing for the storms that I would use to destroy my enemies.

"Come on," Alice said, dragging me along. "We can play with toys later. We have a goal!"

We marched on, but out of the corner of my eye I kept watching Bearshark. One of the window-drooling boys tried to get inside but was denied by the burly security guard standing at the door. The guard asked the kid for his government-issued Hero Card, just to mess with him. The kid handed him a fake, and the guard laughed in his face, tearing the plastic rectangle into pieces of confetti. Hero Cards are impossible to counterfeit. The boy slipped back into his group of friends like a defeated mall warrior. Alice noticed me staring.

"Those guards are dicks," Alice said, definitively.

"I guess. But that kid was stupid, too, right?"

"Yeah, but he didn't have to be so showy about denying him admission. Stores like that just make the gulf between Heroes and everyone else more obvious. And it's not, like, always a problem. Look at you, bridging the gap with your mystery Hero on Friday night."

"Bridging the gap? What does that mean?" I felt awkward.

"Aw jeez," she said, blushing a little, her blonde hair covering her face. "I didn't mean anything by it. It's just that he's a Hero and he asked you out. On a date. That's really cool, but also so weird. Who dates? I have never, ever read about dates on Rookie. At least not that I can remember."

Who dates? I thought. I hadn't ever really had anything close to a date, or a boyfriend since lunch time with Tyler Friedman one week a couple of years ago. "I guess Freedom Boy can date. Because he's Freedom Boy and it's super retro or something."

"I knew it!" Alice said. "Yeah, Freedom Boy can do whatever he wants."

Alice pulled me into American Hero. It was a Hero fan store, filled with all sorts of Hero-themed memorabilia: cheap plastic knickknacks, posters, documentaries, and crappy ceramic collectibles. I got my Black Zephyr poster from here, years ago. Toward the back there was the supervillian section, which was like the obverse of the Hero section. All the clothing was black and sinister looking. It was really popular with the goth kids. I've avoided Hero stores since they removed all the Lady Outstanding gear and put a Lady Oblivion dartboard in the supervillian section.

Alice stood in front of Hero family pendants. "Look, Sarah," she said. "Don't build this up too much. He's just a Hero, standing in front of the daughter of his father's archenemy, asking her to go see a movie or something. It's probably not going to lead to marriage." There was a Freedom family poster behind her.

"When you put it like that, it is weird," I admitted. "And nerve-racking. Have you ever been on a date?"

Alice blushed. "Um, no. I was hooking up with someone from Hoosick for a bit last year, but that was pretty much it. I don't really get teenage boys."

"Yeah, me neither," I said. "And what about his dad? He probably hates me. Or his Hero friends? Or... Or..." I got breathy. Panic set in.

"Calm down. Right now that's out of your control. What isn't, is what you can wear on the date," she said.

"So, all-knowing one, what should I wear?"

Alice took me into boutique after boutique. She picked out clothes that were too fancy for my taste, like a silver dress that made me look like a fish. Besides, I had a year left to live on my summer ice-cream money, I couldn't blow it all before October. We went to teen stores and tried on the best combinations of jeans and fancy tops. My favorite was a royal-blue tank top made out of some crazy fabric with ruching on the sides. I didn't feel that comfortable in anything.

"I look like a doily," I said, as I put on the white lace dress Alice picked for me. Alice looked at me and frowned, a small "hmmm" coming out of her mouth.

"We need you to be comfortable."

"And attractive," I added. "I'm terrified of Freedom Boy."

"We need you to wow him," she counseled. "And also to have lots of topics that are interesting to talk about. You should do homework on that, maybe."

"Get to the clothes, Lofting."

Exhausted, we slipped into the last store, MadeGreat. It was filled with clothes for athletic, horsey girls. Classics that were a little bit faded and edgy. I was in love. Alice rifled through the sale rack. "We have it, Robertson!" She held up a wild miniskirt in hot pink, with small black hearts dotting the fabric.

"No," I said. "Really?"

"Go get one of those soft, perfect black T-shirts."

I went into the dressing room and put on the skirt. The plain black T-shirt calmed the print down and looked pretty awesome. I felt like a queen. Or a smarter, better version of myself. I stepped outside.

"By George, I think we've got it!" Alice said. She smiled at me. "It only took going to every single store in the mall."

"Sorry!" I said. "I just don't know who I am," I joked.

"Painfully obvious," she replied. We walked down the hardwood floors to the store's cash register.

I gave the bored cashier my card as Alice explained what was next. "Makeup."

"No!" I replied, shocked.

"Eh, put on your best lip gloss and you're fine. Every time one of my cousins gets dolled up with makeup they always look like a tramp. Let's go minimal. Great skin is your right, as long as you don't breakout or anything."

"Seriously, though, Alice, what am I even going to say to Freedom Boy? What do you say to a dude whose official products you can buy at the mall?"

"You'll be fine, Sarah. Besides, it's an experience. How many girls get to go on a 'date' with Freedom Boy?"

A lot of them, I thought. At least that's what I could tell from the many Family Freedom documentaries, tabloid stories, and rumors. But I didn't say that to Alice. She was being really awesome. I liked hanging out with her.

I hit her on the shoulder, and we walked back out to the parking lot. A smile crept across my face. I couldn't wait for the date. But I was also pretty excited to maybe be making a friend.

ELEVEN

BUZZ MAN was a coffee shop in what passed for the downtown of Doolittle Falls—that is, Main Street. It was arty and Hero worshipping, all at the same time. Maybe due to the décor, which featured both: large Warhol prints of famous town heroes on the walls. I'd grabbed a table in the back between two giant red chairs and nervously shredded a napkin into paper strips. I had decimated a small forest when Freedom Boy walked in. He waved and went right to the counter.

Carrying a couple of lattes, Freedom Boy came over and sat down in the opposite seat. He looked at me. He was too attractive for words. The light was dancing off his blond hair, which looked particularly good today. I tried to make small talk. I had no idea what to say. What would interest him? What would make him interested in me?

"So how is school going?" he asked. He looked so happy to see me. Not serious, like in his press photos. It was throwing me off my game.

"Okay. The usual first-week introductory stuff. It doesn't ever feel like it really starts until the end of the second week."

"I know. It is the same at the Academy. You would think it would always be nonstop action—that is how it is always portrayed—but most of this week was spent on paperwork and going over basics like bullet avoidance and this very boring class about The Paladin Act and Criminal Procedure in the Modern Era" he said, taking a sip of his coffee.

"That sounds terrible," I said. "What does it even mean?"

"Basically the rules of being a Hero," he said.

"That sounds a little interesting."

"Not really. It is taught by this blowhard who claims he was a Hero in his day, who goes by "The Lawyer." When anyone acts up he says stuff like 'Watch out, I got a PhD in Street Justice' or 'I did my dissertation on kicking butt, Mister' but his only power seems to be boring us to sleep."

I laughed. "Okay it does sound pretty bad."

He nodded. "Do you have to take that civic responsibility class? Dr. Mann actually explained it to us. It is a new initiative for people with powers, whoever they may be." He grinned. "I think it is pretty necessary. And progressive. What do you think?"

"It's kind of cool, though our teacher hasn't shown up yet." I gulped down my latte. It burned the tip of my tongue. But it made me feel like I had to keep talking. "She's still at some conference or something, so the principal has been reading the materials like a robot." Freedom Boy just looked at me with those green eyes like I was super interesting. "A lot of the kids seem to resent it though. I don't know why," I added.

"Misshapes do not trust the Bureau of Superhero Affairs." He stopped and blushed, embarrassed by using the M-word in front of me. "I mean, people with powers who are not Heroes."

"No, you're right. They are Misshapes. Most of them have silly powers that are more annoying than anything." *But I'm not a Misshape, am I?* I thought. This class made me think otherwise. Or the fact that I wasn't in the Academy this year. I didn't know what category I fit into.

I glanced around the room. People were pretending not to stare at us. One of them came into focus. Doodlebug. He was just straight-up staring. He didn't seem to approve of our date. When I caught his eye, he scowled and looked back down at his magazine.

"Like what?"

I told him about Butters, about Alice, about the way that Hamilton's shutter shades were always dripping paint from his paintballs. The coffee kicked in and before I knew it, I kept talking. It was funny, the whole time I was anticipating the date I imagined him regaling me with amazing tales, and now that it was happening, he wanted to know about me. He kept asking me tons of questions about myself. It was like he was interviewing me for something. We didn't have any awkward pauses. He just kept gazing at me. Some of the coffee shop patrons looked over at us, quizzically. Seeing Freedom Boy in the flesh was a big deal for some people.

He avoided asking me about my family. I ignored the fact that he had a dad. A dad who was the mortal enemy of my mom. A dad who wanted my mom dead. We skirted the issue, but it was in the air, surrounding us. When we came close to the topic, like when he mentioned Innsmouth or I said something about his family, we were struck silent and looked away from each other.

"So, did you catch the latest episode of *American Hero*?"

"No, I do not really follow it," he replied. "It is nothing like that with real Hero teams, whether it is the Amazing Eight or Hero Squad. It just seems so scripted."

"Are you going to try out for one of those groups?" I asked.

"Not really. These people are practically immortal so it is rare that there is ever an opening. Also, I kind of have a spot reserved for me on the Justice Marauders, which my granddad founded. I'm sort of a legacy."

"So," I asked, "why did you ask me out? I mean, we haven't really talked. Ever. We have no reason to talk, really." I squinted my eyes. "Doesn't your family hate me? Wouldn't everybody?"

"You are not your mother, Sarah." Freedom Boy looked into the distance. "If I thought that you were your mother, I would be a terrible person. People are not their families." He paused for a second, and more alert, took my hand. Sparks shot up my arm. "Sarah, you are an interesting person. You were the only person who had any honor at Hero Camp."

Huh? I thought. How do you have honor as a nine-year-old at camp? What was he even saying? "Was I a particularly impressive camper?"

"You stuck up for Carter," he said, softly.

I can't believe he remembered that. It was so long ago. Fourth grade. My parents had sent me to this stupid summer camp in Maine for Hero children. But everyone there hadn't gotten their powers yet, so it was a bunch of potentials hiking and swimming and talking about how great they were going to be when they got powers. Mom, as the dean of the Hero Academy, was probably pressured into it, because even she thought it was a little silly. Johnny told me that it was the worst thing ever and showed me some escape routes.

But I stuck around, and I didn't take those escape routes into rural Maine, and I met Carter. His parents were on the Future Team, one of those big-shot Hero groups. He was kind of nerdy and no one really paid him any attention. In our second week, somebody found out about a scandal with Carter's parents blowing up in the real world. They got kicked off the Future Team because his father was caught with a power booster and his mother was accused of helping to cover it up. After that, it was open season on him. I guess I defended him once or twice. It made me sick to see how Carter was treated and I wanted the bullying to stop. It didn't stop, and it never stopped. Carter moved away soon after.

I was so embarrassed by the attention that I changed the subject. "You said you had a surprise. Um, in your text. So what is it?"

"I figured we could check out the aurora borealis if you were interested. If not, we could go see a movie. I think *Super High* is still playing."

"You mean actual northern lights."

"Yes! They are caused by solar winds in the northern hemisphere."

"But aren't they far away?" I blurted.

"Yes. We will have to go to northern Maine."

It didn't make sense to me. How would we get there?

"Check them out with me?" he asked. "Don't make me beg, Sarah. It's the best thing you'll ever see."

"Won't it take over five hours to drive to northern Maine?"

"I wasn't thinking of driving," Freedom Boy said.

My eyes grew big. A shiver of excitement ran down my spine.

He relished this part. "I was thinking of flying."

TWELVE

THE WORLD fell away and there was just sky. Doolittle Falls disappeared below us in a mess of inky blackness dotted by some lights.

I wrapped my arms around his neckline like a kid ridding piggyback. The wind rushed by so loudly I couldn't hear anything else. Even though my mouth hovered over his right ear, he could barely hear me talk. It was so cold. The only thing keeping me warm was his body. He seemed to radiate heat like the sun.

When I had a question about flying, Freedom Boy slowed down to answer it. It had something to do with gravitrons, or some particle that makes gravity and his ability to manipulate them. "Some writer named Douglas Adams said it best: Flying is just learning how to throw yourself at the ground and missing."

The few times my bare flesh peeked out from under a glove or face mask my skin immediately felt like it was going to freeze off.

"Sarah," Freedom Boy said, sounding more authoritative than he had previously.

"What?"

"See those buildings down there?"

All I saw was night.

"I don't have super eyesight there, guy," I replied.

"They look dangerous. I think they may belong to Admiral Doom," Freedom Boy said.

"I'm going to take us down a bit. We need to check this out," he said. "Be prepared and hold on!"

We whooshed downward like an eagle going in for the kill. For a second, I felt like I was going to puke. I think, even on a super date, that's bad etiquette. The ride got bumpy. I held on to Freedom Boy as tightly as possible. Below us, a cement box with a turret-mounted laser cannon came into view.

A cannon that was aiming right at us.

As we zoomed toward the earth it fired a red beam. The red beam shot between us. Freedom Boy took a hard right. I tried to keep my arms around him but the force from the turn was too strong. My arms were wrenched away from him. As I plummeted, the

red light grew smaller until it was a razor-thin line.

The seconds stretched out over a lifetime. The air swallowed my screams. I was falling. It was terrifying. The tiny bunker with the laser below me got larger and larger. It had stopped firing. Perhaps it knew that gravity would finish the job. As the ground got closer and closer, I could see it was in the middle of a field. The only building other than the turret was an old red barn. I could start to make out the details of objects. A mass of green became a field of grass. A gray wall became individual cinder blocks. A brown barn roof became a series of wood beams and slats. As I looked at the world come into tighter focus, it took a minute to click: I could die.

I tried to remember what he told me to do in the zero-percent, never-going-to-happen chance that I fell. It was something like stretch out your body, lie flat and parallel to the earth, and try not to spin. It was hard to maneuver in the air while I was freaking out about certain death. Freedom Boy guaranteed that flying with him didn't mean certain death. Then again, why did he tell me what to do in case I fell?

I felt myself moving faster as I fell. Accelerating toward the earth, like my body was gaining distance on my mind, faster and faster.

Down.

Down.

Down.

You can really stretch out time by falling to your death. I was a whirlwind of emotions. My body sparked like a Roman candle but my mind grew oddly calm.

Then something strange happened. I stopped falling. Not because Freedom Boy saved me or because I crashed into the ground with the expected splat. I just stopped falling. The wind grew silent. I was stretched out as wide as possible and suddenly my body just snapped back. It was like I was a horse that just had its reins pulled.

Was I dead? Was this the afterlife? I looked up. I was still in the sky. I pinched my arm. It hurt.

I wasn't dead. I just wasn't falling anymore.

I looked around as best as I could. I spotted Freedom Boy flying toward me. But he wasn't getting any closer. It looked like he was struggling. Like he was trying to fly to me but was stopped by some invisible force field.

I kept lying flat. Afraid that if I moved, if I changed my position even an inch, I would start falling again. I floated in place. Fluffy clouds billowed beneath me. Beads of sweat rolled down Freedom Boy's perfect cheek. The muscles on his neck bulged.

He tried to shout something. His lips moved but no sound reached me. All I could hear was growing wind pushing up from below. It appeared to be keeping me aloft. I looked down toward the earth and all I could see were clouds. Foggy wet air was everywhere. Forming a blanket around me and slowly hiding Freedom Boy from sight.

For a moment I was completely lost in my own world of white. I felt like I was going to be suspended forever. Trapped thirty thousand feet in a prison of clouds. Forever separated from Freedom Boy. Forever separated from everyone I knew and loved.

It grew dark. The white clouds turned gray. Then black. Everything disappeared. Everything grew silent. I was above the earth but nowhere. No light remained. I touched my fingers to each other to make sure I was still there. That my body hadn't abandoned me. Suddenly a hand reached out of the darkness and grabbed me.

I shrieked.

It squeezed tightly around my arm. It felt sinister. I struggled to break free. It pulled me toward something. Something large and powerful. Another hand grabbed my other arm and jerked me forward. The force was so great I hit something solid, and large arms wrapped themselves around me. I put my hand up. It was saying something. My name.

"Sarah....Sarah...Sarah!" it said.

"Who are you?" I demanded.

"It's me. Freedom Boy."

I looked up. Through the fog I could see the outline of his face. It wasn't some

monster. He had reached me. Finally.

"Where the hell were you?" I demanded, now back in his arms.

"I tried to get to you but the wind was too strong," he said. "I don't know what hit us. And I didn't know you could fly!"

"I can't fly," I said. The wind pushed us around like rag dolls. The air cleared up. We could see each other. And we could also see a quick-moving blur headed right for us.

It was a shard of wood. Freedom Boy pulled me out of the way before it hit me. We looked down. More things came into view. Pieces of debris were starting to spin and fly toward us. The wind was no longer holding us up. It grabbed at us like it wanted to toss us around and then rip us to shreds.

"What in the world is going on?" he asked.

"I think I did this. That's what saved me, and why it's so hard to fly."

"You can create wind this strong?" he shouted back, impressed. "Amazing!" A small scrap of metal flew toward us and he shot it away with a laser pulse from his forearm.

I thought about it for a second and realized what I'd created. An updraft! I guess terror equaled updrafts. Studying had paid off. But suddenly I remembered the second part of the chapter on updrafts. It wasn't pretty. Pictures of leveled trailer homes and ripped-up towns and houses with roofs torn off. In my excitement and fear I'd created some kind of massive storm system. An updraft strong enough to hold me up meant one thing. A tornado. A giant one. And we were in the dead center of its spout.

"I got some bad news," I shouted. "We're in a tornado!"

"What about Toronto? We're not going there."

"*Tornado!*"

His expression changed. For the first time he looked genuinely scared.

A giant wooden picket fence spun in the air, a splintering threat, while the growing darkness descended upon us again.

Freedom Boy held me close. All his muscles were tense. I could feel them twitching beneath his suit. He must have been straining with all his force to keep us from being torn apart. If we separated, I don't think he would ever find me again. Not until the vortex spit out my lifeless body.

Bam! A blinding lightning bolt exploded. It was so close to us that I could feel the heat. Unable to hear or see, I clung on to Freedom Boy out of instinct.

More lightning exploded around us. It created a quick flash in the dark cloud that illuminated the dark border of the tornado. The center was calm, or at least safe from debris. Whenever we moved toward the edge, the wind picked up, trying to tear us limb from limb while blasting us with dirt and debris. We were unable to think or figure out what to do. It sounded like a freight train.

A stop sign flew at us out of nowhere like a ninja's throwing star. Freedom Boy deflected it, moving his forearm through the air in a slicing motion and it shot off behind him. It was sucked into the dark walls and lost in the blackness.

We couldn't see the world outside our prison of wind.

I wanted to make it stop, find the shut-off switch or the emotion that would make it fizzle out. But I didn't know what to do, what thought or feeling could stop it. It had become bigger than me. Bigger than the both of us.

"We need to do something. Can you slow it down?" he shouted to me.

"I don't know how. I'm sorry. It's too powerful. Can you fly us out?" I screamed back.

"The force is too strong," he yelled. "I can't hold on to you." His face lit up and he reached into his utility belt and pulled out long nylon straps with loops at each end. "I have an idea." He held the straps with his one good hand, motioning for me to put my hands in them. He tightened the straps like handcuffs around my wrists, and then he bound us together. I was on his back, tighter than before. He was pressing against me with each deep breath. I could feel his shoulders swell and his chest fill up with air. It was like we were a circuit, with electricity passing between us. It felt good, I had to admit, but why hadn't he done this before liftoff?

"That should keep you attached," he said.

"Just don't rip my arms off!"

He tried to fly out of the tornado from the center but he kept getting sucked back where we had started. The lightning was growing stronger and steadier and we had a few near misses.

We both looked around, trying to figure out how to escape. I could tell what he was thinking. There was only one way out. He would have to go up. Shoot his body into the sky and let the tornado pass below us.

He gave me a knowing nod. "Hold your breath."

I sucked a large gulp of air into my lungs. It pushed my boobs firmly onto his back. My brain took a second to notice that and wonder whether he noticed it as well.

His chest puffed up and we shot into the sky.

Objects kept flying at us like miniature rockets. He kept deflecting and dodging them as we fell. His hands moved like a blur.

We shot up into the clouds and emerged above them. It was freezing. We had a view of the extent of the storm—my storm—and the dark cloud stretched out for miles. I had no idea my fear could create something so massive. What else was I capable of if provoked, I wondered. Above the cloud, there was an enormous canopy of star. They stretched out in every direction, like we were leaving the earth. We watched the storm in silence, clutching each other just to ensure we were both still alive.

Then something strange happened.

From the top of one of the clouds, a large red stream of light shot up like a rocket into the universe. Then there were more red streams, only lasting for milliseconds before disappearing and leaving a bright crimson trail behind. I tried to figure out what they were aiming at, but it was impossible.

Out of the corner of my eye, it looked like there was a person in a sleek red poncho and a blood-red mask standing behind one of these streams of red light. No, he was floating, still, and staring at us. In the time it took for one of those red streams to appear and disappear, he was gone.

We floated above the earth for a few more seconds, drifting down, pillow feathers in soft freefall. Then Freedom Boy held me tighter in his powerful arms and yelled, "Hold on!" and shot down like a bullet into the earth.

He draped his arms over my head to keep any remaining projectiles from the tornado out of our way. We smashed through the roof of a barn with a loud crash that shook every bone in my body. We fell into a heap of hay. Splinters and dust floated in the air. Pieces of obliterated beams fell from the ceiling. The tornado was moving off toward the horizon and sputtering out of existence. It was safe now.

I looked up at Freedom Boy. His face was cut. A thin line of blood ran down his cheek. Something must have hit him. I lifted my hand up and wiped away the blood. All my residual anger and fear dissipated as I touched his skin. He was just so beautiful, and here he was, protecting me. He removed his arms from above my head and pulled me closer. My arms wrapped around him like we were still flying. Like if I let him go I would fall to the earth from our perch.

A few seconds later, I kissed a boy for the first time.

THIRTEEN

ONCE I kissed Freedom Boy, it was all I could think about. The kiss. It didn't matter what class I was sitting in. I couldn't pay attention. The kiss played on a constant loop in my head.

It began with me on my side in the dirt, shivering, fear and adrenaline pulsing through my body. Freedom Boy hovered above me like a broad warm sun. I wrapped my arms around his wide shoulders, and he placed one hand on the small of my back and ran the other through my hair. I felt so small compared to him.

Ever so slowly he leaned down toward me, coming so close that I could feel his warm breath, still heavy from the exertion, brushing against my cheek. And then, in an instant that passed like an eternity, contact.

His lips were soft and gentle, in striking contrast to his heavy muscular body. I couldn't breathe. Rays of light surged through my chest, radiating down to my toes in the dirt—

"Sarah," Alice said, hitting my shoulder, "you should pay attention." We were sitting in civic responsibility, and Ms. Frankl was glaring at me. She was a thirtysomething teacher, with a penchant for dark eyeliner and bright red lipstick, which brought out her porcelain skin and oversized features: big eyes, big lips, and a ski-jump nose. She looked like a Disney cartoon heroine.

"Everybody," she announced, "today I need you to fill these

out. Write down your name, address, and what your power is." She motioned at Butters and passed out some index cards. "This includes you, Sarah Robertson."

"Why?" Johnny asked her.

"It's an order from the Superhero Bureau, class. You have to do it or you fail. It's out of my hands. I suggest you fill out the card."

"Not going to do it," said Hamilton.

I didn't have as much of a problem with it as Johnny, but the way she said that order didn't sit right with me. I tapped my pen on my desk and thought about it for a few minutes.

I was still having a hard time figuring out civic responsibility. It wasn't the gateway to the Academy that I envisioned at first. It felt like the opposite. If I was in a class with all Misshapes, did that mean that I was—straight up—a Misshape, too? Couldn't I just be Normal until proven Hero? That's what I wanted to be, when I thought about it at night.

Also the class sucked. Ms. Frankl was awkward, slogging through epic history. It bugged me because if the class was, like, taught by Dr. Mann, it would be awesome.

As I wrote my info down I saw Johnny scrawling on his card. He didn't seem to be filling it out correctly, and from the sound of his chatter he was encouraging his neighbors to do likewise.

After she collected all the cards she put them on her desk and said, "Okay, I hope you don't think we're racing through things, but today we're doing a short history of the Hero Academy system in America."

I asked, "Is Dr. Mann coming in? Since he's the Academy dean, wouldn't it make sense?"

Ms. Frankl replied, preoccupied, "He chose not to come in. He thought it would be best that you guys learn about the Academy in an unbiased environment."

"But wouldn't he have better information so we could learn more about the place?" I pressed on, disappointed. Ms. Frankl just wasn't an insider like Dr. Mann. "Really?" Ms. Frankl started, but before she could get out a full answer, Kurt interrupted her. "Learn what, that they're better than us?"

The words came tumbling out of my mouth before I could think about it: "Well they are, aren't they?"

The class was silent. Johnny narrowed his eyes at me and glared, and Butters' Spectors let out a disapproving, "Oooooh." Outside, a great gust of wind knocked over a metal trashcan.

My brother broke the silence. "Do you really, sincerely, think that the Heroes are better than us?"

"Well," I stammered, "isn't the guy with extraordinary abilities technically better than the guy without those abilities? Wouldn't that make him valuable?"

Someone muttered from the back, "More valuable than the genetic freak?"

Johnny switched into preacher mode. "That's the type of theory that leads to fascism, sis."

My voice shook as I tried to come up with a better reply. Fights in class made me want to crawl back into my shell. The trashcan rolled around outside in the wind. "Well, you're arguing for"—I searched for a comeback and came up blank—"arguing for some kind of commune utopia. It's delusional—"

"C'mon, guys," said Ms. Frankl, trying to be a voice of reason.

Alice piped up: "Look, I don't think Sarah meant that Heroes are better than us on a value level, per se. They're not better than us as people, just like we're not better than Normal people even though we have skills. But you have to admit that most of them have talents—extraordinary talents—that easily lend themselves to fighting crime and changing crappy things about the world. Right, Sarah?"

"Yes!" I said, in a voice that was too loud. Different argument completely, but I was going to go with somebody on my side. "That's it exactly. Like, I'm just as cool as a football player, but nobody's going to pay me several million dollars to throw a football, right?"

This argument seemed to work. The others had calmed down. I think Alice had talked us out of that hole, although I still felt like my foot was in my mouth. She was really good at arguing.

Ms. Frankl changed the topic. "Good job, guys. That's what this class is here for—to talk about the issues. Now, who wants to see a Bureau DVD about how to be safe around flying humans?"

Before we could respond, the lights were out, the screen was down, and the DVD was spinning in the tray. A large seal for the Bureau of Superhero Affairs, an A with a sword through it, flickered on the screen. The film started. It was so dated. The footage was grainy and looked like it had been taken on an old camcorder. It was a Laserdisc transfer, copyrighted in 1996 and 1985. A narrator came onscreen. He had a large mustache and spoke in a newsman's baritone and kept a somber face the whole time. He reminded people to look three ways when you're in an area with known flying activity, and if you're flying, always call out appropriate warnings if you're ten feet above the ground. A boy ran up to thank him and he patted the boy on the head without ever taking his eyes from the camera. "Well done, Jimmy," Jim, our announcer, said.

As a man in a gray flannel suit showed the correct way to signal when a Hero is flying in your direction, I felt a tug on my shoulder.

"Sarah," Ms. Frankl whispered, "can I have a word with you in the hall?"

"Sure."

We tiptoed out of the room. I was pretty sure that I was going to get in trouble for the argument in class.

In the hallway, Ms. Frankl eased up. Her face relaxed. "Sarah, I'm sorry about what happened earlier. I'm usually in better control of my classes. This one is just…particularly difficult. How are you feeling?"

I was taken aback. My first instinct was to apologize. "No, I'm fine. I'm sorry for interrupting class and arguing and getting my brother mad—"

She put her hand on my shoulder. "Sarah, you have nothing to be sorry about. Just understand that you have to be respectful of the difference of opinion in class when it comes to the Academy and the Heroes."

"Okay."

"I have an assignment for you. I need a book report in a week." She handed me a paper with a series of numbers on it.

"Secret code?"

"ISBN. Give it to the librarian at the Edward Kennedy Library and she'll hook you up."

I nodded and put the paper in my pocket. "A book report?"

"Book report. Two pages, one thousand words, next week. I'll count it as extra credit but it's mandatory. You should get on it quickly, too, since the book is long and can be pretty dense. Don't worry, I think you'll enjoy it."

I nodded and followed Ms. Frankl back into class.

FOURTEEN

SCHOOL ENDED and I booked it to the library. Outside, there was a pleasing chill in the air, with a bite that indicated fall would be coming soon. My favorite sort of weather. Even though I knew that temperature, wind, hail, and all sorts of things could change according to my mercurial moods, I still couldn't stop fall classics like leaves changing color.

A blanket of light gray clouds covered the sky. I nestled my hands into my coat.

I made it to the gleaming white pillars of the Edward Kennedy Library and walked inside. After a few minutes I found the book, *A Misshape's History of America*, by Henry Winn. It was thick and heavy, with yellowed tissue-thin paper and a red embossed cover. Four hundred pages with small type. It would take me all weekend to finish.

With a short history of oppressed people weighing down my bag and hurting my back, I went out the library's back door. I stopped for a moment on the stairs. There was something weird in the air. I could feel it pressing against me, but couldn't quite explain it.

Doolittle Falls looked like a picture-perfect New England town smothered in rolling clouds on a cool September day. I peered upward and followed the cloud blanket with my eyes. Something out of the ordinary caught my attention—a neat hole cut in the clouds as if by scissors and a beam of sunshine cutting through and shining on a spot in the middle of the woods.

The sunlight wasn't too far away from the library. I decided to investigate. The woods were thick and filled with great brambles, rambling bushes that caught on my pants. It was the type of thing that Indiana Jones would fight his way through. After a few slips, one of which left an unsightly dirt stain on my jeans, I came to the edge of the sunned area. The sun stung my eyes and I found myself squinting. The light was coming down around an enormous tree. And what was that at the base of it? It was mesmerizing—a naked boy sitting cross-legged in the middle of a sandbox. Not a stitch of clothes on his perfectly tanned skin. I shrieked.

The boy jumped up, defensively, pulling a blanket off the ground to cover him.

"Whoa, whoa, whoa," he said loudly, one hand in the air as a stop sign. "Don't call the cops. I don't want to start anything." He babbled incoherently. "I didn't mean to be…I mean, I'm sorry. My parents live up the hill. I'm a good citizen." He must've thought I was a cop or a parent.

"Chill. It's okay. But don't pull anything, because I have a phone ready to call the cops, and mace," I bluffed. Then I went into the light so we could see each other better. I felt awkward, but I thought it might calm him down.

"Hi," I said, sheepishly, raising my hand in a semi-wave. It was nice and warm in the circle of light.

"Oh! You're not the cops. Or an angry mom—"

"Yep, not a mom. It's cool," I said. I had questions: Had he found the one spot with sun? Or, better yet, had he created it?

At first I couldn't find the words to ask because he was so stupid hot. I felt dopey in the radiance of his attractiveness. He had sharp cheekbones that drew you into his golden eyes. I had never seen abs like his before, either, outside of cheesy underwear ads. They were perfectly symmetrical squares, heading toward a deep V-line that led all the way below that blanket. I felt faint. I'm sure I was beet red.

He was waiting for me to talk. When it became pretty obvious that I was just staring, he tried to intervene. "Look, I'm sorry you had to see me like this—"

In my head, I responded, *There is nothing wrong with that* while looking at his chest. His compact but well-developed chest. Sigh. Focus, Robertson!

I literally had to shake my head to get my thoughts out and said,

"Um, the sun. Sun! How did that happen? You made it." I shook out a few more thoughts and then got out an actual question. "So, did you make the sun appear?"

"Nah, you got me all wrong," he said and laughed. He continued in a faux stoner voice: "God made that, maaaaaaan."

"You just found the one spot where it was shining?" I asked, a bit more composed.

"That's not exactly true. I did draw it out of the clouds to play," he replied. I smiled. I'm not sure he realized it, but he just made my day with his words.

He was like me. He had to be.

"So you did it. You made this little light box. How?" I needed to know if he was who I thought he was.

"The clouds, I just make them go away," he said with a smile.

I knew it. It was Sam, the Sam I had been hearing about from Lindsay and Dr. Mann. He was the Academy's most recent Hero with weather control. Lindsay wanted me to replace him at the Markowitz party. He graduated last year and supposedly left town. Why was he here? I wanted to be nonchalant after outing him, but was too eager for my own good. "Show me how you did it!" I ordered.

"I'm a Hero. That's how," he said. "Why are you so curious?"

"You can change the weather like me. But you can control it," I said, standing up straight. "How do you control it? I need someone to teach me."

"Oh, oh, oh," he said slowly, looking me over with new eyes. "You must be Johnny Robertson's sister. Awesome!" He tried to high-five me with his free hand, but I was too far away. "I love that dude. He told me about you a couple of times. Like you're my mini me. I'm Sam. Sam Albedo."

"I know," I said. "I'm Sarah. And forgive me for sounding slightly incredulous, but you like my brother?" I didn't want to sound like a jerk, but I thought everyone just hung around him so they could get free drinks. I gathered up my courage and took a big step toward the tree, the sandbox, and Sam, my thumb running back and forth along the straps of my backpack.

"Your brother," said Sam, "was the only kid with courage in a school full of Heroes." He grinned at me and offered me a seat in the sand. I took it.

It was the first time I heard anybody talk with real respect about Johnny. Dad always had this note of disappointment in his voice every time he had to deal with him. Sam's tone was different.

"Thanks. He never talks about his time there and he's been moody since he got kicked out," I said. "Well, he was moody before too, but he hid it better."

"The Academy can be rough. Not like all those movies and fanboy sites make it seem. But your brother was a champion for the underdog. Even the snottiest of the Marston Heights kids, born with golden capes on their backs, admired him." Sam grinned. "Can you believe it?"

"No," I said. I couldn't help but smile a bit. His enthusiasm was infectious. I would've given Sam a hug, but he was pretty naked. And the word "fanboy" stung a little bit, even though I'm sure it wasn't meant that way. I shrugged off my backpack, took a seat next to him, and put my hands in the sand. It felt good. I was sitting in a sandbox next to a naked man. Weird. "Shouldn't you be in school now?" I asked.

"I was going to John Henry College but I wasn't really into that. Studying wasn't my thing."

"Oh, the Hero college." I had done a little research on it. New York seemed like the perfect place to be a Hero. All those tall buildings to fly by, and all that history of crime fighting. Gotham City.

"Why are you here, though? You could be anywhere."

"I got a gig at PeriGenomics. It's, like, a dream job. I get to do real stuff."

"How is it?" I said. It was the main employer in our town, and did so much to help Innsmouth. Although Johnny had some insane theory that it was responsible for what happened with Mom. And there were the occasional news articles about it that painted its research in an unflattering light.

"PeriGenomics is a great company. Every major Hero in this town, probably country, is on the board," he said.

Yup. I knew that, thanks to Dad. "What do you do for them?" I asked.

"They don't really publicize it, but they do a lot of charity work in developing nations. I get to travel to all sorts of places on their dime helping fix weather patterns. It's amazing." The way Sam talked, I wanted to be employed by PeriGenomics. It sounded cool when he described it. Not like the drudgery I imagined from my dad's occasional complaints.

"So you're there when you're not naked in the woods?" I asked.

"Hold on a second and stay in the pit," he ordered. "I'll put on some clothes." He went behind a tree to change. He picked an elm tree that was shedding its leaves. I could still see his body flailing around as he jumped into his jeans, his chest heaving.

"I'll cover my eyes!" I offered. I felt a little awkward. I peeked over at Sam. He was still beautiful.

Sam popped out from behind the tree, fully clothed, his floppy black hair perfectly messy. I wanted to run my fingers through it, but I thought about Freedom Boy and felt guilty for a second. "How's Johnny doing? Are you enjoying the Academy?"

He didn't know that I'd been rejected. I didn't want to tell him, to let him know that all I knew about the Academy and the real world of Heroes was from the media and my brother. But I needed his help and I thought honesty might work.

"Johnny could be better. He's at Harris High. Well, we both are, actually," I said, sheepishly.

He sat down next to me. He put a hand on my arm. Electricity surged through me, ending at my fingertips. "Not the Academy?" he asked. "That's completely wrong. If you're like me, you have a pretty useful skill."

"Not useful enough to get accepted. I guess I'm not developed enough," I said.

"What do they know? Half of those kids are legacies whose greatest power is having famous parents. You, you can control the weather." Another grin. "It's great, Sarah. We don't have to be mopey about our abilities."

"I can change it, but I wouldn't really call it control. More like it responds to me. How do you do it?" I asked.

"Control the weather? Well, to simplify it by, like, a million, I think about something like 'rain,' and boom, I get rain."

"Oh, that's not me," I said. "Controlling the weather with your emotions blows."

"I guess it would." He thought about it for a second. For someone with an instant *rain* thought button in their brain, the idea of emotions must've seemed odd. It didn't seem like Sam ever got that sad in his life, either. "That's got to be really hard. Most people with powers that control things like the weather or magnetism or gravity just do it with thoughts or concentration," he said, deflating my hope of potential help.

We were silent for a few minutes. I felt a little wounded. The idea that I may not be that powerful rattled through my brain. Maybe the Academy was right in not taking me. Maybe it wasn't a vendetta against the Robertson family name, but a vendetta against me and my so-called skill. I looked over at Sam. He was deep in thought.

After a while, he spoke up, uncertain at first. "You know, in reality, that might be pretty cool. Even people who control their powers with their thoughts still need to control their emotions. It's like a system." He seemed to savor the word "system." "Yeah, it's like an exchange between how you feel and how you think. Most people think it and it can happen, but to do that, they have to feel it. Then they control their feelings so they can think more clearly. Like, for me, I can make lightning, but when I conjure anger I can make stronger lightning."

"Really?" I said, snapping out of my funk. That idea sounded promising.

"Yeah, thoughts and feelings go hand in hand. You just work differently from other weather people, but it doesn't mean you're weaker."

His speech gave me a boost. Yes! So I'm wired differently. After that tornado, I knew the extent of my power. I just needed control. We sat silent for a moment. Then I asked him a question. "Can you teach me how to channel my powers?"

His enthusiasm dropped. "Well, I'm busy with PeriGenomics and may have to travel on a few missions. It's not that I don't want to help; it's just…"

He wasn't getting out of it now. "I just need a little help. Just some basics. We can even do it online. Like, when you're not busy." I just needed my foot in the door. "You're so powerful and anything you could teach me would be soooo helpful," I said, trying to charm him. "I really could use a mentor." As I looked at him, I worked out a plan in my head. If Sam could teach me how to understand my power, the Academy would want me. As it was, this civic responsibility class had me dangerously close to Misshape status at Harris High and in Doolittle Falls. "So, Sam, would it be weird if I e-mailed you sometime or something?"

"Uh, sure. It's Sam at Sam dot sam."

"Awesome," I said, happy that I'd at least be able to bug him online. "Funny e-mail address."

"Don't make fun!" he said. "That's the first lesson."

I pressed my luck. "So what's the second lesson?"

"You're going to be trouble."

"No, I was just hoping you could show me something before I headed out." I held up the book. "As you can see, I have homework."

"Okay, one trick, then you go."

"Then I go," I agreed. "For now."

He shooed me out of the sandbox and scooped up a small pile of sand. He looked me in the eyes and said, "Now, pay careful attention to all the wind vectors. They are constantly shifting. You must keep them flowing in the same direction or you'll lose control. It's about keeping everything under your power while excluding all the outside forces."

He threw his arms up into the air, like a cheerleader in first position about to say *Ready, okay!* His face tightened up and he made fists out of his hands. Some of the sand particles began floating in the air, above the sandbox. They started out slowly, and then they twisted faster in a circle. Sam's hand was attracting the sand like a magnet. The swirling circle of sand went up, higher and higher, pulling more sand with it and forming a small tornado. After a few seconds, the small tornado became a full-blown twister, spinning grains of sand in an upward spiral into the air, a mass fizzling out at the top of Sam's hands.

"That's so cool!" I exclaimed.

"Put your hand in it before I run out of sand," he said. "Quickly."

I placed my hand in the tornado. It felt both painful and good, like I was being blasted by a hairdryer and like someone was trying to scrub my flesh off at the same time. I pulled my hand out. An instant later we were both showered with fine particles. It made the air around me shine like I was surrounded by a thousand little stars. I closed my eyes to protect them from the sand, and when I opened them, Sam was smiling at me.

"So that was your first real lesson."

FIFTEEN

FREEDOM BOY and I were hanging out at a hot dog on the South Shore of Massachusetts. He'd flown us over there, using hand straps this time. I'd never seen someone eat so much in my entire life. I guess flying burned a lot of calories. We had gone all the way to Boston this time. He had picked up five tremendous hot dogs and a jumbo Coke, which the guy referred to as the Freedom Special, from some place in South Boston before flying us to a beach.

It was our third date-type thing. We were on our sixth round of kissing so far. Yes, I had been keeping track.

"Sam's a great guy," Freedom Boy said, before downing his third jumbo hot dog. "You'll have a lot of fun with him." I was a little pissed off that he wasn't jealous.

"Were you friends at school?" I asked.

"Sure. Everyone was. Girls, especially. If you wanted a tan you hung out with Sam." He kind of sang this last part, or cheered it or something. Like everybody at the Academy said that phrase all the time.

I could just picture Sam, walking around the halls of the Academy shirtless, getting asked to the beach by every girl in cleavage-bearing Lycra. The more I heard about it, the more I realized that my relationship with the weather was more complicated than Sam's. It was, I don't know, sort of similar to my relationship with Freedom Boy.

But still, I couldn't see a shred of jealousy on Freedom Boy's face. I thought he'd feel something if I mentioned that I was meeting up with Sam tomorrow. I had been pestering Sam for lessons for weeks, and I finally snagged an invite to his lab at PeriGenomics. I thought it would be the type of information that would get some sort of reaction out of Freedom Boy, whether territorial or at least curious about us spending time together. Especially considering Sam's former player status.

But Freedom Boy remained placid, chuckling slightly at some old Sam story that he remembered and chowing down on another hot dog. "What do you think of Sam's skill? It's kind of like yours, huh?"

I rolled my eyes. I wanted something to happen. I guess we were "hanging out." I didn't really know what that meant. Once a week we went on something like a date. It was mostly talking and some kissing. But it didn't seem serious, at least on his part, even though I really liked him.

How could I not?

But I wondered if it was Freedom Boy I liked, or the idea of Freedom Boy.

We usually flew somewhere together and hung out. He liked secluded places, and it was quick enough to fly out to a place like Plum Island. He told me that he wanted to avoid stares from fans. But I was just starting to feel like a secret. Newspaper gossip columns and tabloids showed pictures of him almost every day attending galas, documentary openings, and fund-raisers, and at each event there was another beautiful Hero or starlet hanging off his arm. He always said it was for show. Something his parents and his handlers made him do for sponsors and fans. But it made me feel terrible.

The waves crashed against the rocks. This beach was incredibly relaxing. I didn't know why it was so empty; it was September, and the water was almost warm. "Hey, I'm going to dip my feet in," I said.

I wondered what Freedom Boy saw in me. A little girl who once stood up to bullies at camp? I was just a potential Hero, teetering on the edge of being a Misshape, and he was America's Golden Boy. I looked at him sitting in the sun, and reminded myself that the why didn't matter. It just mattered that he saw something in me.

SIXTEEN

THERE WERE things, however, to keep me distracted from the curious case of what was happening with Freedom Boy. The book Ms. Frankl had me read was so dense and long I had to stay up really late for three nights to get through it. It was a meticulous, and sometimes ponderous, examination of the history of America from the perspective of Misshapes. I actually found it interesting, in between naps. I'd never read anything about how Misshapes were treated throughout history. Most schoolbooks were about intelligent leaders and brave Heroes. Winn wrote about the real lives of Heroes and how destructive some of them were. He also wrote about real-life Misshapes I'd never heard of and how important they were in shaping America. I handed in my book report on *A Misshape's History of America* to Ms. Frankl. Then I turned my attention from being a Misshapes to becoming a Hero. What was the magic thing that would make Sam like me? And it hit me, with a eureka that had me jumping out of bed in the middle of the night: The way to Sam's heart may be through his stomach.

I poured hot coffee over a big hunk of dark chocolate in a pan. I looked over to Mom's cherry-red mixer, which was whipping butter, sugar, and eggs. Then, I went back to my chocolate pan, grabbed a wooden spatula, and stirred it around, willing the chocolate to melt into the coffee.

Johnny came up behind me and stuck his finger in the mixing bowl. He licked a glob off of his finger, smacking his lips. "What's with the baking?" he asked.

Pushing him away with my elbow and an "ew," I flipped the spatula at him. Some batter dribbled onto Johnny's shirt.

"No! Not my Captain Moron shirt!" he squeaked, his voice cracking, and then he ran off to the laundry room. Dad giggled from his vantage point on the couch. He was watching Maximum Fighting again. The bloodthirsty crowd on TV roared behind him.

"It's for Sam, not you and your grubby fingers," I said, shouting to Johnny in the laundry room.

"Don't you already have one Hero boyfriend? Do you really need a second?" he said, returning in a different Captain Moron T-shirt.

"Shut up! He's going to be my mentor!"

Johnny looked at me. "Mentor, eh?" He made the word sound dirty and leering.

"Donde esta tu chiquita Rosa?" I fired back. That would get him.

Johnny turned red. Boom! I knew it! The tables had turned and I had the upper hand. I knew the copy of five hundred Spanish verbs he'd been carrying around since the party meant that he had a thing for Rosa. He was even taking Spanish this semester. "Well," he said, walking away, "save a piece for me and Dad. If you're not too busy picking which guy to swoon over."

"Fine," I said. Johnny could get one brownie. Just one. But these had Sam's name on them. I would spell it out in red frosting if it'd make him like me better. And if that wouldn't seem stalkery.

It wasn't like I was courting Sam or had a crazy crush, either. Maybe just a normal-size one, but I had Freedom Boy, sort of, I guess. Sam was a guru. A hot yogi. I wanted him to give me some lessons in controlling the weather. Even something as small as figuring out how to make the occasional rain clouds over my head go away when I was sad. Like Dr. Mann said, I had to make a choice. Sam was part of that choice.

The sound of the mixer whirred me into a happy lull. I poured the chocolate into the batter. It looked like marble. These brownies were going to be amazing.

I waited at the front gate of the PeriGenomics complex for the guard to call my name. I put on a baseball cap and some sunglasses. I had to be kind of incognito—I didn't want to run into my dad. My bike was leaning against my side and the brownies were wrapped in aluminum foil in my bag, still warm. The guard read my name on the chart, spoke to a few people, than came out to inspect my bike and belongings. He pulled out a brownie, smelled the foil, and said, "I'll have to confiscate one of these to make sure it isn't a deadly bomb or something. You can go in. Building five, on your left."

I walked my bike toward building five and turned around to see the guard eating my dangerous explosive with a big grin. The PeriGenomics complex was huge. There were ten airport hangar-size buildings in a room with pipes and tubes protruding out of them, in a row. In the center was one large office building twenty stories high (and reportedly fifty stories deep) and all glass. Smokestacks and electric poles shot into the air from all the buildings. Dad worked in the main building fifteen stories below the ground, in a windowless lab. He didn't even have clearance to go to building five. He'd worked there his whole adult life and Sam, fresh out of school, was already more important to the company than him. I felt like I ran a low risk of running into him, and I took off my sunglasses.

I made my way past the parking lots and toward the campus area, which was filled with manicured lawns and park benches to make it seem like a place people would hang out, and not a workplace. The park was completely empty.

I locked my bike to a rack in front of building five, a giant cube made out of blue corrugated metal, then made my way inside. The doors opened into a small room with two armed guards at the desk. Security was super tight at PeriGenomics. The fact that Sam could easily put me on the list, having been there for only a few months, meant he was worth something to the company.

I had to donate ten more minutes of waiting and two more "explosive" brownies before Sam arrived. He was wearing red PeriGenomics overalls and had an ID card hanging over his bare chest. Sweat glistened off of him and he was huffing and puffing.

"Hi," he said, between gasps, then took my hand. "Let me take you to my cubicle."

"I have brownies," I said. "For you."

"Hey, thanks!" He picked one and threw it into his mouth without looking. "These are awesome." He looked in the package. "All one of them."

I shrugged. "Security is tight. And hungry."

The hall was plain as plain as can be, with a low ceiling, gray doors, and white walls with nothing on them. It looked like a storage building. We got to a big door at the end and he swiped his card over a pad and put his face up to a retina scan. The door popped open with a whoosh.

A wave of heat came gushing out. It was hard to breathe the air. My hair stood on end. It took a moment to catch my breath and open my eyes. When I did, I saw that the room was the best thing I'd ever seen. It was tremendous, with large pools of water along the floor, huge fans lining the walls, and massive air vents across the high ceiling. Giant iron fixtures with big glass bulbs hung from ceiling bars. We walked toward a complex control panel against one wall with a computer attached to it.

"So this is my playpen. I prefer the sandpit but this gives me more options."

"Like what?"

"I can recreate any weather condition, at least local conditions. I've been simulating famine conditions from western Africa."

"I can tell," I said.

He hit a button. The lights dimmed, the machines whirred, the air became cool, and there was a gentle breeze. My hair calmed down. It felt like the perfect fall day. It sure beat my humidifier.

Sam led me to a shelf in the corner that was stocked with energy bars. He grabbed one and inhaled it. "Work makes me hungry," he said. "And we should probably have a lot of water."

"So how many people have our power?" I asked, taking an energy bar.

"There are a few of us around, some with different levels or specific skills. Maybe a couple dozen. Not too many with real power, though."

"Really?" We were coworkers jawing at the office kitchen. I was surprised by how comfortable I felt around Sam.

"Yup. We have a union, the Anemoitian Union. You and me and all the other weather controllers can make big money for airlines and Hollywood. Or agribusiness."

"That's nuts. I could do that? Could you?"

"I've been thinking about it, but my gig at PeriGenomics is kind of perfect. They don't pay me a lot, but I do get this awesome room for play and practice, in exchange for helping their agriculture division." Sam pulled at his ID card. His hand was shaking. He was itching to start working, I could tell. But I had more questions.

"So you're not going to fight crime?" I asked.

"Some of us do. There's the Black Zephyr." He paused. "But I'd have to get back in school and go through the whole Hero Card process. And I hate studying for tests. Besides, most of that Hero stuff is flashy showmanship and the real heroes work behind the scenes, making life better for people."

"Cool," I said, thinking about the possibilities. I never realized how many ways I could use my powers, that is, if they ever got strong enough to be worth anything. My mind was always tuned to the superhero channel.

"So there's something that's been bugging me about our power," I said. "How much control do you have over the weather? Could you stop global warming or prevent hurricanes?"

"Nope. People like us have local impact. Maybe ten miles at most. That won't create any kind of global meteorological transformation, but a localized impact of that magnitude can have a major effect on a massive dynamic system with so many variables—"

"Hey there, you're nerding out. Can you talk about it in normal terms?" I asked. That's how I learned best.

"Sorry! Um, what about the butterfly effect?"

"Oh that, doesn't that have to do with time travel?" I asked, remembering some stupid movie I saw on cable.

"It can. Basically it explains complicated systems. Take weather. Major variables can affect how it's going to be. But each one of those variables is impacted by uncountable other factors that interact with each other on big and small scales. Something as big as a volcano or as small as a puddle can alter the weather."

"Where does the butterfly come in?"

"The butterfly's the central metaphor. Something as small and insignificant as the flapping of a single butterfly's wings can create or prevent a tornado," said Sam. "So, Sarah, it's like this—you and I are very large butterflies."

"I feel like a caterpillar."

He laughed. "Everyone does at first. Now it's time to get you out of that cocoon you've wrapped yourself in."

He darted toward the sandbox, kitty-corner from the door. I followed, dutifully, a spare energy bar in my hand. When I got there, he grabbed a small rod and used it to make a graph in the sand. "The weather has three controls—pressure, temperature, and water. What do you get from that? Everything from awkward daily small talk with your neighbor to a world-destroying tsunami. The Academy gave me the skills to quiet my mind and figure out how to affect these three factors."

"So is this going to be some Zen stuff where I could learn how to stop being an emotional girl and really, truly control the weather?"

"Hey, emotions aren't bad," Sam said. "You just don't want to be led around by them like a puppy. You want to be in control. Are you powerful? Could you do what I did the other day?"

"I've made rain. Lots of rain and some lightning," I boasted. "But only when I'm furious. I want to make thundersnow happen. But mostly because I like the word." I kept quiet about the tornado for some reason, even though it was the biggest thing I ever did. Maybe it was a fluke. Or maybe it was the company.

"Oh, me too," Sam agreed. A smile crept across his face. "It sounds to me like you are powerful, Sarah Robertson."

I wanted to kiss him. Not because he was beautiful (even though he was), but because he was the first person to tell me that—and I believed him.

SEVENTEEN

AFTER TALKING about the butterfly effect, Sam put on his teacher's cap. Literally. He pulled a battered Red Sox hat out of his gigundo overalls pockets and told me that it was lesson time, and today's lesson was lightning. We were going to figure out how I could make it come out of the sky.

"I think you're going to need a bigger canvas," he said. He walked over to the controls and pushed a button. When he did this, the ceiling opened up. Large sheets of metal folded back, like a piece of paper, until there was nothing above us but sky.

"That should do. Now, for me to help I need to know how your powers work. You said it was controlled by your emotions."

"Yes."

"So what emotion makes it rain?"

"Sadness usually. The more sad, the more rain."

"Okay. How about lightning? Have you ever created lightning?"

"Not intentionally. Usually they're the result of thunderstorms, which happen when I go from sad to angry."

"So what do you think anger would do?"

"Well, anger makes the storms, but not individual bolts. I did get a bolt once or twice but it was weird. It came from this strange place between sad and angry. I called it smad."

"Good. So you're going to need to get really, really smad. But try to observe yourself when you do, so you can figure out what about it controls the direction or strength of the bolt."

In order to make a big cloud for lightning, I was going to need to tap into a deep well of emotions, emotions that would charge the cloud with electricity. "Embrace them," said Sam. "Make a list of things that make you sad or depressed."

> *My list:*
> *Being jerked around by the Academy*
> *The dartboard with my mom's face on it*
> *Fighting with Johnny*
> *Watching Dad struggle without Mom*
> *Being treated poorly by Lindsay*

At first I thought about them, but nothing happened. I'd built up a lot of walls to protect myself. Then, I tried to remember specific instances and details to recall how I felt. The towel draped on the door in the bathroom at the Markowitz party; the word supervillian streaming under the picture of my mom on the evening news; the texture of the paper Academy form letter in my hands. It worked. A couple of minutes later I was bawling uncontrollably and a large thundercloud was forming overhead.

As I wiped tears away from my face, Sam explained that for a lightning bolt to strike, a charge on the ground was needed to reach up toward the charged cloud. Then the electrical charge creates friction, separating into positive and negative. Maybe my anger could create the charge difference.

I was crying too hard to even think about what made me angry. In a hysterical stammer, I said, "It's just suh-suh-sad!"

"It's also unfair," said Sam, trying to goad me like a coach for team depression. "Yeah, it's sad and it sucks, but doesn't it piss you off?"

"Yuh-yuh-yes." I wiped my eyes.

"Aren't you angry?" he said, not even knowing what I was angry about.

He was right. I was. His question flipped a switch and I saw everything in a different light. I tried to focus my anger. Train it on a single object. I thought of Christie's mom in her stupid scarf on WXBS news talking about how they should catch and execute my mother. How cavalierly she dismissed any calls of dissent and summarily condemned my mom. I thought of her heavy makeup, needle-like voice, theatrical outrage and shock, stupid red lipstick and nails. I tapped into sheer rage.

My face, loose from crying, clenched up. I formed a ball of fury at the front of my head. I could feel it pounding like a headache.

Just as that ball grew, I heard Sam scream, "No!"

He grabbed me and fell to the floor with me on top of him. I heard a deafening crack, and at the same time, a blinding flash went off. *Lightning.*

The bolt flowed down from the clouds and diverted just above our heads.

After a few long minutes, we got up, staggering like a bunch of drunken sailors. Still dazed, with my hair sticking out everywhere like Einstein's, I said, "That was close. We are so lucky."

"Luck?" Sam snapped. "*Luck?* I had to move that thing so it didn't kill us," he yelled. He looked genuinely terrified.

I felt terrible. My first real lesson and I almost ended my mentor. He would never teach me again. He probably thought it wasn't worth the risk. "I'm so sorry."

His tone softened. "For what? That was amazing. Besides the almost getting killed thing. I've never seen lightning so strong created by someone." He paused. "It's just, next time, we have to be careful. And not die. That was *really* dangerous."

"So, next time?" I said with a smile. I was trying hard to contain my excitement. I had gone from being worried he hated me for almost killing him, to beaming with pride at my lightning.

"Yeah. Let's call it a day for now. I don't think I can take another one of those."

I said my good-byes to Sam and ambled back to my house, sneaking peeks at the spot that I had nearly destroyed with my very own lightning bolt. I felt like I had conquered something. Like I was, ever so slowly, learning to be a Hero.

EIGHTEEN

CIVIC RESPONSIBILITY was incredibly boring in comparison to my actual life. It just didn't seem like the class for me. Ms. Frankl would lecture about Heroes and powers, and I'd imagine sitting in the tony Academy classrooms. Or my mind would wander to Freedom Boy and our latest adventure. Everything had seemed pretty low-key after our first near-death experience, but flying with him was always exciting. Much more exciting than class. But every time I pictured us flying, my thoughts would crash into the latest glossy magazine cover of Freedom Boy saving a scantily clad damsel in distress.

I wanted to learn about Heroes while surrounded by the best and brightest. When I wasn't in school, I felt like I was getting closer, whether it was working on my powers with Sam or flying with Freedom Boy. I knew that Dr. Mann was going to give me the call any day now. Sometimes I looked to the sky and imagined I'd get some sort of bat signal in the air.

Adding to the remedial feel, Ms. Frankl tried to hold class outside all the time. For October, it was unseasonably warm. I think Sam may have had something to do with it. Or maybe it was just New England being weird.

For Friday's class, she led us to a shady spot, where we sat in a semicircle under some trees that lined the perimeter of the baseball field. It was just on the edge of a small sketchy wooded area where people would drink and hook up.

We were taking turns talking about how we felt about our powers. Some of the kids seemed to genuinely resent them. "It's not like I have a real power," Hocho said. "It's more like I'm just…set up to be part of my family's restaurant. I want to be a surgeon, but they want me to make sushi."

Backslash nodded, gravely. "Exactly. Do you know how much I want to just…run fast, one day? With having to be chased?"

George Herbert, the quiet freshman who tended to disappear when he got embarrassed, chimed in. "I just want to exist. All the time. People forget about me," he pointed out.

The class nodded. We had forgotten about him for the past few weeks. He flickered in and out of civic responsibility, never saying much.

"But can't you do cool tricks, George?" Butters asked.

I kept my mouth shut. Tom Doodlebug rolled his eyes when anybody said anything. Admittedly, I was right there with him. A silence settled over the group. A lone bird chirped. It was awkward.

I turned my attention to Kurt, who was avoiding everyone in his own little corner. He was in a shredded pair of Levis and a black T-shirt and slouching against a tree. He had a scuffed-up Nalgene bottle filled to the lip in his right hand. It had HARRIS HIGH TRACK TEAM written in white lettering on the side. Kurt didn't run track, or do any other school activities. He, like the rest of us, wasn't allowed.

He dipped his finger into the bottle and watched as a cold smoke wafted out. It looked like he dropped dry ice inside. He poured the liquid out into one hand. It flowed slowly, like blue lava. When the goo touched his hand, the water turned into ice.

I wasn't the only one staring at Kurt. The whole class had grown quiet as Ms. Frankl droned on. Kurt paid no attention to anything. Just his water. Then something distracted him. A small green frog was hopping around by his feet. Looking at the frog, Kurt squeezed his fingers together and the ice turned back into water. It splashed to the ground. The animal was startled, letting out a loud croak and slowly hopping a couple of feet away from him. In one quick motion Kurt leaned down and grabbed the frog in his free hand. He held the frog up to his face.

It was frightened, trying to leap away. It looked like its feet were frozen to Kurt's wet hand. He flipped his hand over and the frog remained suspended from his hand. I was grossed out, watching the poor stuck frog and its trembling legs.

A thin line of a smile crept across Kurt's face. He turned his hand back over and then poured the water onto the frog. It turned bright blue. Crystals crept across its skin. I looked over at Alice. Her mouth was open in shock and disgust. Kurt balled his fist around the frog, pulled his arm back like a pitcher, and tossed it like a baseball at a tree. When it hit the tree it shattered like glass. It made a loud thump and green fragments flew in every direction.

The class flinched. "Why the hell did you do that?" Alice screamed.

Kurt woke up from his wicked dream. "What? It was only a frog," he responded.

"It was a living thing, you psycho," she said.

"Whatever. There are lots of living things. If I didn't do it, a hawk would have probably finished him off. Different predators have different reasons," Kurt said.

He walked slowly back toward the class, swinging his hips like a cowboy, the bottle still in his hand. Alice looked sick. I glared at Kurt. I did not like him.

"Kurt, go to the principal immediately," said Ms. Frankl. We watched him swagger away into the school. "Would anyone like to give us a positive demonstration of their powers?" she asked.

Johnny stood up and announced, "Check this out." I was surprised that he volunteered, but maybe he was trying to make Alice happy again. He grabbed a bottle of water, took a swig, pulled out a lighter, and then blew an enormous fireball. Everyone gasped, and then they applauded.

As he began to take a bow, Johnny grabbed his stomach and stumbled around a bit. He had that familiar and distinctive dead-eyed stare he can get when his disorder acts up. I think the stunt may have triggered it. He got up from the semicircle and stumbled away from the group to the green bench in the dugout. Dazed, he sat down.

I rushed over to him and put my hand on his arm. His skin felt warm and clammy.

"Johnny, are you alright?" I shook his arm. "Do you need your pills?" His AlcoMeter was bright red. I rummaged through his pockets, looking for the jar of meds he always kept close by.

While I was doing this, he must have regained some of his

composure because he suddenly snapped at me, "Stop touching my stuff!"

"I was just looking for your medicine."

"Leave me alone. It was just that trick. I'm fine."

I crossed my arms and glared at him. I was just trying to help.

He got up, using the bench for assistance, and announced, "I'm going to go take a breather."

I felt obliged to yell after him, "Are you sure?"

He turned around, said "*Yes!*" and continued to stomp away.

Alice came bounding over. She had seen the whole exchange. "Ms. Frankl's worried. You two okay?"

"Could you check on my brother? I know he said he doesn't need any help but he needs someone to look after him." I added, "Not me."

"Is he going to be ornery?" she asked.

"He'll be fine. Look, walk over and make sure he's taken his medicine and isn't incoherent or passed out. Sometimes his power can flush his body with alcohol. I get nervous."

"On it," she said and ran off. Johnny did not like being helpless or seeming weak. I think it cut into some kind of primordial male pride thing. Sending an attractive girl to help him might work.

When I got back to the semicircle, Ms. Frankl was concerned but I told her not to worry; he'd be fine. I didn't want her to get the nurse involved because I knew Johnny would just resent it.

A few minutes later Alice and Johnny returned to the group. He looked more like Johnny, not flush and sickly.

"Do you need help?" Ms. Frankl asked.

"No, I'm fine," said Johnny, with a weak smile.

"Great," she said, looking at her watch. "We have five minutes, but I have to tell you something before we go back inside. I'm starting a club—civics club—for everyone in this class. Every Tuesday. I know you can't play sports and I think you need a place to talk about civic responsibility or practice your powers. You can benefit from participating."

"Robertson the minor shouldn't come," Doodlebug blurted. "She thinks she's better than us."

"Ooooh," said the Spectors. Butters looked confused. "What did she do to you?" he asked.

Doodlebug, arms crossed, kept talking. "She didn't do anything. She's just a sellout. I've seen her—"

Ms. Frankl interrupted him. "Come on, Tom, that's enough. And if you keep it up, you can join Kurt."

I was just embarrassed. I wanted to disappear. Like George. I looked around and saw George's books floating through the air. Maybe he was embarrassed on my behalf.

Ms. Frankl got up, following George, and she led the class back inside.

NINETEEN

CLASSES BECAME routine. Not boring, just not as exciting as everything else in my life. Between practice with Sam and dates with Freedom Boy, my plate was full. But there was more Sam than Freedom Boy these days. Heck, these days Freedom Boy was more of a figure on the newsstand. He texted me occasionally with a *What's up?* and then I wouldn't hear anything back from him, and I tried not to care. I had practicing to do with Sam, and that was more important.

I still couldn't get my finger on what the point of civic responsibility was. It was fun learning about Heroes in history and the rules that apply to them, but for the Misshapes in the class I didn't see the value. If they weren't going to become Heroes, why force them to learn about Heroes? I thought about the book that Ms. Frankl made me read and how none of what Winn had written was in the Bureau-approved curriculum. Most of class, somebody would be making snide remarks or mocking the lesson from the back of the room. Usually it'd be Johnny. But Ms. Frankl never kicked anyone out like our other teachers would. She had a "talk" with Kurt after he nearly hit her with a red paintball. And she tried to engage with Kurt. The only person who should be engaging with that kid is a prison warden.

Johnny might've complained about it, but it felt good to me to know that I was taking the same class as Heroes. That I wouldn't be behind once I got into the Academy. That technically we were taking the same class together. They just had better company.

I split my time after school between training with Sam and a few clubs that were fun and would look good on my college application. Nerdy as this sounds, the one I actually loved was science club. Once I got over the boys who wanted nothing more than to fire off rockets on the football field and look down my shirt, I found it amazingly fun. And useful. It was like an academic supplemental to all the practical learning I was doing with Sam.

The club was run by this crazy professor type named Dr. Reveala. He had a shock of white hair that always stood up at an obtuse angle and intense eyes. Apparently he had once worked at PeriGenomics, but left to pursue teaching. He seemed to be most comfortable at the white board, writing out long equations and turning around on occasion to explain something. He was so smart he usually blew past high-school-level explanations and shot straight toward PhD-level esoteric. On occasion he would turn to us during one of these mini-lectures and ask very seriously, "Too far?" and the students, if he had gone off the deep end into Feynman diagrams or Lie algebra, would yell back in unison *"Too far!"* Then he would backtrack and give us more elementary explanations.

Every chance I could, I would try to steer the club toward some meteorological topic. Some of the kids complained that meteorology wasn't real science, that it was something for weathermen, but Dr. Reveala came to my defense.

"You know, the most important part of rocket launches is meteorology. Weather conditions need to be precise."

He had them at "rocket launches." Soon after, we were out on the field collecting rainwater and measuring wind velocities. I even got some lessons on fluid dynamics and pressure systems, although in exchange I had to build a three-stage rocket. Luckily Marcus was in the club as well so we were able to work on it together.

On Tuesdays and Fridays I made my way to PeriGenomics for more hands-on learning with Sam. The factory was only a couple miles from Harris High—toward the Miskatonic—so the bike ride wasn't too bad. The night before, I would have to make brownies to assuage the guards and keep Sam from wondering why he was helping me.

Once I forgot to bring them and I had to get a full-body scan at a building way on the other side of the campus before they let me see him. I hoped no supervillain found out that the way through PeriGenomics security wasn't lasers or explosives but chocolate and sugar.

Lessons with Sam were intense. They lasted for only an hour but they left me physically and emotionally exhausted. I longed to be able to control the elements with my mind, instead of the stupid whims of my heart. Sam was very patient, although a little more cautious after our first lesson. We'd been working on winds for several weeks. Wind, as I learned on my Freedom Boy date, was the product of fear. And fear is a hard emotion to control. We tried all kinds of winds: breezes, gales, gusts, light, strong, moderate, hurricane, monsoon. We practiced creating them and destroying them and using them in combinations. There were so many combinations of pressure systems and elements. The PeriGenomics room could recreate practically anything. My hair was always a rat's nest afterward, full of knots.

I was slowly mastering all the elements. In addition to fear, I learned the precise amount of sadness for rain, the level of anger for lightning strikes, and the range of joy needed to create sunshine or disperse rain. Snow was becoming my white whale. I kept trying to make it happen. I kept failing. I imagined stunning my enemies with blustery gusts but instead of blizzards I got drizzle. I tried to use some of the lessons from Dr. Reveala. He had taught me about a thing called nucleation, which is how snow forms. Apparently when there is water in very cold clouds it doesn't automatically condense to produce snowflakes. Snow only forms when there is a place, called a nucleation site, where the ice crystal can form around. The sites can be anything, including living material or live bacteria that gets absorbed with water vapor.

Armed with this knowledge I tried to create snow, but I couldn't do it right. Sam said I was thinking too hard, that I needed to clear my mind and function on instinct and feeling.

As the lessons progressed I felt a strange friendship growing with Sam. Like he was a mentor and a friend and something else, something I couldn't place my finger on. Whenever I succeeded at some new manifestation of my power he would high-five or hug me, but quickly turn back to being professional and professor-y. The professor thing didn't quite fit his surfer-boy demeanor but it got the point across. He couldn't be my teacher and my friend, or whatever it was he was becoming.

One Tuesday, mid-October, Sam had to cancel on me last minute. When school got out, I didn't know what to do so I went to Dr. Reveala's classroom. He let me work on my balsa-wood bridge in the back of the room while he tutored students in chemistry and physics. It did cost me one brownie, but I had a few to spare. At 2:30, I heard a song coming down the hall. The sound of four women harmonizing wafted into the classroom.

"Bonds, I'm locked up in bonds / The kind that you can't see / Bonds of love / Holding on to me".

Butters walked into the classroom, followed by his Spectors.

He said, "I'm here for some extra help on..." but Dr. Reveala cut him off.

"Give me a second," the teacher said, concentrating. "I can get it."

The Spectors continued to sing: "Bonds, I can't break from these bonds / Can't run cause I'm not free / These bonds of love / Won't let me be."

"Chains. Chains. Hmm..." Dr. Reaveala said. "I've got it! You're here about covalent bonds."

Butters looked embarrassed. "Yes."

"Excellent," the teacher said. He talked to the Spectors. "Thank you, that was fun." It was the only time I'd ever seen a teacher—besides Ms. Frankl—acknowledge the Spectors' specter-y existence.

"Don't mention it," the lead said.

Butters interrupted them. "I only have twenty minutes to learn." He turned toward his ghosts. "Then we can go. Then we can see him."

They began to sing, "Twistin down the street..." and they evaporated.

"Very good. Very good," Dr. Reveala said, and brought over some books to his desk. Butters noticed me in the back of the classroom and waved. I waved back and returned to my bridge.

They discussed chemical bonds and electrons while I cut and pasted small pieces of wood on my bridge. I had big plans for it, but in the end it looked like a mess of triangles. It wouldn't stand a chance against the weights it would be made to bear. Bridges weren't my strong suit.

Dr. Reavela and Butters finished up just as the Spectors appeared.

They seemed impatient, which made Butters impatient. He was a little bit rude to the teacher as he ran out of class. He was never really that rude to anyone, ever. I was intrigued.

I put some glue on the ends of two sticks and put my bridge in a storage nook. When I turned back around, Butters and the Specters had gone. I pattered down the hall, looking for him, and I got my last glimpse as he turned down the stairwell and headed for the door. Fired up with curiosity, I kept on his tail, following him down the stairs, and I wasn't even looking and ran right into someone. Alice.

"Was that Butters?" she asked.

"Yeah," I said. "What are you still doing here?"

"Tuesday is debate team. My parents only let me play the drums if I do something academic after school. I figure learning to argue might have some benefits."

I looked down the stairwell. "Where do you think he's going?"

"Not sure," she said.

"We should find out."

"Sure. Sounds like an adventure!" she replied, then looked at the tin foil poking out of my bag. "Hey, are those brownies?"

We quickly caught up to Butters, but kept our distance. It was pretty easy to find him, what with the singing and all. He seemed too distracted and annoyed to notice us lurking in the background. The Spectors were singing up a storm. It was a pleasant cacophony of sound.

Whenever he started to turn, we ducked behind a garbage can or a hedge. We must have looked ridiculous. Two girls following a boy and his four backup singers.

As he got closer to his home, they grew louder and louder. They were singing two songs. One was about a postman twistin' down the street, the other about a postman looking for a letter. He kept asking them to quiet down, and they just ignored them. When anyone saw him, they either laughed or tried to refrain from laughing. I must admit we almost gave ourselves up a few times.

When he finally got home he sat on his front stoop while the Spectors continued to sing. We tried to duck behind a recycling bin but were easily spotted.

"Sarah and Alice?" he said.

"You caught us," we shrugged.

"What are you doing?"

"Trying to find out why you were in such a rush," Alice said.

"I wasn't," he said. "They were." He pointed to the four women in silver sequins.

We walked up and sat next to Butters on the steps. The Spectors were vibrating, freaking out.

"He's coming!" one of them whispered. "He's almost here," another one said. Finally we caught on to what they were talking about. Butters's mailman had parked his truck down the block and was lugging a large blue bag. He looked up and waved at us.

"Hi!" Alice and I said. Butters said nothing. His Spectors thrust out their hips, smiled widely, and said in unison, "Hello, Mr. Postman. We've been waiting for you."

Alice and I laughed hysterically.

Butters just looked down and muttered, "Every damn day with this."

TWENTY

"**H**OW DID you beat me home?" I asked, flabbergasted. Johnny had a job at our town's tiny used-record store, which always seemed like it was about to close. "Didn't your shift just end? Doesn't somebody need a used Barry Manilow joint?"

"Special powers, little sis. You snooze, you lose," said Johnny. "Use the computer if you want to watch TV."

"It's too small to see anything. And it always does that annoying pause-y thing that makes it feel like stop-motion." It was kind of true. And I wanted to watch *The Next American Hero*, which wasn't streaming. I know. It's a crappy reality show but it's so campy that I love it. "Johnny, come on, this week Bella Morte teaches the wannabes how to look sexy while flying. It's supposed to be hysterical, better than this mess." I hated picking fights, but he was occupying some sacred space.

"It's not lame. Who are you to judge the artistic merit of *The Dead Walk Slowly*?"

"What merits? They eat brains and groan." I hated horror films, and the one Johnny had on was particularly gross. I had to turn away from the screen to avoid seeing some bloodied chicken parts being eaten out of a fake stomach wound.

"It's a metaphor for the human condition. How the world makes us into the undead. See that group eating that man's head? That's a commentary on that *Omnivore* book you forced everyone to read,"

Johnny said. "Also, that show is such crap. It's not like those kids ever go on to be real Heroes. Most of them just end up stopping one bank robbery and doing mall signings for a few years. The real Hero teams don't televise recruitment. That would be stupid."

I caught the screen out of the corner of my eye. "That is so disgusting. Zombie films are so tired," I said. "But I'm glad you read that—"

The screen was filled with *braaaains*. I felt like I was going to puke. Johnny laughed as I turned green.

"Okay, you win. I'm going to go make dinner now. But don't go away. You gotta add your magic to the penne sauce."

Johnny grinned. He won.

I was busy setting the table when Dad walked in. He tossed two grocery bags on the counter and went straight for the TV, clearing his throat.

"Maximum Fighting?" said Johnny, tossing the clicker over.

Dad switched it over to ESPN Ocho, with a groan. "Oh, it's just normal grappling. I want to see Captain Moron!"

Dad and Johnny were pretty obsessed with Maximum Fighting. I didn't get it. They liked it because it was one of the few sports leagues that let Heroes and even Misshapes fight, in the no limits division. "Captain Moron is *our* hero!" Dad said. He had been on a big Captain Moron kick lately. I think he thought it was good for us.

"Great name, too," said Johnny.

"The Irish and Jewish immigrants had boxing heroes when they were first fighting for acceptance in America. We have Captain Moron. Rough and tumble folks from humble origins who just want it more. Those are the best boxers, unlike those fancy-pants Heroes. When you come from a place where one hit levels a block, and then Captain Moron puts the whole world—the whole world!—of hurt on you, you cave. Instantly."

It was a big speech, but Dad was a man in love. He believed fervently in Captain Moron, and that his popularity would make the world safe for Misshapes, safe for people to be who they are. Dad never really expressed any kind of Misshape pride. He was always more of a nerd than anything else. And with Mom around, he didn't need to be anything else. But after Mom left and Johnny donned a Misshape identity—even though he was still in the Hero Academy at the time—

Dad joined him. I'm not sure if it was to show support for Johnny one of the only ways he knew how, or out of genuine outrage at the Hero community for abandoning his wife. Either way, Captain Moron gave him and Johnny hope, and that was a beautiful thing to see.

I wanted hope, too. But the pasta was more pressing. "Johnny, get in here. I need you," I said.

Johnny made his way into the kitchen, thrust his hand into the saucepan filled with cream and tomato base, and clenched his jaw tightly. I dipped my finger in and tasted it. Yum. He licked his finger and headed back to the TV.

Dinner was ready soon after, and I told Dad and Johnny to get to the table.

The men in my life got up and slouched their way over. Watching them, I realized that Johnny's whole essence is likely hereditary.

"How's school?" asked Dad.

"It's going okay," I replied, quickly. I didn't want to talk about it with him.

"Okay? It sucks," Johnny said. "Civic responsibility sucks. I don't know who decided to keep an eye on Misshapes this year, but I don't like it. We should be treated like free-range chickens. They treat us like veal."

"Ew. Gross metaphor," I said. "What's your problem with the class? Leaning about Hero stuff is important."

Johnny snapped. "Way to fall for it."

"What are you talking about?" I replied.

"They're separating us for a reason. Every Misshape at Harris High got outed. The Academy's after us and they don't ever lose."

"Brother, have you been watching *History's Mysteries* again? You know the answer is always a cover-up for aliens among us."

Dad looked confused. He had no idea what we were fighting over.

Johnny sneered at me. "And you still think you can go to the Academy? It's so gross. Accept that you're a Misshape, Sarah. Because you are. You're a freak."

"Johnny, use better language with your sister," Dad said, butting in.

"Language?" Johnny was full of disdain. "Who cares about

language when we have a traitor in our midst?" He glared at me. "You buy into what the Normals and Heroes think about us. They don't let you into their silly school or their cliques except to use you, and you're okay with that."

I got up from the table and headed toward the kitchen. I didn't want to look at my brother.

"Johnny, lay off your sister," said Dad.

I paused, midstep. The words started spilling out of me. "It's not fair. I should've been in there. It's your fault I'm not in there. I should've been a legacy—" It was true. If Johnny hadn't been expelled from the Academy, I would've gotten in. I knew it.

"This whole town is under the spell of the Hero Academy. They get to decide who's special because you let them have power. We have powers too, but they think that we're nothing—"

"I don't want to hear this!" I said, and ran off to my room. But our house was too small. There was nowhere to hide—you heard everything—and Johnny kept talking. "You don't even have any friends, Sarah. They're all at the Academy and left you behind." He took a bite of my pasta, which shut him up.

I wanted to add some last words or something. Point out that Johnny was thrown out of the Academy and the only reason people invite him anywhere is to use him. The human liquor store. But I opened my mouth and no words came out.

My head felt like it was going to explode. I looked up at the skylight. There were no stars at all. Clouds were forming. I ran to my room and slammed my door shut with a satisfying crunch punctuated by a thunderclap.

Outside of my door, I heard fragments of an argument. There were some of the old classics. *You need to stop missing school. Do some work around here because Sarah has been cooking all the time.* Then there was the main argument, the same argument that they'd been having for months. Dad scolded Johnny for getting kicked out and my brother said it was a terrible place that only taught kids to feel superior.

"You could've been amazing," Dad said.

"And I'm not now?"

"I'm not saying that," he sputtered, "but you could've learned so much there and gone on to great things."

"A lot of good that did her. That place is a den of snakes. There's nothing they can teach me that I want to learn from them. The things they said about Normals and Misshapes, Dad, it was disgusting."

"You could've made it better if you weren't so rash. So much like—"

"Like Mom? Yeah, I know. I'm not clueless—"

I heard my brother's door slam and Dad turned the TV back on with a loud sigh.

After a few minutes there was a knock. I rolled over in my bed, putting my pillow over my head.

Johnny's pale face peeked through the doorway. He had some ice cream on a plate as a peace offering. "Dad sent me. Sorry. I know things are tough."

"Dad told you to say that."

"No," he said sheepishly. "No, he didn't. There's a lot going on and I sometimes forget you're younger and might not be aware of some of it. I didn't mean to accuse you of being a jerk."

"Whatever." What did he mean, things I wasn't aware of? What sort of amazing knowledge did he gain in our one-year difference?

He started to talk again and then looked back down at his feet. He offered to make dinner for the next week. I told him not to sweat it. He's an awful cook. There was a pause and he walked away again, leaving the door slightly ajar. I turned over and pretended to sleep.

TWENTY-ONE

MY FIGHT with Johnny ate at me. The only thing that distracted me was the arrival of homecoming weekend. It wasn't the homecoming for Harris High. It was the Hero Academy Homecoming weekend. The Harpastball Homecoming was our *Friday Night Lights*, our excuse for a high school game at a stadium. Our tiny little town felt like the center of the universe, as people traveled from far and wide to crowd the streets, buy our maple syrup, and enjoy the sheer spectacle. It made the Summer Spectacular look like a swim meet. News outlets from as far as Japan and Russia covered the action with live satellite feeds. There was even a Hero parade. Not wanting to compete with the Heroes, Harris High always scheduled its Homecoming football game for the following weekend.

I was so excited. I had a ticket for the stands. I thought this time I could handle the stands. I had experience. Freedom Boy hooked me up with a ticket, and I'd get to go with Betty. I'd barely seen her since school started and I missed her. It was going to be perfect.

I found a spot near the middle of the parade route and caught the early-bird floats. They were mostly Golden Age Heroes and Academy alumni that I didn't know about. They were active in the twenties through the fifties, with names like The Sun Beam, Adventure Boy, and The Dark Rider.

I snapped to attention when I saw THE ORIGINAL FREEDOM MAN AND FREEDOM MAN II written on the side of a convertible. There were two very old gentlemen sitting in the backseat with the same strong chin and sharp eyes as Freedom Boy—his great grandfather and grandfather, probably. The crowd cheered loudly for them.

After the retired Freedom Men wheeled on by, the parade kicked into high gear. The marching band for Academy West played a deafening version of "When the Saints Go Marching In" on loop. They featured ridiculously large instruments that were so loud they must have required Herculean lungs. It felt like the drums were coming at me in surround sound. They had some hot-steppers with dance moves that shook the ground.

I made my way forward, weaving through people, closer to the Harpastball field's iron gates. Then, suddenly, someone yelled my name. I turned around but I couldn't see anybody. I kept going and there it was again: "Sarah Robertson." It sounded like Alice.

All I saw was a steady stream of flag-waving people. I yelled back, "Hey, where are you?"

"Look down!" Alice replied.

There she was, chilling with Butters, Markus, and Hamilton on a bright blue inflatable couch facing the street.

We were interrupted by a deafening roar from the crowd. Something hit my head and I picked it up. It was a candy. I looked up and there was Freedom Man, flying over us, tossing candy from a giant blue bag. The kids loved it, jumping up and down like they were pogo sticks on a sugar high, cheering like their lungs were going to burst.

Markus looked at a piece of candy on the couch, picked it up, and tried to throw it back.

"Do you have any chocolate?" he yelled, drowned out by the cheers.

I looked up, and I could've sworn that Freedom Man gave me a courtly nod. But maybe I was imagining it. I was sure Freedom Boy hadn't said anything about me. I was even more sure that I was a secret non-girlfriend girl who he had been hanging out with on a weekly basis. So why would he nod at me? I felt more confused than ever when it came to where I stood with Freedom Boy.

I asked Alice if I could sit down. The roar had dulled as Freedom Man flew toward the field.

"Sure thing," said Alice. "Pull up a seat. You're floating on plastic-encased air. It's sort of like you're flying, too."

I plopped down and bounced up slightly.

It took a little bit to get adjusted to the plastic, which stuck to everything. "What are you guys up to? I didn't think I'd see you here."

Butters responded, "You can't miss this. It's like a stupid summer movie. You want to make fun of it, but you still need to go for the spectacle."

"So we do both," said Markus, chewing on a piece of RPG Lou bubblegum that had rained down on his head from the sky. "We made plans at civics club."

Oh. Yeah. I missed that. I was practicing with Sam.

"Are you heading to the game?" I asked the group.

"Yeah. Come with us! Markus knows a way we can sneak in through the woods and not have to pay," said Alice. "It's my first Harpastball game."

"Me too," said Butters.

"Aw, I'd love to but I got tickets to the stands. I'm going with my cousin Betty," I added. I felt a little guilty. I didn't want to say that Freedom Boy got me the tickets. Alice had been telling me to dump him, and that being a secret non-girlfriend meant that he wasn't really into me, but I didn't want to do that yet.

"Rollercoaster! Of Luv!" the Spectors sang. "Say what?"

"Too bad," said Alice. "If you need a break from all that excitement, meet up with us. I need another girl with all these boys around. We'll be hanging out by the other team's pool." She paused. "It's so weird there are pools."

"Your brother and his friends are coming, too. They didn't want to but I told them about a back entrance I learned of when I played for the team. I think they couldn't pass up the chance to sneak in," said Markus.

"I'll try," I said.

Just then, the float with the Academy Harpastball team cruised by. The athletes smiled and waved. The team was outfitted in matching uniforms of skin-tight blue Lycra with gold lettering, thin sparkling gold helmets, and shin, elbow, and knee guards. HERO ACADEMY was emblazoned across their chests, with numbers and names on the back. I recognized Humungulous, who, even sitting down, towered above all the other players.

Freedom Boy stood on a pedestal at the end of the float. He looked like royalty, giving his curt half-wave to the crowd. People cheered wildly and he waved with his right hand. His left hand was wrapped around the shoulder of a buxom Hero who I'd seen on TV named Dangerous Girl. She wore a skintight red costume, its most notable feature a boob window that revealed ample cleavage. It seemed very un-aerodynamic.

The boys gawked. Alice glared at me. I averted my eyes.

Then I caught Dr. Mann in my peripheral vision. His Grand Marshall float had a large chair in the middle, like he was Santa or something. He wasn't in his usual suit, but dressed down in a leather motorcycle jacket and jeans. Alice let out a whoop and I smiled at her.

I was staring at his perfectly shaped head. He was ridiculously good looking and pulled off the bald thing.

I was so distracted that I didn't even notice the weather turning. I looked around nervously, hoping no one blamed me. This time it wasn't my fault. I tried to fix it a bit, but despite my lessons, the weather was just too strong for me today. Maybe it was all the Hero energy in the air.

A thick cloud ran across the sky and hovered over Dr. Mann's float, plunging the bright day into dullness. It started to drizzle and a collective sigh swept across a section of the crowd. Dr. Mann, seeing the disappointment, raised his hands up to the sky. He scrunched up his face, and in an instant disappeared into a cloud of green dust. The green dust floated upward, joining the rain cloud.

Thirty seconds later, rain fell. Instead of splashing, the drops just materialized into ants. They all ran toward Dr. Mann's car and formed a giant black sinewy mound. The mound grew and grew and then took shape, like a scarecrow made out of tiny black insects.

It was a massive stupid-animal trick.

Suddenly, Dr. Mann burst out of this formation, like a mermaid emerging from a dark, churning pool of water. It occurred so fast it was hard to register what had happened. Stray ants continued to crawl up his skin and merge into his flesh, like he was absorbing them. I was grossed out. I had always hated ants.

Before I knew it, Dr. Mann was back. Everything was fine. He roared, and the crowd responded with wild claps and hoots of approval.

But I was still a little disgusted.

TWENTY-TWO

FTER THE parade, I had to meet up with Freedom Boy to get my ticket, which meant lingering around the athletes' entrance. There were other girls there in FREEDOM BOY T-shirts waiting as well. I felt like a creepy fangirl. He jogged over to me. "Here you go, ma'am, have fun," he said. He winked at me, and then turned around and jogged into the entrance. The other girls glared. I felt like I had whiplash. A gust of wind whipped my hair in a circle. I heard Alice in my head, reminding me that he's a jerk. But he had to like me if he got me tickets for the Harpastball stands. Freedom Man would be there and everything.

When I got to the stands, I was shuttled to the nosebleeds. I had the idea in my head that my seats would be good seats, near the field, but instead I had to go to the tippy-top. As I started my hike, I passed the Freedom Family holding court, Freedom Man whispering and pointing at the field. Probably talking strategy with somebody. I put my head down and rushed by them. Betty sat down next to me, with her giant foam finger and a Freedom Boy commemorative jumbo Coke. It felt like he was avoiding looking at me, totally embarrassed by me.

I was really excited when I saw Sam sitting in the alumni section. I stopped over to talk to him and he was friendly, but seemed skittish about talking to me around his former classmates.

"Good to see you, Sam," I said.

"You too. Glad you got a spot in the stands."

"I have some ins. Though the seats leave much to be desired," I replied.

"I'd offer you a spot but it's alumni only."

"That's fine," I said, then leaned in with a question that had been bugging me. "Hey, do you know what was up with Dr. Mann and that trick at the parade?"

"Oh that. He loves that power. He devolves into some real basic organism and ascends into the cloud."

"Like bacteria in water vapor," I said, thinking of what Dr. Reveala had taught me.

"Yeah, I guess," he said, distracted. He looked around nervously at his friends. I knew the look. I took it as my sign to leave.

"Well, I should go," I said. "Good to see you. Sorry I don't have any brownies."

"Next time," he said as I walked off. He might've winked at me. I couldn't tell.

I waved when I saw Lindsay and Christie picking their way through the stands. I don't know why I did it. I still hated them. They ignored me completely, sat down next to a few girls, and all giggled together as they tried to surreptitiously look back at me.

"What's that about?" I asked Betty.

"They're just a bunch of spoiled jerks," she said resentfully.

I had no idea how things had been going for her at the Academy. Before I could ask, the players took the field and a roar spread through the crowd. They faced the stands and waved at family and supporters. I tried to wave at Freedom Boy. He waved at his parents in the front row. It felt like I was going to make a fool out of myself, eventually. My face turned red. The stands weren't fun today. Not like the summer.

I looked along the field boundary line at the enormous crowd of Normals. I would never find my friends among that mass. But then I noticed some small figures at the far end of the field, by the opposing team's pool, on the same side of the field as the stands. As I squinted I could see Alice and the Misshapes hanging out. Even though they were tiny figures in the distance they seemed like they were having fun. The place they were sitting was off limits to people not on the team or officiating the game. It was on the other side of the magnetic rail for the stands and required getting past two fences—one on each side of the rail. Despite my best instincts, I kind of admired the effort they had put into flaunting the rules.

"Do you want to head out of here and meet up with some of my classmates?" I asked Betty.

This question would have been unthinkable this summer. Sitting in the stands was such a rare honor we wouldn't ever, ever, ever part with tickets.

But without hesitation, Betty said, "Yeah," and moments later we were walking toward the exit.

I was surprised by how eager Betty was to leave the stands. I always imagined that the Academy was a magic place that would solve all of life's problems. With all my pining for the place, and resenting Betty for getting in, I never considered what the actual experience was like for her.

"Do you like the Academy?" I asked Betty.

"I think so," she said, cautiously. "But it's really overwhelming, like, ninety-nine percent of the time."

"Yeah, the stands were terrifying," I said. "Like a nest of vipers."

"I feel like all the Hero kids are just waiting for you to say or do the wrong thing so they can make fun of you," she said. "I just wanted to enjoy Harpastball, you know? And now, it's like this, this social gauntlet. It's always like that."

I still held on to my visions of super friends hanging out, fighting crime, and forming lifelong friendships. But it seemed like Betty's experience was miles away from that.

"I'm not sure if this will be better," I said. We were heading toward the scariest part of the journey—sneaking through a fence, crossing over the track, and then sneaking over the second fence. "I have one friend here, I think, and the rest are just vaguely hostile."

"That's school," Betty said. "People can suck." Considering her remarks about the Academy, I think her dance card wasn't much better.

Alice heard us talking and ran up to the fence on the opposite side. The fence and the Harpastball pool beckoned across the gulf.

"You're almost there," Alice said, eyes gleaming. The metal plate track stood between us, shiny, silver, and intimidating. Any minute, the stands could fly by and decapitate us. Several sets of muddy footprints zigzagged across the sparkling plates.

"Betty here doesn't want to cross," I shouted.

"I don't want get kicked out of school. Our family doesn't have the best track record," said Betty, giving me a look.

Alice directed us toward a small gap in the fence that we were able to shimmy through. We timidly walked to the track before stopping to stare at it.

"What's taking you so long?" Alice asked.

"Give us one second," I said, glaring at Betty.

"Okay, but you go first," Betty replied.

I had to admit that my mind was coming up with the many gory ways that I could die crossing these tracks and stepping on the electromagnetic rail, but I steeled myself to pretend that I was totally together and not scared for Betty's sake. Looking both ways, I checked three times for the bleachers. They were at the other end of the field, fifty feet in the air. I placed one foot on the first track. And then the other. My shoulders relaxed slightly. I carefully tiptoed across the metal. I heard Betty following close behind.

When we got to the other side, Alice pointed us toward another hole in the fence. We crawled through and she greeted me with a bear hug. Betty got a handshake and a few introductions. I saw some other kids milling about: Butters, Markus, and Johnny. My brother had brought along Hamilton, Backslash, and a glowering Kurt. The Spectors said, "What's up girl!" in a sixties Motown riff. I was glad Doodlebug hadn't shown up.

"What up, Robertson?" said Hamilton, bounding up to Kurt like a puppy. "And…"

"Cousin. Betty," she said. "You two are Johnny's friends?"

Hamilton said, "Me and Kurt spent some time in the clink together. We took the fall for a night of partying with the Academy. The usual, put the blame on the Misshapes from the poor part of town."

"That sucks," I said.

"How's the Academy?" Kurt asked, acidly. He said the word "Academy" with a palpable contempt.

"Eh," Betty said, and I pulled her away to join Butters and Alice on the side of the pool. I took off my shoes and placed my feet in the water. It was nice, considering the air had gotten chilly. Markus plopped down next to me and Betty took a spot next to Butters. Johnny and his crew were busy playing War or some gambling card game.

"So, Markus, I heard you used to play?" I asked.

"Yeah, they let me play in JV scrimmages when I was in junior high. Before the Academy got fascist."

"Fascist?" asked Alice. "Were they planning a clampdown?"

"No, just tightening up their 'rules' on who could and couldn't play. Before, they would let some Misshapes join in, but now it's only

Academy-admitted Heroes. They told me it was because they could only insure students," said Markus. A red hat hovered in the air behind him. It was George Herbert, the invisible boy. It had to be.

"Hi, George!" I said.

"Hey, Sarah," I heard a small voice reply. "Nice to see you here." George flashed back into existence for one second, blushed, and then disappeared again. I turned to Markus.

"So, if you used to play, can you answer a question that's always bugged me? How are these guys flying?" Betty was about to speak up, but she let Markus explain. They probably told her at the Academy.

"Two ways!" Markus said excitedly. "Biologically, like me and birds and stuff, or supernaturally, like Freedom Boy and the other strikers. The supernatural dudes can warp a gravitational field. Except over there," he said, pointing above the pool. "That's where they block warping to make it unnavigable for the strikers. If you try to fly in there you end up disappearing, falling, or shooting back in some crazy zigzag pattern. Usually kids start getting sick, and it's like projectile and gross. There's the anti-anti-gravity device that makes flying there nearly impossible…"

Betty chimed in with her explanation, which sounded right out of some textbook. "The rules require that a device be placed above the pool that inhibits flying above the aquatic portion of the playing cube. Over the decades, elaborate netting made out of adamantium was used, until the development of the Graviton Bosonic Field Manipulation Inhibitor by PeriGenomics in 1998."

"A graviwhat?" I asked.

"Graviton Bosonic Field Manipulation Inhibitor," Betty repeated.

"One of those," Markus said, and pointed to a large black ball with a blinking green light mounted on a metal post across from us. "Everyone just calls it an Aerofail. They prevent flight of any kind, including leaping. They are very rare and very expensive. It's a rite of passage for Harpastball players to accidentally end up there and wind up at some completely different place along the field, puking their guts out. See? Watch," Markus said. He curled up a program that was lying next to him on the ground and threw it up above the pool. The paper ball disappeared for a second. Then it popped back into the atmosphere and came flying back down to earth, hitting Butters in the head.

"Dude, not cool," he said.

"Hey, I just know where they go up, not where they come down," Markus replied.

Butters got up and said, "I gotta pee. Where's the bathroom?"

"Follow me," said Kurt. He whispered something to Johnny, Hamilton, and Backslash. They ventured over to the edge of the pool, about twenty yards down from us, toward the goal.

The boys proceeded to unzip their flies. I heard an "Oooooooh" from the Spectors.

Alice was the first to realize what was going on.

"Eww!" she screamed and quickly pulled her legs out of the water. "Not cool, not cool at all."

They were peeing in the pool. It was so gross! I pulled my legs out as quickly as I could.

"If it feels good, do it!" crowed Backslash, as the pool became a toilet.

"Yeah!" Johnny chimed in. "Revenge!"

"Revenge?" I turned to Alice and Markus. "What's he talking about?"

"Dude. Your bro has issues with this place," said Markus. "Ergo, pee."

The Spectors had come up with a full-fledged song in response to Kurt, hiding behind Hamilton, Butters, and Backslash at the edge of the superpool: "*Payback! Revenge! So cool! Peeing in your super pool!*"

Markus and Alice were starring glazed eyed in the distance, trying to watch the game, or more accurately, trying to ignore the whole peeing thing.

"Guys, I can't see anything. Who has the Harpastball now?" I asked.

My voice was drowned out by two sets of silver stands hurtling down the sidelines like a train, chopping through the air with a deafening whoosh.

A ball—and a speeding vision in blue and gold—was headed our way.

TWENTY-THREE

THEY MOVED so fast we didn't register what was going on. Freedom Boy zoomed through the air with the Aqua Kid in his arms. They were chasing something rolling on the ground. The Harpastball. It was one thing to watch the game from the safety of the stands, but it seemed so much more brutal and real when it was in our face.

In one smooth movement, hovering three stories high in the air, Freedom Boy swooped down and Aqua snatched the ball from the ground. An instant later, Freedom Boy was right in front of me and tossed Aqua in the pool. The impact into the water would've killed anyone. Anyone but the Aqua Kid. He entered the water like a torpedo and sped to the other end.

I got splashed. All of the Misshapes got splashed.

Freedom Boy stopped at the edge of the pool, pressing his feet into the ground to hasten his halt. Markus was right. That anti-flying field was not to be messed with.

I tried to follow Aqua's movement in the pool and saw Hamilton still hanging out on the sidelines. Paint was dripping off his shutter shades and onto his face. He wiped his face off and yelled, "Come on! Watch yourself!" Johnny and Butters stayed next to him, but Backslash sped away from the action in fear. It was beautiful. He looked like an Olympic sprinter with his power in motion. Who knew where Backslash would end up. Maybe New Hampshire.

Then Hamilton's luck took a turn for the worse. A referee, who must have had superpowers herself, sprinted along the sidelines behind Freedom Boy. When the ref reached the pool, she smacked right into the distracted Hamilton and knocked him into the water. The water that he had just peed into. Gross!

"Oh no," I said. The Aqua Kid did not play well with others. Seconds later, the Aqua Kid grabbed Hamilton in a bear hug from behind and screamed "The hell? I should destroy all of you right here!"

A giant wave rose in the Aqua Kid's wake, furious and cresting. At its height, you could see an angry bearded face with its mouth agape. Before I could think, *Danger! Move!* There was water. Everywhere.

We all got hit by the reach of Poseidon's mouth. It didn't matter whether we were by the edge of the pool or hovering around by the fence. It was like having water from a fire hose hit you in the face. The force of it knocked me to the ground. Markus, Alice, and Butters were similarly disheveled on the sidelines.

While I was trying to get up in a dignified manner, I heard Freedom Boy trying to calm his friend down. "Aqua, Aqua, *Aqua!* Put the kid away and score the point. I got this. We will handle this situation."

Aqua yelled back, "These Misshapes need to be dealt with!"

"Do not worry about that now, Aqua Kid. We have a Harpastball game to win. Such behavior will just get you a red card!" The referee had slowed down and could see the action. The game was catching up to them.

"Fine," said Aqua. The wave disappeared and Aqua continued to the end zone, a scrum of players following now. Freedom Boy lingered on the sidelines.

"Are you okay?" he said to me.

I went in for a kiss and he pulled me in for a hug.

"Fine," I said.

"Okay. I must return to the game. I will see you again," he said.

Freedom Boy motioned to Hamilton. The Hero let out a huge gust of wind from his mouth, drying us off and then turning to the graffiti kid. "It is chilly, my friends. No time to take a swim," he said, flying away.

"Thanks, Freedom Bro!" yelled Hamilton.

"So, what's with the cold shoulder from Freedom Boy?" Alice asked.

I huffed loudly and then asked the group, "Does anyone want to ditch this and get some food? Let's get out of here."

TWENTY-FOUR

"LET'S GO to Psycho Loco Taco," Hamilton insisted.

"Hell no!" Alice replied. "I am not going to a fast-food joint named after an ex-supervillain. That ground beef is sketchy enough as it is without my having to worry about some evil plan being cooked up with the new Pobre Gato meal." She took a breath. "Also, one crazy is enough."

"Awww, come on," Hamilton persisted. "I heard the Pobre Gato combo is amazing. They have zombie sauce in between their three crunchy shells,"

"I'm with Alice," I said. "Especially now that you mention the supervillain and zombie sauce thing. Let's go to the diner."

Butters' Spectors chimed in: "No no no no no psycho psycho loco! Redundant!"

I agreed with them completely.

As we walked toward the car I overheard Kurt grumbling, "Psycho Loco wasn't a villain. The LAPD just didn't like someone actually keeping the gangs in check and stealing their glory." He paused, muttering, "All with a fricking crossbow, man, a crossbow."

We split up into two cars. Betty, Markus, Alice, Butters, and me in one. Johnny and his posse in the other, minus Backslash. We probably wouldn't see him for a few days. George, of course, had disappeared. I had no idea where he was.

"Yo, we're going to be later than you. We have something to do," said Johnny. "Markus, when you drive your car home, drive by State Street. Write it on your hand so you don't forget."

Walt Jr.'s Diner—home of the all-day breakfast—was on the western end of the main drag of stores and shops in town. It was a marvel of chrome and glass, open until one o'clock in the morning.

A glowing neon sign in the window blinked HOME OF HERO FRIES and a handwritten sign under that indicated they were twenty-five percent off for Harpastball Homecoming weekend.

The sun was just starting to go down when we walked into the diner. Many of the booths and tables were filled with Harpastball fans. I looked around, worried that we wouldn't get a seat, especially for a crowd so large. But a funny thing happened when the hostess saw us. She came over and gave Alice a big hug.

"So great to see you Alice," she said. "It's been too long."

"I hope you don't mean what you could mean," Alice replied.

"No, it's been under control just like you promised. We give them the drop-off, and they don't show up in the kitchen. We got a C+ on our last health inspection."

I tugged on Alice's sleeve and whispered, "What are you talking about?"

She turned to me and said in a low voice, "I make some extra money helping out local restaurants with pest problems. Kind of like a negotiator between the animal and human world. This place had a huge rat problem."

Gross. Maybe I'll just have a milkshake.

"Hey, mind if I check in on the kitchen and bring my friend?" Alice asked the waitress, whose name tag said Wanda.

"Sure, hon, you're always welcome back there. Should I get you a table?"

"Yeah, there's gonna be, like, eight of us total," she said as she dragged me toward the kitchen.

It was a pretty greasy-looking place, not the shiny metal kitchen I had seen on all those cooking shows on TV. The chefs said hi to Alice and I felt kind of cool, like a Walt Jr.'s Diner VIP.

Alice swaggered toward the exit door. "Hi, guys," she said. "Mind if I say hi to our little friends?"

"Sure thing, Alice," one of them said, looking up from his cutting board. Alice chirped out something incomprehensible, and a high-pitched squealing noise came back in response. I couldn't figure out where it was coming from.

"What was that?"

"The rats. I arranged a peace accord where they would take the leftover scraps at a drop-off point if they didn't touch anything in the kitchen. I just asked how it was going," she said. "They warned me, if they see any traps, the peace accord's off."

"Wow," I said. "That's pretty cool that you're using your power for good." "I guess. Keeps me with some spending money and comfort when I eat out," she said and then chirped out something else.

"What was that?" I said

"Just told them that we're eating here, so don't touch anything or I will personally oversee their death," she said.

Some Harris Highers, decked out in varsity jackets, had taken over several diner tables. They glared at us while we walked toward our friends at the back.

We took our seats. I couldn't follow the eight different conversations at our table. I felt a tap on my shoulder. It was Butters.

"What's the deal with your cousin?" he asked, while Betty was talking with Johnny and Markus.

"Betty, oh, she goes to the Academy. Same power as Johnny," I replied. "But she's, like, responsible."

He nodded. It looked like he was going to say something to her, but then his arm brushed her arm and he looked down at the floor. The Spectors began singing, sweeter than usual: "Baby love, my baby love." He whipped his head around and, embarrassed, squeezed out a darling little "Shut up!" The Spectors giggled, standing around our table. The color drained from Butters's face. "No words, please. Please, no words. 'Las,' 'bops,' 'bahs,' and stuff like that is fine. I'm just eating with my friends, you know?"

The lead started in: "Well, well, aren't we Mr. Big Shot. I've worked with the best and you cannot lecture us—"

"Please, please, please," Butters pleaded. "It means the world to me."

Struck by Butters' sincerity, they teased him. "Okay. We hear you. But only because we like you, lil' Butters!" He blushed.

Alice asked Hamilton, "Why did you guys come late?"

"You'll see it later. I was doing an ongoing public service for the town," he said.

I caught onto what he was saying. "Didn't you get arrested because you posted your graffiti on your Facebook page a few weeks ago?" I asked.

"Oh that, well, they just don't appreciate street art. I have to go around cleaning up my work all throughout town. Punk cops."

"Ham," I said, "your avatar was a picture of you giving the thumbs up to your own graffiti. You have to admit that's kind of ridiculous. Sort of funny, but ridiculous. The cops were watching that house, right?"

"Well, I've learned and adapted," he replied, suavely. "Decided to go more anonymous, Robertson."

The waitress came over and we ordered two plates of Hero fries and a round of milkshakes. Hero fries were a local specialty, a giant plate of french fries slathered in American cheese and then doused in gravy. It was big enough to serve four and leave them all stuffed. And, more important, it was cheap.

"Guys! Wait!" said Markus. He just got a text about the game. "Hero Academy won it one hundred and two to ninety-nine." He read aloud from ESPNs recap: "Aqua Kid got the MVP award, but the true champion of the night was student coach John Joel Glanton V. He really showed an unheard level of strategic play, magnificently—"

He was interrupted by the waitress, who had our shakes and platters of Hero Fries. We picked at them all night, hanging out and chatting until closing, when they threw us out. Wanda was particularly apologetic, but we understood. I had never been out so late.

"Okay, don't forget to drive down State Street!" Hamilton yelled. "You have to see my handiwork."

Markus took us to the super-big PeriGenomics billboard on State Street. It was an ad with one of their positive statements accompanied by a picture of a happy family in front of a perfect house and their logo. It said, "Helping you create promising tomorrows for yourself and your children."

But Hamilton had been to work. The family was missing some teeth and the dog had blood coming out of its mouth. His graffiti changed the statement to "Helping you cr a p yourself." I laughed and couldn't stop. The rest of the car joined in.

In the hubbub, Betty whispered in my ear, "Your friends are pretty cool."

"My friends," I said, letting the word reverberate in my head. I leaned over toward Betty and gave her a proper reply. "They are pretty cool."

She squeezed my hand and gave me a smile.

TWENTY-FIVE

MY CELL phone ring pushed its way into my dreams. I was flying with Taylor Swift's "I Knew You Were Trouble" as a soundtrack, and then I crashed, opening my bleary eyes to the blackness of my room at…oh god, 5:45 a.m. I grabbed at the glowing green light on the table. It was a text from Freedom Boy. *How's the most powerful girl in Doolittle Falls doing?*

I chose to ignore him. Freedom Boy had not been acting fantastic and I didn't feel like texting with him. I just wanted to get through the day and practice with Sam. I zombied through my morning until I got to school.

First period was odd. Anytime I answered a question in class, I heard people talking and whispering. I thought I heard the words "Misshape slut."

When second period rolled around, I went straight to Alice and Butters. It just felt like all the Normals were whispering and staring at me. I didn't get it.

"Alice, do I have a 'kick me' sign on my back? What's going on?" I felt like I was being watched.

"You didn't hear?" she replied, "Oh, it's not good. Not good at all. Butters, do you have it?"

"Here you go, Sarah. Don't let the teacher catch you with it," he said, giving me a crumpled-up newspaper.

I put the paper on my lap, and the *Doolittle Daily Star* headline screamed Misshape Scandal Ends Harris High School Football Season! I gulped. So that explained the freeze-out.

In all the Harpastball excitement I had forgotten about the big championship football game at Harris High. There is a strict rule against allowing people with powers, any powers, from competition in events with Normal athletes. According to the newspaper, there was a secret Misshape on the football team. An anonymous caller phoned in and the game was canceled. After an emergency meeting Sunday night, the Massachusetts High School Athletic Association suspended the whole school for the season.

It was one of the linemen, someone I didn't really know. He tested positive for the genetic marker of powers. The report said he had the ability to become completely immovable, like a tremendous boulder. Sounded like a solid Misshape power, and the paper even labeled him as one. Nobody knew him. He had somehow managed to fly under the radar, which is why he wasn't required in civic responsibility.

I gave the paper back to Butters. My paranoia was growing stronger by the minute. The looks that the kids shot at Butters, Alice, and me made it clear that they were blaming us for a ruined football season. It wasn't a secret that we were in the civic responsibility class. Thanks to that class, every Misshape at school—save our new lineman comrade—had been outed, and now everyone at school hated us. Officially.

"There's more as well," Alice said. "I'll show you later. But just ignore what they say, okay? It's them, not you."

She looked sympathetic. Like she wanted to let me know she was there for me. But I didn't know what she was talking about, and I was scared to find out.

For the rest of the day, I stuck to Butters and Alice. We sat together in class, we walked down the halls together, and we ate lunch together, saving some room for the Spectors. When lunch came around, the Spectors sung, softly, some song called "Trouble in Mind." One of the kids from the football team, I think his name was Peter, came over to our table.

"I can't believe they still let you in this school. It's freaks like you who screw it up for the rest of us," Peter said.

Butters replied, meekly, "Look, it wasn't me. I don't even know the kid—" and his Spectors interrupted him with "Let me lay it on the line. I got a little freakiness inside." That set the Peter off. He grabbed Butters by his collar and pulled him off his seat.

"Stop!" I said. I couldn't stand by.

"Shut up, freedom whore," someone shouted. It sounded like it was directed at me, but I couldn't understand why they would say that.

"Get your hands off him," growled a voice behind me.

It was Kurt, flashing his sharp teeth and looking as unhinged as possible.

Peter dropped Butters and took a huge swing at Kurt's head. Kurt grabbed Peter by the wrist and squeezed. Peter seemed enraged at first but his scowl quickly turned to a look of horror. As Kurt squeezed, Peter's hand turned grayish blue, followed by his arm, then his neck. The color spread and grew darker and darker. His whole body shook. I thought Kurt might kill him. Peter let out a spine-tingling howl and Kurt just squeezed harder. His whole body seemed frozen, like it could shatter into pieces in an instant.

It took three jocks to pull Kurt off the footballer. Peter quickly regained his color, but his arm was still bluish and tattooed with the white imprint of Kurt's hand. All hell broke loose. The lunchroom monitor tried to calm the room down. Everyone was out for blood. Kurt was threatening to take on the entire team, and the only thing stopping them from pounding on him was the sorry state of their friend. Other kids joined the mob in front of Kurt, looking for revenge: for the football player, for the team, for every misfortune they blamed on people with powers. Kurt stayed in front of us, ready to fight the world. Then there was an announcement: *Will all civic responsibility students come down to the auditorium immediately.* The lunchroom monitor came over and ushered us out.

When we got there, Principal Holloway and a school board member were waiting for us. They ignored us and talked in serious tones on their cell phones. The football ringer, Lou Ferlinghetti, sat a few rows behind us. He was monstrous but no more so than any other linebacker. He looked like he had been having the worst day of his life, like he'd flinch if someone said hi to him. The principal shot Kurt a look and he picked up his things and left.

Holloway spoke, abruptly. "I'm sorry to do this—especially after the recent incident in the cafeteria—but we must address some immediate concerns. The school board convened last night regarding the story in the *Doolittle Daily Star*. It was determined that, starting today, people with special abilities will not be permitted to participate in any after-school activities that involve a competitive element or could pose a danger to other students. This includes debate club, science club, academic bowl—"

"Damn it!" I muttered, a little too loudly. "They were going to smash my bridge today."

"Mine too," Marcus said. He looked so sad.

"Is there some problem?" our principal said.

"No, sir," we answered in unison.

He kept talking, but I couldn't hear anything. My head dropped into my hands. It made no sense, really. Our powers didn't affect things like Alice's debate club or my science club. A knot formed in my stomach. I was immediately plunged back to the days after my mom was accused. I knew what it was like to have a whole town turn against you. You want to disappear. It's exhausting. My friends didn't deserve to be treated that way.

"And for your own safety," Holloway continued, "and because of the unfortunate incident in the cafeteria, your lunch period will now be taken in the AV room. We may have to move your schedules around because we can get a monitor for only one period. I have contacted your parents and told them that you have the rest of the day off. If you can't get a ride, you can study in Ms. Frankl's room. She volunteered to watch over you."

Alice grabbed my hand. I think I was white, or as pale as I could be, considering. This news was major. Misshapes were officially persona non grata at Harris High.

Johnny gave me a knowing look. My phone buzzed. *See? Who's the conspiracy theorist now? Come to a civics club meeting. Your loving brother.*

I hadn't gone to a civics club meeting before. It bugged me. Why should we separate ourselves from the school? I didn't want to drop out of the social fabric—it did count for something—and just full stop become a Misshape. I wasn't a Misshape. I was that girl with that weather thing that would be at the Academy soon. Dr. Mann all but said it to me.

Then there was the other side of it. I shivered. Thinking about her cruel, cutting words, Christie's Betty Boop squeak repeated in my head, mocking me: "It's not like she has real powers. Just a Misshape who isn't a criminal yet."

TWENTY-SIX

WHEN WE were set free from the auditorium, Alice grabbed my hand and dragged me to the library, with Butters following close behind.

"What are we doing?" I asked.

"We need to suspend our online profiles," she insisted.

"But why? I didn't do anything wrong." I said, trying to diffuse the tension.

"Look, we haven't seen the worst of it yet. People at school know we're in that class but it's not like we stick out," she said. "Unlike Butters here."

The Spectors went off. "Hey, I'm gonna do me. You'll be mad, baby!"

"She's right, if they know you're dead. Better to stay off. Privacy's important."

"But I can ignore it," I argued, and then I asked the real question. "What are you even talking about?"

"Dude," said Alice, leveling with me. "We're going to be harassed. We're known Misshapes."

"I guess," I said. But I didn't believe her. "You sound like that stupid cyberbullying assembly."

"Fine, check your page," she said, getting up from the seat to give me the computer.

"Gross!" Butters said. "Why are people so mean on the Internet?"

Alice winced, looking at her page. "This is pretty brutal."

I pulled up my Facebook page. Alice and Butters looked over my shoulder. On my Sarah Robertson wall, there were a bunch of links to a fan page called one thousand strong for throwing out the Misshapes. On that page, there was a list of people who wanted us expelled from Harris High. People were talking about the ruined football season and writing awful comments. I scrolled the members page and it was basically everyone in Doolittle Falls.

But the worst was yet to come. Someone had posted a photo of me standing near Freedom Boy outside of the locker room at the Harpastball game. It was taken from Christie's blog, and as I clicked over to her blog, there was gossip. Gossip that involved me and Freedom Boy. She talked about me like I was nothing. Just a fan who got lucky. Like Freedom Boy was slumming. I was referred to as either "The Misshape Girl" or "Supervillain's harlot daughter." The headline FREEDOM IN CHAINS? GOLDEN BOY FALLS UNDER SPELL OF VILLAINESS' DAUGHTER.

Minute by minute, people were adding comments to my page. They all referenced the column. And someone had written, in all caps and bold:

HERO SLUT

It was gaining strength, like a meme. "Hero Slut" was written all over my page. I didn't even know the status of our relationship. But apparently the Internet knew something I didn't.

It hurt, seeing all these made-up stories. I needed to go anonymous.

"You're right," I said to Alice.

"I know. People suck," she said, glumly.

I went through the steps of deleting my account. Everything. Photos, memories, little quips about day-to-day stuff, all lost to my status as a Hero slut.

"Good," said Alice. "Now come to civics club. I know you've been avoiding it. I think we all need it."

"I have been practicing, just with Sam." It sounded lame when I said it, even though practicing with Sam was my ticket to the Academy.

"There are things that no power, no matter how strong, can help. You need to be with your friends right now," Alice said. "I need to keep an eye on you!"

After school, she took me through the sketchy woods behind the baseball field. After five minutes of twists and turns, we came to a clearing. It was like a scene from Robin Hood, with people hanging out on rocks and tree stumps or congregating under branches. Everyone in civic responsibility was there, like Henry, Backslash, and even Kurt, conversing in the corner with Johnny. My eyes went straight to Ms. Frankl, who was talking animatedly to Hocho, Markus, Wendy, and George.

"Hey, Ms. Frankl!" I yelled.

"I'm so glad you could make it!" She came over with a big smile on her face.

"Thanks. After everything today, I figured I should."

"You're telling me. I felt awful for all of you. I'm so sorry," she said, switching tacks. "I've got to get back to my discussion. Feel free to join us."

Alice and Butters got a hug and then she scampered back to her group.

"Mrs. Frankl is pretty cool out of class," I said to them. "That's new."

"Oh my god, she's so awesome," said Alice, gushing. "I'm just sorry you haven't come sooner."

"I've been busy being a Hero slut, I guess," I said. "And all that Sam stuff and my extracurriculars and, well, what now? What do we do?"

"We practice," said Butters.

Butters, Alice, and I took up a spot near a dead elm tree that had shed all its bark and looked like a telephone pole. Alice convinced a few chipmunks to make a cheerleader-like pyramid and then play a game of leapfrog. I asked her whether she ever thought about taping these shenanigans and putting them online. "You could be rich!"

She said, "I know I could, but it would be so disrespectful. So I don't."

Johnny punched my shoulder. "Nice to see you."

Butters tried out some tricks next. He did a sort of mental karaoke with his Spectors, leading into a cover version of "My Way," by Frank Sinatra.

Johnny said to the Spectors, "Hey, I know this awesome version of the song that Sid Vicious did. Want to get into it, ladies?"

Sitting next to Butters on the ground, they said, "No way, baby. That version's a travesty," and then they disappeared for a minute or two.

"I pissed them off with Sid Vicious?" asked Johnny.

"No!" said Butters, laughing. "I'm improving at making them disappear. They're *my* mental projections."

"What's Wendy up to?" I said, pointing to my classmate, standing in the middle of the clearing. Little Wendy Slothtrop, who was four foot five at most, levitated above the ground. Then she shot up like a rocket and flew in a small arc. Markus stood under her like he was ready to catch her if she fell.

"I didn't know she could fly like that," I said to Alice. "She rarely talks. Why isn't she at the Academy?"

"She's kind of amazing, but she told us last time that she can only fly across a set trajectory, and once her body is in the air, she can't change her path. So if a bird or plane or something gets in her way she's going to hit it and drop like a bug. That's why she rarely flies," Butters explained.

Markus flew, popping up into the air to practice his own version of chicken flying. His arms flapped spastically and the minute he got up in the air, he seemed fated to smash into the ground.

I wanted to play along. I wanted to do something cool. It was cold enough for thundersnow. But I had no idea whether I could pull it off, alone.

I pulled Alice aside. "I'm afraid of trying anything. I don't want to look like an idiot."

"Don't worry," she said. "This is a safe space. Everyone else already thinks you look like an idiot."

Okay, I thought, here goes nothing. "I'm doing thundersnow!" I said.

I stood very still. Thundersnow required a combination of both rage and calm, two opposing forces, creating my personal favorite weather system. The sun peeked out from the sky. I looked over at a smaller tree at the beginning of the woods. It was a baby compared to all the other trees. As I looked at it, I realized how I could access some serious rage.

I thought about Mom. How she had betrayed the family, how she had just up and disappeared without any warning, or even any good-byes. How Johnny became a faux badass after she left and how Dad looked smaller and older by the day. The way it felt to walk through Doolittle Falls with people glaring and murmuring cruel words to my back. The longer Mom stayed on the front of the newspapers, people looked through me, like I didn't even exist.

The cloud grew dark and rose higher into the sky. There were ice particles inside it, hitting against each other and building up massive frictive charges. Okay, next I have to take it down a notch. Change that air into snow with total calmness.

Boom!

A huge lightning bolt shot down from the sky and split the tree clean in half. Smoke rose in the air. The tree was on fire. The air smelled like burned leaves.

"Oops," I uttered. My aim still left much to be desired.

"Oh, Sarah," said Ms. Frankl. "You should probably plant a tree!" She shook her head, her mouth agape.

"That was the biggest lightning bolt ever," I said, shaking my head. Maybe I was starting to get it.

TWENTY-SEVEN

I WAS SUMMONED to Dr. Mann's office. Again. And this time, I had no idea why he wanted to talk to me. I walked over to the Academy, with a midnight-blue cloud trailing behind. Some raindrops fell right on top of my head. I tried to get my Dr. Mann game face on, but it was getting harder and harder to feel like Hero material in light of going to school and dealing with the daily parade of Misshape drama.

He wasn't even in his office when I got there—the secretary took me into the room and went to a long bookshelf, lined floor to ceiling with large tomes. Running her finger across a row of leather-bound books with Latin titles, she settled on a modern text in glossy white that read *Architectural Praxis of Contemporary Lair Design*. She pulled it halfway out of the shelf. With a loud creak the entire shelf opened outward like a door. She grabbed the edge of the door, pulled it open, and announced, in chirpy tones, "Dr. Mann will see you now."

The door opened into a dark corridor with dim gaslights running along the walls. The entrance to a dungeon. I walked forward until an enormous room opened up in front of me. It had walls of TV screens and computer monitors, large black computer towers, and shiny chrome tables. In the center of the room was a holographic globe, green and partially translucent, that rotated slowly on its axis. The globe was larger than me. The room itself was as big as my school's gymnasium. I marveled at how this sheer amount of space could be completely hidden. I wondered what other hidden corridors and spaces existed in the Academy. On the opposite side of me, I could see Dr. Mann staring up at a bank of computers, waving his hand in front of it to manipulate documents, videos, and images.

"Come over, Sarah!" he yelled to me, as he pulled up a security video that looked oddly familiar. As I drew closer to him I could see that everything on the screen was somehow related to me. There was a large section with what looked like a bunch of snakes mating that read "Sarah Robertson Karyotype. Applicant." There were a bunch of graphs and charts attached to my name. One was labeled "Ev capacity," one "HrO genetic screen," another "Physical test results." Each screen seemed to pinpoint me on a scale of average people and average Heroes.

"Sit down," he said and pointed to a chair next to him facing the bank. He was looking at the video. From up close I could finally see what it was. Me. And Sam. At PeriGenomics.

"What? How'd you get that?" I asked. It came out more hostile than I intended it to, but I felt annoyed. On top of the Hero slut blog and this—I felt violated. No privacy at all. People shouldn't be able to access surveillance footage of your day-to-day life.

He swiveled his chair toward me. "We have eyes everywhere, Sarah. We're always on the watch for Heroes and potential Heroes. And we're always watching people who interest us. And, as you know, *you* interest us."

"Did Sam know?"

"Who knows, really? If he did, he probably thought nothing of it. He's used to being watched by the Academy; he should expect the same from PeriGenomics."

Was he? Did he? I thought Sam was too much of a do-gooder to be a spy, but, then again, he was working for PeriGenomics. I was feeling a little pissed off at him for not telling me. I thought our practice time was a safe space. I suddenly realized that if Dr. Mann saw me practicing at PeriGenomics he must have seen the lightning. He must have seen my power. My breath grew short. Maybe he invited me here to say yes, he's pulled the strings, and I'm in. Hope blossomed in my chest.

"I've been reviewing some of the data we got from PeriGenomics and other information we've picked up from our other monitors around town. And I went over it with the admissions board concerning our ability to get you in next semester…"

He turned to pull up some more charts, graphs, and electrical readings. This was it. He was going to tell me I was in. Excitement pulsed through me. I couldn't sit still. Just as I was about to jump up to give a celebratory "Yes," he frowned.

"And they were not impressed with your results," Dr. Mann said.

I was shocked. He had dangled the promise of the Academy right in front of me and pulled it back. Like I was Charlie Brown trying to kick a football. It just didn't feel right.

"Look, Sarah, I pleaded your case. I really did. But based on these numbers you just don't merit acceptance in their eyes. I know you have it in you. But right now we have ten to fifteen kids who can shoot lightning. And if you look at these numbers…" He pointed to a chart with me and the other students listed, with names like Young Sparky and Shocker, "You score low on voltage, and your accuracy leaves much to be desired."

This was a complete misrepresentation of my talents and what I could do. It was my first time practicing. I had gotten better. I sputtered, "I don't get it, sir. I don't just have lightning. I have weather, the whole of weather. If they let me in, I could train in all of it."

"I know. That's what I told them. And your potential is great. But it's not enough. Not now. If it was freshman year, potential would be enough. But now we need to see results. If we let you in, you'd be at the bottom based on everything. And also they were concerned about your screenings."

"What screenings?"

He pulled up a genetic profile, the mating snakes and a screen with a series of As and Gs and Ts and Cs. "This. Look there, at the end. That is your HrO genetic grouping. Your Hero gene. Based on the number of markers, you might have the potential to be a great Hero or you might not. They usually want definitely Hero. Granted, most of the greats, the geniuses of the Hero world, were mixed, like you. But they only understand what they know works, not what *may* work. You're too much of a risk right now. Your environment leaves much to be desired. Lack of control runs in your family, as does poor decision making."

I wanted to cry. The more I knew, the worse I felt. There was nothing, absolutely nothing, I could do to convince them. It was in my blood. In my body. It had nothing to do with how much I wanted it or how much I tried. It was like being mediocre was a disease, and I had a fatal case.

"To be blunt, we need to be sure that with you we're getting a Hero and not something else. But," he said, changing his tone, "you still have a chance. Not for this year but for next. That board owes me. They owe me big for some of the crap I've had to accept here. Don't tell anyone this, but we accept students all the time with less power than you and absolutely no potential. I've tried to put a stop to this, but their parents donate, and they keep this place running. If we had fewer of them we could take more of you. And Sarah, we need more of you. But you need to meet me halfway. You need to help me show them that you don't just have potential, that you're more than your mother or your brother. You have true power and the strength to rise above."

"And," he continued, "when the time comes, I just may need you to help me with these, these lesser Heroes. Clogging up the system."

He thrust out his hand and shook hard, then directed me out of his hidden lair before I could ask him any questions. I turned around before heading down the dark corridor and watched as he pulled up similar charts and videos for other students and applicants. I stepped outside into a torrent of rainfall. It fell as if heaved from large buckets in the sky. Wind blew the leaves—which were just beginning to change—off the trees. Puddles formed in every crack and crevice. I had imagined that when I left this time I'd be leaving to the sunniest fall day in the world. Instead, as I tried not to sulk on the way home, my clothes became leaden from the downpour.

Another meeting. Another failure. What kind of person would I have to be to get the Academy to accept me?

TWENTY-EIGHT

FTER WE got kicked out of all school activities, Ms. Frankl veered off course in class. It got interesting. It felt like it all happened at once, but it couldn't have. "Many people around the world have powers," she said. "It's probably in the millions. Still, out of all those people, only a relative handful are considered Heroes. In countries far and wide, some people with powers are considered Heroes, and others, the more numerous, are considered Misshapes."

The class flinched. I sat up in my seat. She had never said that word before. She had talked about Misshape history, the roles of Misshapes in society, all while managing to work her way around the word "Misshape." Maybe she was afraid of offending us. Maybe she was afraid someone like Butters would think it was a slur, or that she was labeling him as officially a Misshape. But the rules had changed. We were officially ostracized.

"Misshapes have as much to offer as Heroes. Or they should. They're subject to the same restrictions as the Heroes: not being allowed to play sports, not being allowed to hold elected office, not being allowed to practice law in a courtroom." She coughed. "But they're not given the same privileges, benefits, and rights as Heroes. It's because you're considered inferior by your government. There's more to being heroic, to being valuable, than arbitrary judgments by private school boards and the Bureau of Superhero Affairs." Her voice grew passionate, fervent. "You need to look inside yourself to find true power, not rely on the judgments of others. That's what I want to talk about in class today."

Her lecture echoed some of the points made in the book she had assigned me, *A Misshape's History of America*. On the page, they had seemed like an exercise in academic writing, dry and repetitive. Hearing them made by Ms. Frankl was something different. It felt inspiring.

She moved to the back of the classroom, where she had her MacBook and projector set up. "Butters!" she trilled, "please pull down the white screen, okay?"

Butters ran to the front and pulled the screen down by the metal loop. He had to jump up to get it.

She clicked on her remote control, and a photo of some Heroes appeared on the screen. The photo was old and hazy. The women were in shapeless floral dresses. The men wore a lot of plaid. It looked like some kind of Hero parade in the nineties. I was confused. I couldn't see the connection she was trying to make.

Ms. Frankl moved to the screen in the front of the class and used her clicker as a pointer. "All these people in capes? They're Misshapes."

The class let out a little "Oooh." It was a big deal for a Misshape to dress in a Hero costume. Generally, shiny fabrics, Lycra, and capes were the exclusive provenance of Heroes. Anyone else in costume, Normal or Misshape, just looked crazy. Hero wear was sensible for crime fighting but silly anywhere else. It was a little shocking to see the people on the screen and know they were Misshapes.

Ms. Frankl continued: "The nineties was a historic time for Misshapes. There was a big surge of Misshape pride after years of overt and subtle cultural oppression. Sometime in the mid-nineties a group of them decided to take over Halloween and use it to celebrate their identity." She pointed at the USA map. "In San Francisco there was a Misshape parade in a neighborhood called the Mission with a lot of Misshapes. Everyone dressed up in their own superhero costumes designed to reflect their own unique power. It was a whimsical celebration of their powers. For a brief period the trend spread to other cities, and then it died out."

As silly as this may sound, it was an amazing thing to hear. Halloween is mostly celebrated by kids before they get their powers. At that age they dress up however they want and no one minds. But for teenagers and adults, Halloween takes on a whole other meaning. What you dress up as depends entirely on who you are. Heroes dress up as historical political figures or Normal athletes. Basically, things they can't be. Normals dress up as ghosts or standard Halloween fare, including the occasional famous Hero.

But Misshapes are usually caught between two worlds, especially in a town like Doolittle Falls. They wouldn't dare dress up like Heroes. It was such a social faux pas it felt like it was practically illegal. And dressing up like they were Heroes themselves, in their own costumes, it gave me the chills just thinking about it.

Ms. Frankl clicked to the next slide. There were two Misshapes in bright red capes, the man and woman both in tights, holding the hands of a grinning little girl. "Look at this," said Ms. Frankl. "Really look at this one."

I didn't think there was so much to see: The man had on an eye patch, and the woman had a mask. The little girl had her hair in pigtails and wore a blue-and-white gingham dress. She had a basket with a toy pooch in the caddy. Really, the only thing notable about the picture was how adorable the little girl was.

"There's something about Halloween. It's a very freeing time of year. If you're not yourself on a daily basis, you can be yourself. If you're too shy to talk to people half the time, you can dress up and talk to that person in their Spider-Man outfit. It's a magical night, I've always thought," said Frankl. She paused for emphasis.

"And that little girl in that picture? That's me."

The class gasped again. This time even louder. I wondered what kind of rebellion Ms. Frankl was trying to stoke. And what brought Ms. Frankl to Doolittle Falls?

Ms. Frankl flipped through more slides of the Misshape Halloween. After a few minutes I felt a slight tug on my arm. I looked down to see Alice's hand pulling on my shirt.

"What's up?" I whispered to Alice.

Alice said, in a barely audible voice, "We need to do this."

"We need to do what?" I whispered back, looking around like a guilty man.

"Halloween. It's coming. We've got to do this."

"Maybe," I said.

Once I turned thirteen, I had declared myself too old for that day and stayed in with my dad watching cheesy Halloween movies. I guess I always assumed that I would be dressing up as some historical women, like Betsy Ross, if I ever went out again.

The slide show ended and Ms. Frankl handed over the projector to Hamilton. She had been giving kids in the class the opportunity to teach their own lessons. Hamilton wanted to talk about how Heroes are depicted in films, like the hugely popular Hero documentaries. He stood in front of the class and began to expound on the *GrappaMan* series. "It's like Roger Ebert said, you know? These films reinvigorated the Hero documentary genre with their brutal realism."

"*Brutal realism! You said it, H!*" the Spectors enthused.

"I hate those Freedom Man documentaries because he's so perfect," Hamilton said. "It's like he's running for office. But the *GrappaMan* filmmakers had this guy drinking and beating people up side by side with newsreels of him fighting villains and saving people from fires. He was a huge jerk and he still saved Italy from evil, like, a million times! It's awesome."

Secretly I had seen every single Freedom Man documentary. There were eleven total. And that was just for the newest Freedom Man, Freedom Boy's dad. The Freedom documentaries were the longest-running Hero series of all time. They broke records every time they were released.

My phone buzzed in my pocket. I flipped it open quietly under my desk and saw a text from Alice. *No maybe. We're doing this!!* I eyed her and typed back *Fine. But no parades.*

"What else do the *GrappaMan* films have to offer?" asked Ms. Frankl, pointing to the screen. Hamilton had stopped the film on a particularly beautiful still, where *GrappaMan* was punching a guy so hard he nearly flew. You could practically see the *Pow!*

"Every film ever is ripping off shots from this one. You have to watch it if you want to know anything about films," said Hamilton.

No parades, just the right clothes. A last gasp of childish frivolity. Misshapes nineties style? I wrote.

Yes. With better hair, she replied.

She took furious notes in her notepad.

After the bell rang, Ms. Frankl bid us good-bye and Alice picked up where she had left off, walking next to me down the hall, "I just think it's important, you know? And this is like a 'don't let the bastards grind you down' to the town. A show of unity. A political statement."

"So our politics will start with a trip to Party Time?"

"I'll be at your locker," Alice said, with a smile, "and you better be ready to buy something embarrassing."

TWENTY-NINE

HALLOWEEN WAS days away, and Party Time was a wasteland. All the good costumes and decorations were already purchased and we left with an assortment of skanky costumes that were either too risqué or too random, like a sultry aardvark costume that Alice found on the ground. We made the best of it and headed to the craft store to get supplies for more homemade affairs.

Later that afternoon, while I was training with Sam, I built up the courage to ask him about what Dr. Mann had said.

"Hey, did you know Dr. Mann was watching these?" I said, pointing around the room toward cameras I couldn't see.

His face clouded over. It was the first time I'd seen him angry. "Are you serious? Why would you ask something like that? No. I had no idea."

I felt attacked. It wasn't my fault Dr. Mann was spying. "He said you would have, you know, considering the Academy and their monitoring."

"That's bullshit. Him and his little police state always watching the students. Online, offline, with spies, with cameras. That's the kind of thing that got to Johnny, and I don't blame him. I thought once I left it would be over." Sam smiled at me, a terse curve in his mouth. "But I guess it's never over."

He was on my side. And Dr. Mann was not all that he appeared to be. I shouldn't even mention Dr. Mann in front of Sam. It changed his easygoing personality into something darker, something I couldn't put my finger on. In a blatant effort to change the subject, I brought up Halloween.

"So, should I go?"

"Of course, you should go. That sounds awesome," he said.

It was settled.

Two days later, I was standing in Alice's room in a silver unitard while she smeared greasepaint on my face. Her room was an utter mess. Clothes were spread everywhere, a bra hung off the snare of a small pink and black drum kit in one corner, and the walls were filled with posters of fierce-looking women from bands I had never heard of: Sleater-Kinney, Helium, PJ Harvey, and countless others. It was like her wallpaper. The whole place felt like it was a green room at a punk club. The unitard was from her ballet days. Dark days, she claimed. She had been kicked out when she had a bunch of squirrels join her for the "Nutcracker Suite." Once she was booted from ballet, her parents let her play the drums.

"Let me see a demi-plie," she teased.

"You're mocking me with dance! How did you even dance in this?"

"It's not *dancing*," she said, giving me her best pirouette. "It's ballet." She stopped. "And dancers don't have boobs."

I looked down. Boobs. As a result, I looked more hooker-y in Alice's childhood costume.

"I could take some scissors and make it look more like Dangerous Girl if you're still hung up on Freedom Boy."

"No, thank you!" I said. Change the subject, Alice, I thought. I bit my lip.

"I feel, like it's a good thing we're meeting your brother. Because I want to see how he's going to make fun of you."

"I'm getting cold feet," I said. I felt like a bride on her wedding night. "I can't walk around like this."

"You can't back down now!" said Alice. "You're committed. You have silver toxins all over your face that make you look like an adorable disco ball."

"But I look like I'm a space hooker," I tried to argue.

"Enough with the pity party, okay? It's a great idea. You look great and every time you disagree you make me feel worse about myself because I can't even fit in that silly thing anymore, which is a terrible thing to do to a best friend." My ears perked at the words. Best friend. I smiled.

"So here's what's gonna happen," Alice continued. "I'm going to zip up the back of your top, and you are going to stop complaining, hold your head high, and roam the streets of Doolittle Falls on this lovely All Hallows Eve with me and our friends."

I nodded and I sat down on Alice's bed. She moved the battalion of makeup and potions out of my way. "You're fifteen and your way of shedding your youth is to take a strong stance against party-size chocolate bars. I dread the day I can't walk around and get free candy," said Alice. "I think half the reasons people have kids is so they can take them around and get back in on the free-candy thing."

"Fine. But no houses around my block."

"Deal! Halloween is ready when you are," she sang. I would've joined in if I knew the song.

We walked downstairs together. Alice was dressed as a sexy monk in tribute to St. Francis of Assisi, the patron saint of animals. She wore a short skirt and a long jacket, necessary for a Doolittle Falls Halloween. Small animals were attached all over her brown frock coat like a psychotic Disney princess. Before we walked out the door she asked, "Can you make sure none of my birds end up copulating accidentally when their pipe cleaners bend?"

I took two of the birds in my hand and made a humping motion with them. I tried to make some sexy tweeting noises but I just ended up laughing.

We walked out the door. It was freezing. My getup provided no protection from the October chill: I had a skirt on over my unitard, covered in cloud-like cotton balls, gold lightning bolts drawn on my face, and a golden eye mask across my eyes. I tried to warm up the air but when a cloud shot toward me, I stopped short. It was time to think warm thoughts. Thoughts about love and happiness and things like that. Thoughts that avoided Freedom Boy, because we were apparently off at this moment. He didn't call or try to get in touch. I tried to ignore the situation. It wasn't ideal.

"Everyone goes as what they can't be on Halloween," Alice said, trying to calm my nerves. "We're celebrating who we are and what our powers are. We can be ourselves and make other people know that we think it's awesome. Our super selves,"

"Thanks, teach!" I said.

"You and your sarcasm, Sarah. You sound like your brother. Why don't you go back to suffragette city?"

"I have no idea what you're talking about half the time."

"Ziggy!" Alice exclaimed.

"Nobody reads that comic strip."

When we hit Main Street, we could see our friends loitering in front of the closed CVS. They looked spectacular, shiny, glittery, and fantastic. If I didn't know any better I would have thought I was approaching some kind of short and skinny crime-fighting team.

Butters had on this amazing lounge suit. He must have gotten it at Cannibal Jacks, the town's vintage store. It was framed by a gold-sequined cape that matched the dresses of his backup singers. He had taught them a call-and-response theme song to sing for him, which they did on cue.

"Check it out," he said as we approached. "Ladies, who's the smoothest cat on the block?"

"Butters," they cooed back.

"Who's the super man who churns his enemies out like—" he said.

"Butterrrrsssss. And we can whip it!"

Johnny had on his usual leather jacket and jeans. But he hadn't completely wimped out. He had made a red-and-white-checkered cape that looked like an Italian restaurant tablecloth, and a homemade jug handle that jutted out of his T-shirt.

George Herbert was wearing a trench coat and a mummy bandage around his head. He disappeared the minute he saw Alice.

Markus focused on the chicken factor for the night, wearing a chicken costume that was marginally better than the ones they make people wear when they try to convince you to come to their new fast-food restaurant on a street corner. Johnny joked that any getup playing on his ability to read the minds of mothers would just come across as sketchy.

"I made a MILF Man costume but my parents saw it and wouldn't let me out of the house," Markus said.

"Nice outfit," said Hamilton, nodding my way. He looked like a cat that had seen a Jackson Pollock painting and tried to recreate it in neon vomit on a tracksuit. I felt like I had vertigo just looking at his costume.

After milling about for awhile, we started by heading toward the bigger houses in the neighborhood because Butters thought we might get something other than fun-size candy bars. They were south toward the Harpastball field. We ended up snaking our way up and down streets and around cul-de-sacs, picking up an equal amount of finger-size chocolate bars and weird looks.

Wearing a Hero outfit felt kind of strange. Even though it was a dime-store version of the real Hero outfits we saw around town. After a few blocks I began to feel like I could actually be a Hero. As I argued with Alice about whether that razor blade in the apple story was true I noticed that I wasn't the only one looking perkier. Butters, Johnny, Markus, and Hamilton were all holding their heads up a little bit higher. It was the first time since the football incident that everyone looked happy. I was happy for them. But I wondered, idly, where Lou had gone to tonight. We'd invited him out, but he said no. He had become a loner.

When I looked at the groups of little trick-or-treaters walking around with their parents, I was able to forget that those same parents thought of my friends and me as freaks every day. For one night, they looked at us like we were Heroes. Tonight, the Misshapes were in charge, patrolling the community, protecting good and fighting evil.

A couple of hours later, we had made our way to the edge of Doolittle Falls. We divvied up the remainder of the candy and watched the sunset from the steps of the library. Johnny had to take some extra medicine because all the sugar made his alcohol conversion thing get all wacky. Fleetingly, I thought about texting Sam. We were close to his sandbox. A thought popped into my head about Freedom Boy. He hadn't bothered to text me since the Hero slut thing broke. I was so mad at him. I heard a clap of thunder behind me.

I wanted to lapse into a sugar coma on the steps, but I decided that we should keep moving. Johnny led us down a dead-end street at the base of the Marston Heights hill. When we turned back toward the main road, we saw a big group approaching us. In the dim light of the lone lamppost, it was pretty obvious that they were from the Academy. That Humungulous kid stuck out. The sight of an eight-foot-tall Winston Churchill with a ninety-inch chest, absurdly large hands, lips, jawline, and tongue really was something special. His thumb was as thick as my whole body.

"Wasn't King Kong dressed up as Eisenhower last year?" asked Alice.

"Dude!" I said, poking Alice in the side. "You do not say things that could be construed as teasing regarding that extremely large man. You are asking for trouble."

George added, "Humungulous always goes as WWII figures. I guess it's symbolic."

"I want to know where he shops," I said. "You have to look far and wide for a hat that big."

Humungulous led the way and the rest of the Academy kids came into focus. The Aqua Kid was dressed up like a football star and was walking with Megan, who was dressed like a sushi platter. Lindsay had on a slutty business suit. Christie was dressed up as a First Lady. I didn't know which one. The others were outfitted as TV pundits and talking heads. One guy even dyed his short buzz cut silver. And then there was Freedom Boy. He was dashing and heartbreakingly handsome as a chiseled Thomas Jefferson. But something still thrummed inside me when I saw him, some sort of charge or electricity even though I was still pissed at him for ignoring me, especially in public. I felt like my circuits were going haywire.

"Well, if it isn't the valiant Misshapes, led by the brave and noble leader StuporMan," proclaimed J5. I had no idea who he was dressed as. But he was wearing a perfectly cut suit.

Johnny tried to charge at him. Johnny tended to snap into crazy if you even said the name J5. There was something so smug about him. He crawled under your skin with his tiny smile and upturned nose. Hamilton grabbed my brother's shoulders to prevent him from starting a fight. They could pulverize all of us in a matter of seconds.

Johnny pulled out his Zippo and said quietly, "I will end you." He pulled the trigger and a small plume of fire rose up out of the lighter. Then he hocked a huge loogey toward J5. When the spit passed through the flame it caught fire, and a small glowing ball of flaming mucus landed near J5's shoe.

He chuckled and stomped it out with his foot. He didn't flinch. In his soothing serial-killer monotone, he said, "Nice fireball, Mario.

Where'd you get the fire flower, from one of the question mark boxes?"

"No, your sister," Johnny shot back.

J5 turned to Humungulous and asked, "Are you going to let this stand?"

Johnny pulled a bottle of water from his pocket and unscrewed the cap.

Humungulous's brow dropped and he squinted at Johnny like a gorilla preparing to charge.

Freedom Boy put his arm out and blocked him. "Now, things should not get out of hand," he said. "Sorry about J5, Johnny. He is not so well trained. Huge should know better." He smiled at us. I swooned, despite myself. "Great to see you out tonight."

"It'd be better to see you—" Johnny said, but Hamilton shut him up by putting his hand over his mouth.

Freedom Boy looked over at me, checking me out. "Nice costume."

"Thanks," I mumbled through my teeth.

He took some tentative steps over my way. Alice glared at me for falling for it. She was not on Team Freedom Boy. The rest of the Heroes followed his lead. Some of them complimented my friends on their costumes, while others like J5 held back and whispered to each other. Johnny sneered in the corner, glaring at J5.

I wasn't really paying attention. The air was toasty around Freedom Boy and me. I didn't even need my jacket. I tried to think good thoughts, pure thoughts, but I just wanted to make out with him. He looked really, really good.

"What have you been up to?" he asked.

"The usual tonight. Wandering around and getting some candy bars," I replied.

"Awesome. It is a little hard for us to trick-or-treat, though we did score some full-size Kit Kats from people in the houses that we saved from a fire." He laughed a little. "They could not say no."

There was a shuffling behind us, and my brother broke in. "Nice to see you, J5 and crew, but we gotta get going. People to save, you know how it is." He obviously wasn't up for the impromptu mixer.

Before I followed them, Freedom Boy pulled me aside, and said, "Join us for a while."

Whoa. Whoa. I looked at his hand on my waist. He had large hands, powerful and gentle. They had saved so many people. A little voice in the back of my head said why would he want to hang out with me but I ignored it. He smiled. A special small smile just for me.

I was torn. I didn't want to be a girl who ditched her friends for a guy. Even if this was a chance to be like a real Hero, not a Misshape. It was like I was choosing between two identities. I liked Alice and Butters and the rest of the Misshapes. They were becoming good friends, people I could rely on and trust. But I just couldn't say no. Even if Johnny would probably make me cook incredibly fancy meals as penance. But this was bigger than him. Freedom Boy seemed on the verge of acknowledging me.

Maybe Alice would get it. If she really thought about it.

I turned to the Misshapes, blurting, "Hey, um, I'm, ah, going to hang with them for a bit. I'll see you later, okay?"

Johnny looked at me like I just shot the family dog. "What?" His voice was low.

"I'm just going to tag along with them for a while," I said, going toward Freedom Boy, who was waiting for me.

Alice looked up and glared at me, then muttered, "Whatever. See you later, Sarah. Maybe I'll send you a text about where we are."

Johnny didn't respond. He just turned around and continued on with the Misshapes. Alice made her way over to my brother. I figured they now had something to talk about. How much of a traitor I was. It felt awful.

I watched my friends walk away, and turned toward Freedom Boy. He took my hand and said, "I'm so glad you came."

"Me too."

In the distance I heard a phone ring and Butters' Spectors singing, "*Bring! Bring!*" I glanced over and Butters was peeling off the crowd, headed toward some other destination.

He ditched Johnny, too.

Walking away, I felt my phone buzz in my purse. I pulled it out.

Sure? Alice wrote.

Yes! I typed back, quickly. But her question lingered in the air. Was I sure?

I might have felt like a super elite walking through the streets with the Misshapes dressed up as a Hero. But when I walked about town with the actual Heroes, the Academy-certified superheroes of tomorrow, it was like a whole other level. Even in their silly outfits there was the feeling that they ruled the world. They talked casually about their superhuman tasks and abilities. Like "Oh, so I was flying the other day and the strangest thing happened." Because the flying wasn't at all the strangest thing that ever happened.

I felt invincible, walking and talking next to Freedom Boy. It felt like being famous or something. As we made our way around the same suburbs I had wandered earlier with the Misshapes, the few remaining children who were out stopped to gawk in admiration at the group. A lot of them came up and asked for signatures.

Freedom Boy got the most requests. A steady stream of little boys interrupted us while I tried to make conversation about Doolittle Falls and school. Some even had the first name Freedom, which just felt strange. Little Freedom Smith or eight-year-old Freedom Daniels. About half of these kids came with mothers, who blatantly tried to undress the Hero with their own eyes. Those moms all gave me the filthiest looks, like my mere presence was interrupting their fantasies.

Cougar town aside, I was still having a great time. The other Heroes, while not exactly nice to me, were at least accepting. I even got to see J5s black collar up close. It was made of interlocking pieces of metal and had the words PROPERTY OF BUREAU OF SUPERHERO AFFAIRS: PSYCHOKINETICS CONTROL DIVISION written in white letters on the side.

We continued walking for an hour until the sound of an overly dramatic German opera burst my bubble. It was coming from J5's pocket. He grabbed the phone, had a short conversation peppered with "okays" and "be right there," and then hung up.

"The dean called. We're needed at PeriGenomics. There's been some attack by the Dragoons and they want our help."

"What about the ShWAT team or PeriSecurity?" asked Freedom Boy.

"The team is off hunting down Admiral Doom and can't make it for half an hour. Security is overrun, they need backup, and they need it now. We're close. Let's go."

Freedom Boy instantly switched into Hero mode. His posture changed. A grave look crossed his face. He walked ahead of me.

"I guess we are needed," said Freedom Boy. He said sorry, turned his back to me, and put on his gloves and lightweight thermal coat.

"We have to go now!" yelled J5.

The Hero group headed toward J5's car. Freedom Boy took off into the sky, with a wink in my direction.

I didn't know what to do. There went my in. I followed the Heroes to the car.

"Where do you think you're going?" the Aqua Kid snapped.

"Wouldn't I come with you guys?" I felt stupid just saying the words. I didn't feel like walking around in a very short skirt at this hour. "Can I at least get dropped off somewhere less empty?"

"This is a case for the Hero Academy. Not the anti-Hero Academy," said J5.

The Aqua Kid gave him a high-five. "Besides, no groupies," he said.

I just wanted a ride and I didn't think that was too much to ask. There was no sympathy on any of the Heroes' faces. If only Freedom Boy hadn't flown away. He just left me with this group of vipers.

"Sorry. I just thought because I was here with—"

"Fans, no matter how slutty, don't get admission. What would Dr. Mann do, bro, right?" J5 snapped, jingling his keys. "Can we just get going, please?"

"Good luck." I turned on my heel and headed toward Main Street.

Really? That's what they thought of me? My phone had a new text from Alice: *We're at the Miskatonic Bridge. Come meet us!*

I clicked my heels together and took off toward the river.

THIRTY

THE OTHER Misshapes were gathered around the glowing tinders. The air had been flirting with rain all night, but when I arrived and saw my cold reception it began to drizzle. The precipitation didn't make getting the fire going any easier.

Everyone glared at me when I took my place around the fire pit. Even Alice. There was a distinct chill in the air. The warmth I had created disappeared the minute Freedom Boy left me. I crossed my arms in front of my unitard. The sad little fire, unsuccessfully stoked by George Herbert, didn't look like it would provide much heat.

"Where's Butters?" I asked.

Alice was the only one to offer an answer. "We haven't heard from him. I'm worried." She looked over at Markus.

"What? He's probably fine. Got distracted and went home or something," he said, defensively.

Looking up at the sky with his hands out, Johnny pretended that I wasn't even here and said, "I can't believe she ditched us. Butters ditched us too."

"I'm right here," I protested. "And what do you mean, you don't know where Butters went?"

"We just don't—" Hamilton muttered.

"—know," finished Markus.

Johnny dialed Butters several times but had no luck.

"Look," I said, "we gotta go find Butters. It's really weird that he's not picking up the phone. Didn't he get a phone call and ditch you?"

The group grumbled.

"Come on!" I said. I walked toward town. They'd come after me, eventually. Despite their resentment, I was right.

We hoofed it all over Doolittle Falls searching in vain for Butters. Each street and destination led nowhere. It got to the point where Alice decided to check in with the animal kingdom. She interrogated a few robins but they had no information.

Most of the critters out at this hour proved just as useless, but a few gray mice talked her ear off about a battle they were having with Mrs. Hodgkinson over their god-given right to live in her walls and eat her spilled peanut butter. They had lost a small garrison to a glue trap earlier in the day.

Their comments were all so useless, according to Alice. She was polite but it was getting late and I was worried about Butters, so we kept going.

Finally, a raccoon poked its head out of a trashcan and said he might be of some help.

He hissed. Alice nodded like he was lecturing on some important topic. "Thanks!" she said.

I pulled her sleeve. "Any leads?"

The raccoon had heard strange singing coming from behind the Dumpster in the back of the ShoppingTown supermarket. Sounded to him like an old time R&B or soul group.

"His backup singers," Alice blurted. Markus and I looked at her. "We're going to ShoppingTown."

We arrived, breathless, at the vacant lot. A faint sound of women harmonizing wafted through the air. I could hear the music coming from behind the ShoppingTown Dumpsters. "He hit me, and it felt like a kiss. He hit me, and I was glad."

Markus pulled the farthest Dumpster away from the wall. We found Butters, weeping quietly to himself. He was curled into a ball on the ground in the fetal position. His clothes were ripped and bloody, and beneath the tears in his pants and shirt his skin had been lacerated. His left eye was puffy and his cheeks were heavily swollen.

Johnny walked over and leaned next to him, wrapping his lanky arm around Butters' slumped shoulders. "We got you. You're gonna be okay," he said, in the gentlest voice I had ever heard.

Butters looked up, and wiped his tears away with a shaking hand. "You're safe now, okay? You're safe." Butters hugged him limply, and Johnny tried to help him get back on his feet, but he was dead weight.

When he got upright he let out a loud wail. "Put me down, put me down!" Johnny lowered him back to the ground.

"I think they're both broken," Butters said.

Johnny rolled up Butters's pants legs and turned greenish. He looked away from Butters and said, "I think you're right. We need to get you to a hospital."

I called 911 and the dispatcher said they were backed up because of an attack by Admiral Doom, but we should try to get him to the hospital since it was only a mile away.

I called Betty, the only person I could think of who had access to a car. Her house was only a few blocks away.

"*What?!*" said Betty. There was a pause, I heard a sniffle, and Betty said, "I'm there. Give me a second."

"Butters, my cousin Betty will pick us up," I said. "Let's just wait here by the supermarket. We're safe by the twenty-four-hour supermarket."

"Nooooooooo!" Butters said weakly. His singers said, "Ooooooh."

We gathered around Butters and tried to comfort him, his Spectors quiet. "We're going to get you to the hospital," said Johnny.

His pain was getting worse. He was wincing more, gritting his teeth, and grimacing.

"Who did this to you?" Alice asked.

He looked up, squinting through swollen eye sockets, and responded, "Dragoons."

"Admiral Doom's henchmen?"

"I was in their way. I think they were headed to PeriGenomics or something and they saw me and started in. So many of them..." His voice trailed off, getting weaker.

"You're lucky to be alive," said Johnny.

"You must have given them a hell of a fight," Markus added.

"I think they just got tired of beating on me and needed to get to whatever it is they were doing." He coughed up some blood and winced.

"Should we let someone know?" I asked. "They're out there and dangerous."

"PeriGenomics has its own security force. Tougher than Dragoons."

He was interrupted by the *screech!* of Betty's car. It careened into the parking lot, leaning to the left like it was in an old movie chase scene. She stopped short right in front of the bench. Betty handed us a large wooden board she had found in her garage.

"Stretcher?' she said.

All of us, as delicately as possible, slid the stretcher under him and put him in the backseat. Johnny was elected to go to the hospital. We walked back toward our houses together, for safety.

There was nothing else to do. I went home. But I couldn't sleep. I sat up in bed wondering why the Dragoons would attack Butters, a Misshape who posed so little threat. Or did he? What danger did he pose? Was he just in the wrong place at the wrong time? I decided that I would wait up until Johnny returned home to ask him how Butters was doing. I sent Johnny a text and I tried calling him but I think his cell phone was off. Hospital rules.

I hoped that Butters would be okay.

WINTER

THIRTY-ONE

OR WEEKS after the Halloween revelry, my mind was stuck on the Butters channel. Playing the same show over and over again.

Butters. Bloodied and curled up. Like an injured animal. Every class, I would look over at the empty desk that he should've been sitting in, and that memory would return, as vivid as if it were happening again. I didn't care about any class. Teachers just sounded like *Peanuts* characters, droning in an endless *wah-wah*. I knew it got bad when it was hard to pay attention in science class. Mrs. McDonald was doing some experiment with Mentos and Coke and making a total mess, Coke flying around the room like a—

BLEAT! BLEAT! BLEAT! BLEAT! BLEAT! BLEAT! The room turned red and blue with blinking lights. The sirens and lights meant that it was a Doom raid.

"Line up, children," said Mrs. McDonald. She was still wearing her goggles from the interrupted experiment. "Line up, for safety's sake! And put your fingers in your ears if you hate the noise."

A door off the boiler room led down to the shelter, built especially for the school by PeriGenomics, according to Dad. The shelter was dank and smelled like wet pavement. It was a subterranean imitation of our cafeteria. It had flat-screen TVs in every corner tuned to WXBS and a choppy audio feed pumping in the latest news about what villain was striking Doolittle Falls from the town's Division of Super Defense.

The radio voice—the Official Voice of Doolittle Falls—bleated over the loudspeaker: "WE ARE UNDER ATTACK! Reports are light right now but Admiral Doom and the Dragoons are descending upon the city!"

Admiral Doom. He was back. That man was an enemy of the Robertson family. He was the man who had, supposedly, been in cahoots with my mom. Johnny thought he probably framed her for the destruction of Innsmouth. He was involved in some way.

And it had to be his goons who beat up Butters and put him in the hospital. They were notorious bullies, toughs who fought people just for the hell of it. They made a point to inflict pain wherever possible in Doolittle Falls. But he'd been quiet since the Innsmouth incident. He disappeared like Mom did. Until now.

I walked to the TV in the left corner. All the TVs showed the scene outside: Admiral Doom had on a shiny metal suit that had a bronze tint and a giant chest plate. He hovered above the dirt and fired small rockets from his arms at the base of PeriGenomics's cement smokestack. His Dragoons—fashionably attired in bronze jumpsuits with military lapels—were positioned around the campus, trying to break into heavily secured buildings. The scene was familiar to me from training with Sam. But this was a much different situation. It made me sick to see it. They were locked in battle. Guards littered the ground, limp.

The action was hard to follow until a Dragoon grabbed a guard. He flung the guy more than one hundred feet, and he went *smack!* into the middle of a laser turret. It exploded in a flash of green and orange smoke.

The whole mess looked like a gruesome video game. It was hard to hear what the commentator was saying because the shelter was quickly filling up with the whole school.

Megan stood next to me. Alice had run off to some table in the way back with other Misshapes, far away from the action. Unlike them, I wanted to know what was going on. Didn't they see that this had to be connected to Butters?

"I know it's gross. Do you want to know what's happening?" I asked.

Megan replied, "Ugh, this is the worst. Tell me when my boyfriend gets there. I know he's going to save my father's company." I wondered how the Aqua Kid could do in a fight on land. She paused. "So, how's Freedom Boy?"

I cringed. I wouldn't know. He had been off on some mission or another, evasive as ever. Halloween was like a little blip of something, and then he had to go fight evil again.

"I saw some super-cute photos of you two. Are you making the leap from just a fan to super fan?" she followed up, hitting me in the heart with that line. There was a palpable sneer in her voice, like she knew what was going on.

"Sorry, I'm going over there. To my friends," I said, making a beeline for the Misshape table. It was for the best. The news was starting to repeat itself, hypnotic and gruesome, in that way the news does with incidents and accidents. I knew the pattern well.

"Hey there, lady," said Alice. "I missed you. Way to ditch the Queen B over there," she said, referring to Megan. The Queen B was watching the TV through her fingers, like it was a horror movie.

"Eh, you've seen one explosion, you've seen them all," I said.

Frank, one of the quieter Misshapes, pulled out his deck of cards. He was wearing his typical fedora and suspenders. He generally slept through civic responsibility. Supposedly he ran a gambling ring around Doolittle Falls. "Tin Arm," he announced. "Let's *do this!*" He had deadly accuracy with nondeadly weapons. He could hit a bull's-eye with a paper airplane at a hundred yards, but he couldn't really throw knives. He worked at a casino over the summer and constantly wanted to play cards.

He shuffled and dealt the deck, which flew out of his hand like balls from a pitching machine, landing in perfect piles in front of the poker players. He sang, "The boy with the tin arm steps up to the plate, fifty-two paper balls and a fistful of fate." The cards shot out until the whole deck was spent.

There was a cheer from the kids in front of the TV, and we whipped our heads around. The news report showed a broadcaster in front of a wild scene. Buildings were on fire and people flew through the air in the background. "The streets are shaking with fear today as Admiral Doom descends upon the city—but wait! We have reports that there is a counterattack from up on the hill at Hero Academy. Freedom Man and his sidekick, Academy A-squad member Freedom Boy, are leading the good—the good!—in a counterattack. Perhaps the town will be safe again soon."

Johnny, perched on the top of the table, yawned loudly and pulled some beat-up novel from his back pocket. "Guys, call me when there's actual news of stuff actually happening and less of this green screen fake news stuff," he said, burrowing into his book.

"Shut up, Misshape!" someone shouted.

"Yeah, isn't that your mom's partner in evil? You're probably rooting for him," someone else yelled.

That set Johnny off. "No, it's your mom's partner in bed. At least one of them," he said, leaping off the table and lunging toward the kid. Kurt and Marcus held him back.

"You two, detention," Principal Holloway shouted at Johnny and the instigator. "And if you keep it up, you're expelled. This is a crisis situation. I can't have this behavior."

I rolled my eyes. I had things to say, too. I wanted to fight. I wanted to defend Johnny and Mom, but I would have just gotten detention as well. "So what's the game?" said Alice, looking at the neat little deck in front of her on the table.

"B.S." said Frank.

"Sounds good to me."

Frank volunteered to start and laid down two twos. George Herbert laid down two sixes, which didn't cause any suspicion until he looked up and vanished into thin air. "Bullshit, George!" I shouted, slamming my hand on the table.

"*Sarah Robertson!*" Holloway yelled. "Detention!"

"Damn it," I uttered to myself. Alice suppressed a snicker and made a goofy face while trying not laugh. Megan whipped around from her perch in front of the TVs and gave me a look.

"Sorry, Mr. Holloway!" I yelled.

"Principal Holloway, to you. Don't let me hear that language again, young lady. Take this seriously. Our town is in peril. Have some respect."

I was absolved, but everyone else added a "sorry." When we looked back at the table, the cards in the center were moving to George's seat, seemingly on their own. He slowly rematerialized, giggling.

"You know you have the worst poker face I think I've ever seen," Frank said to George.

"It's terrible!" he replied. "Anytime I'm the least bit embarrassed, poof, I'm gone. It's got to be the worst power I can think of."

"Can't be good for your social life," mumbled Johnny, flipping through the pages of his book. George heard it, and started to flicker away.

"When you say girls don't notice you, you actually mean it," Markus teased.

"They are blind to him, Markus, blind," Hamilton joked. George was still invisible. Then Markus squealed. "Ow! Who poked me? That hurt."

George came back to earth, giggling.

"No, really though, your thing is not that bad, George. You know what skill isn't that useful?" said Markus. "Being able to fly the length of a football field. What can I do with that?"

"Avoid being caught by the cops!" said Johnny, who slid down closer to the group of card players and put his book down, "and then failing. You do have your telekinesis, though."

"But I don't look cool when I fly," muttered Markus, "and only being able to read the minds of super-hot mothers has done nothing—nada, zip, zilch—for my love life." He looked around for a reply.

"At least your power has some purpose," I chimed in. "Mine just means I need a raincoat all the time."

"It's not that bad," said Hamilton. "I've seen you do some cool stuff."

Alice said, seriously, "I have to listen to the inane chatter of squirrels. They are the most boring creatures imaginable. If I shot them all with a BB gun no one would care."

Time slipped by and the Admiral and Academy seemed to be at a standstill. Each had a secured a position. The occasional laser or explosion shot across the screen and Normals would cheer in response. The same old sound bites and a bleached-blonde woman trying to do her best "concerned face." Our card game grew more and more silent. We were all thinking about Butters but not saying anything. I felt so pent up and stir-crazy, watching that iron-clad jerk run roughshod throughout town. We were stuck in a basement that was "safe," when we needed to get revenge. This jerk had attacked one of us.

Us. I had never thought of the civic responsibility class as an "us." I looked over and Alice was grinning at me. We were a united group. I maybe had my first set of real friends. And I was mad. I wanted to fight for them. To fight for Butters.

I started to formulate a plan. It was entirely possible that if I made a break for it, maybe I could fight alongside the Academy. Be hailed as a Hero. A rogue Hero, but still—a Hero.

"This is killing me," I said. "I need to get out of here."

"Planning a prison break?" said Johnny.

"Anything, I can't stand just sitting around playing cards while the world blows up," I said.

"Dude, help 'em out, Weathergirl!" Frank enthused. It was the first time someone gave me a name. I liked it.

"I can at least watch the show," I said, getting up from the table. "Anyone with me?"

"Count me out," said Markus, followed by a chorus of "me toos," including my brother. That surprised me. I walked around the table, stretching my legs, and then I heard a small voice pipe up.

"I'm game," said Alice, meekly.

I stopped short. "Sure?"

"Yeah," said Alice. "What's the plan?"

I fiddled with the saltshaker on the condiments table. Like a maracas player in a terrible band. Shake, shake, shake. Plan, plan, plan.

Hamilton spoke up.

"You can sneak out. I had detention a few weeks back and they made me clean the place up after hours. I went to take a nap in the room where they store the food. There's a false shelf with fake food against one of the walls. Pull on the giant tomato can and a door opens up to the utility stairs."

I looked at him and smiled. Hamilton looked to the left. His eyes were hidden behind his sunglasses as per usual. "Dang," I said, still standing, restless leg jiggering: Holloway's table was right in front of the pantry entrance.

How we could leave without anyone noticing? While I thought about it, I watched Frank shuffle and shuffle, displaying feats of dexterity. He dealt again, and the second card slid perfectly under the first.

I grabbed the deck.

"Hey!" protested Frank.

"More important things, Frank." I had an idea. "More important things. So, do you think you could hit that switch from here?" I said.

Alice's eyes lit up.

"The light switch?"

"The one a few inches from the principal's head."

He picked up a card and twirled it around his fingers. Next, he flipped a series of cards in the air, catching them with a snap of his beefy digits. His brows furrowed as he thought about the challenge. After a few more seconds, he looked up and said, "Yeah, I can hit it. No doubt in my mind. But if the lights go out and a card is lying near the switch I'm as guilty as Cain. No one could pull that off in this joint but me."

He had a point. I needed Frank right now.

"Besides, what's in it for me?" asked the cardshark.

"I promise to get your card on the way out and..." I looked at Johnny and he reluctantly nodded back. "And Johnny here will buy you a drink for your services."

"She good for it, Johnny?" he asked.

"Hell, if it gets her out of my hair and leads her to break the laws of man and school, I'll give you the Big Gulp of your choice." He mimed crying and uttered, "I'm so proud."

"I'm in," said Frank. "Pick a card."

I pulled out a card and flipped it over. It was a jack holding a sword aloft in front of his face.

"One-eyed jacks are wild," said Frank, before pinching the card between his thumb and forefinger and flicking it forward with lightning speed. It flew across the room and hit the light switch dead on.

THIRTY-TWO

THE LIGHTS went out. The Normals screamed as if the world were ending. Someone shouted, "Admiral Doom! He'll kill us all!"

I sprinted for the door. Alice trailed behind. We stuck to the wall, avoiding any panicking students. Alice kicked the card on the floor over to me and I picked it up in one smooth motion. Alice grabbed the door handle and pulled me inside the pantry. It was pitch black inside and we put our arms out, feeling around for the shelves.

A light flickered under the door. The lights had come back on in the bunker but we could still hear chaos. There was a high-pitched scream and an "It's okay, Megan!"

The flicker of light seeped into the pantry, and I got my hands on the fake shelf with the tomato can. I pulled the can toward me and heard a loud creak. The door to the dingy stairwell opened wearily.

What was the purpose of this room? If this really was a 1950s fallout shelter, it'd at least have real food and supplies.

"We're on a movie set," I said.

"This is ridiculous. Everything is fake," said Alice. "If there were an emergency, these kids would be left to starve. It's just trying to comfort students with normalcy if a supervillain really attacks and tries to destroy the world." She charged up the stairs and I followed behind.

We got to the top of the stairwell and Alice paused. "Sarah, should we go out there? We could get hurt. We don't know what's going on."

"Don't worry. We'll be fine," I said. "Now, let's *do this*!" I pushed on the door's heavy wheel handle, like a sailor steering a ship. The door screeched open, and we ran out of the school.

The world was silent. Blue skies and empty streets. No birds chirped. No signs of life.

There were no people anywhere. I guess they were in the community Doom raid shelters. Tumbleweeds danced down the streets. I felt like a sharpshooter in a Western strolling through a ghost town. I wanted commotion. Signs of life or signs of war. The blue and white emergency lights—letting people know they should go to a Doom raid shelter for safety!—were still flashing atop large metal poles, but the sirens had subsided.

We walked toward Alice's car.

"Sarah," said Alice. I jumped at the sound of her voice. "What's the plan? We could drive over to PeriGenomics and jump into the fight, I guess. Will they even let us do that?"

"I doubt it. The police probably have the whole area blocked off for safety. But I don't need to get that close to help out. Just half a mile away and I might be able to hit him with some wind or a strike."

Alice let out a sigh. "Fantastic. Seriously, I was worried you wanted to go toe-to-toe. We're friends and all, but I don't think secret squirrel attacks would help against the people who beat up Butters."

"Don't worry, you'll be a safe—" *Cring! Cring! Cring!* My voice was drowned out by a strange mechanical clanging that echoed throughout the town.

"What was that noise?" Alice asked.

"Not sure. Maybe we should inspect."

"Are you sure? Shouldn't we notify someone?"

"Who? Everyone is fighting at PeriGenomics," I said, then realized something: "That's it. The fight is probably a distraction for whatever that thing is. We can just observe. No getting close or fighting."

"Sarah Robertson, you are going to get me killed, aren't you?"

"Never," I said. Sure, this may have been dangerous, even foolish, but I felt weirdly happy. It sounded like the strange noise was coming from the direction of the Academy. We jumped into her car and drove toward the Harpastball field. All of the streets were completely empty. The only sound was the blare of sirens and Alice's crappy car galumphing down the road.

We cut across town and up Main Street. With the streets empty we could speed and run lights with impunity. Alice was pretending to be a race-car driver, even though her car topped out at forty-five. When we reached the Harpastball field she screeched to a halt in front of the gate as I yelled, "There it is." I pointed toward something strange and frightening hanging over the school.

It was a cloud. A cloud that was truly bizarre. It was a deep purple with an amorphous black object swimming in it. To the naked eye, it looked like an octopus and a cloud had mated.

We got out of the car and tried the front gate. It was chained closed but we could open it just enough to slide in. Once inside we scrambled over to the edge of the grounds. I kept my eye on the cloud. Some tentacles poked out, emerging for a few seconds and creeping back in. The tentacles were sucking up the light—every time they poked out of the cloud, the day got darker and the cloud stretched out.

Alice noticed it too. "Ewwwwwww! Those tentacles are getting bigger!"

"I don't think it's native to Doolittle," I said. I didn't want to say anything else. It was highly likely that my voice would crack and Alice would realize how nervous I was.

Purple smoke was rising from something in the center, like there was a campfire going. I squinted into the distance, trying to get a closer look. The smoke was coming from a black box, pouring into the air from large slats on the side.

"Sarah, where's that cloud going?" asked Alice. We looked up. The black creature was gaining in power, warping the purple cloud, which kept changing shape and moving around so quickly that tentacles seemed to be the only thing in the sky. I couldn't even see what was happening. It screeched.

"We gotta get away from it!" said Alice. "We'll be okay over here."

I ran away from the noise, grabbing Alice and pulling her back toward the woods with me. "What was that?"

Ka-boom!

After a few minutes cowering behind a tree, a squirrel hobbled by using a twig as a crutch. Alice asked it what was going on. They chirped at each other, Alice clucking with her teeth.

"What'd he say? Anything?" I asked.

"It was just gibberish," Alice said. "He's traumatized."

We poked our heads out from behind the tree and saw that the entire ground below the cloud was completely black. Devoid of life.

I took my phone out and snapped a photo. The circle's diameter was almost the length of the field. The earth had been charred, burned and dead. Several trees were completely bisected. The field's mainframe—the goal posts, the stands, the fence—were completely intact. I couldn't believe it. The first words out of my mouth were "What's going to happen to Harpastball?"

Alice looked at me, confused. "Are you in shock? There's more important things!"

I snapped out of my daze. "You're right. Let's go to PeriGenomics. If this weapon is Admiral Doom's, we need to warn them." Maybe it was foolish. But I wanted to be the Hero so badly that I could taste it.

We jumped into her car and sped to PeriGenomics. When we got to the gates the fight looked far from over. The Admiral was positioned with his Dragoons at building seven, trying to storm building eight.

Sam had told me that building eight was where they did their munitions and weapons research. Every time Doom tried to fly into the building he was repelled by a group of three students who shot out a combined reddish energy blast—which looked like a giant piece of bubble gum—that blew him backward to building seven. Some of the Dragoons were trying to make a ground assault on building eight and were fighting hand-to-hand with the Heroes. Stray laser pulses in greens, purples, reds, and blues flew through the air. Loud explosions detonated every few minutes, sending bodies soaring in every direction like limp dolls. White and blue flashes blinked in the air with the explosions.

Some of the Dragoons were lying prone on the ground and the police carted them off. The Heroes tried to counterattack and take back building seven, but Admiral Doom repelled them with his massive electric whip, which cracked in the air and sent a shock wave so strong it knocked them off their feet.

Maybe this was my opening. It seemed like there may be a space for my power.

"I have an idea," I said. My heart pounded.

"Should I find someone? Tell them about the cloud?" asked Alice.

"No. Everyone's busy. And this is our fight as well," I replied.

"What?"

"I'll take out the Admiral," I said. I felt calm and powerful.

"Don't you think we should leave this to the Heroes and then tell them what we found? You know, at the field?" Alice asked. A reasonable request, I guess.

"I can do this," I insisted.

Alice stepped back. I stared at Admiral Doom's masked face bobbing in the sky. I tried to conjure up as much hatred as I could and focus it at his little bronze-winged ears and electric hair. I thought of Butters, left for dead behind a trash bin like a piece of garbage. I thought of Mom, who had always been there for me. And how once this fool framed her, the whole town turned on her in an instant. I thought of Freedom Boy treating me like crap, like I wasn't worthy of being seen in public with him. My anger made clouds form in the air, I was sure of it. Electricity surged in my body. I felt like I was going to burst.

The clouds started to rumble. My mouth stretched into a smile. I wasn't a slave to emotions! I bore down one last time and clenched my teeth. A huge lightning bolt escaped, aiming for the ground.

"Yes!" Alice yelled.

My heart stopped beating for a second.

I was breathless. I may actually get him!

Then disaster struck.

My happiness ended the bolt midstrike. It exploded in the middle of the air, looking like glaring midday fireworks, blinding the Admiral and everyone within a few hundred square yards. The electricity shot everywhere. A few electrical transformers at the company's substations blew up and black smoke began pouring out.

I grabbed Alice and ran toward the relative safety of a brick wall, left over from an old water pump. It felt like I was blind and deaf. I put my hands over my ears and stared at the red stone.

When the world settled, emerging, anew, I could see that the Admiral had escaped.

"Oh no," I said. "I did that."

I puked onto the grass.

Blue hail fell from a brilliant orange sky.

THIRTY-THREE

THE NEXT day, I felt like I'd been hit in the head with a boulder. My whole body ached. My ego felt worse. I'd screwed up and let Admiral Doom escape. I flipped on the TV and Anne Glanton stood in front of the work crews repairing building seven and building eight.

"I am here today reporting from Doolittle Falls, Massachusetts, the scene of Admiral Doom's latest attack on PeriGenomics. The Admiral is fresh off a series of West Coast attacks and appears to have headed east. Most noted for his destruction of Innsmouth with his sometime partner Lady Oblivion, the Admiral is no stranger to this region. The fight ended when a stray lightning bolt exploded, incapacitating many on both sides. It is not clear whether it was the result of Admiral Doom, the Heroes, or as, some are suspecting, a rogue Hero. The Bureau of Superhero Affairs has sent agents to determine the cause of the bolt and see if an unlicensed individual was utilizing powers."

I gulped hard and turned off the TV. If anyone found out I would never get a Hero card or get into the Academy. It would confirm everyone's suspicions. They probably would lock me up in one of the super-prisons they have for villains like The Luthor.

In fifth period, I got a text saying that we had the all-clear: Friends could go see Butters at the hospital. I was psyched. It had been a long wait. The only news so far had been the occasional updates from his family.

When I got to the hospital, Betty was sitting in the waiting room. She looked pale and nervous, huddling in a Hero Academy sweatshirt. Her hair, normally pin straight and perfect, was pulled off her face in a scraggly ponytail.

"Hey, cuz!" said Betty, brightening. "This is a nice surprise!"

I sat down next to her on the uncomfortable red waiting room chairs. She turned toward me, her big brown eyes worried, and half asking and half pleading, said, "Go up with me?"

We stood together and approached the desk.

"Sign here," said the nurse, holding out a clipboard. Betty grabbed it from her and filled it in.

The nurse typed our information into the computer and made us stand in front of a small camera. She gave us two IDs with terrible black-and-white photos with VISITOR written in large red letters. "Keep these on during your visit."

We had to walk past the chronic exochositis unit to get there. It made me want to cry just seeing those words. That was the unit for the people born with powers that were slowly killing them. They had bad HrO mutations. It brought back memories of a sad doc called *The Purple Boy* about a teenage boy slowly dying of a form of exochositis that made his skin glow an incandescent purple. I couldn't help but tense up.

In Butters's room, the light was low, the shades were drawn, and the overhead was dimmed. When the nurse said he had visitors, Butters propped his head up on the bed.

When I saw him, I gasped. He was in bad shape. His left leg was in a full cast and held aloft in traction. He had a sling over his right arm, which was also in a cast. One of his eyes was greenish blue and his cheeks were puffed out like a chipmunk's from all the bruising.

"Hi, ladieshh," he said between clenched teeth. "Shorry I can't talk to well. Zhey wiyred my jaw shhut. Zhey alsho put meztal zrods in my legz and armz."

"I am Iron Man!" sang his backup singers, before fading out. They looked the same: sixties-era fab, but they all had red eye patches on over their right eyes.

"Are you okay?" I asked. I felt stupid since I knew he wasn't okay, but I didn't know what to say. It was good to see him. "I'm awshome," he said. "Zhey got me hooked up to morphine. I can't feel a thing. My shingerz, when they're around, can't even keep a tune."

I laughed. "Nice to know you're in good hands."

"Zhe best. Zhough I kind of rezhent being on zhe kids ward. Nuthing makesh you feel more like a man zhan wallpaper with teddy bearz and vizhits from clone doctorz."

"What's a clone doctor?"

"Not clone, *clone*. Shilly outfits, red nozez, and shtetoshcopes." Clowns. The worst. They're terrifying in any form.

Betty hadn't said anything. I turned around to see her crying softly in the corner. I grabbed her by the hand and drew her closer to the bed.

"Betty, sho glad you made it," said Butters.

She wiped her face and replied, "How could they, how could they?"

"Djon't worry about it. Living in a shuper town means rishking getting shuper beat up," Butters joked. "It happens. Stupid Admiral Dzhoom. Dozhen't even have a zhip."

After a pause, Butters said, "Your shirt iz great, Betty."

"Johnny made it," she said.

She opened her arms wide and bent down to give him a huge hug. The shirt said YOU CAN'T WHIP OUR BUTTERS.

He groaned slightly when she pressed against him but he didn't push her away, even though he was cringing in pain. She apologized. "I'm so sorry, I'm so sorry." Butters protested that he was okay.

I stood awkwardly against a wall. I knew this feeling. Like I was an interloper in something that had already started. That's when it hit me like a laser blast to the chest. I don't know why I hadn't figured it out already.

Betty and Butters weren't just friends. They were dating.

THIRTY-FOUR

FTER THE Hospital, Betty spilled everything. They'd been seeing each other since the Harpastball game. When the Academy found out, they forbid her from dating him. So Butters and Betty dated secretly. It was why she hadn't told me anything. I was so obsessed with my own things—Freedom Boy, training with Sam, the Academy—that I hadn't figured it out. Sometimes I was dense. It was weird, however: Why would a school meddle in Betty's love life like that? Why would they even care? The following week was my birthday, and I sent Alice, Betty, and Sam an e-mail asking them to meet me at Buzz Man at 3:30 for a pastry and one of those coffee milkshake things. I lingered at the computer, feeling like I should maybe send Freedom Boy an e-mail, but good sense prevailed. I didn't need someone who was going to make me feel bad about myself hanging around on my birthday. Besides, I wanted to do something in public, not thirty thousand feet above the earth.

Betty couldn't make it. She had been spending most of her time at the hospital. Butters was going to be released at the end of the day. And Sam was on some mission for PeriGenomics. Which left Alice and me.

The day started out great when the sweet and salty smell of heavenly bacon woke me up. My nose led me toward to the kitchen, where Johnny and Dad were cooking.

"Happy birthday, Sarah!" said Dad, attacking the bacon.

"Happy sixteenth," said Johnny. "Try not to get pregnant and on some dumb reality show this year, okay?" He was working on a plate of pancakes. "I made these with extra love."

"Ew," I replied. "Do not want!"

"I meant chocolate chips!"

I had slept late and I was pretty sure my hair was sticking upward and outward in a variety of different angles like I had a triangle head. I felt kind of goofy in my pink sock-monkey pajamas.

"No, you want," said Dad. He had on a Kiss the Cook apron. "They're good." "I didn't set the table for you for nothing!" Johnny added. He was right—there was a placemat set out, my favorite Hello Kitty plate on it, a balloon tied to my chair, and a fresh copy of the *Doolittle Daily Star* and a padded envelope on top.

"Aw, you shouldn't have!"

"Check that envelope," Dad said.

I studied it for a little bit.

There was no address on it. Just "For Sarah" written in the center, in meticulous block letters. It looked like it could have been from anywhere. Maybe even—oh, I couldn't hope.

"Where did this come from? I thought the mail doesn't usually come until at least one o'clock?" I asked.

"It wasn't delivered by the mail guy. It was just on the front step next to the newspaper," Dad replied.

Johnny emerged from behind me and sat at the table. He took one look at the envelope and then avoided my gaze. Like it was toxic or something.

"Aren't you going to open it?" My father looked on, as Johnny studied the tines on his fork.

"Nope. I think I'll save this for later." I had a feeling that I shouldn't open this envelope in front of Dad. I asked, "What's the birthday spread?"

"Dad's got the bacon covered," Johnny said grandly, getting up and returning to the kitchen. "I'm on the delicious pancake station."

After breakfast, I was in the mood for an early siesta. When Johnny and Dad tried with breakfast, they were really good. Johnny even wrote "Happy 16!" in maple syrup on my first pancake. I was pretty sure that a solid thirty percent of me was waffle, with a good ten percent made up of a variety of syrups ranging from boysenberry to caramel.

Three o'clock rolled around, and I put on my favorite dress, a simple royal blue shift, a black cardigan, and cute silver flats and headed to Buzz Man.

My favorite barista, Max, was behind the counter. When he saw me, he grinned. "Sarah Robertson," he announced to the store, "it's your birthday!"

"How do you know?" I asked.

He held up a card. "You put it down on your comment card. Don't tell me you didn't expect a free cupcake."

Sweet. I grabbed a table at the back of the café. My phone buzzed with a message. Alice was late. Fine. I could open the envelope without anybody watching. Johnny was acting really weird about it.

I turned the envelope upside down and a necklace fell out. I held it in my hand and studied it. The pendant was made of a bright turquoise stone with metallic flecks that caught the light. It had a strange shape, sort of like a key. At the top was a flat circle, which ended in a long bar that, toward its bottom, was bisected by three parallel bars. The bars rotated, but it took a bit of effort to turn them. It wasn't a thing that you could buy for five bucks at the mall. There was some sort of light or spirit or energy coming from it and it was slightly spooky. It felt like a live thing in my hand. I pulled out a sheet of paper. I gulped. Holy smokes.

To my beautiful daughter,

Happy birthday, honey. I'm sorry I am not around to celebrate with you on this special day. That I cannot be there for you is one of the saddest things in the world to me. I am working to fix this, but I don't want to give you false hope. I just want to let you know that you're an amazing daughter and stronger than I could ever be. I know you want to see me and learn more about what happened, but doing that would put our family in too much danger. Even this letter is risky. They have eyes everywhere.

I know you must be kicking ass at the Academy this semester alongside your brother, Johnny. I always knew you were going to be strong and brave. For your birthday I have included a small gift for your protection. It's a necklace and a beacon. If you are ever in danger, twist the base of the device and help will arrive. Use it sparingly; likely you have enough strength to help yourself at this point.

My greatest wish for you is that you live your life to the fullest. Do not seek to help me or uncover the traitors who betrayed me. It is too dangerous and not your burden to bear. It would break my heart if you were injured trying to pursue justice on my behalf. Revenge is a fool's game.

I'm sorry for having to leave you. I wish I could tell you the truth of the situation but I've already put you in enough danger as it is. Watch out for Johnny for me. He wasn't as good as you at keeping out of trouble.

Love,
Mom

I was crying by the second line. My mind swirled with all the possibilities that my mother's letter hinted at. I had so many questions. I didn't know what she'd think of me right now: going to Harris High, ridiculed as a Misshape. My throat closed and I felt like I couldn't breathe.

"Hey, girl!" It was Alice, standing in front of me and my optimistically big table. I wiped my eyes and tried to smile, but it felt like a grimace.

Alice saw my distress and gave me a big hug. "Sarah, what's wrong? Birthday problems? Freedom Boy?"

"No," I sobbed. "Everything's just so weird!" I told her. I'd never spoken to anyone about Mom before. Even in our house we always discussed it in a kind of improvised code. I missed her so much, and needed to share that with someone. Just talking about it with Alice made me feel a little better.

We were interrupted by Max, who took our order. He took one look at my tear-stained face and said, "You really hate the food here, huh?"

"You know the most annoying part?" I said to Alice. "She asked me to look out for Johnny, my *older* brother, because I'm good at keeping out of trouble."

"So?" she said.

"Well, maybe that's not a good thing. Maybe I shouldn't be well behaved and following the rules. It hasn't helped me so far."

"Are you forgetting the Doom raid? Sarah, you're already on the wrong path. You're totally planning to go all badass now that you're sixteen," she said.

"Maybe a little," I said.

"And she gave me this." I showed her the necklace and she helped me put it on. Max came back with two cupcakes and lattes. "On the house," he said. We thanked him and he rushed back behind the counter.

"You know he's flirting with you, right?" Alice asked.

"Who, Max? Nooo," I protested.

"Sarah Robertson, sixteen-year-old heartbreaker," she said. We laughed and dug into our cupcakes, gossiping about school and trying to forget for a moment that my alleged archvillian of a lost mother had just sent me a birthday card.

When we stepped outside I was greeted by another surprise. It was Freedom Boy, in his full costume, standing next to his dad's custom-made car.

I gave him a look. I tried walking the other way. He gave a small little wave and ran up behind me, tapping my shoulder. "Look, I am sorry, Sarah. I have acted like a jerk, and I wanted to make it up to you. I figured we could drive this time."

I looked at him, again. I didn't want to betray any emotion with my face.

"And..." he added, looking at his stocking-clad feet. "Happy birthday?" Suddenly, he seemed shy. Vulnerable. "I sent a photo of balloons to your Instagram page," he added.

A sort of public acknowledgment. Hmmm. Not a big one, but it was something. It changed things. Maybe we could go on a date. It was my birthday, after all.

Alice, standing behind me, shook her fist at Freedom Boy. "If anything happens to her on her birthday, you drop her, you abandon her, you split an end of her damn hair, I promise every squirrel in this town will be on your nuts." She furrowed her brow and muttered, "Literally."

Freedom Boy looked a little taken aback. He was not used to girls threatening him.

"I promise nothing bad will happen," he said,

He pushed a button on his keychain, and the passenger-side door flung upward like a wing. I stepped into the car. The doors descended, and I waved good-bye to Alice.

It was going to be a late night.

THIRTY-FIVE

I NSIDE THE car, there were dark plastic-looking seats with harness belts. The dashboard looked more like an airplane cockpit than a car. I jumped in, pulled the belt over my head, and tried to figure out what all the glowing switches, knobs, and buttons did. Instead of a steering wheel it had one of those half-circle controllers that they use on planes. I hadn't the faintest idea.

Freedom Boy strapped in next to me, pushed another button and the winglike doors descended and closed around us. The windows were tinted so dark that the only light inside was coming from the red glow of the dash. It felt intimate and eerie, like a sketchy motel from the future.

"So, where are we going, a make-out spot?" I teased.

"No. I would not do…I mean, I want to and we…Let me start over. I thought we could go fight some crime. Team up."

I looked at him quizzically. "Really? Am I even allowed to do that?"

"If you are with me you can. I just got a new level Hero Card a few weeks ago with sidekick privileges so I can now patrol. And what teammate would be better than my girlfriend?"

I blinked my eyes. I couldn't believe he used the G-word. Girlfriend.

Awkwardly, but he used it. He also called me teammate but I chose to ignore that.

I guess this is what happens when someone avoids you. After radio silence, they randomly show up and call you their girlfriend. Pretty sure Kate Middleton had to deal with this sort of off-and-on stuff with Prince William.

But it paid off for her. She's a princess now. She'll be the Queen of England.

I was on the right track too. Freedom Boy—*Freedom Boy*—was my boyfriend. I had no idea how to respond.

"I am so sorry how my friends treated you," he started. "They think that they are better just because of their powers and their money and their school. But you are amazing, Sarah. Amazing. From what I have seen, you are better than any of them."

He paused. "And I am sorry about how I treated you. I know it is no excuse, but with the media and my father and the Academy, it can be a lot to take sometimes."

I regained my ability to speak and stuttered out, "We're boyfriend and girlfriend?"

"Yes, I guess. I mean, if you want, because I want to and—"

"Yes!" I responded. "And as boyfriend and girlfriend we're going to fight crime."

He pushed some buttons, and he placed his hand on a throttle that was between us. I moved my hand to place it on top of his, but before I could do it, he pulled the lever back and we took off like a rocket.

It felt like we were in a revved-up motorboat, if a motorboat could fly over all the buildings in town. My body was thrown back against my seat from the force of the acceleration.

After our launch the ride got a lot smoother, almost like we were cruising down a highway. As he pushed various buttons and reviewed monitors, Freedom Boy tried to explain how the vehicle worked. He needed a small-aircraft license to fly it, along with a regular license and his Hero Card, a veritable wallet full of IDs and paperwork.

After flipping a large switch that said AUTOPILOT, he turned on the radio.

"Do you even get reception up here?"

"We get everything. Radio reception. But I have to put on a crimewatch channel."

"What's that?" I asked.

"It is a broadcast put out by the Federal Paladin Oversight Division, or F-POD, an agency under the Bureau of Superhero Affairs. They are the ones that issue the Hero licenses and do all that testing, and they have a broadcast for all people with licenses that blends local police radio scanners with information on crimes committed by people with powers."

The radio was staticy and filled with jargon. It reported on the locations of crimes in progress, and occasionally a crisper voice would chime in, saying a power was used in the commission of a crime. Like "Car theft on fifth and Lincoln, frozen ice projectile used."

"Why 'paladin'? What's that even mean?"

"It was an old word for hero, usually used for knights and warriors. When the organization was started in the early days, it was the term for superhero."

He looked over to me and smiled. His eyes wandered downward. Was Freedom Boy staring at my chest?

"Where'd you get that?" he asked.

"What?" I said, blushing and putting my hand over my cleavage, only to realize it was something else that had caught his eye. "You mean my necklace?"

"Yeah."

"I got it from my..." I stopped short. "I got it from a friend. For my birthday. Do you know what it is?"

"Yes, when I was a little kid..." He trailed off. "That must be some friend. It is called a Djed, the symbol of one of the oldest superhero groups. Also, one of the most secretive. My dad does not even know if they exist or are just a legend."

"Oh," I said, clutching it tighter. "I think she got it at a thrift shop or something. Um, he. He got it." I couldn't tell him anything else about it.

"Could be a knock-off or something," he said. "But if it is not, I would like to ask that person some questions."

I bet he would. As would his father, my "friend's" nemesis. He looked back at the wheel and turned the volume up on the radio. A report was repeating itself. Maybe the sign of a big one: "Break-in at the Massachusetts Institute of Technology. There is a break-in at the Massachusetts Institute of Technology. Classified radioptics division, Galileo Way and Broadway..." Then that authoritative voice came in: "MIT radioptics break-in. Suspected presence of Admiral Doom. Be cautious, possesses flying capability, laser weaponry, and extra-ballistic protection."

Freedom Boy entered the information on a keypad embedded into the steering wheel. A map of the region came up on the windshield and information streamed down next to it about the location, security, and layout.

"So are we going after that bastard?" I asked.

"They could probably use our help. The Boston police do not have a good history with the Admiral."

"Hell yes! After what he and his bully Dragoons did, I wouldn't mind watching you hurt him! Or doing my own damage," I added.

I didn't mention Mom. It was still unspoken between us. His father, my mother, and this mysterious villain. Maybe if we caught him I could get some answers. Also, I wanted payback for the royal screwup at the PeriGenomics fight.

"Right. He hurt Butters," Freedom Boy said.

"It was awful, you know," I said. I was touched. Freedom Boy remembered Butters. He remembered that my friend got hurt. He has to care.

"I bet. Well then, let us go."

Superheroing seemed like so much fun. I wish I could be as blasé.

He took the controls and increased the speed so I was pushed back into my seat again. The car descended and I could see the skyline of Boston approaching us, the Charles River glittering below.

We landed on the highway next to the river, in the midst of an entire brigade of police, firemen, and SWAT cars. When Freedom Boy opened up the doors and got out, a police officer with broad shoulders and all sorts of insignia on his arm came over and slapped him on the back.

"Good to see you, Freedom Boy. We could really use your help in there," he said, with a broad Boston accent.

"What is the situation, Captain?"

"Admiral Doom set off the alarms while trying to steal some expensive prototype that the geeks won't even tell me about. They just said it could be very dangerous in the wrong hands."

"Is anyone in there with him?"

"A couple of henchmen. We cleared out most of the civilians but there are still some injured. We have the place surrounded with snipers but every time we send someone in, they come out in pieces." I hoped he meant that figuratively.

"Well then, looks like for a job for us."

"Us? Who's your little friend?" he said. I glowered at the captain.

"She is with me—do not worry, she is under my card for this mission."

He produced a card from his pocket and handed it to the captain. The captain inspected it closely, pulled out a laser scanner, and scanned the card.

"Okay, good to go," the captain said. "I'll just need your information, miss."

I gave the inspector my name and address while Freedom Boy walked over to the car and pressed a couple of buttons. The captain wrote down my information and eyed me suspiciously as I joined Freedom Boy. The car made a whooshing noise and a little drawer popped out of the side. In it were two blue vests with his logo on them, a pentagon emblazoned with FB. There were also a pair of goggles. I grabbed the smaller goggles and vest and put them on. They fit like a glove.

"It will keep you safe. That and me," he said.

He pressed another button and a display case of weapons came out. He ran his hand across a few before settling on one and handing it to me. It was the size of a pistol but seemed to be made out of bright red plastic.

"That should be a good start for you. It's nonlethal, all of them are." He said, half to me and half to the captain. "Just point it and shoot."

"And what comes out of the other end?" I asked.

"Energy pulses. They look like bright red bubbles. You ready?"

"I guess," I said. An indoor fight with a criminal mastermind wasn't really playing to my strengths. Outdoors I could at least make it rain, trip him up with a puddle, and then run like hell. Inside, not so much. The idea seemed foolish, but Freedom Boy had faith in me so I wasn't going to back down. But there was a part of me that wanted dinner and a movie, to be treated fancy, like a future princess or something. But Freedom Boy was an adrenaline junkie.

"Okay, cool. No tornados," he said, with a smirk. He grabbed a much larger weapon, which looked like a futuristic rifle, and charged into building seventy-three.

THIRTY-SIX

ONCE WE were inside the building, Freedom Boy switched from sheer bravado to quiet cat burglar. Building seventy-three was so creepy and cavernous, even the squeak of my sneakers echoed down the hall. I took every step super carefully, trying not to make a sound at all.

A siren was going off and bright white lights flashed intermittently. It reminded me of the Doom raid sirens. We made our way over to a door with a picture of stairs on it. Freedom Boy motioned for me to stand against the wall. I was getting more and more nervous. The alarm was really getting to me. My gun was vibrating slightly. My hand was shaking from clutching it so hard.

He reached over, opened up the door, and walked in, weapon-first. It was clear. We made our way down the stairs to the basement. At the bottom of the stairwell, we made like cops once again, but the only thing on the other side of the door was a long hallway.

The basement was destroyed. Lab equipment spilled out of doorways. The floors were covered with broken glass beakers. The lights flickered on and off. We tiptoed through the halls, carefully slipping by open doors. I felt like I was in an underground labyrinth with an infinite number of halls and rooms. After a few twists and turns, we heard a strange moan coming from the end of one of the halls. We followed it to its source, an injured scientist lying on the ground, clutching a wound in his side.

"Are you okay?" asked Freedom Boy.

"Yeah, I just can't walk and everyone ran out. Everyone except that metal thug and his crew down there destroying my lab and stealing our stuff."

He looked pale. And not the I-work-like-a-mole-underground pale but the I-lost-too-much-blood pale, as evidenced by the red pool underneath his body.

Freedom Boy reassured him. "We will get you out of here. Just stay alive." He grabbed his radio, quickly reporting to someone about the hurt scientist.

"Okay," the scientist said quietly. I gave him a quick smile and followed Freedom Boy to the door. Noise could be heard behind it. I looked back at the scientist. That could be me and my blood. What was I thinking? This was a real fight, not some documentary. We were about to fight a real supervillain and his henchmen. And this time up close.

I looked up at Freedom Boy walking ahead of me, his shoulders back, his head high.

"Are you ready?" he asked.

I nodded, grabbed the door, and pushed it open, my gun in my hand. The place was in complete disarray. Tables were turned over, machines were broken and spinning out of control, henchmen were everywhere rummaging through cabinets, and Admiral Doom was standing by the weapon, flanked by two henchmen. He was shorter in person, nearly my height. The henchmen fired at the door. I instantly realized my huge screwup. My gun was at my side. I left myself wide open for an attack.

As Freedom Boy yelled, "Sarah, don't!" a large globular red ball flew toward me. I couldn't get out of the way. Even though I swore it was moving in slow motion. Or maybe I was moving in slow motion.

I hit the wall with a thud. My body was immobilized by whatever the Dragoon had shot at me. I slid down the wall and slumped over on the floor. Freedom Boy grabbed me by the arms and dragged me down the hall and away from the attackers.

The world went completely white.

"Mer mu mowmay?" he asked.

I drooled in response to his question.

"Mer moo mokay?" he screamed back, shaking me slightly.

"What?" My whole body was ringing. I squinted and things slowly came into focus.

I could make out simple shapes.

"Moo may?" I asked.

The world was starting to vibrate less.

I was alive.

Freedom Boy seemed nervous. "Mokay! Okay? Sarah, are you okay?" he said.

"Yes, yes, I'm okay," I finally answered.

Thank goodness for the vest. It probably saved my life from whatever that Dragoon attacked me with.

"Thank god. You need to get up, because they are coming for us," said Freedom Boy, handing me my gun back. "Protect yourself!"

"What?" I asked, but didn't need an answer. The thunder of a group of Dragoons came racing down the hall. They ran toward us in lockstep. One of them was holding the weapon that shot me. Freedom Boy, seeing their approach, flew over to them and took them out like a series of dominos. He grabbed the weapons from the knocked-out Dragoons on the floor, including the Sarah flattener.

He took on hordes of them at the other end of the hall. I dragged myself behind the relative safety of the stairs, still clutching my gun.

I shot toward the Dragoons and took a couple out. They dropped like zapped bugs. It was kind of awesome.

"Keep shooting, Sarah!" Freedom Boy yelled, while knocking several of them unconscious. They kept streaming through the doors while Freedom Boy fought. He was so elegant in the heat of battle, almost like a ballerina, with his high kicks and graceful dodges.

When the stream of Dragoons became a trickle, Admiral Doom emerged from the lab with some kind of device in his hand. I assumed it was the classified weapon the cop had told us about. It looked like a nutty professor type of device with metal coils and digital clocks and antennae all over the place. The Admiral had on his usual bronze chest-plated getup. He wore a slash of a smile that stretched across his face. He must really like stealing technology.

A large piece of drool was hanging off my lip. I wiped it away. My motor functions were coming back. My head still hurt and my hair felt electrified. I must've looked awful.

Freedom Boy came bounding back to my hiding spot. "Sarah, do you think you can cover me while I go after Doom?"

"Cover you? But you're so much bigger than me!"

"No, not like that." I realized how dumb I must have sounded. That thing must have knocked me stupid. He continued: "Just fire that gun at the two remaining Dragoons."

"Sure," I said.

He handed me a grenade and sprinted down the hallway.

I popped up and fired. My shots missed the Dragoons but were close enough to slow them down. It felt magnificent for just one second.

After my third shot the red pistol made a fizzing noise and started to smoke. It stopped firing. I looked at the gun as Freedom Boy flew past the Dragoons blocking his way to the Admiral.

When the smoke cleared, the Dragoons looked at Freedom Boy. Then they looked at me.

They sprinted my way. I screeched and ran to the end of the hall. The Dragoons were going to kill me.

Behind me, I heard the sounds of Freedom Boy attacking Admiral Doom—"We meet again!" Freedom Boy yelled—as they struggled for control of the device.

I kept pulling the trigger on my gun, trying to hit the Dragoons, but the whirring just grew louder. And then they were gaining on me. I threw my grenade at them as a last ditch. It hit the ground and went up with a flash.

The boom pushed me to the floor. When I recovered and poked my head up, all the Dragoons were gone and there was no sight of Admiral Doom.

A large hole was torn in the concrete wall. They escaped. Again.

I stood up and saw Freedom Boy at the end of the hall, device in hand. Smiling at me like I was the only person in the world. He ran over and gave me a hug. My ribs groaned in response.

"You are a fighter," he said, happy.

When we staggered outside, he gave me the honor of returning the machine to a bunch of scientists in white coats waiting eagerly.

"Thank you so much, Freedom Girl," one said. "You have no idea how dangerous that could have been." Another chimed in: "He could have blown up half the city, or worse, ruined my thesis dissertation."

"You're welcome," I said.

I tried to keep a straight face long enough so they would believe I was the cool girl who fights evil. Freedom Boy was filling out some paperwork with the police while I got to soak up some super glory. My adrenaline was racing.

After the fight, we drove to an industrial part of town. Freedom Boy stopped the car and we got out.

"So what now?"

"I thought we should go on lookout on one of these buildings to get a better view to see if anyone is committing any crimes in the city," he said.

"Sure," I said, and jumped on his back. "Top floor please."

"Right away, miss," he joked back, and then leaped up and flew to the roof of the building as the wind blew my hair behind me.

We landed softly. I grabbed his hand and we walked over to the edge to look out on the city. It was a bright, clear night and the skyline was laid out like a postcard before us. I looked down at the street to see if there were any crimes being committed.

I couldn't find anything suspicious going on. In fact, I could see only a few streets. All the dark alleys were blocked by the big buildings.

"I don't really think I can spot crime going on from up here," I told him. "Do you have some kind of super crime sense or something?"

"Not really. Without the radio, it is just luck."

"Wait, you didn't really bring me up here to spot crime, did you?"

"I think we have had enough for tonight," he said, turning toward me.

We locked eyes, and seconds later, lips. The city screamed and wailed around us as we made out on top of the world. Two superheroes. Me and my boyfriend, Freedom Boy.

THIRTY-SEVEN

FREEDOM BOY dropped me off with a kiss. I floated into the house. The lights were off. I quietly made my way toward my room.

"Sarah." It was Dad, sitting on the sofa. He was very still.

Crap. I'd been caught. I was hoping I'd get a pass, it being my birthday and all. Isn't it an unwritten rule that curfews are softened when you age up?

"Yes?" I said, continuing over to my room.

"Young lady, stop right here," he said. "You are not—"

"Not what, Dad?" I said, crossing my arms.

"You are not a crime fighter!"

"What? How would you know?" I sighed, realizing that by trying to defend myself, I had just incriminated myself.

"Look, I do not want you flying around town with that caped crusader, risking your life," Dad said.

"I wasn't risking my life. We were safe," I said.

"If he was protecting you, he would have taken you for a coffee or something. Not a crime scene with supervillains!"

"We were safe. We both had on protection," I said, before realizing how bad that sounded. "We had on bullet- and laser-proof vests."

"They didn't keep that from happening," he said, pointing to the large black-and-blue bruise that had formed on my leg. His eyesight was lethal. Even in dim light. And it could be classified as a Misshape power.

It was a nasty bruise, as long as my thigh and in the shape of a fish. I hadn't even noticed it. I felt no pain.

"I'm a klutz. I can be klutzy, you know." A lame defense but I had nothing.

"Sarah, I know it's exciting to be part of his world. But you're not ready to fight. Even if you were in the Academy." He huffed. "I don't understand why the great Freedom Boy would be so cavalier about your safety."

"He's not cavalier; he thinks I'm a Hero. Unlike some people."

"You're sixteen. I worry about you when you come home with a giant welt from a date with Freedom Boy. A date, mind you, that I heard about on the ten o'clock news, because of the whole fighting a supervillain thing. I have a right to be worried and annoyed."

"You're just mad because his father is a big respected Hero and everyone loves him. Nobody loves Mom. She's a villain. She's a villain and she abandoned us. We needed her and she just left us," I said, my voice rising. It wasn't the fight I meant to start and I was almost shocked when the words left my mouth.

His face sunk. "Do you really believe that?" he asked meekly, his former fire gone.

"I don't know what to believe. We never talk about it. It's, like, this big secret thing that nobody can ever talk about even though we all know what happened. The whole town knows what happened. The whole world. And then you don't even act like Mom existed. What am I supposed to believe if no one ever tells me anything?"

He sighed. "I know. I'm sorry. It's hard for you. It's hard for me too. I wish it wasn't. I wish I could make it better, but I can't." His voice grew reedy as he kept talking. "You have to know that she didn't abandon us. She would never do that. And she didn't do anything to that town. If she's gone it's to protect us. And you know what? At least we have each other. She's out there, on her own. She's completely alone."

My head sunk down. I hadn't thought about Mom like that. "I'm sorry."

"Don't think you're getting out of it just because you changed the subject," he said.

"What?" I asked.

"I'm still annoyed about your date." His mood turned on a dime. Back to angry. "I don't want to be mad at you—especially on your birthday—but that's no excuse to act recklessly. That's not showing you're growing up. And don't forget what his father did to this family. They are not welcome here. Ever."

I'd never seen my father so angry before. He finally said, with a huff, "I don't care if he is America's sweetheart, if the boy of steel as much as lets a hair on your head split I will smelt his invulnerable behind."

I laughed at his threat, and he began to chuckle. He came over and hugged me. "You're grounded."

"Aw, man! I thought we just had a moment."

"A moment doesn't get you out of a grounding. No going out at all next week. Not unless it's for studying, and then you have to be back by nine o'clock at the latest." Then he got a look on his face like he had eaten a sour candy.

"Johnny and I were going to be out on Friday."

"I guess I'll have the run of the—" I said, before I looked up to see his eyes gleaming. "No, no, no. Don't make me go with you." I groaned.

"It's settled. Friday, family outing, a great way to cap off a grounding."

THIRTY-EIGHT

ON MY way to my room, I veered off course and knocked on Johnny's door. He told me to come in. He was on his bed, playing his cherry-red guitar into a pair of stereo headphones. When I poked my head in, he finished a few chords, put the guitar down, and slid off the headphones.

"Johnny, did you get a letter from Mom on your birthday?" I asked.

He became serious. "Yes, a year ago. I take it you got one too."

"Yeah. That's what the letter was—"

He interrupted me. "That's what I figured."

"What did she say in yours?" I asked.

"To be careful. Be nice to Dad. That usual crap," he said. "I kind of hated her for a week after that." The words lingered in the air.

"I really miss her," I said.

"I do too." He muttered it, and his eyes grew glossy. We looked at each other for a minute. As simple as it was, we had never said it to each other. I ran over to hug him tightly. He wiped at his eye, but when I pulled away he tried to look like his cool composure hadn't broken.

"Hey, um, so, in your letter, was there anything about a secret, or the truth, or your getting in trouble?" I asked.

He looked down at his shoes and muttered something while nervously rubbing his right heel against his left toes.

"What?" I asked, ducking my head down so I could take a peek at his face.

He looked up. "I'm not supposed to tell you. Mom made me promise." He stressed the next word. "*Dad* made me promise."

"Tell me what?" I asked. "If it's about Mom I have a right to know."

"I agree. But they don't think it's safe. They didn't want me to know. I had to find out myself."

That's what she meant by getting in trouble. Johnny *had* to investigate. It was his nature. He had to find out what really happened while I was happy living like what they told me was truth. Mom had the two of us pegged.

He grew quiet and conspiratorial. "There's more to it than they were willing to tell me. More to it than they know themselves."

"Can you at least say anything?"

"Look, I didn't tell you, so don't go running off to Dad or trying to find Mom, okay? But she wasn't some evil supervillian like they made her out to be. There aren't heroes or villains like all those movies and news stories want you to believe. There are just people who make choices. And Mom choose to stand up to people with power and now she has to live in hiding and we are the town pariahs and never get to see her again."

He got up, went over to his desk and pulled out folders brimming with papers. Then, he walked over to a Ramones poster and pulled it down to reveal an elaborate chart with circles and arrows all over it. He was *Beautiful Mind*-ing it all over the place. He looked insane.

"Don't tell Dad," he said, "but I've been doing some research."

I gave him my word.

He pulled a box out from under his bed and opened it. Inside the box, there was a stack of pictures with lines drawn all over them and newspaper articles cut out and highlighted in crisp stacks. "Admiral Doom is not who everyone thinks he is. I think he set Mom up. I don't even know if he exists. Or maybe she didn't exist. Wait, no, she existed. But if Admiral Doom…"

He handed me another piece of paper. "Mom existed," I said. "You know that."

"I didn't mean it that way, Sarah." Johnny's eyes lit up. "Did you know the Innsmouth attack was his first? And since then he's only been involved in high-profile failures. Lots of media attention so people remember him and don't start asking questions. And PeriGenomics, there's a ton on them. They're suspect. And the school. The whole town is suspect."

He walked over to the chart and pointed out connections. "They were heavily involved in Innsmouth. Freedom Man, the savior, is the chief of the board. And you know Mom was sponsored by them in her Hero days. Pre-Academy." The words came out in a rush. He took a breath. "I don't know what this all means, but I'm not giving up."

It was the most animated I'd seen him since he'd started going to Harris High.

"Is that why they kicked you out of school? Did you find something they didn't want you to find?" I asked.

Johnny paused. He looked reflective. "I can't say anymore. It's better that way. There's not much we can do." Johnny tried to calm down. He reached for his headphones. "Now let me figure out this song, okay? 'Night, Sarah."

I walked out. But as I left, I could tell he wasn't thinking about music.

THIRTY-NINE

THE NEXT day, I tried to cover my bruises with a long-sleeved plaid shirt. But I couldn't get anything past Alice. She saw a flash of bluish flesh creeping out when I was getting my civic responsibility books out of my locker. She grabbed my arm, right on the bruise, and I winced.

"Freedom Boy's into some kinky stuff," she said.

"Eww, no it's not like that. It wasn't him," I protested. I blushed.

The bell rang and we headed down the hall toward class.

"Sarah, you can tell me: Did Freedom Boy take you to a Hero orgy? One of those masked things with terrible piano music and people flying around banging each other?"

"No. We got into a fight," I said. She stopped short, a look of shock on her face. "I will kill him…" she muttered.

"No, no, no, you got it wrong. A fight with other people! We took on the Dragoons. And kicked their ass." I smiled, thinking about last night.

"I know," she said, and then handed me a folded-up newspaper. When I unfolded it the front cover had a picture of Freedom Boy and me emerging victorious from the MIT building. The headline read FREEDOM BOY AND MYSTERIOUS GIRL SAVE THE DAY!

"If you knew, why did you—" I asked.

"Because you're too fun to screw with. You like the headline?"

"It's a lot better than 'Freedom Boy and Mystery Slut,'" I replied.

"Oh, that's the *Herald*'s headline," Alice added.

"Really?" It just came out. I didn't really believe her.

"No. But you are cropped out of the photo."

The rest of the day I walked around with my head held up a little higher. I even rolled up my sleeves to show off my battle scars. As my last class was ending I got a call. It was from Dr. Mann's secretary. He wanted to see me. *ASAP.*

School got out and I ran over to the Academy. I made a beeline to Dr. Mann's office. My hands were shaking. I was a little nervous he knew about the incident at PeriGenomics. The day's headlines had to be on his mind.

"Congratulations, Sarah," he said, as he swiveled to face me. "I've heard nothing but good things. Granted it was a bit on the margins of the rules, but I can let that slide. And not too bad at the PeriGenomics building either."

"You know about that?" I asked.

"Of course I do. Who else could have caused that kind of meteorological damage? You're starting to outshine our former student Sam Albedo, who I believe is also your mentor."

"Yes, we've been working together. I'm sorry I let him get away," I said. "Admiral Doom. I hate him."

"That's okay. You were doing a better job than my A-squad, and that's quite the compliment. I don't say that lightly," he replied.

"Thank you," I said. Silence.

He whispered, "Don't let anyone know I told you this. But after last night, I think you'll be a shoo-in for next year. I have a meeting with the admissions committee and you're my number-one priority."

I gave a little yelp, inadvertently covering my mouth with my hands. Hopefully he didn't notice. I could literally reach out and grab my dream. It was within my grasp.

"I just need you to remember what I said," he continued. "If you want to go to the Academy there are certain choices you'll need to make. Some harder than others."

"I think I have made my choice, sir," I said.

"I think you have too," he said.

As I walked home, elated by the compliments, I got the feeling that we were talking about two different things.

I looked up at the sky and the clouds had started to shift. Some strange pattern. They looked like jellyfish. Maybe it was a warning. Or a coronation.

But as soon as I noted the clouds changing, they flipped back to normal. The feeling passed. I was a lot more than just a Misshape. Next year I would be attending the Hero Academy.

I was going to be a Hero.

FORTY

THE WEEK was so exciting, in spite of the grounding. But Friday still rolled around. I had to fulfill my family duty.

"Thank god you're here," I said to Alice.

"We are going to have a heck of a night," she said, waving a Captain Moron flag back and forth. "We will find the kitschy fun in this."

We were sitting next to Dad and Johnny in the upper stands of a midsized arena somewhere on the outskirts of Worcester. Below us was an eight-sided ring surrounded by a chain-link fence.

Now, I like half-naked men wrestling around as much as the next girl, but Maximum Fighting was not my cup of tea. At least Dad sweetened the deal with an extra ticket for Alice.

I tried to catch the neon-orange cheese as it dripped off my nachos with my mouth. I managed to get some of it before it splattered on the rest of the chips. Johnny elbowed me as he stood up to cheer for Captain Moron, and I ended up with a streak of safety-cone orange across my face.

The crowd was deafening. People held up signs, flags, and all sorts of merch-table goodness for the honorable captain. Misshapes from all over New England showed up for this event.

A chant of "Mo-Ron! Mo-Ron!" started in the crowd and grew to a tremendous roar. A man walked into the middle of the ring and held his hands aloft. He was wearing a great purple cape, a purple

Renaissance-like mask with a bulbous fake nose, and a dunce cap with "moron" scrawled on it.

To the chants of "Mo-ron" he stripped off his costume and threw the pieces over the fence until he was wearing only a set of purple shorts, his hairless chest oiled and gleaming.

An announcer walked out next to him. "Ladies and gentlemen, Captain Moron!"

The crowd went wild. I heard some strange noises, like a whooping bird, and realized it must be coming from some Misshape. I looked over to see a little boy holding a Moron banner with birdlike plumage on his face.

He grabbed the mic from the announcer. "Thank you," he said, above the cheers. "Especially my fellow Misshapes out there." The crowd exploded again.

A shadow flashed across the entrance hallway for the stands nearby the bird boy. It was the silhouette of a perfectly shaped bald head. The man was pacing back and forth, looking nervous. I thought the guy might've been Dr. Mann. But there's no way he'd be here. Or maybe I was hoping that the guy was Dr. Mann.

The announcer took the mic. "Tonight we had an open call for challengers in the no-limits division. Many brave men and women tried out, but only one emerged as the obvious champion. So tonight, for the first time in Maximum Fighting history, I present you with… the Great Ape!"

The audience began to boo loudly before he even got from the dressing room to the ring. A tremendous man—at least I thought it was a man—came out wearing a gorilla mask and brown shorts. His limbs and body were all out of proportion, and his muscles were massive. As he got into the ring the boos grew louder.

"Johnny, does that look like the kid from the Academy? Humungulous?"

Johnny replied, "Same size, sure. But what would he be doing here? The Academy is strictly against stuff like this."

The fight began. Captain Moron had a drunken way of fighting, which Johnny said was actually a style and not a state of intoxication. It helped him trick his opponents. But his true power was his ability to sustain abuse. He had slightly flexible bones, so normal locks and pins didn't work on him.

Captain Moron lurched forward stumbling and then at the last possible moment delivered a blow out of nowhere. Every time one of his strikes hit, the crowd cheered, and I even got into it.

After a few minutes we were certain that Captain Moron had his opponent bested, and then things took a turn for the worse. The Great Ape escaped some sort of leg head hold thing and hit Captain Moron square in the temple. The sound could be heard throughout the entire arena. It was loud and dull. He flew across the ring and hit the fence with a clatter. He lay still for a moment as the crowd sat silent, holding their breath, and then he stood up, wobbling with the aid of the fence. The crowd let out a loud cheer as the ref went to check on him.

The ref let the fight continue after a few tests of his coordination, and within a second another loud, shocking punch landed squarely on Captain Moron's chest. He fell down, but the fight continued on the ground as they rolled over each other. Before anyone knew what was happening, the Great Ape was on top of Captain Moron, pulverizing him with hit after hit right into his head. The ref came over to try to call off the fight. An errant move by the Great Ape's elbow sent the ref flying into the fence. There was the sickening sound of another wallop on Captain Moron.

The cheers stopped. The stadium was united in queasy disgust and horror. It was odd of the crowd to go from wild to silent. I looked at the hallway where I thought I saw Dr. Mann. While everyone was transfixed in horror, I watched as the shady figure slinked away into the shadows of the corridor. I felt like I was the only person who noticed it.

It seemed like the world had paused, until an entire team of large men in black shirts ran into the ring to pull the Great Ape off Captain Moron. He let out a horrific scream, and then allowed himself to be escorted out of the arena to boos and a shower of beer cans. A team of medics came out to attend to the ref and Captain Moron. They were able to get the ref out of the ring, but Captain Moron lay still in the center.

The crowd went silent. It was absolutely gruesome. Alice looked like she was going to throw up. Dad and Johnny sat stone-faced as the medical crew came and took his still body out of the ring.

After taking his pulse, they put him on a gurney and carted him away. The lack of medical attention was telling. When they got to the entranceway across from us, everyone could see them pull the white sheet over his legs, across his torso, and over his head. I turned to Johnny and saw that his lower jaw was trembling. Dad sniffled.

I looked around at the crowd. My eyes settled on the bird boy. He was crying uncontrollably, his I Love Captan Moron sign torn and sagging at his side. His parents stood on each side of him and tried, unsuccessfully, to comfort him.

FORTY-ONE

I WAS WORRIED about my brother. Johnny had always been volatile, but since Maximum Fighting, he was different. Catatonic. His eyes were blank, lacking their usual fire.

It went on like this for a bit. Until Johnny snapped in a civic responsibility class.

Hocho was presenting a paper on the history of Misshapes in the film world when Johnny yelled, "Bullshit!" out of nowhere.

Hocho blurted, "What? My paper's great!"

"Johnny! Do you want to go to the principal's?" Mrs. Frankl admonished. I was just shocked that he talked. He had spent most of class with his head in his book, ignoring everything and just reading and taking furious notes. He was wearing his homemade Captain Moron Forever shirt. He had worn it every day and it was stinky, dirty, and had a hole in the back, right where his shoulder blades met.

"I'm sorry, there's just no other word for it. Unless you have a thesaurus handy," Johnny said. The catatonia had left him.

"Johnny," Ms. Frankl scolded, her voice rising.

"My phone would know," offered Wendy, holding up her phone with the thesaurus app open. "Let's see. Nonsense, crap, baloney—"

Johnny looked at her with a glare. "Don't you all see it? This Captain Moron thing wasn't an accident or some isolated event. They're after Misshapes. They're attacking us in the streets." His voice wavered. "I was at that Captain Moron fight on Saturday night. I can't get the images out of my head. They're killing our icons." He pointed to Butters, back in school and sporting two large boots and crutches.

"Butters isn't my icon, dude," said Hamilton.

"I'm talking about Captain Moron," Johnny said. "One of the few Misshape icons in the world."

"How do you know the whole Maximum Fighting thing was some planned attack? It looked like an accident to me," Markus said.

Ms. Frankl, having lost control of the class, chimed in, sitting on her desk. "This is a good thing to talk about, guys. It relates to you as Misshapes. Let's discuss it."

Johnny continued, walking to the front of the classroom, pacing back and forth. "Nobody's looking into the death. The papers said it was an accident. It's the first death ever in Maximum Fighting. Why was it Captain Moron? I don't get why it isn't a big deal. It should be in the tabloids. The Bureau of Superhero Affairs should be looking into it."

Markus said, "Johnny, conspiracy theories are your thing—"

"Shut up!" Johnny yelled. "You weren't there. You didn't see it." Markus looked a little frightened. My brother was weirdly emotional.

Johnny was right. Captain Moron's death was one of the worst things I'd ever seen in my life. Alice and I were shaken up pretty bad and my dad tried to comfort us, but Johnny, he just snapped. Shut down. I thought it was going to be like that for awhile but now he's snapped back into some other realm.

After his outburst, Mrs. Frankl placed her hands on his shoulders, trying to calm him down. "It's okay," she said. "I think you should go down and have a chat with Dr. Feinberg. Would you like to do that?"

"Okay," Johnny demurred. Dr. Feinberg was the school counselor. It must've been a good idea if my brother wasn't even putting up a fight.

I was worried about him. We needed to figure out what was going on before he snapped, again. He was probably one drop of crazy away from burning down the Academy. He was obsessing so much over the fight and stuff about Mom the other night. I needed to protect him.

I snuck into his room one day when he was at the record shop. His wall of crazy looked worse. I knew that he was convinced that something was up with the Heroes, the shadowy presence of Dr. Mann at the Captain Moron fight, and the Great Humungulous-esque Ape.

I thought Johnny was wrong. I think. It seemed like a series of coincidences. A fighter who looked like Humungulous, of course a fighter is going to look like a huge dude if they're in that tiny ring. And Dr. Mann. Probably just someone else who looked similar. It was far enough away that I could have been mistaken. I have been basically obsessed with him. Maybe I wanted to see him. I willed him into the arena.

The Academy was the best thing going in the town, the country even. It regularly graduated people who would make the world better, sometimes by saving it entirely. But then I had class with my brother. I saw his face. His sunken eyes. I felt this weight on me.

I had to look into a potential Academy connection. For Johnny's sake. Besides, I was probably the better detective. Johnny was too susceptible to crazy theories and ideas perpetuated by Internet wackos.

Against my better judgment, I decided that the best thing to do was research and question people I knew at the Academy, which boiled down to Freedom Boy and Betty. I started with Freedom Boy.

We met up at Seymour's Scoops after school. I was early and grabbed a stool at the counter, and Freedom Boy showed up a few minutes later, with a big goofy smile. He sat down next to me and the waitresses brought him two sundaes for free, winking.

I dove into it.

He looked at me. "You look hungry. What is up?"

"Conflict makes me hungry." I paused. "It's been crazy. My brother's on edge since that fight we were at last week."

"Oh, the Maximum Fighting thing? I heard about that. That must have been tough to see," he replied. "I heard that guy was a hero to Misshapes. And to watch anyone get killed, even if it was an accident..." His shoulders shook and he made a face like his hot fudge with whipped cream suddenly became gross.

"Have you ever been to one of those?"

"A Maximum Fight? No, never," he said, dismissively. "Not my thing. Besides, we are not allowed to go. Academy rules."

"You're not allowed to fight?" I asked.

"Official policy. Dr. Mann put it in stone. Now we cannot even go to one, let alone participate. Dr. Mann says it sullies the Hero name in the community. Fine by me. I kind of agree with him," he said.

Why would a Maximum Fighting hater be at a fight? I pressed him for more information.

"So what's Dr. Mann like?" I asked. "Besides cryptic meetings once a quarter, I really don't know much about the guy."

"He is a fine man. And an excellent teacher."

"Teacher? I thought he was the dean."

"Both," he said, taking a bite of his sundae. "My dad is always going on about how great he is for the place."

I wasn't getting anywhere. "So, is your civic responsibility class the same as mine? Tell me about it."

"It is okay," he said. "Look, why are we talking about boring stuff? I'll make you feel better. We can fly to the Cape and check out the Academy's submarine base."

It was tempting, but I wasn't in the mood. He was trying to distract me. Like he was trying to get out of talking, or having any sort of conversation. Our dates weren't this stiff and awkward. I didn't get it.

"I have a lot of homework. And I should get going on that. Big paper due tomorrow," I said. I just wanted to go home.

"Okay. Do you want a ride?"

After Freedom Boy dropped me off with a quick, frustrating kiss, I gave Betty a call and told her to come over immediately. I wanted to get these grillings out of the way. I wasn't a natural detective.

Betty sat on my bed's bright green comforter Indian-style. I sat across from her on my swivel chair, angling my desk lamp so it shone in her face. Betty tapped her fingers on her knee.

"What's up?" she asked. She looked a little sad for some reason, looking down at the floor.

"I need to know what the deal is with Dr. Mann," I said, getting right to the point.

"The deal? I barely see the guy. He's usually behind the scenes or at assemblies or stuff. He doesn't talk to plebian students. Only the elite kids in his special class."

"What special class?" I asked. "Civic responsibility?"

"He wouldn't dare teach that. It's kind of like study hall," she said, rolling her eyes at the lameness. "Dr. Mann has a class for the top heroes. It's secret. No one really talks about what goes on and they're always meeting after school and on weekends. But we all know about it." She made a face. Betty wasn't so into the Academy. It was simultaneously endearing and annoying.

I wanted to talk about that with her, but I had to stay focused. Figure out what was going on with Dr. Mann. Whether there was a link between him and Captain Moron and general anti-Misshape stuff. "Who's in the class?" I asked.

Betty pulled the sleeves of her sweater over her hands. "The Aqua Kid, J5, some kids who are in the papers all the time. I think Lindsay's in it too, but I have no idea why she's elite."

I breathed a sigh of relief, smiling at Betty. She hadn't said the name I was expecting.

"Doh! How could I forget?" Betty gave me her first smile. "Freedom Boy's in it too. Obviously."

FORTY-TWO

ETWEEN BETTY and Freedom Boy, I was convinced something was going on at the Academy. And all signs pointed to Dr. Mann. It didn't make sense. He was one of the good ones. The only person to truly care about my potential and help get me into the Academy.

Johnny's room had become a psychotic mess of newspaper clippings and Post-it Notes filled with theories. He spent his nights at his computer, trying to figure out who, exactly, killed Captain Moron.

"Sarah, come and look at this," he said, calling me over. He had a bunch of blurry images and photo clippings in small boxes around his computer screen. He told me he was ninety percent sure the other fighter had been Humungulous in some kind of disguise. "The hands, look at the hands," he said and pointed at the screen. That's when I decided to tell him that I thought it was probably Dr. Mann at the Maximum Fight. My brother punched his pillow. I cringed in the doorway.

"It's just a suspicion. Besides, what do you have against Dr. Mann? Everyone at the Academy loves him and he's been nice to me," I said.

"The evil drones at the Academy think he's great. That proves *my* point. And you don't find that odd? He sure is treating Lady Oblivion's daughter well. Why?"

"He thinks I'm special. That I belong there. Unlike you!" I said, and stormed out.

A few minutes later he knocked on my door to apologize.

"You're right. We need to learn more," I said. "But don't go into this blaming the Academy or Dr. Mann."

"Fine," he replied. We were at a détente.

Over winter break, the Misshapes met up at the quarry to come up with a plan. I told them everything about the links between Captain Moron, Maximum Fighting, and Dr. Mann.

We spent hours talking about how we could learn more, each plan more preposterous and unworkable than the last. Finally a tiny voice spoke up.

"I can help," George said. "I can sneak into the special class."

George was right. The only way to find out what exactly was going on with Dr. Mann was to get someone inside the Academy who could sit in on his elite and secretive Hero class.

The plan was simple. First off, we'd need Betty to figure out where and when the class was located. That required one day of following Lindsay around.

Once we got the logistics, George would sneak into the Academy, find a spot in the back of the classroom, and record the whole thing. Betty, who really wanted to help, could give a layout of the place and suggestions on where he could best hide in a typical Academy classroom.

There was one hitch. George would have to be invisible the whole time to avoid detection. The *whole* time.

Alice, with a great big smirk on her face, offered a solution. She volunteered me as her helper. Her idea was to give George an earpiece and keep saying things to him that would ensure his invisibility.

Getting it right required a lot of trials. We needed him invisible for at least an hour. He made a lot of weird rustling noises when he was invisible, but Johnny had a solution: George would make less noise if he wasn't wearing clothes. And at a school with superhearing, we had to take every precaution. We started with tests: Butters, Markus, or Johnny would follow George on some course they laid out for him and we would try to find the best way to prevent him from emerging. We had tried all sorts of voices, stories, and sounds. Most things worked at first, but after twenty minutes nearly everything wore off and a naked

George would appear. But George's potential public nudity was its own fail-safe, causing him to vanish again, giving him enough time to escape.

It felt like we'd never figure it out. Until we found the secret. Alice had discovered a cache of scripts from seventies-era erotic films online. They were such a perfect combination of cheesy and dirty that we couldn't help but turn beet red while reading them. "There is no way in hell I'm saying that," I exclaimed, when I read the first one.

"Come on, Sarah, it's for a good cause. Besides, I'm the one who answers the door for the plumber. You just have to say the thing about not realizing your roommate had a guest." She handed the paper back to me with a big smirk on her face.

I was amazingly embarrassed. I could only imagine how George Herbert felt.

We texted Johnny on his phone. *Can you see GH?*

He shot back, *No. Must be workin'!*

I gave Alice a thumbs-up, and she giggled again while talking about the pipes in her apartment being too large for a woman to handle without a plumber's assistance.

We met the hour benchmark, and I texted Johnny and the Misshapes. *Mission accomplished. Give him pants and meet at Buzz Man now.*

We picked next Friday for spy day. It was Annihilation Day, a Massachusetts-only holiday celebrating Monsignor Annihilation's single-handed salvation of the Boston harbor during the War of 1812. Public school kids had the day off. The Academy didn't. Johnny said it was so they could ratchet up the yearly pro-Hero propaganda.

The Misshapes met up in a small abandoned building by the river, one of the control stations for the old mill. Johnny suggested it. I think he went there to smoke cigarettes sometimes. Markus and Butters took over most of the room, syncing up their laptop and speakers to George's video signal. Alice and I got a corner, where a microphone was set up to send our embarrassing signal. Johnny was off on the hill showing George a secret back entrance and giving him a final pep talk before heading back to our makeshift headquarters.

When Johnny came back, he told us to start when George gave the camera a thumbs-up. I kept my eye on the laptop. So far it was dark, even though we had a George's-eye-view of the world. According to Johnny, George was climbing through a vent in the back that led to the Academy basement. Once he got in, he could walk up a set of stairs and be next to Dr. Mann's classroom.

George walked down the narrow basement hallway. Right before he got to the stairwell, he passed a heavily padlocked door with a numerical keypad in the middle of a giant metal wheel. Then two thumbs appeared in front of the screen. Alice and I knew it was go time.

She mimed smoking a cigarette and easily slipped into an absurd sultry voice, saying in a faux smoky baritone, "Hello, Georgie. Do you come here often?" His hands instantly disappeared from the screen. She hadn't even started on the scripts.

George climbed the stairs, walked through the hall for a minute, and snuck into the classroom. It was my first real glimpse inside the Academy. It looked so plain and normal. Lockers, educational posters, industrial lighting.

It took an entire dirty movie before Dr. Mann's class shuffled in, in their Academy uniforms. Alice and I were whispering about the engine on a hot rod. Some of the kids were familiar: Humungulous, Aqua, J5, Lindsay and Christie, a Harpastball player from Markowitz's party. One girl in a black body suit walked right through the door without opening it. The girl with green hair from the party followed behind her. A boy floated in on a small circular board and landed in front of a chair.

All the seats were filled save one. I looked at that seat and hoped that it wasn't for Freedom Boy. It was a naïve thought. I knew he was part of the class. He was the Academy golden boy. It's just that—if he was in the class, that meant he lied to me and he lied smoothly. I hoped Betty was wrong.

The bell rang and Freedom Boy strode into class, his shoulders square and a huge smile on his face. He had on his crisp navy blue pants and a freshly ironed shirt with the Academy insignia on the breast pocket. I felt sick. I didn't want him to be involved in any nefarious schemes.

Dr. Mann walked in wearing a white lab coat. The feed was crystal clear. He went up to his desk and shuffled some papers around before announcing, "Good afternoon, class, and happy Annihilation Day. Today, in honor of the holiday, Glanton would like to give a speech about the event. Please take the podium."

J5 got up. Dr. Mann walked over, took something out of his pocket, and adjusted the boy's collar. Then J5 said, "Before I begin, let's give a round of applause to this semester's independent learners. They have been crucial for the Academy, and humanity." He recounted the exciting events of Annihilation Day, taking every chance he could to diss Misshapes in his flat voice. It didn't seem like J5's powers of persuasion translated on camera, because I was bored out of my mind. By the end of the speech, I was mentally calling it Mediocre Day. Who really cares about some Frenchman torpedoing ships with his bare hands?

"Thank you, J5. You really are doing a tremendous job, but I wouldn't expect less from a Glanton boy," said Dr. Mann.

A smattering of applause came from the group. They resumed their normal postures. J5 went back to his seat.

Dr. Mann took the floor. I was too busy murmuring in George's ear about how I wanted the pizza delivery right away, hot and fresh, to pay much attention. He just kept talking and talking.

"I would like to say a few words in the spirit of Annihilation Day myself. We have trained you in these hallowed halls to hone your natural skills, your powers, so that you may protect the world. And you've done well. But can you really say you've made any progress?" He looked around the classroom.

"The word 'progress' has become a dirty word in the modern vernacular. In academia it is seen as 'elitist.' Why? Why is progress considered filthy?" Dr. Mann pointed straight at Freedom Boy. "Because progress requires improving the world. Making it a better place. And to make a place better requires judging something wrong with the world." He paused. "Judging some people as wrong."

"There are too many imperfections that are tolerated. I am unable to ignore those things. I am incapable of looking past them, seeing the world as beautiful in its imperfections." He sneered like he had smelled something bad. A chill ran down my spine. "I hope I can instill within you this feeling. This feeling that the world is not right as it is."

He sounded like a preacher. "Your greatest achievement is not your fighting of crimes or your saving of innocent lives, but rather your mere existence. You are the next step in humanity. You are progress. We are progress. And yet we have not advanced beyond relatively small numbers. Why, if the fittest are to survive and breed, are we not the dominant among the world?" He was addressing the camera. George's camera. Dr. Mann's ears grew long like a dog's and he made a high-pitched noise. This was not the suave, confident Dr. Mann who I had met; this was a different Dr. Mann, a Dr. Mann who believed every word he said in a way that scared me and sent chills down my spine.

"No," Markus said, shaking his head. "He's playing to the cheap seats."

"What is this?" Johnny asked.

"Those noises. He's onto George. I think he senses him somehow."

"How?"

Alice cried, "He's seeing with sound. Like a bat does." She blurted that into the mic. I saw the flicker of George's flesh.

"Oh!" I said, loudly. "Oh, Georgie!" I was laying it on thick. I heard a small "gross" burst out of Johnny's mouth.

Dr. Mann continued: "There are some little insects that may work their way into even the highest places. Little flies on the walls that need to be stomped on. Insignificant little nuisances."

I knew George wanted to run, to get out. Looking at the screen I wanted to do it for him. But Dr. Mann moved across the classroom and stood in front of the door. The exit was blocked.

"Vermin need to be destroyed or they will grow from small nuisances to large problems. A simple moth can destroy the most elaborate computer in the world."

As he spoke, he transformed into a giant humanlike spider hybrid. His legs multiplied, turning shiny and black. His face stretched out, and his eyes transformed into large black circles. His mouth made some strange back-and-forth motions before large, sinister fangs poked out of his tarlike gums.

We lost it for a second. Alice shrieked. I was in shock. We stopped reading. And then George's terror overcame his embarrassment. In an instant, he was physically there, naked in front of the class, shivering in fear. Time was frozen. Then the class laughed. It finally hit him that he was standing naked in front of Heroes his age. His hands disappeared and he had turned invisible again.

Before anyone could react, he was pulling up the window, jumping outside, and running across the field. A loud clatter. The camera dropped. The screen went blank, a close-up of some fuzz on a linoleum tile.

Johnny bolted out the door to find George.

In the cabin, we were all fighting.

"Screw those heroes!" said Hamilton. "You can't trust them."

"I liked Dr. Mann," said Wendy in a small voice.

"But he doesn't like you, honey," said a Spector.

A noise from the computer made us jump. The camera was down but not out. We could still hear what was going on in the classroom.

"Well, that was a distraction," said Dr. Mann. The class laughed. "How's the mission going, Freedom Boy?" My ears perked up.

Freedom Boy replied, "It is going well. No new news to report, sir."

"You're doing important recon on Misshape habits and ways. It's very important. I need to know how they—"

"Way to date for your Academy!" someone said to him.

"You're getting in Robertson's pants, right?"

It took me a second to realize what was going on. Even though he basically said it.

Freedom Boy wasn't dating me for me. He was dating me to *spy* on me. On us.

Everyone stared at me.

Alice gave me a hug. "He's stupid. Forget him."

It started to click.

Our whole relationship was a lie.

He was off and on for a reason. Not because of inner pain or important missions or anything. He was just getting information for Dr. Mann. That's how he knew everything. All those missions and dates. A setup. He wasn't interested in me at all.

I typed a quick message: *Don't ever talk to me again, Freedom Boy!!! – S*

Alice grabbed the phone from me before I could hit SEND and she read the message.

"You know I've wanted you to tell him this for months. But not now."

"Why?" I asked.

"Sarah, they'd know. You know they'd know. They're watching you."
She wrapped her arm around me.

It was like a Mack truck hit my chest. Dr. Mann walked toward the
camera and lifted his foot. A loud shriek blasted out of the speakers,
and the screen went black.

FORTY-THREE

WHEN JOHNNY got to George he had run halfway across town but was fine. It had already started to rain when Johnny found him. And it didn't stop raining.

Over the next few weeks, the streets of Doolittle Falls became dank with rain. I turned on the weather channel and the meteorologist showed a map with clear skies everywhere but a five-mile radius over my head.

It took some time for it all to sink in. Dr. Mann was after the Misshapes. He was not to be trusted. There seemed to be something going on with J5 and brainwashing, too. I looked up the collar and apparently the Superhero Bureau requires all people with mind-control powers to wear collars to prevent them from having undue influence on people's actions.

Then there was Freedom Boy. I waited a week to send the text I wrote that day. He never sent a response. I hated that this bothered me the most, but this wasn't a case of someone dumping me and making me feel like crap. It's the idea that our whole relationship was built on a lie. That it never really existed in the first place, even though I had feelings for that jerk. I had gone through so much for him, for us. I knew I was getting attacked on blogs and Freedom Boy fan pages, and it was just so he could spy. His car was probably bugged. All those Academy kids got to listen in on my dumb girlish excitement about being his "girlfriend." I bet they were all laughing at me.

Everything in town reminded me of him. Buzz Man, where we had our first date. His stupid face on the Harpastball booster poster, plastered in every shop window. The statue of his grandfather in the park. The spot on the Marston Heights hill where his house lights shone, twinkling over the town.

When I walked by the Hero fan store I almost lost it. One look inside, with its bounty of Freedom Man and Freedom Ex-Boyfriend paraphernalia and I was crying hysterically. I had to sit down on a bench to catch my breath.

The next day I got a call from Dr. Mann's secretary. He wanted to see me that afternoon. I was nervous and tried to put it off, but she said he wouldn't take no for an answer. I thought I was done for. Now I had seen his true face. I knew how intense and creepy he could be when he wanted something. But what choice did I have? We still didn't know what he was planning.

The whole day we tried to make sense of what we'd seen. I kept welling up whenever anyone mentioned Freedom Boy, and Alice had to console me in the girl's room for a record three times in one day. Johnny was convinced they wanted to kill us all. Kurt agreed with him and said we should strike preemptively.

"You mean kill them first?" Alice asked incredulously.

"Well, if it comes to that sure, why not. They have it coming," he said.

Markus and Alice thought it was bad, but not that bad. George, the only one who had been there, disagreed.

I didn't tell anyone about Dr. Mann's call. I thought it would worry them or they'd try to talk me out of seeing him. I wanted to march into his office and demand answers, and an apology. I was worried it was a trap.

I sat in his waiting room until I was led into the office. Class was still going on so people were flying around the halls like any normal day. I had this vision of me slamming my fist down on his desk, telling him, "I know all about your evilness," and playing the hero. But the cat got my tongue. I felt like a mouse.

He called me into his office. He pulled out a seat for me, and sat at his desk. He looked me square in the eyes and said, "Let me cut to the chase."

I held my breath. Waiting for the sword to drop on my head.

"I want to offer you a spot in the second-year class at the Academy next fall."

I was stunned. I'd waited my whole life to hear those words. And here they were, coming out of the mouth of someone I no longer trusted, out of the mouth of someone who considered people like my dad and Butters to be wrong. Vermin in the way of true progress. It made me sick.

He continued: "Now, you'll have some catching up to do over the summer, but we can provide you tutors, so you're not behind your peers. But we've seen tremendous growth in your skills over the past year and I've convinced the board that your abilities should outweigh any lingering concerns about your family and friends."

All I had to do was keep my mouth shut. It would have been so easy. Shake his hand and begin my life as a Hero. Not after what I'd heard. Not after what I'd seen. He was right: I had grown a lot. Enough to not let a line about my family and friends slide.

"What concern was there with my family and friends?" I said. "They mean a lot to me."

"Sarah, you have great potential. And an offer for a place in the Academy. Don't blow it because you're surrounded by people who you're better than: Your mother is a menace to this country, your brother is a delinquent, your father is a lowly Misshape with a factory job." He looked at me for a moment, encouraging me to think about it. "And all your friends are Misshapes without futures."

I grimaced.

His voice grew in power and strength. "Here, this place, this is your future. I know you may be conflicted. That is good." He chucked to himself. "But remember, those are just the people you've been forced to associate with because of the problems with the Academy. Not problems with you. The people here, this school here, *this* is your destiny. We chose you, Sarah."

I stood up. "Thank you for the offer," I said. "I'll need to think about it."

He stood up to shake my hand. When he clutched mine, his skin transformed into reptile flesh, scaly and green. Small spikes poked out of the backs of his hands and his hair bristled. As he began to speak, his perfect flat teeth turned into sharp fangs.

"I know about your little spying adventure. We take that very seriously here and because I see great strength in you I won't hold that against *you*. Like I said, there are choices you need to make." His temples pulsed. I could feel an animal strength in his grip. "So far I've been impressed with you. I expect you won't disappoint me. You have until May to decide."

He released my hand and then returned to normal. I was shaken but tried not to show it. As I walked out he called to me, "My secretary will show you the way out."

His secretary saw me, smiled, and slowly peeled off her gloves. She reached out and touched my hand. I realized I had never seen her without gloves and never touched her skin, just as I was passing out on the floor. The last thing I remembered was the drop ceiling of the office.

I woke up later in the middle of the Harpastball field. I didn't know how I got there. I checked the time on my phone. An hour had passed.

My right shoulder was sore. I craned my neck around to look at it and saw a small black-and-blue mark. I also noticed some gauze and a Band-Aid in the crook of my left arm. I pulled it off and saw the small purple mark over a vein. They had drawn my blood and given me some kind of shot. I was about to put away my phone and head home when I got a text message from Johnny.

COME HOME IMMEDIATELY, it said.

He never wrote in such a forceful tone. I rushed home, clutching the welt on my arm.

He was sitting in the front yard in a lawn chair. He looked at me and his face dropped. "Sarah, we're going to the quarry."

FORTY-FOUR

A TEXT MESSAGE seems so weightless. It's just a bunch of characters on a small screen. Numbers, digits, exclamations, and emoticons. Insignificant, right? But sometimes that string of letters and words, so ephemeral and fleeting, can crush you.

After I read those three words I never looked at my phone in the same way. I'm not sure if I reevaluated text messages or the power of words to communicate something horrible. To carry with them the weight of the world.

Something's happened to George at the Quarry.

I sat silently in the passenger seat as Johnny raced through the streets, over the Miskatonic crossing, and through the woods.

Hamilton had sent the message. Fifteen minutes after his thumb pressed the square SEND button, we were pulling our car up to a makeshift parking area. There were sirens blaring and red and blue lights flashing. It was surreal to see a place, usually so empty and serene, filled with so much sound and light.

Hamilton was standing alone. His face was ashen. His eyes were bloodshot and filled with tears. The only other people there were paramedics or police.

As we approached him, we were stopped dead in our tracks by what was in front of us. What Hamilton was staring at. A small body lying on a stretcher, motionless and covered with a white blanket. It was George. It had to be. And George was dead.

SPRING

FORTY-FIVE

I WENT NUMB after George's death. The days blurred together. The weather went haywire. It was early in the spring, but the air around me was a terrible freezing mix of hail, frozen rain, and very high wind. It was like a cold blast on my face every time I stepped outside. I had to wear a balaclava to keep from freezing my face. Lightning clapped erratically and the sky filled with odd clouds that looked like blue eyeballs. Tulips, half in bloom, froze in the ground. The small buds on trees froze. Branches became heavy and cracked off trees. Sometimes I thought the blue eyeball clouds were staring at me.

I couldn't think about anything. I could barely breathe. It was worse than anxiety; it was like being a rat in a cage. Half the time I gnawed at the bars frantically. The other half of the time I just stared at them.

The cops talked to every Misshape. It was intimidating, but it didn't amount to anything. George's death was first labeled "mysterious" and made the front pages. I wanted to tell the cops to talk to the Academy, to show them that this accident had to be retaliation from Dr. Mann. Johnny told me to keep quiet. It would implicate us more than them. I hated him for it but he was right.

When the coroner's report came out, George was sent to the back of the paper. The blurb said he drowned to death and had a large amount of alcohol in his bloodstream.

It happened every year. Another drunk kid at the quarry.

We fought about it in civic responsibility.

"From missing person of interest to just another punk kid who probably had it coming," said Johnny.

"George never drank. He wasn't a punk kid. That report makes no sense at all," I said.

"Sarah," said Alice, "Johnny's right. To them, he was just a teenager—a Misshape—screwing around. What can we do?"

"We have to do something!" I said.

There was no reply.

George's family banned the Misshapes from attending his funeral. They wanted it to be small, immediate family only. We sent flowers. I wanted to be there. I wanted to run up and pound on the casket like people do on TV. I wanted to scream at them for not demanding the authorities investigate. But who was I to say what they should do? They had lost a son.

School had a vigil for George outside. It was run by the principal and the student government. They told us that counselors would be available if needed. The last of the snow had melted and everyone tried to politely deal with the massive mud pit that used to be our football field.

We lit candles while some terrible Sarah McLachlan song about angels played. I knew the song by heart since it was always soundtracking touching TV moments. It was about a drug addict stuck in a terrible hotel room dying. It didn't feel applicable to a teenage boy. The song played and all the kids who had ignored or hated George held their candles and clutched at each other. Megan gave a speech, tearing up beautifully. The clouds formed small bulbous eyeballs, which turned a lurid red. They stared at us like a field of devils.

A curfew was put in place in the town for all kids under eighteen. Harris High blamed the Misshapes. We ruined football and now we had ruined nights. They had forgotten about the forced camaraderie of lighting candles in the gym.

Time crawled by. Winter was gone, spring was nonexistent. It was hot all the time. I wasn't sure where the year had gone. The Academy tried getting in touch with me. I didn't reply to their phone calls or letters. I let my voice mail fill up and I hid the letters in the corner of my room.

I wore a rotating series of drab dresses to school. I put them on mechanically, like a uniform. I was just so hot all the time that I couldn't think.

All of the Misshapes were on edge. Every time I looked outside I saw those creepy eyeball clouds—mammatus—staring at me from the heavens.

One day, I was walking down the hall with Markus. A few lacrosse kids in front of us were griping about the curfew.

A player said, "It's not fair that we're being punished for some stupid Misshape who can't handle his booze. What the heck was he doing swimming in March anyway?"

Another interjected, "Just like a Misshape. They're such a pain in the ass, with their worthless powers, and all the accommodations our school has to make. And what? They just act like idiots and go and get themselves killed."

Markus walked faster. Toward them. I was very uncomfortable. His hands balled into fists. "Markus, just let it go?" I said.

One of the boys continued: "They should have had a party instead of a vigil for that kid because it's—"

Markus's right fist hit his jaw. The kid dropped like a wet sack of flour on the floor.

Markus yelled, "Anyone else think George deserved to die? Say it now, because I will take on every single one of you bastards."

A teacher had to pull Markus off one of the other lacrosse players.

The rest had already fled. Both Markus and I were sent to the counselor. He talked to us about loss and appropriate coping while I stared out the window, watching one of those sticky summer rainstorms in April, when even the air clamors for relief. The great world flooded. I wanted to wash it all away.

The air was thick with ghosts. When I got home, there was a letter sitting in my mailbox, addressed to Sarah Robertson. It was Sam. He was in Boston.

I needed to get out of town.

FORTY-SIX

A FTER I read Sam's letter, I gave him a call. He told me to come to Boston. Just get on the bus. He was going to India in two days for some PeriGenomics-related charity work. Something about crops and the monsoon season.

I told Dad and Johnny that I needed to get away. They didn't want to let me leave, especially after everything that was happening, but I promised them that Sam would take care of me. They figured I would be safe under his care.

"Just as long as you don't go see that Freedom Boy," Dad said.

I hadn't told him what had happened.

"I never want to see him again," I replied. "You don't have to worry. We're done."

The trip was long. Too long. Partly because the terrible weather followed me, and, therefore, followed the bus. My mind was racing as I sat on the bus to Boston. It wasn't much better once I took the car ride out to the facility on the shoreline. I had a list of problems. The last thing on my mind was the offer to enroll in the Academy. I couldn't really believe it. It had consumed me most of my life and now it was way down on my list of concerns.

So many things had happened so quickly. George was gone. Freedom Boy...that just hurt. The horrible Maximum Fighting bout. And then there was Dr. Mann. Seeing him in front of that class, talking about the Misshapes like that, like they were nothing. And then he summoned me and told me that I was in. An Academy attendee, a Hero-to-be. Thanks to him. Just like that, with a snap of his fingers. My mind felt like a giant cloud of random thoughts, just ping-ponging around.

"So what are you going to do?" Sam asked.

"About what? Freedom Boy, the mysterious plan to destroy all Misshapes, and, you know, whatever the deal is with my not completely disappeared mom?" I said.

"No, Dr. Mann's offer," he replied. "Because it's, like, a good place to train and all. But there are other options."

"What other options?" I asked. It came out more mournfully than I meant it to sound. But it didn't seem like there were other options.

"Let me show you," Sam said.

We wore giant orange parkas with fur-lined hoods, like we were in Antarctica. The parkas said PeriGenomics in black lettering on the front. He had "borrowed" them from work. The field was empty. The wild grass had frozen. It crunched under our feet. The company owned a plot of land along the coast, with some small research buildings, and a rocky coastline abutting the Atlantic. It shouldn't have been so arctic; it was April. But Sam and PeriGenomics were using this little corner of the coast for something.

Sam and I held hands in a circle of two. The mittens were so heavy I couldn't even feel his hands beneath them. Just a handlike shape. I closed my eyes at his instruction and we started to concentrate. It was hard, focusing and managing all the emotions, but I had Sam there to support me. We were in it together.

Very slowly I felt the air start to lift. A small cloud formed and grew. It pressed on, expanding second by second, so slowly that it felt like an eternity passed. Dusk turned into night.

I heard Sam whisper. "Focus," he said. His words carried in the crisp air. It was the first time I had felt crisp air since George had died.

I could feel our powers converging. Starting to build together.

The cloud rose and rose. Even though it was outside me, I could feel the cloud like it was in my chest. Like I was the sky and it was growing inside of me, filling up every part of my body. Even though it was well below freezing, I felt warmer and warmer.

I removed my gloves and reached out for Sam again. I touched his hand and my small hand curled inside his warm hand. A spark shot up into the sky.

The cloud spilled from horizon to horizon, growing darker with each space it filled. I was burning up. Sam was, too. Beads of sweat were forming on my forehead. I wanted, desperately, to unzip my parka, but we were in the middle of something big.

Snow fell. When it got near our circle, it sizzled, creating a mass of foggy water vapor. The world whited out around us. When Sam let my hands go, I threw off my parka and hat, slipping out of my boots. He stripped down to his underwear. We were in a protective bubble of warmth.

Energy started to build in the cloud. Its hollow interior spun around and around like a whirlwind. With each rotation it grew stronger and stronger. Steam built up around us. Encasing us like a blanket. We had to breathe heavy to get oxygen back in our lungs.

I could feel the power of the storm grow. We were making it grow. The air under the anvil was ready. I just had to focus. Sam clutched my hands tighter.

"Now," he said.

I reached into myself and let go of everything, every last bit of energy, strength, fear. It poured out of me and filled the sky. And then, with a deafening crack, a huge bolt of lightning shot down and hit our bubble. The electricity flowed all around us.

Bright blue light was everywhere. Our shield kept us safe, but I could feel it surge around me. It seeped into the ground and melted the frozen world. When I finally let go of Sam's hand, we were surrounded by a soft wet earth and a halo of char.

FORTY-SEVEN

W E PASSED out from exhaustion in our warm bubble. When we awoke, the sun was shining and there was dew on the grass, which was now soft and warm. Sam looked at me and said we needed to get going.

Back at the PeriGenomics facility we ate some breakfast, and then some more, and then more. Piles of fruit and cereal and eggs. We were both starving.

Sam turned to me and said, "Come with me."

"What?" I asked. It was the first thing he'd said, really, all day. "Where?"

"Come with me. To India. I can get you a ticket through the company. I'm sure they'd put you on if I asked." He smiled.

"Is this what you meant by other options?" India. Not Doolittle Falls.

"Yes. Train in the world. You don't need an Academy or those institutions. You saw how powerful we were together last night. Imagine if we teamed up; we could do so much good in the world. I need you. The world needs you." Sam looked at me, his eyes soft. There was an opportunity here.

I wanted to say yes. It was so easy. So convenient. Sam and I, traveling around, solving problems, and probably becoming a thing at some point. There it was. Right in front of me. I just had to say yes. I wanted to say yes.

But I couldn't. Sam was just an escape. I thought about Johnny, about the crazy look in his eyes. He needed me. Everything I had and knew was in Doolittle Falls. I needed to go back. I needed to help out.

"Sam, I want to. I really do. But people need my help. Running from them would be the most cowardly thing I could do, even if it is to help the world. I couldn't live with myself. A storm's coming. I need to be there to help stop it." If I wasn't there, I don't know what would happen to my brother.

He looked at me with his gentle eyes, ran his hand down my hair, and said, "You really are something special." They were good words, setting down somewhere, small and sure, inside my heart.

Sam gave me a ride to the train station and I headed back to Doolittle Falls. I slept for the whole bus ride.

When I got back to Doolittle Falls, the weather was finally approaching normal. The next day, in school, Ms. Frankl handed out permission slips. She said we needed them signed by tomorrow because she had arranged a field trip for us in lieu of class, and we'd get to miss all day at Harris High. I wanted it to be tomorrow already.

"Where are we going?" a stray voice asked.

"The quarry," she replied.

FORTY-EIGHT

I HATED THE quarry. I could picture the sirens and swarms of police and EMTs. A shock of yellow police tape still clung to a tree and flapped around in the wind when we arrived. It was unsettling.

We sat down in a semicircle. I took my usual spot between Ms. Frankl and Alice.

Ms. Frankl pulled a small, rectangular wooden box out of her satchel. She opened it up and called out students' names. When someone's name was mentioned she handed them an index card. I got mine after Hocho. As I grabbed the paper and looked at it I realized what she was handing out. Our index cards. The ones we had to fill out on the first day of class. I read mine quietly to myself.

Sarah Robertson
Can control the weather with my emotions
200 Robin Lane
Doolittle Falls, MA 02212

There it was, staring at me. I didn't know what she was doing. I looked around to see a similarly puzzled expression on everyone else's face. What was she up to, and why did she pick the quarry to do it in? It was where George died.

After she got through the whole class she began again, this time handing out index cards. I was thoroughly confused. I got my second index card and read it. It said:

> Dorothy Derringer
> Can fly up to one foot for ten seconds
> 10 Park Street
> Doolittle Falls, MA 02212

As I tried to figure out who Dorothy was and why I had her card, Ms. Frankl began to talk. She was holding up a card. "George Herbert. Can turn invisible when embarrassed. 18 Boylston Street. Doolittle Falls, MA 02212."

"Class," she continued, "I have given you two cards. One is the card that you gave me on the first day of class. The second one is a card that I made for you with a fake identity on it. As the teacher of your civic responsibility class, I am required to hand over the cards you filled out to the local Bureau of Superhero Affairs. This is my job and my responsibility. I was not told what they will do with this information, and all my requests for clarification have been met with silence." She stood up.

"George's death is a tragedy and a waste. It's awful. Just awful." She had to take a moment to regroup and blot away some tears. "I know that everyone seems to be trying to help you through this, while at the same time they are treating you like you were responsible in some way. The anti-Misshape sentiment is high. You're being treated like trash and it's unacceptable and I wish I could do something to help other than to tell you things will get better. But that's not true. We need to make them better. We can't wait." She opened the box again.

"These cards may mean nothing. They may just be a way to keep attendance. But if you have the same feeling that I do, they mean something greater and far more sinister. No one outside the school knows who's in this class. The administration keeps those records confidential. I'm going to ask you to put one of the cards back into this box and then place the other card in the center of this circle."

She walked around and we weighed our future in our hands. What do we do—keep doing what we're told? Subjecting us to an oppressive system that kills our friends? Or would we resist?

For me, the choice was easy. I put Dorothy in the box that Ms. Frankl was sending to the government.

After all the cards were collected, Ms. Frankl lit George's card on fire and placed it on top of the pile of other cards. They all burned. Sarah Robertson burned. The girl from Robin Lane who could control the weather with her emotions. The girl who had been weak and unsure of herself. Who looked to the outside for approval. To places like the Academy to tell her she was worth something.

I held Alice's hand as we went up in flames.

After the cards were reduced to ash we all took turns talking about our anxieties and remembering funny moments with George. Then I heard the *Ring! Ring!* of my phone. I walked away from the class and tried to turn the ringer off. I was fumbling with my bag when the phone rang again. Betty was calling me repeatedly and it didn't look like she'd stop until I picked it up.

"Hey, Betty, what is it? This isn't a great time."

I couldn't hear any words on her end. Just loud breathing and whimpers. Then the deluge. She was crying hysterically. "I'm sorry, I'm so sorry," she bleated.

I felt bad. I hadn't meant to be so harsh. "Aw, it's okay, Betty. What's going on? Are you okay?"

Sniffle. "No."

"Why?" I asked, pacing back and forth. "What happened?"

The line went silent. She took a deep breath.

"I killed George."

FORTY-NINE

BETTY'S WORDS hit me in the gut. What did she mean by "I killed George"? Did she actually kill him? Give him a free drink before a swim? From the sound of Betty's soft whimpering on the other end of the line, I got the sense she needed to confess. It had been a month since he died. Her voice squeaked and crackled with guilt. Her secret must have been gnawing at her.

I gave her a few reassurances that it wasn't her fault. It didn't feel safe to talk about it on the phone. I was feeling paranoid. The lines could've been tapped. We needed to meet somewhere with no one around. Face to face.

I took a moment to think about where we could meet as she wept over the phone. And then it hit me—midday on a weekday? Johnny's failing record shop. It would be completely empty, I was sure of it. I told Betty to meet me there in ten minutes.

I told Ms. Frankl I had a family emergency and she said I could slip out, as long as I did so quietly.

When I got to the record store, Pete, the owner, was in the back room stacking boxes of vinyl. I waved hi, and he ignored me. Betty was in a corner, listlessly flipping through the Prince section. She was dressed down in a ratty Academy gym shirt and had a makeup-free face. She looked at me with baleful, puppy dog eyes, and immediately cried. I looked around, trying to see if she was making a scene, but there was no one else in the store.

"It's okay, Betty," I said, and handed her some tissues so she could wipe her eyes. "Let's keep browsing and you can talk to me, okay? Whenever you feel comfortable." I flipped through the old albums as she stood next to me, trying to do the same.

When she calmed down slightly, she started talking. "It was so horrible. I was ordered there after it was over. Dr. Mann had been there the whole time, along with Humungulous and the Aqua Kid. George's body was floating on the surface and the whirlpool Aqua had drowned him in was still spinning wildly. I was so scared."

"Did they threaten to hurt you? Is that why Humungulous was there?" I asked.

"No, worse. They threatened to hurt you, Sarah, and Butters. They said that Halloween was just a warning."

"What?" I asked. "Why?"

"When someone at the Academy found out that Butters and I were seeing each other, Dr. Mann threatened to kick me out if I kept seeing him, and a bunch of the A-team beat him up."

"Academy kids beat him up?" I thought Admiral Doom's cronies attacked him. Freedom Boy practically confirmed that to me on our date. But then again, I had no reason to trust him about anything.

"It's all my fault," she said.

"I had no idea. But what does that have to do with George's death?"

She stuck her face in my shirt again for another round of fresh tears. As she caught her breath, she said, "They were just trying to threaten George. Scare him, to send a message. I know they didn't want to kill him. The Aqua Kid and Humungulous looked petrified when I showed up. Humungulous kept muttering that he didn't mean to while Aqua stared at the body like he could make it come back to life. They called Dr. Mann. He was the one who told them to do it, so they didn't know what else to do. Dr. Mann wanted to make it look like George's fault to everyone but the Misshapes who had spied on him. Send a message. He cut George's arm and made me touch the blood that pooled out."

"You're the reason the coroner thought he was drunk."

"Yes. Yes, I am. I'm so sorry."

"Did they say anything about their plan?"

"No, it was big and they didn't want to ruin it."

I was frustrated, and even though I felt bad for Betty, I snapped, "C'mon, Betty. I know you know something. What are they planning?"

The entrance buzzer went off while I was speaking, muffling my words.

A booming voice that could only belong to Freedom Boy bellowed, "They plan to destroy all of your powers. You, and every last Misshape in town."

FIFTY

I DROPPED A record when I heard his voice. It landed at my feet.

So this was it. George got killed at the quarry and then they sent Freedom Boy after me. I guess it was fitting.

I stared at him sideways. "You, you're not supposed to talk to me. Ever."

"Look, I followed Betty here. I thought she might be meeting up with you," he said. He looked guilty.

"Why are you here? Tying up loose ends for your overlord?"

"No, it is not like that," he said, looking ashamed.

"It's not like what? It's not like your teacher bullied my cousin into covering up my friend's murder? It's not like you pretended to go out with me just to gather information for your evil cronies at the Academy? It's not like you went around viciously attacking Misshapes and blaming some supervillain? It's not like what?" I blurted. I saw Pete pop his head out of the back room.

"No, no, no. Not at all," he whispered, noticing Pete was paying attention. "I am not here to hurt you. Why would I do that? You are the only one around here I would even. . . I mean, I am here to help you." He moved toward us.

I held up a Rolling Stones record like it was Freedom Boy armor. He couldn't seriously think that I would fall for this again. "Help? You? The guy who dropped me out of the sky from a mile up in the air? Fat chance, Freedom Tool." He already hurt me. Being here was just redundant.

He looked genuinely hurt when I said that. Maybe he wasn't trying to play me.

Deep down I still wished it was all a misunderstanding.

"Sarah—I liked—I do—like you, really. It was not all some show. And I was not involved in any of those attacks."

"Last week?" It sounded shady. I didn't believe him.

"It was a Dr. Mann plan. A distraction. A way to cover up what he was really doing. He has J5 working on brainwashing the elite class."

"You mean the one you're in."

"Yes," he admitted solemnly. "That one."

"For what?" asked Betty.

"It is not good," he said, shuddering. "I had nothing to do with George. When I heard what happened, I stopped going to school. Sick leave. I cannot even step into that place."

Betty nodded vigorously in front of me. "He's been a ghost."

"Okay, but tell me this—if all the elite kids are brainwashed, how are you *not* brainwashed? How is this not part of the evil plan? I can't trust you."

"Brainwashing is not a switch. For it to work you have to have a willingness to be hypnotized. Some people are just more susceptible to suggestions. Especially when they are working against Misshapes." Freedom Boy, dressed down in sweats, did look like he'd come straight from the sofa after playing video games for weeks.

"Fine, maybe I believe you. I still don't trust you, but maybe I believe you. Tell me the plan and get lost."

His eyes turned down and his face drooped. Every time I told him I didn't trust him it was like kicking a puppy. A muscular teenage puppy that had been okay with ripping out my heart while dropping me so I went hurtling through the sky on our first date, but a puppy nevertheless.

"Look," he said, and scanned the place. "I can tell you but not here. It is not safe."

But even if Pete was watching us, he couldn't hear anything. "Dude. Pete the owner has been deaf since the Rush concert in '79."

"Sarah," Freedom Boy whispered. "I am not worried about him. Dr. Mann has eyes and ears everywhere."

They'd been spying on me, so who's to say they weren't spying on each other? "Fine, but it still has to be public. And I'll want my people there."

"Okay. I actually wanted you to meet some friends who want to help," he shot back.

I thought about it for a second. "Sure. Let's meet. Tomorrow night. Under one condition," I said.

"What?" he asked.

"You have to give me something, so I know I can trust you. Something to give us leverage and safety," I said.

He looked at me and smiled, then walked up and whispered into my ear, "I'm allergic to peanuts. If anyone finds out I'm a dead man."

I smiled back at him. It was so absurd. One of the most powerful superheroes in the world could be felled by a peanut.

"Okay, that buys you a ticket," I said, and walked out with a still-weepy Betty.

FIFTY-ONE

ALICE KNEW exactly where we could hold the meeting. She made some calls, and she got the diner to close for a few hours. In exchange, she had to deal with a raccoon problem that they were having with their Dumpsters. We filed in around eleven, staggering our arrivals so it wouldn't be suspicious. People paired off in booths. Butters and Betty had a love nest in the corner, crowded by the Spectors. We all sat around waiting for Freedom Boy. I was alone, staring at an empty seat.

Then the door swung open with a loud swoosh. Freedom Boy spotted me and walked straight to my table.

"Hi, Sarah," he said and sat down.

I didn't respond. I just stared at him. I could hear Alice whisper in the kitchen. He studied my face, confused. A waitress walked by and put two small white plates in front of us. In the center of them was a peanut butter and jelly sandwich, with peanut butter spilling out of the edge. He looked down at it, his eyes wide.

I lifted the sandwich up to my mouth and took a huge bite. When I put it down the waitress walked around and gave everyone else the same order. They picked up the sandwiches in unison and took huge bites out of them.

"Did you tell everyone?" he asked.

"No. Just Johnny," I said. He looked over at Johnny, who was spreading the peanut butter over his finger and lapping it up while staring at Freedom Boy. "They just think it's an intimidation thing. But I thought you should know where we stand."

"It is not like that, Sarah," he said.

"Then what's it like? Explain to me what spying on me, and pretending to like me even means." I stopped myself. I wanted to scream at him and cry at the same time.

"That is not how it was planned. Dr. Mann found out about our thing and then asked me to discover a few things. I do like you. I want to help," he said.

I didn't want to believe him but he sounded heartbroken. Cheap dinner plates clanged against tables. "Let's just start with what you know."

Dr. Mann had designed a machine. This machine would infect everyone who had weak supernatural abilities—Misshapes—and eliminate those genes from their bodies. It tapped into the specific makeup of the HrO gene. Every Misshape in town would end up losing their powers. People with strong enough genes, the ones they felt deserved to be Heroes, would be fine.

"I saw a machine by the field that made a purple monster out of smoke," I added, lamely. I was still trying to process the news.

"That is it," he said. "They have been experimenting on it for a year. Mostly during Doom raids."

"Why does he want to eliminate Misshape powers? It's not like they affect the Academy. Or Heroes, even." Eliminate. Scary word. Would I lose my powers? I imagined feeling sad on a sunny day. How would I feel about that? Relief?

"He thinks they make Heroes weaker. He calls it ridding the Academy and the world of all the barnacles that are eating at their hulls—"

"Lame metaphor," I interrupted.

"Yup. I think he has gotten annoyed about the legacy students and big donors. He really wants a pure class of Heroes, and everyone else with powers to be eliminated."

"Eliminated like…lose their powers, or something else?"

"The former. I hope. It is unclear how it works, exactly."

But there was one thing I didn't get. "So how does the machine attack only Misshapes?"

"It is designed as a bioweapon to target specific genes. But there's also a vaccine, which he has given to select students in the Academy, and he's convinced some other deans to do likewise, though I'm not sure if he told them his true plan or just said it was for the flu," said Freedom Boy.

I put my hand on my arm where I'd gotten the strange bruise after my last visit with Dr. Mann. Was I immune?

"I think I got one of those," I said. "When I went in to meet with him."

"*Two* of those, you mean. There are two shots," he said.

Damn. Then again, Johnny and I may have genes for natural immunity. But we didn't care. Genetics or not, we were Misshapes.

"Any idea how it can be stopped?" I asked.

"You need to break the machine. It is pretty tough though. I think it was made by PeriGenomics. And it is heavily locked, except when they use it," he said.

"When's that?" I was shredding my napkin.

"Two weeks. Dr. Mann is going to unleash it on the town. He will probably use the Harpastball field. That is where all the tests have been. But it will be guarded."

My mind raced. I wasn't sure what to do.

I said, more to myself than to him, "That doesn't leave us much time. We'll need a plan."

"I can help," he offered up.

It was clear we needed him. We needed all the help we could get. But I didn't trust him. Even after all he'd just told me, and the apology, what he had done still hurt. It was hard to look him in the eye. I felt like I'd start crying or getting emotional. Instead I got mean. "You're probably in cahoots with Dr. Mann. What's in it for you? If you really want to help us, you should just stay out of it."

"I know. You have no reason to trust me after what you saw. But let me at least try to convince you. Meet with me tomorrow." He grabbed a pen and wrote something on a napkin, pushing it at me. "Three o'clock. I will show you why I need to help." He took a breath. "Why you can trust me."

I frowned. Alice murmured, "I got your back. I'll keep your head straight."

Freedom Boy was twiddling his thumbs. "Just this one thing."

"Fine," I said.

He walked off, the door clanging behind him. All the Misshapes rushed to my table. We had a lot to discuss.

FIFTY-TWO

THE PLANNING started in the diner, went all night, and even spilled over to class the next day. "That sounds pretty bad," said Mrs. Frankl, taking it all in. "Are you sure it's all true?"

"No," I replied. "But enough of the facts match up. The shot, the purple cloud, the attacks on Misshapes. It makes sense."

"I've heard from a couple of squirrels that they've seen the purple cloud a lot recently. Like they're preparing for something," said Alice. "They're scared of it."

"Of course it's true. I'm surprised they're not trying to kill us," Johnny opined.

After that, everyone in the class jumped in.

"They probably do want to kill us," Wendy said. "An untested virus targeting our genetic code isn't the safest thing in the world."

"They won't care what it does. As long as it eliminates Misshapes," Hamilton yelled.

"We should get them first," mumbled Kurt.

"We need to warn people," Wendy said.

"No, that won't work," Johnny said, shutting her down. "Remember how George's family responded? People won't believe us. They don't question anything; they just go along."

Everyone seemed to agree. Heroes ruled Doolittle Falls. Misshapes were second-class citizens.

Butters muttered, "Most of them might not fight even if they knew the plan." The room fell silent.

"Maybe we shouldn't fight," Doodlebug said. "Do you really think it's worth it? Taking on superheroes and the Academy to save our worthless powers?"

"But I like my power," said Hocho in the back.

"I don't. Finding water? How lame is that? And in exchange I get a lifetime of discrimination, restricted from all sorts of things that my power doesn't even help me in, get picked on at school. No, thank you." Doodlebug was fuming.

"Maybe he's right. What good have they done us? Maybe we should just let them take it. We can't win," said Lou Ferlinghetti. There was a pause. The words sunk in. A gloom settled over the room, like the fog rolling in over the playground.

I looked out the window, watching the gray clouds. This attitude couldn't stand. Somebody needed to say something. It was my turn. "Yes, we can. Yes, we will. This is our town. These are our powers. This is our fight."

Mrs. Frankl smiled at me. I was finally learning something from her.

"I'll kill them if I need to. My powers, my rights," Kurt muttered.

"I don't think it will come to that, Kurt," Alice said to him.

"Fine, I'll join. But we'll need a hell of a lot more help. I don't think singing do-wop or having small woodland creatures attack them will help us much." Kurt found the jerkiest way to state the truth, all the time.

Alice and Butters glared at him.

"That's enough. We'll have people," I said, quickly.

He was right though. We needed help. And fast. But who could we trust?

FIFTY-THREE

THE NEXT afternoon, Johnny drove me to the secret address. On the way over, we assessed our strengths. Johnny had some ideas on how he could use his powers, and I was getting pretty good at lightning strikes. But we would both need some serious practice.

Johnny had spoken to Rosa. He told me that she was eager to join our side. He was worried about her. "She's not like the other kids. She got into the Academy on scholarship. Her grandmother and father moved up to Doolittle Falls with her from Mexico. If she gets kicked out of school—and Dr. Mann threatens her all the time—it's not like she starts going to Harris High. They deport her and her family." Clearly they had something going on. It wasn't like Johnny to trust anybody.

"What can she do?" I asked.

"Create earthquakes. She told me once that when she got her powers she hunted down the gang that killed her mom and swallowed them whole into the sand. Pretty badass for somebody at thirteen," Johnny said.

"You are so in love. I can't believe you told her all our secrets. She must totally be able to move the earth under your feet."

"Shut up. How about Kurt? He's pretty useful if we're near water."

"Yeah, and a mental hospital. That kid's a psycho. He scares me."

"He's not that bad. He's just had it rough. Besides, he doesn't hold it against you and me even though he and his mom have to stay in the trailer park by the Miskatonic."

"Hold up—he doesn't hold it against you, Johnny." *He's a jerk to me,* I thought. "Didn't PeriGenomics buy everyone houses?"

"They wouldn't take it. Didn't like the terms."

"I still don't trust him." I wanted that to be the last word on the subject.

"I trust him more than Freedom Boy. I don't even know why you're giving him a second chance. Or is this a third? He's probably just being used by the Academy and his dad to find Mom."

"Maybe. But we need him. I want to give him a chance. Call it a feeling," I said. I meant it. There was something new about him lately. Vulnerable.

"Is it his soft, kissable lips?" Johnny took it to the edge.

"Shut up!" I said, and hit his arm.

"Don't hit the driver!"

We pulled up in front of a medium-size brick building. It was down the block from where Butters had stayed and looked like it was part of the hospital complex. A pretty nondescript place to house some dark secret of Freedom Boy.

I opened the car door to leave and Johnny put his hand on my shoulder. "Sis, don't fall for it."

"You got it, dude," I said. "I promise I'm not falling for anything. Not again."

I went into the building. Freedom Boy was waiting for me in the lobby, looking gigantic and dwarfing a couch with a dull blue pattern. There were various logos around the room for the hospital, and a giant board indicating the different medical offices that occupied the building. The fifth floor was occupied by a single unit. Before I could make heads or tails of it, Freedom Boy was in front of me. But he wasn't in costume this time. He was just wearing jeans and a T-shirt.

"You ready, Sarah?" he asked.

"Sure," I said.

"Chill. You seem stressed. No tricks. I'm just here for a regular visit and wanted you to come along." We walked to the elevators. "Let me take your bag," he said. "No photos, electronics, or recording devices."

"Where are we going?" I said, as the doors closed and he pressed the top button on the elevator panel, floor five.

"This is one of the hospital's facilities. It also the home of the Exochositis Long-Term Care Ward."

I thought about the Exochositis walks and the depressing documentary. "Who are we visiting here?" I asked.

The doors opened. He turned to me, looked me straight in the eyes, and said, "My sister."

I wanted to ask him a thousand questions, but the gravity of the situation forced the air out of my lungs. All I could utter was a simple "Oh" as we walked up to a desk where a nurse sat with a clipboard.

He had a sister. A sister who nobody knew about. A sister who never, ever got mentioned in anything regarding the Family Freedom, whether it was press, documentaries, rumors, or the awkward family photos. Why hadn't anyone ever mentioned her?

The nurse said, "Aaron, so good to see you again."

She doesn't call him Freedom Boy? I thought everyone called him Freedom Boy. I guess his name is Aaron. Wow. I can't believe I didn't know his name.

"You too, Nurse Thompson."

"Just call me Fiona. Who's your little friend?"

"Sarah, she's here to meet Linda."

She held out her hand and we shook. "Don't you mean Freedom Girl?"

"How's she doing?" he asked. The nurse's happy demeanor faded.

"Not great. She was doing quite wel, but took a turn for the worse over the weekend. We've had to put her back on the ventilator. The new antigravity device from PeriGenomics isn't working as well as we would have liked. And we have her back on intravenous nutrition." She put her hand on his large shoulder. He looked so deeply hurt by the news. Just seeing his face made me want to cry. "I'm sure she'll pull through this."

He bit his lip for a second and then looked up. He was pulling a brave face. His voice got more bombastic. "Of course, she will. Freedom Girl always does." He couldn't keep up the façade for too long.

The nurse led us down a hall and around a corner. The ward was a lot calmer than the hospital. Rows of glass-doored rooms lined the hall. They hid their occupants with drawn curtains.

Each room had a TV, a pile of complex monitors, and someone lying in a large gurney bed. As we turned the corner, a number of occupants were sitting at a small round table in an alcove playing cards. A few others were watching a communal television.

The nurse walked and updated Freedom Boy. His sister was hooked up to a machine that could read her eye movements, which she could use to communicate with us. She'd been sleeping a lot and may not be up for too much.

"She experiences significantly more gravity than most other people, and she's incredibly vulnerable to even the slightest diseases. The opposite of Freedom. A girl in a bubble," she told me.

When we reached the room, the nurse let us in. She told Freedom Boy that if he needed anything, he could get her or another nurse through the call box on the wall, then she left. He grabbed my hand and led me into the room.

Freedom Girl looked a lot like her brother, if someone had deflated him like a balloon. Her face was pale and gaunt. Above the clear plastic breathing mask covering her mouth there were a pair of deep-set eyes that shone with the same stunning Freedom green. Every part of her seemed frail. Skinny arms, legs so thin her knees seemed enormous, and a distinctly visible rib cage underneath a metal box device with all sorts of buttons and lights. She was lying on something shiny.

She seemed about my age. It was hard to tell. I had never seen her in school. She must have gone to the Pre-Academy Preparatory School when I was at Doolittle Elementary. Freedom Boy walked up to her bedside. For a second, her eyes shone like Christmas lights. I took my place on the opposite side of her bed.

"Hi, Freedom Girl," he said.

Words began to type out slowly on a screen above her head. As the letters appeared, I noticed her eyes were darting back and forth. She seemed to be focusing on a small flat-screen positioned a few feet above her. *Hi, Aaron,* she typed. *I'm so glad you could come.*

"I wouldn't miss it for the world," he said and smiled.

I've been tired, but I wanted to wait up to see you, the screen responded.

"Well, you look great, strongest fighter in the family. Fiona said you'd be better in no time."

Good as new in under a week. The letters were coming out slower every minute she typed. Her eyes shut on occasion, causing the occasional typo.

"I wanted you to meet my friend Sarah. The girl I mentioned last time." She looked at me after his introduction and I wasn't sure what to do. I gave her a big smile and placed my hand in hers and shook slightly. I could feel her return the shake slightly, before her arm went limp again.

Sarah, she typed, before a long break. *It so Good to meet you.* Her eyes shut before I could respond.

After a beat, I said, "I think she's asleep," half asking, half telling.

"She's probably pretty tired." He placed his hand on her arm and she didn't stir. "Yup, out like a light," he said, with a deep sadness in his voice. I guessed he was hoping for a longer visit.

I looked at his sleeping sister. The shiny thing that she was lying on was attached to her by a string around her neck.

"Is that a cape?" I asked.

"Yup, genuine superhero cape."

"Where'd she get it?"

"I gave it to her on her twelfth birthday, a few months after the problems started. It was originally from Dad. He was going to give it as a present when her powers emerged." Freedom Boy paused. "That didn't really work out. After all the doctors and the tests we had to take her here. Dad left on some mission, fighting a supervillain in Vancouver or somewhere, I don't remember. He couldn't deal. My mom tried to push the whole thing under the rug."

This was a different side of Freedom Boy. I was learning far more about him and his family than I had ever learned on our dates.

"I found the box wrapped up in the back of their closet and brought it to my sister," he continued. "She hasn't taken it off since. That year we had a birthday party for her. It was just me and a couple of friends. I gave her a card and said it was from the whole family. She bought the Vancouver story. I don't even remember what excuse I gave for Mom." He was starting to cry.

It was hard to see him cry. I patted his back and said, "It's okay."

He kissed his sister's forehead and we walked out of the room. We sat at the rec room table in silence.

Then, suddenly, Freedom Boy turned to me. "Sarah, look, this is my real life. Not this Hero stuff. Or the Academy. Or the documentaries.

All that seems meaningless. I mean, it is meaningless. This is real."

"I'm glad I met your sister," I said.

"He's been holding it over my head, you know. The whole time."

"Who?"

"Dr. Mann. The same device he's going to use to take the powers away from the Misshapes. He claims he can use that to fix my sister. He's convinced that it's better for the world to take away people's powers without asking them. Like it's his right."

"But why did you stop helping him, if you can save her?"

"It goes against everything I believe in. Powers are a gift. A privilege. You're supposed to use them to help people. I save people. That's what I do. My sister wouldn't want me to give in to him. She'd be ashamed of how much of a jerk I've been to you. To all the Misshapes. I want to do what I can to help the Misshapes. I mean..." He trailed off, resting his chin on his hand. He looked so sad and hollow.

"I face down a bank robber and I do it easily because I'm gifted. I don't know if I could face what you guys deal with every day. People kick you in the face and you get back up again. You're real fighters." He stopped, his voice getting quiet and serious. "If my life means anything, if my stupid costume and all this attention for being the great Freedom Boy means anything, I need to fight next to you."

"Even if it means that you get kicked out of your school and your father disowns you?"

"Yes. Dr. Mann got everyone who knows about it convinced that it's for the good of the school and the world. That it will help people. But I know enough of evil to know that your safety and well-being isn't what he has in mind. I know people could die and he could care less. He might kill Misshapes and no one will notice. No one else sees it, but I do."

I took out a piece of scrap paper from my pocket and wrote down the time and place of our next strategy meeting. I slid it across the table, and left it in front of him. It was fine. He could be part of our team. He would be the best fighter that we'd have.

"Don't be late," I said, and walked off, leaving him at the table.

When I got back down to the street, Johnny was sitting in the car blasting The Reactors and bobbing his head furiously. He turned it down when I got into the passenger seat.

"Thanks for waiting. Freedom Boy is in," I said, never more sure of anything in my life.

Johnny had doubts. "Sarah, he tried to kill—"

"He's in," I said. "We can trust him."

"Okay. I got your back, you know," he said, starting the car and driving us home.

FIFTY-FOUR

WAS I scared? Yes.

I was terrified.

White wispy clouds rose off the grass and condensed in the chilly morning air, edging up toward the smudged thumbprint of a sky. It felt like we were standing in a cloud. This weather was all my fault. My fear made the wind blow wildly and my depression created a permanent drizzle. Combined they formed a deep-set fog, which rendered the world in silvery shades of gray.

We all stood at the six-hundred-yard line of the Harpastball field. Johnny wore his THIS IS NOT A RED SHIRT T-shirt for the occasion. He had made me a T-shirt, with WEATHER GIRL scrawled across the chest. My favorite costume, bar none, belonged to Hocho. Using wire, he had attached shiny knives and scissors, the blades spread open, on a pair of heavy rubber gloves. He looked like Edward Scissorhands, like he could trim your hedges or take you out.

We had been meeting for weeks. Freedom Boy told us that May first was going to be the big day. It was also the day I was supposed to get back to the Academy with my answer. I had one for them now.

A team had come together. Not every Misshape showed up. Frank the Tin Arm bowed out, something about Vegas and a tournament and men in suits. Lou Ferlinghetti grumbled when we asked him to the meeting. He didn't want any part of it.

We met up at the field to take numbers and present a united front: Backslash, Johnny, Rosa, Wendy, Freedom Boy, Kurt, Alice, Butters, Markus, Hamilton, Hocho, and me. Our plan was to kill the machine, any way we could.

We didn't think too far into the future. We knew there would be a fight. What kind of fight, we didn't know.

I assumed that the Academy wouldn't try to kill us. But there was a big wild card. George. He got in the way and he was killed. It was an accident, though. I didn't think they wanted blood. But Dr. Mann didn't care. He was very influential. And from what Freedom Boy said about J5, he gave us a reason to be scared. Then there was Kurt. He showed up because he thought they might try to kill us. He wanted revenge.

We walked, side by side, lockstep, toward the far end of the field. We could see the Heroes. They looked like a row of faint little ants in the distance, standing in front of the machine. As we got closer, their shapes grew larger and more defined.

I could start to pick out who was who. The giant was Humungulous. The tall frame and silhouetted head was Dr. Mann. As we got closer, more and more Heroes came into focus: There was the Aqua Kid, the green-haired girl from the parade, Lindsay, a boy who could phase through things, a kid resembling a hippo, a bug boy, and a scientist in a white lab coat. J5 was encased in a plastic bubble on a Segway, rolling around the field like he was in the Pope mobile, barking out "A7! B29! Red 12!" Christie was on her own Segway, yelling something. The rest of the kids were frozen where they stood.

One more person came into view. I didn't notice him at first. He was smaller than the others. It took a few seconds to make him out. It took a few more to handle the shock when I did. It was Doodlebug.

He told us he didn't want to fight, that he couldn't care less if he lost his powers. I had assumed he would have been halfway to Canada by now. Instead, there he was, standing next to Dr. Mann. I wondered what they had offered him and whether he had snitched on our plan.

There wasn't much we could do about it.

When we got within striking distance of the Heroes, it was time for phase one. The nonessential Misshapes peeled away. Freedom Boy, Markus, and Wendy ran off to their hiding point in the woods. Backslash sprinted away to get the getaway car.

Johnny, Rosa, and I were lined up next to each other, facing the Heroes and the machine.

Johnny turned to me and asked, "You ready?"

I stroked my necklace, filled myself with rage and anger, and said, "Yes."

I stared at the pathetic bald head of the man who thought of me and my family and my friends as vermin. It rained. Large black clouds joined together into the sky and pushed upward to the stratosphere.

They mock us, treat us like nothing, and think that they can get away with exterminating us. They never expected anyone would get in the way of their plan, would just say no, would fight back. He thought he could buy me off with admission. Nobody's ever fought the Heroes before.

The day moved from moody to dystopian. It poured. Rain fell in buckets. The top of the rain cloud pushed outward, forming the perfect anvil. An anvil with an angry face on one end.

That is one badass cloud, I thought, and continued the rage parade. I kept an evil-sounding metal song—"Du Haas," by Rammstein—playing over and over in my head, so I could just think of that when I got tired.

Dr. Mann looked up from the machine and saw us approach. He pushed a button on the machine and purple smoke poured out. J5 yelled through his plastic bubble, "Smokey!" The drones followed suit, holding back and forming a human shield around the machine.

It was time to kill the machine. I clutched Johnny's hand, standing shoulder to shoulder with him and Rosa.

"Ready?" I said.

"Yes!" came the replies.

"Then go!"

Johnny made a fist and punched his hand into the ground. All color drained from his face and he started to pant. The water below us, pooling in the dirt, changed. It smelled noxious. Fumes rose up that were making me light-headed.

Over our heads, Dr. Mann's octopus thing was coming together, forming a large purple cloud with tentacles. It jockeyed with my rain cloud for position in the sky. I focused on my cloud, willing it to the right spot over Dr. Mann's machine.

"Now, Rosa!" Johnny shouted, his voice noticeably weak.

Rosa slapped both of her hands on the ground. It trembled. A large rift emerged from her hands, tearing up the earth and surging through the dirt. The fault line was headed straight toward the machine.

The chasm reached the machine and opened up the ground below it. It fell into the earth with a loud crash, and buckets of Johnny-altered rainwater poured down into the hole.

Purple smoke still poured out, viscous, thick, and evil.

The rumbling earth threw me across the field. I was splayed out on the ground, right next to the machine and a fiddling Dr. Mann. I got up, limping, and brushed the dirt off my pants. I yelled over to Dr. Mann, "I've made my choice. I think I'm going to have to decline your offer."

He grimaced at me. Still formal, even though he was trying to fix his machine, which was screaming in pain. "Sorry to hear that. You had potential. You're not actually here to try to stop us, are you? With your little earthquake and your little rain?" He wiped his brown. "Amateur. Such wasted opportunity."

Staying stoic and strong, I said, "Yes, we are here to stop you."

Dr. Mann replied, "Why? Most of them don't even want their powers. They're a hindrance." He slammed the side of the machine. "I'm giving you a gift. You and the other Misshapes."

The rain whipped our faces as I replied, "That's not for you to decide. That's for them."

"You don't have to be over there. You can be fighting with the strong. Fighting alongside the powerful." He turned his back to me, focusing on the machine.

"I thought fighting for the weak and powerless was what being a Hero meant." Johnny and Rosa ran up to me. Their work was done.

Dr. Mann turned to us. His nostrils flared, his skin turned green and scaly, his finger grew long and sharp. With a deep guttural grunt he yelled back, "Little girl, you have no idea what being a Hero means!"

Johnny whispered in my ear, "Do it now!"

"Get them!" Dr. Mann ordered.

I screamed—I screamed so loud that the Heroes stopped in their tracks. I nearly blacked out from all my rage.

A giant lightning bolt shot out of the sky. It zigzagged through the air and landed with a deafening crack in the chasm, hitting the machine. The charge ignited the alcohol-spiked water and a ball of fire shot out of the hole. The force of the blast was so strong that it knocked everyone on the field down.

The world spun.

My ears rang.

The world split up into multiple images and refused to reunite.

I felt for the ground but I was so confused I didn't know where it was.

I tried to get up but everything was spinning so fast I fell right back down.

A hand lowered to mine and helped me up. It was Rosa's. She helped me out of the grime. My clothes were covered in mud and cinched to my skin. They felt squishy and gross. I looked up to see the sky was filled with my gray angry cloud of rain. But it wasn't alone. The purple cloud, The Beast, was still there. There wasn't enough destruction. It looked weaker, more translucent, and ready to evaporate, but it still clawed at the sky. The machine was burned but still intact. A shower of electrical sparks flew up from it like cheap fireworks.

A few puffs of black smoke poured out, but the purple mist kept trickling upward. Dr. Mann came running at it. He yelled at the Heroes, "Capture them! We can arrest them! Your lives are ruined, Misshapes!"

Behind me, I heard the screech of a car's breaks. Backslash rolled down the window of Johnny's creaky car with a "Get in!" I threw myself in the backseat, next to Rosa and Johnny.

He hit the gas and we went nowhere. The tires spun wildly, kicking up torrents of mud. The car fishtailed left and right, while the Heroes ran after us. Smoke and the smell of burned rubber billowed into the car. We all coughed. My heart sounded like a marching band's drumline. We couldn't let Dr. Mann catch us. Not now. The fight wasn't over yet.

The tires whirred. They weren't catching.

We all silently chanted, "Catch, catch, catch."

Just as Humungulous was about to grab the entire car in his arms, the tires stopped spinning and we shot forward, the four of us pressed against the backseat.

The car skidded off the field and back onto the streets. I looked back and saw Freedom Boy flying off with the machine. Even in his large arms the machine looked huge. Purple smoke covered his face and trailed backward toward the cloud. An angry Dr. Mann cursed him. No one seemed to notice Wendy escaping with the Aerofail. Markus was close behind, leapfrogging with the other Aerofail in his hand, in and out of the air.

I didn't have time to track them as they flew through the sky. The plan was to meet up on the far side of the Miskatonic and make sure that the machine was killed, dead, and ruined with no chance of ever working again. If Dr. Mann or any Heroes caught us, they'd make sure we were put in juvie. Or the Luther Maximum Security Villainry Facility. Thinking about it made me shiver. My eyes were drawn to the large figures behind us. They were coming after us in the air and on the ground—fast and angry.

FIFTY-FIVE

"HIT IT, Backslash!" Johnny yelled from the backseat.

"I'm hitting it as hard as I can!" he shouted.

"Just slam the pedal," yelled Johnny.

The Heroes were rapidly gaining on our tiny little lead. A sharp metal star lodged in the trunk and burst. A chunk of the bumper fell off. I screamed as a boulder flew at us and blew up next to us. I couldn't tell where it came from. Laser beams and projectiles were pulverizing the back of Johnny's car.

More metal stars were coming our way. The girl with green hair was the one throwing them. She was in some sort of lavender superhero outfit that repelled the rain. The stars glowed neon green. When they hit the car, they stuck in the frame and exploded, melting away large sections of Johnny's old beast.

Backslash yelled to me, "Stop the rain! I can't see."

"They can't either. We need this," I shouted, turning toward the back window and shooting off a blinding lightning bolt behind us. It temporarily stunned the kid with laser arms, and he fell to the ground.

"How much farther?" Rosa asked.

"We're almost at the bridge."

"And you're sure there's soft dirt along the southern riverbank?" she asked.

"Yes!" I responded, just before Backslash made a sharp left turn onto the road to the old Miskatonic Bridge. The car groaned the whole way.

Behind us, the ground shook as the lumbering hulk of Humungulous chased us on foot. The green haired girl was still in hot pursuit, attacking with her endless stars. A boy on a blue circular sled came floating up next to her. He stared at the car and then began to shoot some kind of laser beam at the back window right at my head. It wasn't the thin sort of red beam for hot dog cooking, but a powerful, terrifying burst. The windshield glass was starting to melt and drip.

"Gun!" Johnny motioned to me and I grabbed one of the passel of water guns underneath the passenger seat. I opened the cavity of the gun and placed it in front of my brother. He dipped his finger into the cavity and passed it to Rosa.

Rosa leaned out the window and blasted the laser sled kid with a flash. The kid clutched his face and fell off of his device with a sharp yelp of pain. She did the same thing to star girl, who fell to the ground as well.

Rosa shot at Humungulous, but he just brushed it off with his giant hand and continued to chase us.

We had bought ourselves a tiny little lead, but Humungulous did not look like he was about to give up. And it wouldn't take the others long to recover.

"Why are they still following us? Don't they just want the machine back?" I asked.

"We crossed them. We're their enemies now," Johnny said.

"But it seems like they're not trying to capture us. It's like they want to kill us," I said.

"I don't think they want us dead; they just want to stop us. Capture us. Arrest us. They just don't know how to tone it down with their powers. We're not trained to capture at the Academy," Rosa said. "And Dr. Mann doesn't seem to care to teach us."

I wasn't ready for this intensity. The pushback from our aggression was stronger than I anticipated. A fight to the finish with the best Heroes in the country…how could we win?

Our next move was to get across the river and use it as a barrier to protect us. There weren't too many routes over the water so we'd have a tactical advantage. Hopefully, Freedom Boy destroyed the machine by then and could help us fight.

"Hold on, we're close!" Backslash yelled, before skidding into a vomit-inducing ninety-degree left that smushed everyone in the back against the car door. With my head still spinning, I could make out the bridge crossing the Miskatonic. It was an old railroad bridge with iron tresses. Blackslash gunned it to the other side. It gave us a little distance. With the sound of the Heroes racing through the streets, I wasn't sure it would be enough.

We made it to the other side of the river and spilled out of Johnny's wreck.

All the Misshapes were there waiting for us. I was happy to see them. I was hoping we would have good news for them but we didn't. We would have to continue the fight. If we were going to destroy the machine before it got into the Heroes' hands, we needed everyone.

They would attack us. They would fight us to the last man to get it back and not stop until Dr. Mann's plan was fulfilled. This would be our last stand, and the bank of the river across from Doolittle Falls was the best location to make that stand. If we could take out the bridge, we would have a river between us and the Heroes, and with the Aerofails they had no way to get to us. Behind us we had Hopper's hill, a hunk of rock and stone. We could hide there if things got really bad. I refused to look at it.

Alice and Butters ran over. They were glad to see I was okay.

"Did you do it?" Alice asked.

"Well, the plan worked but the machine still seemed to be working when Freedom Boy took it. Hopefully he can demolish it," I said.

"I hope so, too," said Butters.

As he finished, a swooshing noise came at us from above, like a rocket. The machine smashed into the ground in front of us with a loud crash. We all dove for cover. It dented but smoke still poured out of it. Freedom Boy landed beside it, red-faced and breathing hard.

"Damn it, this thing will not break. It is practically indestructible," he said, panting.

I looked up to see the purple cloud creeping toward us slowly. The Heroes were a few blocks away from the bridge, marching in lockstep with Dr. Mann. A small group flew ahead of them. J5 and Christie were on Segways, giving orders.

"Those two can be convincing," Rosa said. "If they're giving the orders for Dr. Mann, this won't be pretty."

I separated myself from the group. It was time to try to freak out the Heroes with weird weather. The sky was still dark and stormy, but maybe, maybe if I felt it, I could make some blinding sunlight peek through the clouds. I took deep breaths. I tried to will myself to happiness. My hands made small fists. Nothing. I would have to keep trying.

The small flying brigade swooped through the air in a tight V-shape. They all eyed the smoldering machine, their faces still red from the dousing. The green-haired girl was swinging an axe-like weapon in her hands, cutting at the air. Laser hands was back up on his floating disc, his face contorted into an angry snarl. A strong gust of wind made him tilt dangerously. All right, I silently thought, go me. A kid dressed up like a bird brought up the end of the air squad.

Freedom Boy stood on the shore, leaning forward, chest out, ready to fight the Heroes if they got near us. His body tightened and his fists clenched.

Just as they were about to fly over the opposite shore, Wendy and Marcus landed and flipped the switches on the Aerofails. Why would they want to fight us, I kept asking myself. Any minute they'll stop.

The Aerofails blinked to life. The green-haired girl blipped in and out of existence several times before being thrown off into the horizon shrieking. The laser-wristed boy managed to appear long enough to fire off a shot at us, but it went the wrong way—straight up into the air. Birdboy went sailing backward, confusion filling his face.

While the air team was feeling the effects of the Aerofails, the rest of the Heroes came marching onto the riverbank. J5 and Christie followed on their Segways. With a "Halt!" they stopped on the edge of the bridge like toy soldiers.

Trying to make the sun blind the Heroes wasn't working for me. I tried to work with the whirling wind that came from my jumbled-up thoughts. If I could only send the Heroes back across the river! Maybe Rosa would make a difference.

Rosa was in place.

"Get behind me," she yelled at us. "And hold onto something stable!" I found the nearest tree.

She spread out her palms and placed them at the base of the bridge pylon. Instead of fissures coming out from under them, this time her hands trembled. And then her whole body. It looked like she was having a seizure. Her hands began to press into the solid rock as she shook.

Nothing was happening. I was growing frustrated. The wind slowed down. I heard a crack of thunder in the air. A small storm grew, centered over my head.

And then the Heroes moved. They ran over the bridge in a straight line. When they got halfway, the ground began to shake violently. It threw the Heroes off the bridge, and they scrambled back to the other side.

I hit the ground hard. This time it hurt almost as much as when the machine died earlier. I knew I was going to need a lot of aspirin tomorrow. If there was a tomorrow. My thoughts were getting fuzzy, dazed and confused. I put my hand up to my face. There was blood on my palm. I had a nosebleed.

I looked over at Rosa, who was completely still. Both her forearms were entirely embedded in the rock.

The bridge undulated violently like a cement wave. I scrambled up to the road to get a better view, hurting every step of the way. Across from us, the ground below the Heroes was spraying all over the place, creating a small storm of dust. It looked as if the dirt was pouring out of a colander. It was literally sinking, uprooting trees and bushes as it separated from the granite. The ground tossed some of the Heroes around like rag dolls—Laser hands went flying backward, soaring through the air, like he was going back into Doolittle Falls proper.

Dr. Mann shook. We watched as he tried to steady himself and screamed, "Get back you idiots." At his words, they snapped to attention and scrambled off the edge of the riverbank, taking refuge on the ruined road.

The bridge stretched into the sky and snapped like a twig. Water splashed up and soaked the land, mixing with the dust that formed a thick, gritty cloud. Where there was once a small road on the other side of the river, it was now an enormous trough. It looked deep. I couldn't see the bottom.

Luckily, nobody seemed hurt. Despite their attack, I didn't want anyone to get hurt. Or even worse, killed. If only they could stop and realize their mistake. These were the Heroes, right?

We needed to hold our position until they retreated. The Heroes huddled together, glaring at us from across the obstacle course we'd created. They looked beat up and weary, hunched over and rubbing dust from their eyes. Everyone except Dr. Mann, who stood tall, staring at us. This was far from over. They were going to attack and keep on attacking until they got their machine back. No matter what it took.

FIFTY-SIX

I F THE Heroes got anywhere near us, that would be it. They would capture us, take their machine, take us back to Doolittle Falls, and hang us out to dry any way possible, if they didn't inadvertently kill us. They had great powers, and because of it, no responsibility. I was breathing heavy. I had never been so scared in my life. The words "juvie" and "supervillain prison" echoed in my mind like a demon chorus. The image of poor George was right there with them. The gloomy thoughts made the rain fall harder.

Freedom Boy was hitting the machine with all his strength, but to no avail. He picked up a large chunk of concrete and smashed it against the thing. The concrete turned to a fine dust, but the machine didn't even dent.

Every Misshape took a turn looking at it and trying to open it up. It was sung at, attacked by squirrels, filled with paint. It was useless. I had to fight the cloud with whatever I had. The cloud kept growing, but I think the rain weakened it. Kept whatever monster lived inside it at bay. But I could feel my powers growing weaker.

Across from us, the Heroes were huddled together, working on something. I couldn't get a good view.

"Alice. Talk to some bird," I said. "They can spy for us."

A few ducks were floating in circles, or curled up in the dirt by the riverbank. They all seemed confused by the massive sections of bridge speeding down the current. Alice squeaked something out and a few seconds later, a duckling came waddling up onto the road, looking for the sound. She made another squeak and the duckling squawked back at Alice.

"What's up?" I asked.

"She doesn't know. They're coming up with some kind of plan. That dweeby kid J5 is coordinating it. Oh, and that song just won't stop."

"Huh?"

Alice turned to Butters. "The duck is talking about some women in sequined dresses. What are you doing?"

"Okay," said Butters, "I have figured out how to make my projections hang out over by the Heroes, singing an annoying song over and over. It may be torturous enough to make them quit."

"The US Army used that on terrorists in Guantanamo, and to flush out some drug kingpin in the eighties who was hiding out in an embassy," said Alice. "Hell of a technique."

"What song are you using?" I asked.

"'Build Me Up, Buttercup,'" he replied. "I know I can't stand that one. My mom used to sing it to me all the time, so I figured by the thirtieth time around they might not be able to think straight."

We were interrupted. "They're attacking!" yelled Hamilton. We looked across the river. Humungulous had climbed into the giant rocky ditch that Rosa had made, his head peeking up over the edge as he peered at the rushing water next to him. With a quick movement, he pulled himself up, landing with a big thud on the outer circle of rocks, close to the water.

On his back hung the Aqua Kid, wearing his form-fitting blue Lycra suit and yellow goggles. Aqua dismounted Humungulous's mountainous form, looking over at us with cold eyes. He knew his enemy.

The Aqua Kid stood on the banks of the river and placed his hands above the water. It rose sharply at a single point in the center, like a wave.

Hamilton and Kurt sprinted down to the river's edge, next to Freedom Boy. Hamilton tried to pelt some paintballs toward the duo, but he couldn't get them on the right path.

Kurt yelled, "He's trying to create a tsunami," and he thrust his hand into the water. His arm turned a deep blue, which crept slowly up to his shoulder. The wave got smaller and smaller.

The Aqua Kid was tense, every muscle in his body shaking and convulsing. He tried to raise the wave, yelling so loudly that it sent a shiver down my spine.

But it was useless. Kurt fought him every step of the way. A slow-moving ripple was all Aqua could conjure.

Giving up, Aqua whispered something to Humungulous, who picked him up by his feet, made several rotations, and threw him with all his force across the water. He stretched his arms above his head into a swimmer's dive. He was more than halfway across the river before he entered the water.

Kurt had just pulled his hand out of the pool. He muttered, "This is not going to be pretty."

The Aqua Kid hit the water, but it seemed more like he was moving through Jell-O. By the time his torso was underwater, ice crystals were forming on him. He moved in slow motion through the river. Sensing the danger, he tried to leap like a dolphin out of the water. Within less than a minute, the surface of the entire Miskatonic as far as I could see was solid and clear as glass. Aqua was in the center of that frozen tundra, with a look of terror on his face and one of his legs splayed in a severe angle. I cringed.

Aqua shrieked and flailed his arms wildly, trying to move across the water. Despite his severe injury, he was still trying to attack us, slowly coming over to our side of the river.

All the Misshapes ran down to the riverbank. "What did you just do?" I asked Kurt.

"Same thing I did with that frog. Only with more water and a bigger animal."

"And so…" I trailed off.

"There goes his leg," Kurt said, dispassionately.

His answer hit me with a dull thud. It was like Kurt didn't feel anything. Maybe they wouldn't realize why. Maybe they'd attack and attack until we all were dead. The response was worse. Humungulous was inflamed. He always seemed like such a comic figure, with his tremendous proportions and long apelike arms. But now I could see him for what he was, a fleshy instrument of pure violence and rage.

His muscles rippled out and pushed his veins to the surface of his skin. I could see his thick neck bulging. It was thicker than three of me. His large hands could easily tear one of my limbs off, or the head of any one of us. The only thing between him and a group of Misshapes was a frozen river.

Humungulous swung his enormous arms and made a huge leap onto the icy surface. He remained motionless when he hit it and let his momentum carry him across the surface. As he slid toward us, the Misshapes froze in fear; there was nothing that we could do.

No matter where my mind went, it just kept raining. I was cold and wet. My body couldn't stop shivering. Every possible weather pattern just emptied out of my head. I looked into the sky and things were going bezerk. There was a cloud. There was the sun. Fog bloomed like a puff of smoke. My power was a remote control switching television channels. I needed to focus my energies and my emotion. It felt impossible.

Out of the corner of my eye, Freedom Boy was preparing for battle.

"You think you can handle him?" I asked.

"That big ape. Sure. Just need to adjust for that," he said, pointing at the Aerofail. I had almost forgot that with it in place, he would be weaker. I wondered if he could truly win against all that force.

Freedom Boy ran to the edge and took a large jump of his own onto the frozen Miskatonic. He hit the surface and began to slide directly toward the monstrous form of Humungulous. Within an instant of contact they were both on the surface hitting each other and wrestling. Aqua helped out as best he could, getting in a punch and pulling at Freedom Boy's cape anytime the fight got close.

For a few minutes I thought Freedom Boy had the best of him. As they slid across the ice he kept getting on top of Humungulous and pounding into his body with his fists. But the punches seemed to do no damage. Humungulous would turn over and get in a few hits. And each one of his hits looked like it hurt like hell. Like it was going to go right through Freedom Boy.

I couldn't tell what was wrong. In a horrible turn of events, Humungulous landed a straight hit across Freedom Boy's face and a bright red stream flew out of his mouth. He looked like he was about to pass out. The awful Maximum Fighting match flashed in front of my eyes.

In between hits, Freedom Boy lifted a feeble arm and pointed it toward me. But it wasn't toward me, but the machine next to me. The Aerofail. I realized what he was trying to tell me. With that thing on he couldn't fight to his fullest. But without it, nothing would stop the Heroes from flying up to destroy us.

I dove on the machine and feverishly tried to turn it off. The wind blew hard and when it came back I had to bat at it.

Freedom Boy mouthed "thank you" and seized Humungulous in a hold. The giant tried to counter and toss him around, but he was surprised to find Freedom Boy at full strength. Freedom Boy deflected the giant and Humungulous popped out of the hold and soared through the air, landing in a heap on his back. Enraged, the giant got up and charged at Freedom Boy. The ground rumbled. Just as Humungulous and Freedom Boy were about to connect and clash together, Freedom Boy stepped slightly to the side, grabbed the giant in a bear hug, and flew straight up into the sky as he wriggled helplessly in his clasp.

Suddenly, we saw Humungulous's enormous body flailing as he flew through the air. He hit the ice with an enormous *boom!* The Heroes looked on in shock. It took the green-haired girl a moment to recover from what she saw before she threw a net out to Humungulous and dragged him to safety. The same Heroes nursing Aqua ran over to help. Another Hero was busy setting Aqua's leg on the ice. It probably wasn't good to move it.

Freedom Boy landed next to me. He was breathing heavy and sweat was pouring out of him. I don't think I'd ever seen him even a little tired before.

"That was hard," he breathed.

"Yeah," I agreed, and looked over to the edge of the quarry. And my heart stopped. Realizing the Aerofail was off, our opponents had an advantage.

The entire Hero Academy A-team was standing on the perimeter of the frozen river. Readying their weapons and fists.

FIFTY-SEVEN

THE HEROES attacked. The flying ones pulled the nonfliers over the frozen river and onto our side. We stayed close to the machine. A flaming star stuck one of the Aerofails. It cracked in two. I grabbed the other Aerofail in my hands. If things got bad we could turn it back on and try to escape. But to where? And for how long?

They rushed toward us.

Betty took a bottle of pills out of her pocket, gulped one down, and handed another to Johnny. They gave each other a knowing look. She pulled out a water bottle and poured the water over their hands. Johnny took out his lighter and lit Betty's hands on fire, then his own. They looked at the Heroes and rushed into battle. The rest of the Misshapes followed behind.

"Whatever you do, do not let them get the machine," I shouted.

It seemed like a lost cause. We were protecting the device that was still working, somehow, draining us of Misshape powers. I was starting to feel weak but not as bad as the rest. The Spectors, still singing "Build Me Up, Buttercup," flickered in and out of existence. Freedom Boy, our best bet for destroying it, was too busy defending it to help cut back the throng.

One by one, every Misshape had a Hero to fight. Some skills were better than others. Hamilton was a combination of brute force and paintballs, firing them off into the faces and crotches of various Heroes.

I bet it hurt, too. I kept eying the machine. That was the real enemy—these guys were just a distraction. I held the Aerofail and retreated toward the woods. I needed to be less scared, so that the weather would be less crazy, flipping from rain to wind to tiny tornadoes at the whim of whatever I was feeling.

Rosa was trying to knock the Heroes over with small tremors. Anything to keep them off balance.

Alice tried to launch an assault but the squirrels weren't complying. Butters just had a stick and was waving it around and yelling. His Spectors had come back to our side, buzzing around and singing their hearts out. The Heroes swatted at them desperately. When the kid who could walk through walls had a direct hit, the air went weird and phosphorescent.

I felt a tapping on my back. "Hey, buddy!"

It was Lindsay. She had made it over the river, dangling from the talons of the green-haired girl.

She spit in my face.

"Ew!" I cried, taken aback. "Why would you do that? We were friends!" I said.

She glowered at me. "Freak."

I sputtered. I had one of the Aerofail machines in my hands. I thought about throwing it at her, but it would break, and we would have no backup. We needed Freedom Boy at full force, although I wasn't sure he would be enough.

Hocho popped up and cried, "I got your back. And her hair!" Hocho had Lindsay's shiny blonde hair in his scissored and knifed clutches. The Lindsay that I knew would've yelled at him and fought her way out of it. But this Lindsay was different. I looked at her. She muttered something, repeating, "Genetic freaks, Misshapes, mistakes. genetic freaks, Misshapes, mistakes."

Her gray eyes were empty. There were no signs of life there, even though she was breathing heavily in Hocho's arms. It was easy to defeat her. Just find her weak spot, her center of vanity.

"Stay like that," I said. "I don't think they'll move." I ran down toward the riverbank, still clutching the Aerofail. I looked at the on switch and eyed the flying Heroes attacking us. Not yet, I thought.

While everyone else was fighting, Betty turned her attention to the machine. She was trying to melt it or burn any liquid inside. It was hermetically sealed except for the vent that trickled smoke. They finally managed to start a small fire inside it, which slowed it down. Now noxious fumes poured out alongside a trickle of purple.

The clash shifted away from the evil machine. The air became thick. It was impossible to breathe.

We were outnumbered and overpowered. I tried to get in front of some Heroes fixing for Freedom Boy, but I was knocked over like a bowling pin.

I hit the ground, landing hard on my arm and the Aerofail. A ripple of pain shot upward. My knees were sticking out of the holes in my pants, cut and bleeding.

The Heroes got to Dr. Mann's evil machine. They grabbed it and held it aloft triumphantly. A smile ripped across Dr. Mann's face.

FIFTY-EIGHT

I LAY ON the ground in agonizing pain. I wasn't the only fallen soldier. Around me were all my classmates, my brother, Freedom Boy, my best friend, people who had volunteered and trusted me, people I had dragged into this fight. The Heroes had succeeded. They were huddled around the machine, ignoring us as we lay on the ground. Dr. Mann pressed buttons and it began to billow purple smoke again. Doodlebug looked pleased.

We had failed in our mission. The Heroes and Dr. Mann would make the machine work again. We'd be completely different people this time tomorrow. I wouldn't be a Hero. I wouldn't be a Misshape. I wouldn't be a Normal. I'd be nothing. We all would.

Alice crawled over to me. She was hurt. Every time someone tried to stand, a laser beam would blast them to the ground.

"You did good," she said.

"Not good enough," I croaked out.

I was growing weaker by the second. The rain had faded. The purple cloud had taken over the sky. I twisted my necklace. I just wanted it to do something, to make magic happen. I needed protection now.

But nothing happened.

Until it did.

Something red was flying toward us. It didn't look like an Academy student. It looked like someone I had seen before.

And then I noticed it. The symbol on his chest. The same one on my necklace. I first saw him that night—when I almost fell to my death with Freedom Boy—above the clouds, watching over me.

He had on a shiny crimson poncho that went down to his waist. His face was obscured by a red eye mask and a black hat with a razor-sharp rim. He looked like a spaghetti Western gunslinger. Underneath his poncho, he had on a skin-tight red bodysuit and black vest.

He flew toward the Heroes. A laser shot out of the sky right at him. He deflected it with his poncho and continued flying right toward them, veering at the last minute and heading to the machine. He unsheathed a long curved samurai sword, which looked like it was made out of a deep crimson metal, and plunged it into the infernal machine. The blade slid through it with ease, like it was made out of water. Nothing even happened until the blade was plunged in, to the hilt. Then it began sparking and smoking. A little at first, but when he removed the blade in one quick motion the entire machine erupted like a fireworks display. Then thick black smoke began to billow out of the neat hole left by the blade. Dr. Mann and the Heroes looked on in horror. The smoke stopped.

Heroes rushed at him. He retracted his sword and brushed them off like dirt on his shoulder. After dispelling some of them, he flew straight toward us. He landed in front of me and came to a soft skid. Then he took off his hat.

Curly black hair spilled out of his hat. It wasn't a he at all. He was a woman. A familiar woman.

I blurted out, "Mom?" I heard Johnny grunt the same thing.

"You called?" she said.

FIFTY-NINE

MY MOTHER tossed something at me. A stick with a ball attached at the end by a slim rope, both emblazoned with her logo.

"For strength," she said, and winked at me. "Now get up!"

Before I had a chance to react properly, the Heroes attacked again. She fought them off with amazing dexterity. In action my mom was incredible. I'd never seen her fight before, only in old movies and the occasional demonstration. She moved like a dancer, knocking down Heroes with grace and speed.

I got up and went behind my mother. I spun the ball around in a circle. "Don't mess with Lady Oblivion!" I yelled. "She will destroy you!" I felt intimidating. For once in my life.

The reinforcement invigorated us. Freedom Boy recovered quickly, following her lead and taking up the fight next to her. They were outnumbered in the air, and the green-haired girl was keeping Freedom Boy busy. Mom flew up to them and pulled out a dark black staff from her belt.

She looked like she was floating as she moved through the air, the staff a part of her. The object itself was so dark, the very definition of black, sucking in all light and color from the surrounding area. It was even able to suck in lasers. I wondered if it absorbed their power.

The green-haired girl pulled out a three-section staff that was radiating blue light. She swung it around like a helicopter blade. She attacked Mom, slicing her staff through the air. Mom blocked it, grabbed her weapon, and before she could let go, flung her like a top into Rosa's chasm.

The Heroes were looking weak. My mother had beaten them down. I had gotten some bops in with my tetherball weapon. It was less of an instrument of hurt than an instrument of hilarity, but it was intuitive and effective.

The Heroes fell and got back up, slower every time. The Aqua Kid, recuperating, gave a yell from the sidelines: "Why are we still attacking them? They broke our machine. I don't want to die for whatever stupid cause you're after, Mann, and I sure as hell don't want to kill for it. Not again."

His message started to sink in for the Heroes. I knew it.

Dr. Mann's eyes grew dark. He had rushed over to the machine after my mother had stabbed it with her sword. Doodlebug was busy tending to it, trying to make it work again. Dr. Mann had created some sort of individual force field around the machine, to protect it from us.

"You will do as I say," he yelled at the hobbling Heroes. "You are the most powerful the world has ever offered up. Are you going to let a bunch of Misshapes beat you?"

J5 joined in: "Now is the time to recoup your strength. That is what you're here for. Fighting the weak and insidious who poison the earth. It's what Heroes do."

"No," said Butters, who had walked up behind J5. "This is what Heroes do!"

He then punched him across the face so hard J5 fell to the ground.

"Doot, doot, doot, that's what Heroes do!" the Spectors sang over J5. He was on the ground, stunned, rubbing his cheek and trying to figure out what had happened.

"Stop it!" I yelled. "We're in this together, guys. You're being brainwashed by Dr. Mann."

Aqua, still semi-trapped in the ice, joined in. "That stupid Misshape is right." It changed things.

Little by little, all the Heroes and Misshapes stopped fighting. We stood shoulder to shoulder, all crowded together like we were at a party. I looked up at the sky and saw a sliver of sun peeking through the clouds.

Dr. Mann and Doodlebug tried to get the machine to work. They flailed at the metal, pressing various buttons, but to no avail. The purple cloud still hung over us but was growing weaker. I felt my true strength return. I put down my mother's weapon. My head felt clear and I was able to make it rain again. The rain made the machine grow visibly weaker. A puff of smoke came out of it.

We rushed forward, a limping army, trying to get at the machine. We couldn't get close, thanks to Dr. Mann's force field, but the Heroes and Misshapes combined their powers. It took Hamilton's paintballs and the strength of Humungulous. Rosa shook the ground again, plunging her hands into the dirt.

And it worked. Somehow. The machine split apart. Some combination of paintballs and rocking ground and Humungulous's huge force made the metal bend and warp. The machine wouldn't work anymore.

Dr. Mann, sensing the destruction, took another tack. He gave a loud bellow, threw his hands above his head, and evaporated into the purple cloud just like at the parade. We looked on in confusion.

I poked Alice. "What was that? Where did he go?"

"I have no idea," she said. "But it can't be good. I don't want to see his backup plan."

A minute later, we had our answer.

The purple cloud, which was barely a wisp when it left the machine, grew enormous. Like one of my super-bad-day clouds. It expanded and expanded until it covered the whole sky in a field of dark purple, like an upside-down mountain range. It rumbled like it wanted to storm. Like the cloud had a desire to rain, not just a physical need. I tried to control it with my powers but it was no use. It had a mind of its own. I could sense it. Dr. Mann was one with the cloud creature thing, and he was angry.

A drop hit the ground. It was big and thick and splattered. I looked up and saw more rain starting to fall.

Betty screamed. A small black creature was in front of her. It had popped up where one of the drops of rain had landed. It stood on its hind legs and had wings and large vicious talons on the base of its claws and feet. At the end of its birdlike face was a black beak with razor-sharp teeth. It looked like a baby dinosaur.

The mini size made it look cute and harmless.

That wasn't the case. In its dark pebble eyes I could see the rage Dr. Mann had shown before.

The creature only had eyes for Betty, like it knew she had betrayed his evil cause. It followed her as she scrambled up to the shore of the frozen river. It was too quick. The creature lunged for her, aiming for her neck. Gallantly, Johnny dove in front of her, getting in the way of its attack, and the creature landed at his forearm. It sunk his teeth into the flesh of his arm. He screamed.

Mom took off the black hat and threw it at the creature with all her strength. It severed in two, spurting blood everywhere. She ran over to Johnny to see if he was okay. Her hat was covered in dark blood. She dropped it.

I heaved a sigh of relief, but too soon. That was only the first creature. As the drizzle from the cloud turned into a downpour, the world was filled with them. They popped up out of the splatter of raindrops. Fully formed and ready to fight whoever was near. By the time someone figured out how to kill one, ten more had taken its place.

They appeared everywhere. The riverbank, the road, the wilderness. Even worse, they had us surrounded on the frozen river. We couldn't get up to the road out of town, or the street back in. It was like the only spot in the world that was infested with these little beasts was the space below our feet. And that space was shrinking.

SIXTY

THE CREATURES attacked. Everyone was pitching in, the hurt and the healthy. Some of the Heroes eyed my mom suspiciously, not sure whether to fight with her or against her. They choose to fight with her for their own safety, but I knew the minute this was over they were coming for the Bane of Innsmouth.

We should have been a force to be reckoned with—but we were exhausted and injured. The army of creatures forced us off the riverbanks and onto the frozen river, where we formed a protective circle in the middle of the lake, our backs to each other, fending off the creatures. Kurt and Lindsay teamed up to make sure that the river was icy enough so we wouldn't fall in.

The injured were placed in the center of the circle to keep them safe. One Hero with healing powers was busy tending to the wounded. She had managed to sedate Aqua. As the minutes wore on, the numbers in the middle were growing and the numbers in the circle were shrinking. Pretty soon the circle was so tight we could reach over the wounded and touch the person opposite us. Freedom Boy was at the end of his strength, same with Mom and the Heroes. Dead beasts were piling up around the circle like chicken wings, and yet more kept coming.

I felt like I was playing a game of Whac-A-Mole and I was terrible at it. My powers weren't helping, either. I felt useless, like I couldn't stop them. My rage was just adding more slippery rain on top of the creature rain.

And then we had a breakthrough.

"I think he's part of it," yelled Alice, clutching a bloody wound on her arm and waving at the sky. "Like during the parade"

It took a moment to click. That disgusting ant trick. Alice was right! I tried to remember what Sam had told me. Something about how Dr. Mann can change into bacteria and then lives as part of the cloud.

"That must be how he's controlling it," I said.

"Yeah, but how do we stop him? We can't kill a cloud," she yelled.

Then I remembered what Dr. Reveala had taught me about rain and snow. If I could freeze the water it would freeze the bacteria.

"There is a way, but I don't think I can do it," I said. "I need to make it snow." Snow would also annihilate the purple cloud and whatever juice it had left, whether it was Dr. Mann juice or evil-kill-all-Misshapes-everywhere juice. But I was far too weak for snow. "It's too crazy. I can't even do it when it's calm."

"If there's any chance you can stop them man up and do it!" Alice said, hitting one of the creatures with a stick. She was right. I swung my weapon around, weakly. The bopping that had come so easily ten minutes ago was gone. I couldn't connect with any creature. They just kept coming at us. The world was being taken over by vicious little beasts.

I felt a hand rest on my shoulder. Mom.

"I believe in you, Sarah," she said.

I looked up at her. She looked tougher than I remembered. Life on the run had aged and hardened her face. I missed her so much.

I felt a thrill settle in my chest. Somebody believed in me.

She was right. I could do it. I had to become the eye of the storm, the center of calm in between all this mess and hysteria. Let go of the world, my own self, and the chaos.

Practically hibernate.

The life of everyone I knew depended on it.

SIXTY-ONE

I LOOKED BACK into the center and saw Johnny clutching his bleeding leg. Rosa rubbed green superpowered healing stuff on his wounds. He looked up at me feebly.

I stepped out of my spot in the circle of defense and took a seat next to him. He clutched my hand, knowing I was up to something, and gave me a reassuring "You can do it, sis, whatever it is." Then he groaned in pain.

My heart was racing. Adrenaline rushed through my veins. The creatures seemed to be herding us together, to our, untimely, mini-dinosaur-pecked death. It seemed like such a small way to go, but clearly the bite of one was enough for a fatal wound.

As the rain poured, they multiplied, squealing and biting. Closing in on us. More kept coming, minute-by-minute. Pretty soon there wouldn't be people mobile enough to defend the wounded. To defend themselves. As much as I was hoping, wishing that cloud would just stop, I couldn't stop the rain right now. It was being controlled by a force greater than myself. Or at least one that thought it was greater than me.

I grabbed my necklace. It was a futile gesture. The necklace already did its magic. It wasn't going to call any great figure to help. That person was here, fighting in front of me.

If we didn't get this cloud, these dinosaurs, we were doing to die.

And it was up to me.

I was the only person who could save the Misshapes. Heroes. Everybody.

As I touched my necklace, I felt calm and powerful. Strong. It reminded me of my mother. Of Johnny fighting for his life, of Alice whomping these creatures with a stick and a toy gun. Of my family. Of my friends. The source of all my powers. The source of my strength.

I closed my eyes and lowered my hands with a deep breath. Around me, people were fighting. They had beaten back armies that were stronger than them, better equipped, armed with privilege and the feeling of righteousness. All united by some genetic freak of nature. We weren't just the unwanted. We had a purpose. The Misshapes had a purpose.

I had a purpose.

I let this goodwill swell up inside of me and release outward. I felt myself empty, my mind numb, my heart slow. I was still, letting the crowd move around me and push me like a leaf on the surface of the ocean. I felt nothing of the world. It was just me and the tickle of air through my nostrils. I jumped into the feeling of total emptiness. I was in this moment, using my hands and legs and feet and brain to be completely calm and still, like water in a glass.

And then a cold damp fleck hit my nose.

It was the most beautiful sight in the world. Snow. My mind flickered past millions of redundant conversations about the weather, about the snow and how it was "awful," "cold," "rough out there," and I smiled. They were wrong.

The clouds became a frosty purple. The creatures began to weaken but continued to fight. They knew their time was short. Ice crystals crept across their skin, formed blue clouds in their eyes, and coated their teeth. Their movements became slow. They were easier to fight. And easier to kill. When the snow hit the ground the new creatures that emerged were deformed. At first, missing limbs and teeth, then jaws and eyes, and finally just lumps of malformed flesh and bone. And then the wind stopped its howling. There were no new creatures.

Dr. Mann was going down with the ship. Those things were a part of him, and every part of him was dying. When I looked into their eyes I saw the eyes of Dr. Mann, enraged to the very end.

The sky looked like amethyst. It grew silent and the heavens slowly shook loose their frozen violet stars..

The snow piled up around us. The Heroes and Misshapes were strewn about the center of the frozen river like broken, used toys. We were battered but alive. And cold.

But what struck me was the emptiness. The silence. I looked at the Misshapes and I felt such a rush of love for them. They were all frozen and miserable, but alive. We were alive.

I looked up to see Freedom Boy smiling down at me. He flew down from the sky and gave me a giant hug.

The world came rushing in.

Mom scooped up Johnny in her arms. Blood still poured out of his wound. She walked over to me. The Heroes looked at her nervously. She watched them out of the corner of her eyes.

"I have to get him to a hospital. Soon," she said.

"Will I see you again?" I asked.

"Yes, honey. But I don't know when." She looked very far away, saying this to me. Like she wanted to say more, but couldn't.

"Why?" I asked.

"Because it's not safe. They're still after me and you won't be safe until they aren't," she said. "And I need you to be safe."

"Who? Who's after you?" I blurted out.

"You did great today. I love you," she said, and kissed my forehead. She then turned quickly and grabbed Johnny, murmuring words in his ear. They flew off together.

"I love you too," I said. I hoped she heard me. Freedom Boy watched her fly away.

"If it means anything," he offered, "I wouldn't have turned your mom in."

"It does, I guess," I said. It meant something. I felt like he had given me a piece of sea glass, found on the beach. Something I'd hold and treasure.

We looked at the damage.

Purple snow piled up and drifted into small mountains. Dead monsters lay bleeding into the snow. The last remnants of Dr. Mann. The Heroes and Misshapes were working together to cart off the injured. Markus had a pile of people in the back of the car headed for the hospital. The machine looked dead, a large gash torn in between the "i" and the "G" in PeriGenomics. Hamilton was already making a piece of graffiti art out of the machine, his paintballs humming. Betty went around lighting the snow, just to make sure that Dr. Mann didn't come back like a crappy horror villain. We had firelight and a purple sky.

We had done it. We had fought and survived. I could see it on our bedraggled faces. Beneath the sweat, dirt, and blood were slight smiles and grins.

I thought of something Sam had told me that day before he flew to India. Maybe I'd fulfilled my destiny in my own way, on my own terms. I looked around at all the people I had helped save, all my Misshapes friends whose lives I defended. A sense of pride swelled in me.

I felt like a hero.

And it was time for the next step. We had to figure out a way to get home.

EPILOGUE

S OMETIMES, SMALL towns have short memories. I thought the incident at the lake was going to mean made-for-TV movies and tear-filled interviews on the nightly news.

But weeks later, it was like it had never happened. It shocked me how much it had never happened. Like everyone told themselves that this incident was imaginary. Like Dr. Mann was some sort of fever dream. Dr. Mann never reappeared and everyone acted like he had never existed in the first place. History can be wiped clean if you try hard enough.

The Academy appointed a new dean, a sharply dressed woman who wore business suits and sunglasses.

Butters was convinced we were going to get a parade. He kept talking about it. "Of course, they're going to throw us a parade, huge, down the Avenue of Heroes in New York City. They did it when Freedom Man defeated the Black Heart. And when the Revengers foiled the Scrabblers's plans to take over the world."

"They're not going to throw us a parade," Johnny would say.

"Well, maybe not in New York, but at least in Doolittle Falls. I bet they're just buying streamers." His voice would trail off, like he was at the parade already. The Spectors would sing, softly, "You Can't Always Get What You Want."

We didn't want to break his heart. Actually, we almost bought into the parade thing. But then Kurt would say, "No. They won't. They don't throw parades for real heroes anymore," which would end the conversation.

Johnny thought it was a conspiracy. He was convinced there was a coverup and every resource imaginable was going into preventing the media from getting wind of the story. I had to agree with him. How could they just ignore the disappearance of Dr. Mann and the mild destruction we had caused the town when fighting for our powers and our lives? They quietly rebuilt the bridge. We each tried calling local and national papers. We got nowhere.

One day, after Johnny had gotten a reporter for the *Herald* to listen to at least part of his story, Police Commissioner Foley of Doolittle Falls came to talk to us. It was in one of our last civic responsibility classes. I had seen him on TV a few times. He was tall, with broad shoulders that looked even broader in his police uniform, and he had a large pockmarked face.

"Children, we've heard that some individuals have been trying to file false reports with the media about an incident with the Academy and a certain former dean. This needs to stop. Immediately. Or there will be consequences. A certain piece of property, a very expensive item I might add, which was owned by the Academy and the PeriGenomics Corporation has recently turned up seriously damaged. Some hoodlums seemed to have taken it upon themselves to try to destroy this billion-dollar piece of machinery. I can tell you now the repercussions of such an action will be severe if those perpetrators are caught."

Kurt smirked. It pissed the commissioner off.

He snapped, "Take this seriously, young man. We are not just talking jail time. Everyone involved will at least go to juvie for the remainder of their eighteen years, but they will likely be tried as an adult and put in the Luther Maximum Security Villainry Facility."

Conditions in the Luther Facility were reported to be abysmal and prisoners were regularly tortured. But no one really knew what it was like inside. Aid workers were always restricted from admittance. It was where they would send my mom if they ever caught her.

The commissioner bid us good day and left immediately. His message was clear. The machine they had tried to use against us was being used again to silence us. Johnny fumed, as did the rest of the class. Mrs. Frankl had to talk us down for the next week.

Rumors of what had happened still managed to get out. The Normals gave us some begrudging respect. They stopped slamming doors in our faces.

Freedom Boy was sent off to Europe and Asia for some kind of Hero Walkabout. From his e-mails, it was more like reform school. I didn't get any good-bye messages, just a cut-off text: *Sarah, I'm in trouble with señor Freedom. I'll be—*

Mom disappeared again. I wanted her back. A week after the incident, a man in a black suit came to our door, flanked by police and a man in a white lab coat. I watched my father speak with them. They had papers in their hands. Dad looked like he wanted to punch them, but something was holding him back.

He showed the men upstairs and as he did I saw the back of the lab coat said PeriGenomic in large letters. A few minutes later they came down with a single box. The one I kept hidden in my closet. It had her old Hero name written in Magic Marker on the side. Lady Outstanding.

The scientist was holding the shiny white skin. Her Hero costume. Even draped over his arm it was a sight to behold. The suit was made of a refulgent white material that was reflective.

When she fought her enemies during the day it would blind them so they couldn't see her while they attacked and were overwhelmed by flashes when she stuck back. During the night it could glow if she wanted it to illuminate something. It was form fitting and gave her a sleek, almost dolphin-like silhouette. She hadn't worn it much, maybe once or twice a year for an event, or if there was a need for her help. I may have tried it on once or twice. It didn't fit.

I think knowing she was still around and ready to fight had frightened someone. There was no need to take her things; she had a new costume now and she didn't need her old stuff. I think they came more to show us their power. To frighten us into giving her up. Their plan, I promised myself, would backfire.

On the final day of classes, when the last bell rang, Alice and I went down to the quarry. It had become a thing for us, a way to relax and put everything into perspective. I still missed George. We both did. It began to sink in over time. He wasn't coming back, no phoenix-like rebirth, even though we still sometimes expected him to pop back into existence, like he'd just been embarrassed for a few months and was finally confident enough to rematerialize. But that was just a comic book fantasy.

We spent the afternoon by the quarry talking about the year and our plans for the summer. Alice was going to start a business helping restaurants with health problems. She had made some flyers on her computer and showed me a few mock-ups. I was certain it was going to be a huge success. I got a job as a waitress at Walt Jr.'s Diner. It seemed like a letdown after the adventures of the year, but it was good money and I knew when I went back I wouldn't be taking any crap from Normals.

Alice tried to get a tan, lazing about in the sun like a cat. I wore a big floppy hat so I wouldn't be hit by any errant rays.

At first I didn't see the small black bird flying right at us. As it got closer, we realized it wasn't a bird; it was some kind of black jet plane that sliced through the air with a creepy silence. It landed with a loud splash and bobbed up and down a couple times before a hatch on the side opened. A boy jumped out of the hatch and onto an inflatable raft and rowed to shore. When he got to the edge of the quarry and pulled himself out I finally recognized him. It was Sam.

He walked over to me briskly, said hi to both of us, and then turned to me with a serious look on his face.

"Sarah," he said, seriously.

"Quite an entrance, Sam. Are you auditioning for a spy movie?" I asked.

"There's a storm coming," he said. His face looked pale. He was wearing a shirt with a tie. This was a very different Sam.

"Okay," I said. "Then why are you here, in Doolittle Falls?"

"It's too powerful for me alone," he said. "I need you."

"Need me?" I asked. "Why would you need me?"

"I realized something after you left. That night in the field. That was the strongest power I've ever felt. Together we can stop it, but only if you come with me now."

"I start work in a week," I said.

"Change your plans, Sarah," Sam said. "I have a job for you."

I didn't know how to respond. I turned to Alice but she just shrugged and said, "Don't ask me. Do you want to work at Walt Jr.'s all summer or do you want to fight storms?" Her smirk said, *Is this for real?*

I turned back to Sam. I had made my decision.

Sam took the wheel while I gazed through the enormous glass cockpit, looking at the town below. Alice waved good-bye, growing smaller and smaller in the distance until she was the size of an ant.

We flew north, over the town, over the Miskatonic, and up toward the clouds. Just as we were about to disappear in the white fog, my eyes flickered on another town down below. My mouth went dry looking at it. It didn't make sense. I couldn't believe what I was seeing.

I thought it would be scorched earth, husks of trees waving. Sheer destruction. But it was just a town, with neat little houses laid out on streets and cul-de-sacs. And two giant gray buildings that looked like binoculars.

"Sam, is that Innsmouth?" I asked.

"According to the nav unit," he paused. "I think it is."

"Where's all the destruction?"

Sam was looking straight ahead.

"What do you mean?"

We flew into the clouds and the town disappeared.

"It was supposed to be destroyed—my mom, you know." I was stammering. "She blew it up. She blew it up. She blew up my life." I shook my head. I couldn't believe it. "But it looks fine."

"Probably just hard to see from this height." Sam was awfully blasé at this moment. I wanted him to see it with his own eyes.

"Take it down," I ordered.

"What?"

"The jet. Take it down. Look for yourself."

"Okay," he said, then tilted the yolk down. The jet dipped below the clouds once again. We both looked at Innsmouth this time.

The town was in ruins.

There was nothing. Just large swaths of devastation, scorched earth, and rubble. The reactor was blown in half; the whale's tail was broken and burning. It was a completely different town.

"Looks pretty wrecked to me," Sam said, then headed back up. "You're making up stuff, Sarah. We need to start our mission." He shook his head, clucking softly to himself.

What was going on? Something wasn't right, or maybe I was just seeing things, making the world like I wanted it to be. I didn't want to know what the truth was.

I took one last glance at the charred husk of Innsmouth. As I looked, a flicker blinded me. The town emerged again, reborn.

ACKNOWLEDGMENTS

Many wonderful people helped this book come to life, including Tobias Carroll, Abby McDonald, George Pedersen, Amy Sprung, Sean Michaels, Andi Teran, Michelle Mizner, Laura Dowell Urban, Alexandra Roxo, Elizabeth Butters, Alex Asher Brown, Janet Ho, Julia Sero our resident Hero geneticist, and Bill Fitzsimmons. Thanks go to Jason Pinter and the team at Polis Books. Above all, we'd like to thank our families for their support, in particular our parents: John and Anne Donnelly, Alan and Sue Ellen Sherman.

ABOUT THE AUTHORS

Alex Flynn is the pseudonym for the writing team of Stuart Sherman and Elisabeth Donnelly. They met at a clandestine book club in Boston, where they broke into a fortified tower in order to discuss literature. They like garrulous Irish writers, Pushing Daisies, Axe Cop, and anything involving The Tick. Their secret lair is currently in a hollowed-out volcano in Brooklyn. In addition to co-writing *The Misshapes*, Donnelly is a cultural journalist who has written for the *The New York Times Magazine*, *The Boston Globe*, *The Los Angeles Times*, The *Paris Review Daily*, *GQ* and many others. She is currently an editor at Flavorwire. Sherman is a bioethicist, health policy analyst and a former contestant on the game show "Who Wants to be a Millionaire?"